THE TORMENT OF RICHARD BREWER

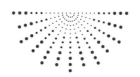

THE TORMENT OF RICHARD BREWER

BREWER

UNTOLD LEGENDS VOLUME TWO

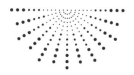

TAMSIN L. SILVER

Charlotte, NC

FALSTAFF
BOOKS
WWW.FALSTAFFBOOKS.COM

This book is dedicated to Richard M. Brewer, who had the heart of a lion and died way too soon.

The series itself is dedicated to the town of Lincoln, NM, that still honors Billy and Richard until this day, and to the amazing people who live there. You all are the reason Billy and Richard have never been forgotten. They live in your hearts so true that the town still vibrates with the love of their history...and that's what real magic looks like.

THE DELUXE CAFÉ

Las Cruces, NM

April 1949

I woke to a lovely spring day and looked out the window of my hotel room in Las Cruces, New Mexico. Glancing up at the sky, I couldn't see the moon, but I knew it had risen. Felt it go up at seven in the morning. That meant werewolves would be about today. They may not have experienced a Spirit Warrior of Scáthach before, which is what I was, but they'd feel a change in the air today and that would make them feisty.

"Nothing says 'fun' like a feisty lycanthrope," I said.

Laughing at myself, I went over and unlocked the room safe, pulled out my weapons, and laid them on the bed before approaching the dresser. Having showered the night before, I got dressed in my favorite pair of Levi's and a clean white t-shirt. Grabbing a casual dress shirt the exact blue of my eyes, I put that on and fastened the last few buttons before tucking the shirt into my jeans.

Taking up my favorite weapons belt made of black leather, which I'd named Lilith, I wove her through half of the loops on my jeans.

Next, I slid the two-gun holster piece that rested at my back into place before looping Lilith the rest of the way through and buckling her up.

Both of Lilith's sides had a bunch of silver half-circles along her bottom where I could attach different accessories. Normally I'd connect a matching rectangular leather bag to the left side and fasten the bottom of it around my thigh. However, I was trying to blend in more today, so I place that and the contents it usually held back into the room's safe.

After putting on my black cowboy boots, I fetched all three of my guns: one from the bathroom, one from the desk, and one from the bedside table. I verified all were fully loaded, yanked up my pant leg, and clipped my Remington 51 on the inner side of my left calf in my boot holster. Easing my pant leg down to cover it, I slid my two Walther PPK/S pistols, one holding silver rounds and one lead, into Lilly's spinal holsters, grips outward.

To hide the PPKs, which is what I called them for short, I pulled on my fitted black leather jacket. Built for me special by a man I met on the job in Poland in the 1920s, the coat hung to mid-thigh and had been lined with a special silk spelled by witches to stop bullets. Not that one could kill me, unless I was out of soul-energy, but they sting like hell, and to be honest, I'd gotten tired of replacing bloodstained shirts.

Almost out the door to fetch food, I glanced at the phone and realized I had to make the call. Thing is, my partner can be a pain in my ass and I'd called him during his vacation and requested he come help me. He was as thrilled as anyone would be. Because of that, I needed to call and make sure he'd gotten his butt on a train. Sitting on my hotel bed, I picked up the phone and made the call. The operator connected me, and my partner's handler answered as per usual.

"Hey, James, is he there or did he head on out yet?"

A sigh on the other end of the line spoke volumes. James was not my number one fan. Hell, he probably wasn't my hundredth fan, but dealing with me was part of his job, so I waited patiently.

"He left to meet you two hours after your first call...against my better judgement."

"Look, I wouldn't have bothered him if I didn't think it necessary. You know that, right?"

James cleared his throat, likely so he wouldn't curse me out in his thick British accent. "He'll be in Albuquerque on March 31st. Early in the morning."

"Good. That's tomorrow mornin'. Thanks so—"

I heard the line go dead.

"—much," I finished saying, and hung up the receiver.

The loud wail of an ambulance approached and passed by my hotel as I stood up and headed out the door. I somehow had to find a way to meet with the dirty sheriff of this town, Alfonso "Happy" Apodaca, today. If the Sheriff of Lincoln County was right, I was going to be hard pressed to get an audience with Apodaca, so my brain was turning over ideas as I headed down to the front desk. As usual, I was probably just going to have to fly by the seat of my pants and make it up as I went along. That's how I did things best though, if I was being honest.

* * *

Lincoln, NM

April 1878

The sound of a man wailing in pain poured out from the open window of Blazer's office gave me a start, causing me to slip on the loose stones of the winding trail to Blazer's cemetery. I fell forward, catching myself with my hands, saying, "Damn it, I'm comin' Dick, I'm comin' to get ya!" Standing, I continued up the incline. "Shouldn't be hard to find you, right? New grave and all?"

Not hours before, my closest friend, Richard "Dick" Brewer, had been shot in the head and likely buried up on this godforsaken hill of rock and shrubs. Thing was, he was a werewolf and that bullet had been lead, so he was lying in a coffin in the ground waiting for me to come give him the all clear.

I went around the bend and smelled fresh, overturned earth. Picking up the pace, I followed my nose to the top and then to the right. The hole was big enough for two caskets with only one inside it, partially covered with dirt. That's when I understood the earlier wailing: Buckshot Roberts had been hit after all and wasn't expected to survive.

"Wait, they're gonna bury him next to Dick, in the same hole? That's just downright wrong."

I jumped down in the space left open for Roberts's casket and lightly kicked the side of Brewer's wooden box. "Dick, I'm here! Tell me you're still breathin' in there!"

When no knock or anything was returned, I panicked. Squatting down, I quickly pried the casket open an inch. Lifting the lid up all the way, displacing the few shovels of dirt that someone had ceremoniously tossed on top of it, I pushed it aside. The big lug was laying there still as death, bandanas still in place.

I leaned in to check for a pulse, like Garrett taught us, when Dick's head turned and his jaw opened wide, as if he were going to lunge and bite me.

I jumped back with a yelp.

Dick sat up with a belly laugh loud enough that anyone walking by would've heard. "Oh, you should see your face!"

"You son of a bitch! That wasn't funny!"

Dick swung his long legs out of the casket and stood. Stretching, he said, "Took ya long enough, you deserved that."

"The hell I did! I've been watchin' Lieutenant Appel try to save John."

"John?"

"Middleton," I clarified. "We really need to give him a new name. Maybe I'll just call him Middleton from now on. But that's a bit long though. Maybe Middle? Mid? Middy?"

"Oh yes, let's see what he does to you if you call him Middy, shall we? Come on, let's get outta here."

I looked at the casket. "You just gonna leave it like that? Create a vampire panic?"

"Oh, yeah, that."

After closing the casket, he hopped out of the hole. "Any chance Mattie is nearby?"

"Not everyone is over six feet, Dick. Help me outta here, would ya?"

"Sure, but—" He stopped speaking and took his hand away just as I reached for it.

"Uh, I rather not stay down here," I pressed, waving my outstretched hand.

"Shh! Someone's comin'."

I heard it now, too. "Damn it!"

Dick bent down and pulled me out. "We need to go!"

I looked at all the footprints below. "Go! Hide. I have to cover this."

"But—"

"Stay close. I might need furry you."

"I hope not," he said, and was gone into the trees.

Seeing the shovel, I grabbed it and started singing a song Dick used to ask me to sing around the fire as I began to shovel dirt all over the casket and a bit into the empty space.

A horse came into view and one riding it was David Easton, the foreman of the mill.

"Billy? Is that you?" David said, staying on his horse.

I tossed dirt into the hole, wiped my brow, and looked over my shoulder like I'd not been caught digging at a grave. "You bet, David."

"What are you doin'?"

"I'm knittin' a bonnet. What does it look like I'm doin'? I'm burying my friend. Havin' a last few words before he is left to rot here." I went back to tossing dirt.

"Well, don't toss too much in there. The other side is for Roberts if he don't make it."

"Really? You'd bury Dick's killer next to him? That's cold, sir. That's mighty cold." Not giving him time to respond, I continued with, "Is Appel in there tryin' to help that scabbard of an hombre who killed my friend here?"

"He is."

5

I casually moved the shovel to my left hand. Then, quick as lightning, I pulled my six-shooter on him. "I should kill him so he can't."

David froze. Either he didn't have a gun handy, or he'd didn't trust I'd not shoot him just for reaching for it. "He said he might have saved your friend. You'd deny the same chance for Roberts?"

I'd saved Middleton, not Appel, but I couldn't say that, so I put my gun back in its holster. "You have a point. I'm just upset. I was just sayin' goodbye to Richard here. I'll be off the property in a few minutes. Which reminds me, Dick's things, where are they?"

"His horse, saddle, and guns?"

"Yeah," I said, tossing more dirt on top of the casket.

"In the stable. I'm sure his family will want his things. Stop by and tell Almer to fetch them for you before you leave."

"Thanks, David."

He nodded, turned his horse around, and headed back down the hill.

Once he was gone, I heaved enough dirt onto the casket so that no one would decide to look inside and then put the shovel back before I headed in the direction Dick had gone. I found him not far away but well hidden, sitting on a large rock, hands on knees, head down.

"Well now, that was a close one. But we should be good," I said. "You okay?"

"Now what?" Dick said without looking at me.

"What do you mean, now what? We go get your shit and we get the hell out of Lincoln."

"You got a smoke?"

"Since when does the great Richard M. Brewer smoke? What does the 'M' stand for anyway? Masculine? Massive? Muscly? Not that that's a word..." I stopped for a second as he looked at me, his face a perfect picture of sorrow. "Morose?"

Finally, he cracked a smile. "You are a pain in the ass, ya know that?"

I pulled out my pouch of pre-rolled smokes and took one to him. "Aww, I think you're...what did Tunstall say? Ah yes, I think you're aces, too. Here." I handed him a cigarette and lit it for him.

Dick inhaled and coughed. "Dear God, these are horrible!"

"Watch your tongue. This is some fine tobacco!" I inhaled and blew it out, unsure how much was smoke and how much was just hot breath on the cold night air. "Ya know, I miss that British bloke. Obviously, I didn't know him well, like you and Rob, but I do miss him."

Dick attempted to inhale again and choked less. "I miss him somethin' fierce."

Silence slid into place like a book snug between others on the shelf, right where it belonged. We stayed that way, and I watched Dick pull smoke in and blow it out without inhaling. He had something heavy on his mind. He'd tell me or he wouldn't.

"William?"

"Uh oh, you're usin' my real name. What is it?"

"What am I supposed to do now? I can't go home. I can't stay here. I'm not about to go work with Dolan. Where does that leave me?"

"We'll head to Arizona or maybe Colorado. You will choose a new name, and we'll take it one day at a time."

"You can't leave here," he said, standing up, purpose behind his words. "You have to stay and finish what you started." In three strides, he stood in front of me, all honor and strength in a towering form that would've given a smart man pause, but I wasn't afraid of Dick. I should've been, but I've never been one to err on the side of caution.

"The hell I do. You think I'm gonna just leave you to your wiles? That's not your thing, it's mine. Let me help you."

"I'm a dangerous man to be around," he said, voice deep and gravelly.

"We talked about this the day after you changed. I don't care that you're a werewolf. I don't."

"Will, you're supposed to kill my kind. You should kill me."

My head snapped around. "Don't you dare say that again, you hear me? I'm not killin' you. Look, you had a rough day. Let's go somewhere and crash for the night. We'll revisit your future after some rest."

"Where the hell can we even go?"

"Home. Last place anyone would go right now is your ranch. Sleep in your own bed a night and see how it all feels after a good breakfast in the mornin', okay? I'll give you a ride to your pretty pony. They'll be too wrapped up with Roberts to notice shit."

Dick tossed his cigarette down and crushed it with his large boot. "Fine."

"I had you at sleep in your own bed, didn't I?" I said with a laugh.

"More like the talk of breakfast," he said with a lopsided grin.

I hummed in agreement. "You know how I love breakfast."

* * *

April 1949

Taking the advice of the bellhop at the Campbell Hotel on where to get a quality morning meal, I walked north on Main Street until I saw the spot he'd recommended. It was nestled between two bars on the left-hand side of the street at about center of the block between May and Griggs Streets. The script on the door called the little spot, "DeLuxe Café," and under that, it read, "Open 24/7."

"This is my kinda place," I said as I took off my hat.

Opening the door, I entered the busy diner and reveled in the sounds and smells of the breakfast crowd. I stood by the empty glass case up front that served as the cash register table and took a moment to enjoy the aroma of pancakes, maple syrup, sausage, and heaven itself: bacon. My mouth watered and my toe began tapping along with the voice of Evelyn Knight as the song, "A Little Bird Told Me" hit my ears, playing on a private jukebox at one of the booths that ran along the wall to my left.

At the far back, I glimpsed the cook through a narrow pass-through opening to the kitchen and thought how similar this set up was to the diners I'd worked in when undercover over the years. It made the long, narrow place feel like home in a way. The café wasn't more than fifty feet deep and twenty feet wide. Even so, they used the space well, filling the center of the joint with four-tops while a long counter graced the northern wall to my right.

The café easily served just enough patrons to be worth stopping in and cozy enough to want to return. Currently, the place was filled with a mix of families or groups of college-age kids, talking and listening to music as they ate.

Looking about for a sign that stated if I needed to wait to be seated, I heard the click-clack of heels approach me from my left as a sweet yet sassy voice said, "Sit wherever you'd like, cowboy."

I turned to see a petite girl with dark hair and brown eyes—the latter of which held a chaotic playful energy that made me smile at her. "Thank you, ma'am."

"You alone?" she asked.

"I am."

"Best spot for ya then would be at the counter. Grab a seat, and we'll be with ya in a jiffy."

"Thank you."

I walked the length of the counter and sat sideways on the last stool so I could keep an eye on the place without putting by back to anyone but the cook. Though my jacket covered my weapons well enough, sitting this way also made sure none of the clientele would notice the slight bulge they made when I sat. From what Sheriff Ortiz told me, and what I'd learned yesterday, I didn't want to upset the lawmen here if I didn't have to.

"Here ya go, darling," a different waitress said to me as she slid me a folded menu. "Coffee?"

"Yes, please."

She placed an empty mug in front of me. "Caf or decaf?"

I noted the name on her tag and, with a grin, asked, "Why on earth would anyone drink decaf, Katie?"

"No idea, sugar," she said with a throaty chuckle and left to fetch a pot of coffee at the other end of the counter.

"Where you from, cowboy?" came a voice from behind me. I spun on my stool until the counter was behind me. Standing there was the pretty brunette from earlier with the mischievous look in her eye. She was waiting on food to come through the window.

I leaned back on the counter. "Silver City originally, ma'am. I'm passing through looking for a pal of mine. I heard y'all serve the best breakfast in town."

"That we do."

I quickly checked her name tag. "Ovida, now that's a pretty name."

"Like any of us call her that," Katie said as she poured my coffee, obviously razzing Ovida in fun. "That there's Cricket."

I liked it. The name fit her haphazard energy. "And why do they call you Cricket, Miss Ovida?"

"Table two redo up!" the cook shouted as a plate of food was set in the window.

Cricket grabbed it. "Thank you, Mel!"

"Yeah, yeah. If they don't like them eggs this time, they can cook 'em themselves."

Katie answered my question. "We call her Cricket 'cause of how she's always in heels, makin' the clickity sound as she walks at a hundred miles an hour wherever she goes."

"Don't your feet get to hurtin', Miss Ovida?" I asked.

"Of course they do, but they make my legs look great!" She winked at me and headed out to serve the plates to table number two.

I watched what I could see of her legs, her waitress uniform hitting her just at the knees, and she was not wrong.

"You gonna order or keep watchin' her legs?" Katie asked.

I turned to Katie. "I wasn't—"

"She wanted you to, so no need to go lying, mister," Katie said with a light laugh. "Tell me, what will you be havin'?"

I picked up the menu and looked at it. Unsure what sounded best, I wavered just long enough that Cricket returned to the back by me.

"You strike me as a simple man who likes to eat the real thing," Cricket said. "Pancakes, toast, two eggs, and a double portion of bacon."

I set the menu down. "It's like you can read my mind. But can you tell how I like my eggs?"

"Table three!" Mel shouted as he set more plates in the window.

"Those are for me," Katie said, grabbing the plates and heading out to deliver them.

"Scrambled. Not runny," Cricket answered matter-of-factly.

"You are not wrong."

She beamed. "I'll put your order in right away then."

"Much obliged, ma'am."

She pulled out a pad and wrote my order down. "Ma'am is what we call my momma. You can call me Cricket, cowboy."

"Name's William, but you can call be Billy."

She ripped the paper from her pad, spun about, and clipped the order to the spindle. "Counter order in!" Food slid into the window with Mel announcing table number four. She picked them up and added, "Well, Billy, your order shouldn't take long. I'll be right back."

Cricket headed to a table on her heels, and I might or might not have watched her legs again. I truly approved of how the length of skirts on women had gone up over time, that's for sure.

More folks entered the diner, and the girls went from busy to slammed, yet Cricket made sure to bring me my food and chat here and there as she went by. I was just finishing my extra bacon when Katie approached me.

"You must be a dangerous man," she said.

"Excuse me?" I said, almost choking on my last bite of food.

She refilled my coffee. "Cricket has taken a shine to you, and though she's not the pickiest dater, she gravitates to trouble. Are ya, stranger? Are you trouble?"

Boy was I ever.

"No, ma'am. In fact, I'm just passin' through on my way to Albuquerque. Pickin' up a friend from the train station this evenin' before we head to Santa Fe. But first I need to meet with Sheriff Apodaca."

"You a law man?"

I grinned. "Just followin' up on a missin' friend of mine."

"Well, good luck with that. Cricket knows Apodaca pretty well, and he's in here often enough."

Her tone spoke volumes to my keen ears. Katie was not a fan. I was about to ask her why when Cricket returned.

"You tryin' to steal my date for tonight, Katie?"

"Your cowboy is leavin' town this afternoon, darlin'," Katie informed her.

"Well shoot, that just throws a monkey wrench into all my plans," Cricket said, the playful lilt of her voice tainted with a hint of disappointment as she gave me some flirty side-eye.

That look alone made me want to pick up my partner on another day all together, but there was no way to change that now. I had no choice but to leave town early this evening, which was a bit upsetting, if truth be told.

* * *

April 1878

B rewer and I rode all night, arriving at his ranch just before daylight. After getting some food and rest, we sat down to discuss our plan.

"Pack all that you want. No one is going to know ya packed it after the trip out to Blazer's."

"What about the sentimental stuff I can't carry right now?" he asked.

"Bury it?" I suggested.

"Where?"

"I don't know...someplace that'll be easy to find later."

He sighed, then said, "Wait, I know a spot. There's a group of young trees, some Lombardy Poplars, out back. I'll bury it in the middle of those."

"We'll do that tonight once your ranch hands head home."

"You expect me to what, stay in here until then?"

"Yes, I do. That is, unless you want to come clean with—"

"No!"

I pulled at my hair in frustration. "Richard, they'd understand!"

"And what if they didn't?"

I rubbed my forehead in frustration. "Look, I have to head into town and make sure Scroggins was able to get the acid for George and deliver it to him. You promise me you'll stay in here?"

"Yes. I'll get some more sleep, then bury my things. Be back before dawn. I'm not safe here… Correction—spring term of court is about to begin…neither of us are safe here."

I nodded. "Agreed. I'll be back before the full moon with everythin' on the list. If somethin' happens, find a way to get me a message, or leave one here and I'll find you."

"And if you don't make it back?"

"I will, trust me!"

"Don't say that! I told you, nothin' good ever comes after you say that!"

I laughed at him. "You're startin' to sound a bit like Charlie… You'll see, it'll be fine."

"You say that, but I know better. Be careful."

"Relax, Barbara Ann. Ya act like I don't know how to take care of myself or that I don't have powers to help me. Now rest. I'll see ya tonight."

* * *

April 1949

"Y ou sure I can't talk ya into makin' it back here tonight?" Cricket asked as she stepped behind the counter and set my check in front of me.

"I wish I could, but my pal's train pulls in around nine o'clock, and he'll be right mad at me if I'm not there to pick him up, seein' as I convinced him to come on out here to begin with."

She leaned over, resting her forearms on the counter. "He the grumpy type?"

I pulled out twice the amount of money I needed to pay the bill and set it down. "Naw, just hates Texas and New Mexico. Too many bad memories, you could say." Leaning toward her with my voice low,

13

I said, "But I'll make ya a deal... Do you and those heels you love to wear like to go dancin'?"

"We sure do."

"Good. Then seein' as I can't stay tonight, and I'll be back in about a month, how about my friend and I take you and Katie out dancin' in El Paso for Cinco de Mayo. How does that sound?"

"Sounds like a date to me."

"Good, so you behave yourself while I'm gone, and I'll be back to town in about a month. All right?"

A smile lit up her face in such a way that my heart gave a thump; I always had a thing for dark-haired, dark-eyed women with spunk. To cover how my throat threatened to close, I slid the money toward her, returning the honest grin back at her. "Keep the change. You've truly improved my visit to New Mexico, Miss Ovida." I tapped her under her chin with a forefinger. "I'll be seein' you soon."

"Cricket?" Katie said. "Could you see what's up with the jukebox at booth four? They say it's not workin' right."

"Sure thing." Cricket leaned in to me, and before I knew it, she kissed me on the cheek. "Travel safe, cowboy. We'll see ya in May."

She rounded the counter and headed off to booth four.

Standing up, I realized she'd not taken the check or money. Not trusting folks, I scooped it up and took it to Katie. "Do ya have a pen I can borrow?"

"Sure thing." Katie gave me a pen.

Watching her open the jukebox and fix it without barely doing anything, I jotted a note on the back of the check with the name and number of my hotel in Albuquerque, in case she wished to call me.

Handing the note and money to Katie, I said, "Be sure she gets all this."

"Can do."

I nodded a thank you to Katie and headed to the door as the voice of Miss Dinah Shore singing "Buttons and Bows" filled the air from the repaired jukebox. Opening the door, I stepped out, put my hat on, and turned back to look at Ovida once more. She, too, was staring back at me, so I tugged the brim of my hat, and with a nod at her, I left. It wasn't yet even nine in the morning and my world had changed for the better.

I headed back to the Campbell Hotel, where I thanked the bellman for the referral, and headed up to my room to find the spell on my door disturbed. Pulling one of my guns, I unlocked the door and cautiously entered the room. What I found inside ruined my perfectly good morning.

2
BEGINNER'S LUCK

April 1878

D r. Appel had left two things of the acid at the Ellis Store, Scroggins only taking one with him when he came through. I picked up the other and began to select a few supplies for Dick and my trip outta town.

"Billy, what are ya doin' here?!" came an intense, whispering voice behind me.

Hand on my gun, I turned around. Seeing it was none other than Doc Scurlock, I relaxed. "Hey there, Doc. What you going on about?"

"Court starts tomorrow. You shouldn't be in town!"

"I'm leavin' just as soon as I get some supplies."

"If they find out I saw you, they'll wonder why you aren't in jail."

I stopped filling the small burlap sack with the potatoes. "What? Why?"

"You've not heard? They voted in Copeland as the new sheriff on Monday, and by Wednesday, he'd sworn me in as his deputy."

"Wait, so the new sheriff of Lincoln is a McSween sympathizer and you're his first deputy?"

"Yes."

I set the bag down, whooped for joy, and pulled Doc into a hug, lifting him off the ground.

"Billy, I can't breathe."

"Oh, sorry." I set him down. "I forget my strength. This is good news! We can finally stop lookin' over our shoulders."

"Not until court is over you can't. You've been charged with Brady's murder."

"What?!" I exclaimed. "I wasn't the only one who shot at him, and I have no idea if my bullet did the job. He wasn't a werewolf, so there was no way I could know if I killed him."

"You're not the only one. It's you, John Middleton, and Henry Brown."

"For goodness sake, Doc..."

"I know, I know! Grand Jury empanels as of Saturday the thirteenth and likely won't be done for a week or two."

"You're sayin' I need to stay outta town for two more weeks?"

"At the least. And ya can't tell anyone you saw me."

I sat down with a grunt. "This is ridiculous. We was protectin' McSween."

"No one will believe that. Besides, Fort Stanton has a new lieutenant colonel in command. His name is Nathan Augustus Monroe Dudley."

"Jesus, that's a long name. Bet he's a pain in the ass."

"No idea. We'll have to wait and see. Give Copeland and me a chance to talk to him after court is over and see if we can get him on our side of all this before you go passing judgement."

"I wouldn't wait that long to talk to him, Doc. But I'll do as you say. I'll deliver this acid to George and then get outta town."

We parted, and I packed up and headed to San Patricio. Once I checked in on George and got news on the rest of the Regulators, I headed on back toward Dick's ranch. On the way, I ran into a broken-down wagon, blocking the whole road.

"Hey there," I said, hopping down off Colonel. "Need some help?"

The big man, a stranger to the area, smiled at me as he limped over. "Could I ever! There seems to be a problem with the undercarriage. Can't tell if it's the bolsters or the reach. Having a hard time seeing it in this failing light."

I glanced up at his wife, who held an infant in her arms. "I can slide under and take a look. Ya got any tools in the jockey box I can use?"

"Sure do. I'll hand them to ya."

"Perfect." I sat beside the wagon. Leaning back, I ducked my head under the bed and pulled myself farther under to examine the axel. Seeing the problem, I shouted, "Come 'round to the other side, hand me somethin' to tighten these bolts. Your reach isn't connected properly."

"On my way," the man said. "Got two things for ya."

I watched his feet as he limped around the wagon. Once he was even with me, I reached both hands toward him for the items. But instead of tools being placed in my hands, two cuffs got slapped around my wrists.

"What the hell?" I shouted as the big man began to pull me out.

Fighting, I found most of my super strength had vanished, and panic set in. Kicking about as my torso cleared the wagon bed, I took a breath to demand what he was doing when something hard as steel hit me in the head, and everything went dark.

* * *

Waking up in a small adobe building I'd never seen before, I sat up and looked around at the simple room. I was laying on a single bed set against one of the four walls of a square room with a dirt floor. In the center of the space was a table with a deck of cards, two mugs, and a small crate. On the opposite side was a wood-burning stove with a kettle sitting on top of it. One sniff told me it was coffee and that was likely what had awoken me.

Shaking off the grogginess that enveloped my head, I stood up with a wobble, only to realize my left wrist was shackled to the bar at the head of the bed. Examining both cuffs, I realized they were made of copper. I chuckled at the choice of metal, seeing as with soul-energy I could easily break free, and pulled hard. Nothing happened. In fact, I felt weak. Correction, I felt *mortal*. Confused, I sat down.

The aroma of coffee hit me again. I slid the cuff along the metallic bedframe to the side closest to the stove. Standing, I stretched for the coffee, but it was about an inch out of reach.

"That's just evil," I said.

Getting a hand on each part of the frame, I lifted it and began to pull it across the small room. Once close enough, I selected a mug from the table, filled it, and took a seat at the table to drink. I was halfway through the cup when the door swung in. Glancing up, I saw Scáthach.

"I shoulda known," I said.

"You are such the knight in shinin' armor, Henry. Saving a stranded family with a newborn on the side of the road like that. Such a good Samaritan." She shut the door.

"Screw you."

"I see you found a way to the coffee without your powers. You always were resourceful."

"Yeah, about that…"

She selected the other mug from the table. "Bed and shackles are made of copper." Saying nothing more, she walked around to pour herself some coffee.

"Thank you, Mistress Obvious. What does that have to do with me not having my powers?"

A look of pure pleasure snaked across her face as she sat opposite me. Quietly she drank, her eyes staying on me over the lip of the mug. Setting it down, she said, "Copper works two ways. Large amounts absorb your power while smaller amounts disrupt your connection to your soul energy. What, you didn't know that? 'Tis more the pity."

"What are you talking about?"

"Cuffs alone disrupt your connection to your well of souls. Larger items, like this bed, work like a bank. But instead of holding your *dinero*, as you call it, these store your power. Thus, leaving you without the ability to heal or any super strength. Meaning, if you die while drained, you die for real."

"Well, this is news to me."

"That's the point," she said, seeming excessively pleased with herself.

"You don't play fair," I pointed out.

"Never have."

Fuming, I couldn't think of what to say.

"However, I find it interesting that you were still able to move the bed across the room."

"Copper isn't that heavy, thank you very much."

"Still…you should feel drained."

"I do."

She lowered one eyebrow into a furrow of curious inquisition and would have likely tested me further, but a knock came at the door.

"Enter."

The man who'd had the so-called broken-down wagon came into the small building. "Mistress, Kamil has returned."

"Ah yes, thank you, Michael. Tell him I will be there shortly."

"Yes, mistress," he replied with a slight bow, and left, shutting the door behind him.

"Well, it seems this chat will have to continue later." Standing, she added, "I must tend to other matters. I'll be back soon, don't you worry."

"Wait, why am I here?"

She stopped at the door and looked back at me. "If you'd stayed out of town, I'd not have had to do this. It's for your own good. Now, you're safe."

"How the hell is this for my safety?" I exclaimed.

"Fall court is in session, and you are up on a count of murder in the first degree. I can't have you captured and taken into court. I need you free if I'm to play my games."

"You have got to be kiddin'—"

"Have no fear. Once court is over, I'll send you on your way."

"I can leave now and be out of town in no time," I pointed out.

She laughed. "I can't trust you. I mean, you were dumb enough to come into town in the first place. No, you'll stay here until the end of court. Besides, you look like hell. Get some rest."

I stood. "This is ridiculous! I have people waitin' who need me."

She thought on that. "Not as much as I need you alive and out of jail for the next part of my plan to go as I wish. Rest and enjoy your stay, my warrior. I will return."

She opened the door and added, "Oh, and there is a bucket there to relieve yourself as needed. Michael will fetch it from you daily. Hurt him, and I'll kill one of your friends and deliver them to you in pieces." She smiled. "See you soon."

She left, shutting the door behind her.

Shouting her name in anger, I slammed my free hand on the table in frustration. But all that did was hurt my hand. I was stuck here for the time being.

Brewer was going to be mad as hell.

* * *

Days passed with a routine I got used to. It was evident that she ran things like an army captain, everything happening at a specific time each day like clockwork. Without windows to see the sun and only portholes at the top of the room for airflow, this military-like behavior helped me to figure out the approximate time of visits and the passing of days.

At eight in the morning, Michael would bring me food and a pail of water for the day. He'd make coffee, leave me a fresh pail for relieving myself, and leave with the one I'd used. He'd return around five o'clock, and it would be a repeat of the morning routine. Occasionally, I'd convince him to stay after one of these visits for a game or two of cards.

"Penalty," he said. "Pay up."

"Damn it," I replied, and began to pay four cards for the ace he'd flipped. In doing so, I sadly didn't play a face card or another ace.

Grinning ear to ear, Michael scooped up all the cards played so far and added them to his pile. "What did you say this game was called again? I seem to be rather good at it."

"Beggar-my-neighbor. British game. Tunstall taught it to us."

"Cool."

"Wouldn't have thought you wolves would like cards," I said, just to razz him.

"I'm not one of them. Never been a wolf a day in my life."

This explained why neither Colonel nor myself had gotten suspicious of him on the road that day, but it didn't tell me what I cared about. "Why are you workin' for Scáthach then?"

He played a card. "It pays well, and my family is hurtin'."

"I see," I replied and played my card atop of his. "So, how is court goin'?"

"I'm not supposed to talk to you about that."

"And it would hurt how?" I said, egging him on.

He thought about it and played a card. "Grand Jury has indicted most everyone who has had charges brought against 'em."

"Oh?" I asked casually as I played my card.

"Yeah. They indicted Evans, Hill, and the rest for the murder of Tunstall."

"Some justice after all. How refreshing."

With a gleam in his eye, Michael looked at his next card. "On Thursday, they'll likely indict you and your pals for Brady's murder." Playing the card, it was a jack of spades. "Penalty on you."

I flipped a two of hearts. "Only three of us up for his murder when nine were present. Interestin'."

Michael scooped up the cards, adding them to his pile. "In two days, you could be a wanted man."

I grinned. Not because of what he said, but because he'd just confirmed for me that it was Tuesday, the sixteenth. I covered my happiness by saying, "I already am."

"Proud of that, are ya?" he asked, wiping sweat from his brow.

I snatched an apple from the crate. "Some days. You want one?"

"No, thanks."

"More water?"

"Naw...stomach hasn't been feelin' so great." Michael played a card. "Ya know, they'll be decidin' about McSween as well as your pal Bowdre today."

"Charlie? What for?" I asked, playing a card.

"Murder of Buckshot Roberts."

"Aww, hell. He was defending himself, and we had a warrant!"

"That's not how the Blazers saw it."

"Roberts killed Brewer!"

"And he'd be facing an indictment on that if he wasn't, you know, deceased an' all." Michael played an ace. "Penalty on you!"

"Damn it." I paid my four-card penalty. "That's the end of my cards."

Besides looking a bit ill, Michael's face lit up. "Woo-hoo! I win! Beginner's luck!"

"I don't believe in beginner's luck," I told him.

"Why not?" he asked.

I didn't tell him why.

The next day, I awoke to find two crates, buckets of water, and outhouse pails. The crate on the table held extra of its usual, which always held a mix of fruit, dried meats, cheeses, bread, coffee, and some sweets. But the second crate, located at the foot of my bed, held something even more precious: books. Inside were the adventure novels I'd read as a kid. A memory Mary would've had, which turned my stomach.

At first, I refused to touch them, but when Michael didn't show up with my breakfast to supply conversation, I caved. Having moved my bed closer to the wood burning stove for heat, I set down the book I'd started to read and made some coffee. I had to admit, it was nice to have something else to do. Maybe even keep me from going mad wondering what Brewer was doing and if he was okay. That's when the extra things made sense.

The full moon must be tonight, and I'd been left these things because Michael would be too busy today dealing with the pack and their shenanigans to tend to me. That also meant Scáthach was probably not here to do so herself. With a fresh cup of brew, I lay down on the bed to read.

Opening the book I'd been reading, I had a thought and cringed. I was attached to a bed that took all my powers away and didn't have a gun or silver on me. Yet, I was about to be surrounded by wolves with no Scáthach to reinforce that I was off limits. This smelled like a setup of Biblical proportions.

"Gee, what could possibly go wrong?" I said aloud to no one but myself and laughed.

* * *

April 1949

I t was the smell of my room at the Campbell Hotel that hit me first. Werewolves can't mask their odor from the likes of me anymore, and this one needed a bath. Though the room wasn't trashed, I could tell my things had been disturbed. Pausing to listen, I couldn't hear anyone breathing, but I searched the room anyway. Finding no one still lingering about, I growled in anger, holstered my weapon, and checked the safe. Thankfully, all my magical items were still there.

Reaching in, I snagged the tracing mist, disguised to look like an old-fashioned perfume bottle, and headed to the far corner of the room. I moved systematically backward about the space, spraying the scentless liquid up into the air in front of me until I reached the door. As it settled, the mist clung to energy signatures, turning them red to my vision, verifying a supernatural other than me had walked about my room.

From the heavier concentrations of color lingering in the air, I could see where the intruder had spent most of his time. In this case, it was near my luggage, the safe, and the toilet.

Standin' in the bathroom, I stared at the reading material I'd left on the counter by the sink. Picking up Arthur Miller's newest play by the corner with only my fingertips, I stared at it in horror. "Why do they always have to touch my things?" Wishing there was a way to disinfect the brand-new script I'd picked up on my way out to New Mexico, I complained a bit more and set it on the dresser in the main room.

With a sigh, I snatched up the hotel phone and called down to the front desk. The young man I'd seen on my way up, Calvin, answered.

"How can I help you Agent Kidwell?"

"I've had a break-in. Someone's been in my room."

"What? I'm so sorry, Agent!"

"Did you see anyone you didn't recognize come up this way while I was at breakfast?"

"No, sir. Did you want to file a report?"

I hemmed and hawed for a second, and then realized that gave me an extra excuse to stop by the sheriff's office later on. "Yes, I'd like to place a report."

"Yes, sir. I'll call them now."

I hung up with Calvin and picked up the play the werewolf had looked at. I inhaled the scent to commit it to memory, then sat down on the bed to pick up reading where I'd left off. If I was going to be a captive in my own room while I waited, I might as well read.

* * *

April 1878

I was halfway through the third book when I heard the noise outside my adobe prison. I glanced at the portholes and noted that the sun was setting. If memory served me right, it would go down at seven o'clock, and though the sun would set just after six-thirty tonight, the moon wouldn't rise until an hour later. I had little time to fortify.

An idea came to mind, and I grabbed the box of candles, the lighter, box of matches, and my box of food and books. Putting all on the bed, I placed the two oil lanterns, two mugs, and coffee pot filled with fresh brew on the table. Standing between the table and the bed,

I began to move both toward the entrance. Soon I had the metal bed frame horizontal against the door with the table at the head of the bed.

I lit a candle and set it on the table and made other preparations as I listened to howls, growls, and the snapping of wolves outside. Soon they left, and I laid back down to read. Not halfway through the story, I heard shouts for help in the distance.

"Damn it."

Hearing the screams grow closer, I sat up, and waited until they were right outside the door. The bed jostled as someone tried to get in. Heart in my throat, I began to go through the scenarios in my mind and their possible outcomes. All of them ended with my death, and as much as I played it off that I didn't care if I died, I did. Not just for me, but for the men I'd promised to keep safe, especially the man who was going through his second full moon by himself right now. That alone brought the mad out in me enough that I found my resolve and shoved down my fear.

The barking and howling of werewolves could be heard getting closer as someone pounded.

"Billy! Open the door!"

"Michael? Is that you?" I shouted.

"They're gonna kill me, or worse, bite me! I don't wanna be like them. Please! Let me in!"

It was a ruse. I knew it was a ruse. But what if it wasn't? He sounded in tears, and for a tough cowboy to reach that stage, things had to be dire.

Keeping to my plan, I quickly lit one lantern and set it on the table. Remembering what Brewer said about how my plans never worked out for the best, I paused. Michael screamed like a girl trapped by men in a confined space. Men didn't scream like that unless they were close to dying, or at least that was my life experience. Fast as I could, I pulled the bed back and opened the door a crack. Michael slipped through and immediately helped me shove the bed against the door just as a wolf rammed into it.

We both sat on the bed, Michael breathing hard.

"Thanks, man."

"Sure," I said. "Why they after you anyway?"

"Full moon craziness?" he offered.

I grinned. "Yeah, that's normal." With a sniff, my smile vanished. "You smell more wolfy than usual."

"Been dealing with those assholes all day and night," he said with a strained laugh. "You wanna play some cards? Maybe my beginner's luck will still hold out."

"Sure, we can try, why don't you grab a chair and—" I cut myself off as I noticed Michael was hyperventilating. "Michael, you're safe in here. They all have orders to leave me be."

"Like they care about anyone but themselves..." he said, tears truly forming before sliding down his face.

"Michael?"

"They said they did it without my knowin'. They only just told me..."

I picked up the lantern. Holding it up to see his face better, I backed away as far as I could. "Michael...what are ya talkin' about?"

"They told me it was miracle salve that healed my wounds last month, and I believed them." His voice caught, and he began to back away from me. Staring at the door, he shouted, "Bastards!"

Putting pieces of the puzzle together, his sweating and upset stomach the day before, the sweats and fear now, I recognized this. I'd seen this last month. "Dear God..."

"They didn't tell me until we were out in the woods, me carryin' their pack with clothes for later," he said, doubling over in pain. "Seems they used their saliva to heal me after that gun fight at the Ellis Store and didn't tell me."

"Fucking hell," I murmured. "This is your first full moon."

Michael fell onto his back and wailed in pain as bones began to break and move. "Kill me!" he screamed.

"I have no silver or powers. I can't do anythin' to help you. I'm so sorry."

"Noooo..." he whined.

Howling erupted from outside, and I knew the moon had risen.

Unlike Dick, Michael wasn't chained up, so as his body prepared for the change, he got up on all fours out of instinct.

"Here we go," I said.

In a mixture of fear and fascination, I watched as the second person I'd known before the infection changed into a wolf for the first time. The pain was excruciating for him, yet I had to admit, Brewer had gone through more issues prior to the change than Michael had. I wondered how much of that was his conscience and how much had been the colloidal silver.

Everything went silent. Michael was now fully shifted, and as his eyes traveled from the floor to my face, the look in them went from pleading to predatory in a second. His soul had left. I could only save it now if I took his life. He just had to get close enough.

Michael howled in response to the pack outside, who responded in kind. I was a sitting duck, trapped in a room with a wild newborn. Even if I could get free, an entire pack awaited me outside. Taking a deep breath, I set the lantern aside, picked up one of the mugs with my free hand, and shoved the table out of the way.

"If you want me, come get me, fluffy butt."

With no self-control or ability yet to consider facts, Michael barreled toward me. At the last second, I stepped out of the way, causing him to slam into my arm, crushing it, my wrist, and hand. Screaming in pain, I dumped the contents of the mug on him before tossing it to the floor.

The smell strong to his nose, he backed away just long enough for me to grab the lantern with my good hand. In doing so, I stepped farther from the bed than I'd been able to in ages. A quick glance showed me that Michael had broken the chain between the cuffs, and though I still wore one, I was free from the bed.

Michael roared at me, unaware of his peril as I threw the lantern down onto the ground at his feet. The oil caught fire and traveled along the ground to the oil pooled around him, and on his fur, from when I'd dumped the mug contents on him. Flames quickly traveled onto him, engulfing his whole body in mere seconds.

The scream an animal makes when dying is heart wrenching. It's even more horrific when you knew them as a person. For a moment, I had mercy, and instead of finishing the deed, I hesitated. In that brief second, Michael flailed about, landing on the bed, catching the straw mattress on fire before falling to the ground in agony.

Soon his human brain must've kicked in, and he tried to roll on the dirt floor to put out the flames, but it was too late, the damage was done. Soon he lay there, unmoving, barely breathing. No longer on fire, his body tried to heal, but like when silver poisons an organ, fire appeared to do the same. Choking on the stench of burned wolf, I dumped the remaining coffee on the mattress and put out the flames.

Unable to see, I reached for the copper cuff with my good arm and pulled it off. Tossing it across the room, I felt all the souls the copper had stored return to me. As if not lightheaded enough as it was, this threw me over the edge, and I fell to the ground where my injuries healed. I could breathe better here, interestingly enough, and in the darkness, I heard Michael gasp for air. I crawled over to him, and he snapped toward me as best he could, but it wasn't enough.

"This is why I don't believe in beginner's luck," I simply said, and broke his neck, putting him out of his misery.

His soul, unblemished by deeds of a werewolf, hit me like I'd taken ten shots of whiskey, and I lay on my back, giggling. "I know this is gonna sound funny, Michael, but your soul feels good."

With laughter that hurt my sides, I stayed low and fetched my box of things from the table, kicked the bed out of my way, and opened the door. Fresh night air rushed in, and I was surprised to find not one wolf outside. Glancing up at the smoke coming from the portholes, I came to the conclusion that they didn't want to be around when Scáthach returned.

Well, neither did I.

Whistling for Colonel, I heard him answer me. Running toward the sound, I found a small stable behind the house I'd been kept in. Colonel was fit to be tied with fear as the smoke seeped out of the house, blowing toward him.

"Shh...it's okay, partner." I patted his neck and nuzzled him for a second. "It's okay...I'm all right." I sent calming energy into him, then tended to his eyes.

Colonel lightly bumped my head in thanks.

"You're welcome. Glad to see you're dressed to go. I have a feeling Her Evilness will be here soon."

Finding they'd relieved my saddle bags of my supplies, I had space for my new things. Once loaded up, I looked about the little barn and noticed a locked chest. Kicking the lock, I broke it. Inside I found my Winchester as well as my belt and both revolvers.

"They took my extra box of silver ammo, Colonel. How rude."

Happy to at least have my weapons, I put my belt on, slid the guns into place, and snatched up my rifle. Leading Colonel out of the stable, I hoisted myself up into the saddle.

"Come on, we still got a lot of full moon to survive, and if we're lucky, we'll find Mr. Brewer before he disappears into the night."

3

THE TALE OF ELIAS STORY

April 1878

Arriving at Brewer's ranch, I found it empty and cold, no one having been here for a while.

"Damn it!"

I couldn't go searching the land at night on a full moon. That'd just be stupid. Instead, I boarded Colonel inside Brewer's big barn, taking note that Mattie wasn't there, and headed back into Brewer's house for the night.

Next morning, after the moon had set, I gathered the ammunition he'd obviously left for me and headed out to find the big man. I visited all of Brewer's usual haunts and found nothing. Deciding to get some help from Zahara, Colonel and I set out for her orchard on Friday the nineteenth.

"You look horrible, Henry," was the first thing she said to me.

Colonel whinnied. "You always look beautiful," she told the stallion.

I rolled my eyes and began to go through the process or removing the damn leather and chainmail armor that showed up in her Forrest of Inner Truth. "Ya know what, from now on, I'll send him with a note and stay relaxing at some hot springs somewhere."

"Aww, your human has had his feelings hurt," she told Colonel.

"*His* human? Really? Oh, for God's sake." I flopped onto the mattress I used when I was there, horribly aware that the bed next to me for Brewer was empty.

"You're so dramatic," she said with a laugh.

I flipped her off.

A gentle hand caressed the back of my head. "You'll find him. I'll help you."

I rolled over to look at her. "How do you…"

"Colonel told me. But first, rest."

"No, I can't. I need to find Brewer."

"You'll do him no good in the state you're in. Sleep."

She waved her hand, and I sneezed on something before passing out. When I woke, I felt refreshed and clear headed. That was until she told me what day it was.

"What do you mean it's Wednesday the twenty-fourth? I got here on Monday!"

"You slept a long time, my young warrior. Your ordeal took a lot more out of you than you realized. If it makes you feel better, it's just now one in the morning on Wednesday, so you didn't sleep two full days."

I glared at her. "Not much better, but some. We need to look for Brewer."

"It won't be hard to find him. Not with your connection. Come, break your fast and we'll get to work."

Sitting by the fire, we ate, and she served a tea to open our minds. It tasted like hell, but it always seemed to work, so I drank it.

"Give me your hand."

I did as she asked, and she stuck me with a pin.

"Ow!"

She shook a few drops of my blood into the small cauldron over the fire. "Don't be a baby. You've been through worse."

"Still, you coulda warned me."

She put a few other ingredients into the pot. "No, I couldn't. You were taken from your path without permission. I had to take the blood the same way."

She said a few things over her mixture, and it began to gurgle, smoke rising out of the pot. Pouring salt from a bag, she made the letter C. Then she made another one, larger, around it. Setting the bag aside, she ladled out some of her brew and filled a stone bowl. Carefully, she placed it inside the smaller C of salt, next to the burning herbs and a small candle, and then turned the C into an O with a handful of salt.

"Sit inside the larger area."

I did as I'd been told while Zahara grabbed two handfuls of salt, stepped into the C, and then closed it to make a second perfect circle. Once she did this, I was surprised to see that the smoke and steam from the items in the smaller O had collected in a bulbous way inside its own salt circle.

She sat across from me. "Take my hands." She reached out around the smaller circle, and I took them, encapsulating the central O between our arms. "We just need to concentrate on who we are looking for. You think of him in human form, and I'll picture him as his wolf since that is how this room knows him. All right?"

I nodded.

"Good. Now, close your eyes. See him."

It felt hokey, but I shut my eyes and pictured Brewer in my mind's eye, looking just like he did on the day we met—riding on Mattie across his land, coming toward me with a look of curiosity on his face.

"Let he we seek, the other half of this warrior's whole, show us where he is. Be he wolf or man, alive or dead, we ask the Earth Mother to see him and show him to us." After a moment of quiet, she added, "You can open your eyes. Just remember, no matter what you see, you cannot break the larger salt circle."

"I know."

"See what she shows us," Zahara said, pointing at the bubble above the bowl.

Clear as day, we saw Richard in human form, fighting the change.

For the half-moon had risen just after quarter past one that morning, and he sat by a fire out in the middle of nowhere. Due to the dark of night, I saw no land markers and commented on that.

"Shh...he seems to be talking to someone..."

"I can't see who."

"We need a bigger bubble. It's very important you don't move."

"Um, okay?"

Zahara let go of my one hand and opened the smaller salt circle. The picture oozed out, quickly filling the space around us, and I could smell the night and the food he was cooking on the fire. As the picture cleared, who he spoke to did as well. It was a man of The People.

I was unable to distinguish his tribe just by the look of him, but Zahara smiled and blew on the smoke of the burning herbs.

I watched as the man of The People stopped speaking mid-sentence and caught the smell of something on the air. He looked around and touched his heart with the palm of his hand.

"Keep him safe. I send his friend. Two days hence."

The man only nodded, and with that, Zahara blew out the candle, and the picture faded.

"Wait, where are they? Who is that? How did he hear you?"

Zahara only smiled at me and let go of the other hand she still held onto. "He is a good man I have known for a long time. You will find Brewer at that same location the day after tomorrow. You will need to ride as soon as the moon sets around noon."

Zahara said a blessing to the north, south, east, and west. Then she broke the outer circle.

"How am I going to find him?" I asked plainly.

"With a little help." She picked up the bowl of what now looked to be simply water and whistled. An echo of that repeated in the distance, and in seconds, Gaax flew into the cavern. Landing on her arm, he danced about.

"It's good to see you, too," she told him.

QUARK-QUARK!

"Yes, I have a mission for you. I need you to take Henry to his wolf tomorrow. Can you do that for me?"

Gaax bobbed his head up and down.

"Good, drink this. It will show you where."

Again, he bobbed and drank of the water. Raising his head, he spoke in many *QUARK* noises, looked to me, and flew off.

"Wait, where is he going?"

"To rest. You both have a long trip to make tomorrow. Drink the rest to stay tied to Gaax."

"I'm already tied to Gaax."

"This will be different. It will help you know where you are going as well."

With a sigh, I drank the water. "Why is nothin' ever easy with you?"

She laughed. "I'm a witch, Henry. Why would you think it would be?"

"You have a point."

"Now come, I have more to teach you. It will prepare you for the next step of your fight."

* * *

D o you even know where we are?" I shouted up at the raven as we approached sunset on our second day of travel. When he didn't reply, I muttered to myself, "I bet you have no idea."

Bird poop landed on my knee, and I looked up. "That wasn't necessary!"

QUARK-QUARK!

"I swear, sometimes..." I shut up, wishing to avoid another assault, and kept riding.

Soon Gaax picked up speed and began dive bombing an area ahead of me. Either it was danger, or it was Dick. Hell, *he* could be the danger, so I picked up speed.

Getting close to the area, I heard laughter and relaxed. Approaching the sound, I found Gaax had taken human form and was sitting naked in front of a fire with Richard.

"There he is. I warn you, he's a bit grouchy," Gaax said.

"A bit grouchy? Me? Gee, I can't see why," I said. "Been ridin' for two days lookin' for this asshole who didn't even bother to leave me a note!"

"And take the chance that someone else would find it?" Dick said. "You taught me better than that."

"You coulda sent word with a Regulator Network guy," I offered. "But oh no, instead, you leave me wanderin' the countryside lookin' for your worthless ass with that thing," I said, pointing at Gaax.

Dick's eyes zeroed in on my pants. "Shit on you again, did he?"

Gaax laughed.

I jumped down from my horse and took steps toward Gaax. "I'm gonna string you up, you little naked bastard!"

Dick stood up and stopped me with a hand on my shoulder. "You're not mad at him. You're mad at me."

Fuming, I looked up at the big man. "Yes, I am! Dammit, Dick. If Zahara hadn't been able to find you, I never would've."

"It's good to see you, too."

I took off my hat and hit him with it. "You're an asshole."

Dick laughed, and I caved. "It's good to see you, too, you pain in the ass. I was worried I'd not find you."

"That might've been for the best, you know."

"Dear Christ, you're not about to go on a speech again about my duty to the world and shit, are you? Cause I've been havin' a rough week."

"I heard. Gaax filled me in with the basics before you caught up."

I didn't know what to say.

Dick sat down. "I'm sorry, but you left me with no choice."

I sighed. "I didn't do it on purpose. Ugh, come on, Colonel, let's get you settled for the night. We are stayin' here, right? I'm beat and so is Colonel."

"Yeah, we'll stay here. It's the best spot to be for now. We'll head out tomorrow."

"What's for dinner?" Gaax asked.

"Always thinkin' with your stomach, bird boy," I said.

"Shifting makes me ravenous. Get it? Raven-ous?" He started to laugh like the fool he was, falling over on the mat he'd sat on.

Dick and I shared a look, rolled our eyes, and fought a laugh.

"Gaax will help me with the leftover deer I've got salted down. You take care of Colonel, and we'll eat when you're done. You can tell me about your adventure, and I'll tell you mine."

I opened one of the saddle bags. "And Gaax will put on some pants."

Gaax rolled his eyes at me. "What is it with you and clothes, man?"

"Pants!" I said, tossing the pair he usually borrowed from me at him.

"Fine...pants...whatever," he muttered and began to put them on.

"Ya know, for a man in his sixties, you sound just like a twelve-year-old."

Gaax flipped me the bird, Dick laughed, and I had to admit, I felt much better...even though there was bird shit on my pants.

"Tomorrow we'll head to Picacho so you can meet Edward," Dick said.

"The man you were with two nights ago?"

"Yes. He's...well...he's a lot like me. You'll see."

* * *

We reached Picacho after the sun set the next day, and Dick maneuvered Mattie through the dark like he'd memorized the land. Me? I had to pull on some of my extra energy to enhance my vision so I'd not run into him out here in the black of night.

"Too bad Gaax decided to head back," Dick said.

"Meh," I said.

"Y'all have a love/hate relationship."

"He loves to hate me?"

"Naw...y'all like each other, but because you're forced to be connected in such a way as you are, you hate each other. Someday maybe you'll both find peace with it."

"Or break the connection," I said, just as I noticed a light in the distance. "Is that where we're headed?"

Dick laughed.

"Something funny I should know about?"

"He said it would be a big party you'd be able to see from miles away. He wasn't wrong."

"Who? Edward?"

"Yes. Come on, he's expectin' us. We'd hate to miss out on all the fun."

"Says the man who prefers to be alone on his ranch most of the time," I pointed out.

"This is different. Come on," Dick said with a huge grin before giving Mattie a nudge and taking off at a good clip toward the light in the distance.

Not to be outdone, I gave Colonel the command as well. "Gonna let that girl show you up?"

Colonel whinnied and took off, causing my hat to almost take a spin out into the dark. Thankfully, I caught it and prayed we didn't hit bad terrain. Closing in on the glow we'd seen from a distance, we discovered multiple fire pits, the one at center shooting flames four feet up toward a clear sky of stars. This was the fire where dancing and chanting were taking place, with other merriment outside the dancers.

The closer we got, I noticed that this was a party of The People, a tribal gathering of sorts, and I had to swallow my fear. Dick always knows what he's about, so I trusted him and tethered my horse beside his before heading toward the four-foot fire. As we approached, members of the tribe would stop what they were doing to stare at us as we passed by.

"Dick?" I whispered, wanting to reach for my gun but knowing better.

"It's all okay, trust me." He then turned to someone and said, "Our presence here was requested by Nantan Lupan."

Many nodded and went back to their revelry while others passed along this request from one person to another. Not ten seconds later, the tall man I'd seen in the magic circle with Zahara emerged from the smoke, dressed in the ceremonial garments of his tribe, which I recognized as Hopi. Though obviously older than Dick or myself, his skin appeared ageless as he moved with the grace I'd only seen in the animal kingdom.

The smoke and people seemed to part for him as he emerged, arms wide. "My friends, I'm glad you have come!"

Dick embraced the man. "There you are! Happy birthday, Nantan Lupan." With a slap on the back, he stepped away. "Billy, this is my good friend who I told you about. Edward, this is William Bonney."

"I've heard much about you," Edward said, his voice majestic in a way only the oldest and wisest of tribe members would sound.

I shook his outstretched hand. "I've heard minimal about you, but I can see why. You would be hard to describe without soundin' like a character from a story."

Edward laughed. "That is the most honest thing I think I've ever heard when meeting someone new." He looked to Dick. "You said he was all or nothing. I see what you meant."

"That makes one of us," I said.

Edward's gray eyes examined my face intently. "It can be understood to be many things, Cheveyo. But for you, I feel the universe means you are all in or not in at all. There is no mid-way with you. You tell it like it is, and you are yourself. True of heart. This is a common trait in your kind."

"My kind? Why, Edward, I didn't know the Hopi had classified poor orphaned Irish boys. What do you call our kind?"

Edward's face said nothing. But he looked to Dick and said, "You didn't tell him."

"That's your tale to tell, Nantan Lupan, not mine. I do not tell other people's stories."

"Hell, he doesn't tell his own, what makes ya think he'd tell someone else's?" I said.

Before Dick could reply, Edward said, "Cheveyo, I speak of her chosen."

My heart skipped a beat, and I casually hooked my right thumb on my belt close to my gun. "*Her* chosen?"

"Scáthach is choosy in her immortal warriors. They all tend to have similar characteristics."

Now my hand did rest on my gun as I glared at Brewer. "What was that about not tellin' other people's stories, Dick?"

"It's not what ya think. He's like me," Dick said quietly.

"Oh, not exactly. I didn't have a warrior claim my soul for me. I earned it back."

"And exactly how long did that take?" I asked.

"For most, it takes fifty years. It took me thirty. This is my birthday celebration you are attending. I am officially one hundred years old today, Cheveyo."

"Why do you keep calling me that?"

He smiled, but it didn't reach his eyes. In the great depths of gray, I saw a deep sadness that I felt in my chest as he replied. "Many moons ago, when I was part of the Hopi Tribe northwest of here, I knew a warrior of hers once before. I called him Cheveyo. It means spirit warrior."

My interest was piqued. "You knew another like me?"

He nodded. "But we shall save that tale for another time when the atmosphere lends to it. Tonight, I wish to celebrate by telling stories of victory and honor. Come, you are my guests tonight. I shall introduce you to my friends. You will eat, drink, dance, and when the sun rises, we will speak more of history and how it is important, Cheveyo."

"I never turn down a chance to dance!" I said with a tense chuckle.

"I am not surprised. Come, eat, we have killed the biggest of the stock and roasted him. He was good to us in life; he will now do our bodies good in death."

I glanced at Dick, and he knew my looks well enough now to interpret.

"You trust me, and I'm sayin' he's a good man."

"Okay...but if they decide to try and kill us later, I'm gonna be mad as hell."

Dick rolled his eyes. "Come on, food awaits."

"Yeah, Edward had me convinced at 'come eat.'"

The evening passed enjoyably. We danced, drank, ate enough for two people each, and in the morning, over the best coffee I'd ever had, I learned why every werewolf out there wanted to kill me.

"His name was Elias Story, and he was old," Edward told us over breakfast. "Sure, he looked no more than twenty, but he claimed to have been born in December of 1600 in Holland. He said he came to this country as an orphaned servant boy, an apprentice, who all believed had died in the winter of 1621. But he did not. And his tale will maybe help you with your own."

Edward sat and poured himself some coffee. Drinking it black, he continued. "Elias became ill like many of the settlers in Plymouth the winter of 1620. A woman who he had befriended on the journey tended to him and was impressed with how hard he fought, how much he loved his life and this new land. So much so that when his fever was high and he neared the end, she asked him if he'd give anything to get well, if he would be willing to let her take him to a medicine woman.

"He agreed. They stole away from the ship in a storm at night, and in an all-consuming fever, he agreed to things he never would have. He was given a potion and awoke renewed. Elias wanted to return to the ship, but she explained how they were both proclaimed dead. He could not return."

"This devious woman, she was Scáthach, I take it?" I asked.

Edward nodded. "She had him trapped. Presumed dead and magically healed, he couldn't return. Instead, he lived with her and two other women. They trained him to be the first Spirit Warrior of the new land."

Dick blew out a breath. "No pressure there."

Edward nodded. "He was miserable, and his growing hatred for Scáthach and one of her women consumed him. The third saw his need to be free, recognizing it in herself as well, and she helped him escape. They began anew, joining a new settlement in New Netherland."

"New what?" I asked.

"Five years later, the Dutch would buy an island of that region from the Iroquois. That area was called Manhattan, and almost forty years later, England named her New York."

"I was born there, or so I think," I said. "I'm not a hundred percent sure on that though."

Dick filled his mug with more coffee. "His shipmates and employer just accepted that what, in his illness, he fell overboard and was washed out to sea?"

"Yes," Edward said. "His name is listed with others who died that winter of the plague that overtook so many. And thus, history has no real record of Elias Story other than that."

"I take it he ended up out here," I said.

"Yes, and as years passed, he decided to hunt Scáthach down to earn his freedom. He and the woman who saved him followed her trail of monsters here to New Mexico. Elias got so close to regaining his soul by sending her back to the Otherworld, but in the end, he loved others more than himself. For as he lay dying, he chose one last selfless act. He used the last of his power to return to the woman who'd saved him all those years ago and then told me to kill him."

Edward paused, emotion heavy upon him. "You see, he was dying anyway. Even killing me wouldn't have saved him. So instead, he died at my hand, the act of which won me back my soul. That gift wasn't free, though. I had to promise him that I'd care for that woman until the day she died. So, you see, Cheveyo, that is why they want to kill you. It will win them back their soul and end their servitude to Scáthach."

This hit me hard in a way I'd not expected it to. "How did you kill him? Will a bite do it?"

"No. A bite will make a warrior of Scáthach go mad unless he can kill the wolf that bit him and kill him by the first full moon after he was bitten. When that occurs, the warrior will age and die a madman, with no chance to save his soul."

"What?" Dick sputtered, the look of horror on his face as thick as an adobe brick. Standing up, he opened his mouth to say something, but instead walked away from the breakfast fire. Hands in his hair, he paced a few times before he said, "There's other options though, right? I mean, what if I accidentally bite Billy?"

Edward's face was grave. "Then he will have a hard decision to make."

I knew Dick was on the brink of running for the hills, so I said, "You never would be that careless. It's not like we wrestle and play like I do with Punch."

"Punch?" Edward asked.

"John Tunstall's dog." I laughed, thinking of that silly boy. "You should see him. He's got this silly tongue that hangs to the side when you—"

"How can you joke about this?" Dick demanded.

I stood. "Because, Worrywart Wendy, you are freakin' out enough for both of us. Look, I'll start wearin' head to toe armor when we hang out if it'll calm you down. Sure, it'll chafe, but I'm willing to deal—"

Dick grabbed me by the front of my shirt with both hands and pulled me up onto my toes. "That wouldn't save you if I lost sight of things!"

I saw the crazy silver glow touch his eyes and knew he was honestly petrified, igniting his animal rage. I could either joke or prove my competence.

"Set me down, Dick. Don't make me ask twice."

"Like you could make me," he said, his voice a partial growl, as he lifted me up off the ground.

"I warned ya, pal."

Channeling soul energy through my palms like Zahara had shown me this last visit, I brought my hands up and brushed past his, sending a shock through his skin, causing him to let go. Free from his grasp, I shoved at his chest with the rest of the energy. Dick flew back from me a good fifteen feet, landing hard on the dirt.

Edward began to laugh. It was deep and genuine. Clapping, he said, "Richard, my boy, never assume you are stronger or more capable than a Scáthach Warrior. They manipulate creation energy through every cell in their body."

Dick stood, the usual ruddiness of his cheeks amped up with embarrassment as he dusted the dirt from his pants, listening to Edward speak.

"Many a wolf has lost their life to a child of Scáthach before guns were brought to this country, and not by an arrow. If a warrior wanted to stop your heart with his bare hands, he could," Edward explained. "The more trainin' he receives, the deadlier he'll be. More to you than you to him."

"Except I'd never kill him," I said so matter-of-factly that Edward looked to me with pause, causing me to add, "What?"

"You wouldn't, would you? You'd go mad first. How interesting."

"Yeah, right," Dick said. "Billy would put a bullet in me if I ate his bacon...if it was his life or mine, he wouldn't choose to be stupid."

"Bacon is sacred," I said, hand on heart. "You eat my bacon, and you very well might get a bullet somewhere interesting." I made my point by sitting down and taking the last piece, biting it in half and humming of glee. "But kill Dick here? Not sure I could do that."

"You're an idiot," Dick said, sitting back down.

"I've been called worse."

Edward turned to me. "I think what he means, Cheveyo, is—"

"See, worse right there. Please call me Billy."

Edward examined me. "You do not find being a warrior an honor."

It wasn't a question. I heard that straight off. Even so, I replied. "No, sir. No, I don't. It's a curse, plain and simple."

"Men sometimes search their whole lives for purpose to find nothing. You've been handed one and yet you don't see."

"I never wanted a purpose. I just wanted to live a life with food in my belly, some cards in my hand, a good horse under me, and a beautiful woman on top of me."

"That is a canned answer," Edward said, disapproval in his voice and on his face.

I stood. "Well, I'm sorry to disappoint you, that's the answer." I tipped my hat. "If you'll excuse me." I walked off without knowing where I was going. Honestly, I didn't care.

I didn't know why I was so upset, so I went to take a leak and wash up in the stream. When I returned, Edward and Dick were talking close. Instead of interrupting a wolfy pow-wow, I snagged a cigarette and went to sit on a big rock overlooking the valley.

With still no answer as to why Edward had upset me, I wasn't keen to going back to talk to him some more anyway. I would've been happy to leave then and there, but I couldn't fault Dick. This was the one person he knew like him and he'd want to learn all he could. Hell, if I could meet another of my kind, we'd probably be as thick as thieves.

It made me wonder about the letter I'd written to Tom back in early March. If he'd gotten it, would he come? Would I like him, or he, me? Either way, I was learning a lot from Zahara, but if one of my own kind were to come to town, maybe he and I could work together to end this curse.

One could hope.

4

THE FRITZ RANCH AMBUSH

April 1878

U nsure how much time had passed, me wandering about in my own head an' all, I was mildly startled by the sound of my name.

"Billy?"

I looked over to see Dick. "Yeah?"

"Everythin' all right?"

"Yeah, just, feelin' off. Sorry if I upset your friend."

Dick smirked. "It takes a lot more than that to upset him. Trust me. Besides, he expected you to be...testy, I think is the word he used."

"Testy?" I laughed. "Yeah, I guess I feel that way."

"He said that our kind can do that to the chosen warriors."

"You don't make me testy...well, not all the time."

Dick laughed wholeheartedly, his face lighting up in a way I'd not seen in a long time. "Yes, I do. I'm a loner, Billy. I'm not fond of spendin' my time with people. You, on the other hand, thrive with an audience to hear your every word. You step into a room and everyone knows."

"Everyone notices when you do, too."

"Cause I'm six feet four, a giant to most around here. Add in that I'm over two-hundred pounds of muscle, and ya can't miss me comin' into a room...where I'd prefer no one saw me at all."

He was quiet for a moment. Toeing a rock, he added quietly, "It's why Mattie felt we didn't belong together. She was a lot like you and wanted a life in the city near family and friends so that we could have people over and attend parties. I wanted to live out on this farm, land my father was giving to give me, and raise animals far away from all those people she wanted to be around."

I could hear the sorrow in his voice under the layer of "understanding" he used as he spoke of something he'd never touched on before. In its own way, it broke my heart, but I said nothing so he would continue.

"I loved her my whole life, more than anythin', but she felt we were just too different for each other. In no way did she want to be a farmer's wife, and I had zero desire to be a merchant in town."

"You were what, my age at the time?"

"A year younger, eighteen." Dick eased himself onto a large boulder, and with his hands in his lap, he looked out at the sky in the distance. "Ten years have passed, and we've written. She married my cousin, and they have a son. She's happy, or she seems to be, and that's all I ever wanted for her."

"Your cousin? Ouch."

Dick laughed lightly. "Yeah, well...Henry is six years older than me, making him three years older than Mattie. I think she saw a young kid wantin' to go live alone on the land, somethin' she had no desire for, and she just couldn't do it, no matter how much she loved me. I can't blame her. She'd hate it out here."

"You don't know that."

"Oh, but I do. Maybe in a hundred years or so when it's all settled with all the comforts of the bigger cities, she'd like it...see its beauty the way I do now, but by then she'll be gone and..."

"And you'll still be around," I said.

His blue eyes now stared at me with heavy intent. "Yeah, I'll still be here, and because of that, I'm very happy she didn't follow me out here. How would I deal with that?"

I shrugged. "I don't know."

He looked up at the sky. "I miss her though. I miss writin' to her, knowin' I'll hear back...I can't write her anymore."

I hurt for him. I wanted to help, so I opened my mouth to offer up an idea, but I never got a word of it out.

Pain so raw and real encapsulated my skull. My hands flew to my head to make sure it hadn't split open. Wailing like a dying man, I dropped to the ground, rolled onto my side, and shoved my palms into my temples.

Dick knelt by my side. "Billy? Oh my God, what is goin' on? Edward!"

Then half of my vision was taken from me, and I knew. "Gaax" was all I could mutter before the raven's view was all I saw.

The aerial view was of the Bonito Valley as Gaax swooped past three riders, making sure to be low enough to show me their faces. It was Frank MacNab, Frank Coe, and Ab Saunders. They were riding along, Coe in the lead on a faster pony, approaching the orchards near the Fritz Ranch.

Once Gaax seemed to understand I knew who he was watching, he flew toward the ranch itself and over the roof. There I saw a large group of horses hidden behind the home, some with men in the saddle, some without, and men on the roof with guns. That's when I understood my friends were riding into an ambush.

I scrambled on the dirt in earnest until I felt Dick's strong hands stop me. Unable to help those I was being shown, I watched as my friends, unaware of the men waiting for them, stopped for a cool drink at the little spring brooklet that ran by the Fritz Ranch. Saunders and MacNab dismounted, and Frank was about to, when a volley of shots by the twenty men in hiding surprised them.

Frank Coe put his spurs to his horse and attempted to ride away at full speed. Almost out of range, a stray bullet hit his horse in the head. After still trotting a few more feet, his mount fell dead. Coe got up and ran for shelter into a gully as Gaax took to the air, following MacNab now instead.

MacNab also had fled into a gully, hand on his abdomen as blood seeped through his fingers. It wasn't his only wound, but it appeared to be a mortal one, slowing him down. Dragging himself up a hill, one of the Seven Rivers posse followed him. I couldn't tell who it was, but I watched in fury as he filled MacNab with buckshot. It was overkill, and I yowled as rage overtook me and Dick's arms gripped me tighter.

Gaax also reacted in kind, his *QUARK-QUARK* holding an anger I'd not heard often. Thankfully, it caused the man to turn toward him, and I saw his face. It was Dolan's number one tracker, Miguel Segovia, a man often referred to as "The Indian."

He took a shot at Gaax but missed.

I could hear both Dick and Edward talking to me from what felt like miles away, but I couldn't find a balance between my real location and Gaax's. Buried deep inside the raven's psyche, I was trapped watching as Segovia turned his attention on Frank Coe. He split the team to flush him out of the gully labyrinth. Frank was no fool, though. He soon understood the only way to save his life was to surrender, so he came out, hands high.

"Where's Ab?" I muttered.

Gaax understood me and flew past the group who led Frank to the ranch to Ab. He was still alive, laying on the ground by the water, gasping in pain as tears slid down his face. The rage in my gut became an inferno. Ab had never been a part of this war. He was neutral, a good citizen, and had never lifted a gun to anyone. Yet, here he was, paying for my sins, my curse.

Gaax turned sharply and beat his wings to gain height. He soared over the posse and landed on a tree next to the ranch. Hopping down a branch to a better vantage point, I finally saw Frank Coe and could hear him.

"Please, Ab ain't never done nothin' to you and he's layin' out there!"

He must've been begging them to help the whole way up to the ranch, for the Seven Rivers posse seemed worn down by his words.

The leader, a man I recognized as Robert Beckwith, sent men down to the spring brooklet. When they returned with Ab in the back of a wagon, I could see he'd been shot in the hip and the pain had finally rendered him unconscious.

Taking a chance, Gaax QUARKED at Frank Coe, who looked up, saw him, and understood.

"Ab, you hold on. Help is comin'."

"Only help he's gonna get is if we take him to Fort Stanton," Beckwith said.

A shot rang out, just missing Gaax. Segovia had also noticed the raven, and as he laughed, he took shots at him, causing Gaax to fly off.

I shouted for him not to leave, but he dropped bird shit on Segovia's head and flew off, returning my sight to me.

When my mind returned to where my body was, my head hurt like Dick had beat me with a horseshoe about the temples. Staring up at the sky, I tried to breathe. As both eyes found focus, I saw Edward and Dick leaning over me, one on either side.

I attempted to sit up. "I need to go." My vision tilted, and I lay back down. "In a minute, I need to go."

"What happened? You were completely gone," Dick said. "And it obviously hurt more than usual."

"I think both are due to how far away he is," I said, my voice sounding like a frog.

"Why, where is your skinwalker?" Edward asked.

"Friz Ranch. The Seven Rivers gang, about twenty of 'em, were lyin' in wait there for any of us who went by. They got MacNab, Frank Coe, and Ab Saunders. I have to go."

"You can't head into that!" Dick sputtered at me.

"I don't have a choice. I have to. Frank saw Gaax. He'll think I'm comin' to help." With this statement, I forced myself up. Wobbling, I reached out and steadied myself on a tree. Blinking a few times, I put my two fingers in my mouth and whistled out my call for Colonel. He came running, slowing down just perfectly in front of us.

Before either Dick or Edward could stop me, I grabbed the reins, put my foot in the stirrup, and threw my other leg over Colonel's back, settling into the saddle. "I'll be back. If I can save one of them, it'll be worth it." I rode Colonel in a small circle. "If you go somewhere else, send a message to me at the Ellis Store. If not, I'll come back here before the full moon on the sixteenth. You have my word."

With that, I urged Colonel to go, and he was off like lightning. I had to get to the Bonito Valley, and I needed to be there yesterday. I went as fast as I could, but because I couldn't waste any soul energy to help Colonel go faster, I didn't reach the ranch until around midnight. Luckily, Gaax spotted me and made a loud enough ruckus to wake the dead. Stopping, I dismounted.

Gaax landed and shifted into his human form. "Got anything to eat?"

"Well, good mornin' to you, too," I said, reaching into one of my bags for what I knew he'd want. In human form, he loved his dried meat, so I handed him some jerky and my canteen.

"Thanks," was all he said, and bit into the deer meat with a hum of satisfaction. Once his first mouthful was washed down, he said, "They left about two hours ago."

"Damn it!"

"Did they take Frank MacNab's body with 'em?" I asked, handing Gaax some clothes.

"Yes. They took all three. But I don't know where they're going."

"I want to head up to the ranch. You joinin' me?"

"Yeah."

I tossed him his pants. "Then get dressed and climb up."

This time he didn't complain. He put on the clothes, climbed up, and we quietly headed toward the ranch.

"Did they leave anyone behind?" I asked.

"Five men from what I saw."

I nodded in thought. "Moon won't be up for three more hours, so that's where I'll start."

Leaving Colonel and Gaax hidden some ways away, I emptied the lead from my second gun and filled it with silver. With both guns in hand, I kicked in the door and quickly sent four of the five souls sitting by the fire to whatever God they worshiped.

I shot the fifth man in both legs and then whistled for Colonel to come before the four souls hit me and dropped my giddy ass to the floor. Laughing, I held my gun on the last posse member and between fits of giggles got the information I needed before taking his worthless life from him as well.

As if I wasn't already as loopy as a child's kite in a windstorm, when the fifth soul hit me, I fell back onto the carpeted floor.

"Well, aren't you a mess," Gaax said as he entered the ranch, Colonel putting his head through the open doorway, whinnying in agreement.

I laughed and raised my gun to shoot at the ceiling. "Five souls in the chamber! Whoo!"

Gaax stopped me, taking my revolver. "Oh no you don't. Come on, help me get you to a bed."

"I'm useless," I said, letting my arms flop out to both sides. Looking up, I swore I could see the night sky through the ceiling, like when at Zahara's, and tried to tell Gaax all about it.

"Never mind, you can stay right here for all I care," he told me. "What is that awesome smell? Ooh, stew! This is my lucky day."

"Night," I corrected him, and then with one last giggle, I passed out.

* * *

May 1878

I awoke to the sun high in the sky and a curse on my tongue. Rolling over, my nose came in contact with a folded note with my name on it. Sitting up with a groan, my head hurting like I'd drank a whole bottle of whiskey the night before, I opened the piece of paper. It was from Gaax, blessing me out for being an idiot, telling me he left me some stew, and that he took flight at dawn to alert the boys in Lincoln.

I placed a few new logs on the remaining embers of the fire under the pot of stew. While it heated, I made my way around the room to each of the dead men and rifled through their things for some *dinero*. Finding five dollars between them, I pocket it, confiscated their guns, and snagged any cartridges they had on them.

Heading out back, I relieved their horses of anything of value before feeding them and Colonel. Back inside, I ate, rummaged the Fritz's pantry for supplies, tossed some sand on the fire, and loaded up Colonel's saddle bags with the stolen food and other items.

Easing up onto his back with a belch that alleviated some of my discomfort, we headed for Lincoln. By the time I reached the outskirts, I was lucky enough to run into George and Frank Coe, as well as Henry Brown.

"Frank!" I blurted out. "So glad to see you're all right. How'd you get away from the Seven Rivers gang? I got to the house, but you all had already left."

George piped up first. "Billy, it's damn good to see you. Thanks for sendin' Gaax with the info...though, next time we best teach the boy which Frank is Frank."

"Come again?" I asked.

Frank Coe laughed. "Seems Gaax got the Franks confused. Told George here that I was dead instead of MacNab."

"Well that got my mad up and runnin'," George said. "So Henry and I went to the roof of the Ellis Store and took a shot at a Murphy/Dolan man we saw spyin' on us."

"Isaac said no shootin'," Henry said. "But you know George."

"That I do!" I said with a laugh. "Bet you hit him right and proper!"

"Did I ever! But that brought on the shootin' from the Seven Rivers fellas, and we shot that out for a while, until Copeland called in for help from Fort Stanton."

"He was too lit to do anythin' else," Henry interjected.

"That's no lie," Frank said, eyes wide. "I could smell it on him down at *The House*."

"You were in the Dolan Store, Frank?"

He smiled wide. "Ain't Dolan's store no more. Had to claim bankruptcy on it when McSween was found innocent of charges on that ten-thousand!"

"What? Great news! But how'd you get away?" I asked.

Frank laughed. "Sons of bitches got so wrapped up in fightin' down at the Ellis Store, they forgot all about me, so I just walked out. Gauss is working there now, ya know, and seein' me, he handed me a gun to protect myself, and off I went, down the street, to help George and them out."

"But he was too late," George said. "Lieutenant Smith rode into town just before that and placed his troops between them Seven River boys and the Ellis Store, haltin' all fire. He then let the Seven River posse surrender and took them all on over to the fort."

"Without relievin' them of their weapons," Henry added. "Just let 'em keep them. Hell, if they'd been takin' *us* all to the fort, they'd have relieved us of our weapons and shackled us."

"How'd you not get taken?" I asked.

Henry took off his hat and motioned back toward town. "I hid up in the hills. That warrant for Brady has my name on it, too...so the minute I saw them comin', I lit out."

Looking mighty proud of himself, George said, "I played sick on a cot, my gun under the pillow, so they let me be. Which I'm glad I did, 'cause Frank here came a-walkin' in not five minutes later, and I was so relieved to see him!"

"Back from the dead," Frank added with a grin.

"You boys made a slick get away, that's for sure. But where's Ab and MacNab now?"

"They took 'em to the hospital at Fort Stanton. Not that they can do anythin' for MacNab, but maybe they can for Ab. Poor boy never did no wrong," George said, his voice trailing off, his inner turmoil evident.

"And McSween?" I prodded.

"Not sure," Frank said. "I'd bet he went to go claim MacNab's body since he wants to bury him by Tunstall tomorrow."

"If that's the case, then I'll stick around for a short bit. I missed John's funeral. I ain't missin' MacNab's. Tell me, how did Ab seem?"

"Doesn't look good, Billy," Frank said.

"Well, Appel will take good care of him, I'm sure."

George nodded. "Still, I wanna get over to see him and make sure."

I looked to Frank and then George. "You two are serious. You want to go into the enemy's camp, where not only the Murphes reign true, but that'd be where the Seven River gang is staying with their weapons at the ready."

"I didn't say it was a smart thing to do; I just said I wanted to do it."

"God have mercy on you, George Coe." With a heavy sigh, I added, "Look, I'll go with ya, make sure you get in and all."

There was a silence that passed between us, and I wondered what was going on, that is, until Frank gave his cousin a nod, and George spit it out.

"We were wonderin'...could you, ya know, maybe help him out like ya did me?"

I didn't need to think about that twice. "Of course I will. I have no idea how much I can do, but I'll do what I can."

Frank sighed in relief. "Thanks, Billy. We just feel so bad. Ab's a good man and neutral in all this. He just was in the wrong place at the wrong time."

I nodded. "I understand. When Gaax showed me what was happenin', I tried to get out there in time. He says I missed y'all by two hours."

"Where were ya at?" Henry asked.

"Picacho, attendin' a birthday party of sorts. Friend of Dick's."

"Did you break the news to him?" Frank asked.

"That Dick was shot?" I said. "Yeah, he knows."

"Poor bastard. I miss that beast of a man."

"Beast?" I asked with a hearty laugh.

"Biggest man in the county," Frank clarified. "If he'd not had the face of an actor, he'd been feared by anyone and everyone."

"I'll be sure to tell him that," I said. Realizing what I'd said, I added, "You know, when I visit his grave. Which reminds me, uhh...do either of ya know what happened to him?"

All three shook their heads in a gesture of honest sorrow.

"He's probably buried there at Blazer's," George offered. "That exdentist has got himself a cemetery up on a hill. Next time we're out that way, we'll have to go see."

"All right, that sounds like a plan to me."

"Speakin' of, what should we do now?" Henry asked.

"Well, I don't know about you, but I'm starvin'!" I said. "Let's head on over and get some grub in San Pat and see if we can find McSween and the others."

We spun our horses about and headed out. I was desperately glad Frank was okay, but MacNab's death sat in my gut all day and night like stone. Because of this, after we buried him next to Tunstall the next day, I stayed after everyone else had headed back to McSween's house.

Removing my hat, I stood over him and John, my heart heavy with emotion I wished wasn't there. I squatted down and spoke in what my mamma called an inside voice. "John, what a mess we're in. If you were here, none of this would be goin' on. Not that it's your fault, it's just..."

I breathed out a sigh. "I fear I'm lettin' you down. I told you I'd get every one of them sons of bitches, and I haven't. I'm workin' on it though. Just hit some snags along the way. But I ain't done yet, not by a long shot. So just hang tight. I'll keep my promise as best I can."

I turned my attention to MacNab. "I'm sorry I wasn't there for you, brother. I promised to help keep y'all safe from them, and now you're gone and Ab is in the hospital. We're fallin' apart. We need a leader. Maybe Doc will step up and do that. The Coes probably think I'm gonna do it. No way! I'll just pull more heat on y'all if I do that. I learned this morning why them demons are comin' for me, and I sure as hell don't want any more of you caught in that crossfire.

"Well, I best be goin'...you two take care of one another up there and say hi to my mom for me. Tell her I miss her fiercely, and I'm sorry I let her down, too."

Standing back up, I put my hat on and walked to join Fred and Charlie. Seeing as I had money to collect and a meeting at McSween's to avoid, we three paired up with the Coes and headed on out, discussing how we were going to get in to see Ab. If his injuries were as bad as they were saying, I needed to try and heal him best I could and soon. If he died before I could get to him, I'd never forgive myself.

* * *

With no more Justice of the Peace in Lincoln, McSween got the one in San Patricio, José Trujillo, to swear affidavits against the members of the Seven Rivers gang for the murder of MacNab and another for the attempted murder of Saunders and Coe.

Next morning, May second, word was Sheriff Copeland would head up to Fort Stanton to serve the warrants. Knowing this, the Coes and I figured no one would notice if we slipped off, and we headed off to the hospital.

"You sure you can't just come in with us?" George asked.

"No way in hell. Trust me. Appel would report seein' me in a heartbeat. Go on in and stick to the plan."

"All right, Billy, if you say so," George said.

I made my way to the other side of the hospital where few tended to roam and waited for the boys to forfeit their guns and be shown to the room. It didn't take long until I heard Frank up above me.

"Psst! Up here!"

Thankful it was just the second floor. I nodded, waved him away, and with the prep Zahara had taught me, I pulled on soul energy and jumped up, catching the windowsill. With each Coe taking an arm, they pulled me into the hospital, and I did my best not to clatter into the room like a drunkard.

Quickly we surrounded Ab, and I sat on the edge of his bed.

"Hey, Billy, good to see you... You didn't need to come all this way..."

George snickered at Ab. "You're as high as a kite!"

"Likely got him doped up on morphine," Frank pointed out.

Laying my hand on Ab's forearm, I said, "I'm going to see if I can help heal your hip."

"I may be the one on morphine, but Billy, that's not my hip," he said with a grin.

"I ain't stickin' my hand down your pants, Ab. I can send the energy through you this way."

"Oh, okay…"

Shutting my eyes, I focused on the soul energy my body housed and sent it as a steady stream into Ab. Interestingly enough, this time I could feel it seep into the wound near his hip and promote healing, reknitting the tissue inside to repair damage and restore blood flow. As I did this, I heard George talking to the patient next to Ab.

It was a man by the name of Charlie Kruling. He'd recognized the Coe boys when he'd come to, calling George on over to have a word. Frank moved to block me from Kruling's view as George walked on over. He, too, stood in Kruling's line of sight.

I heard Charlie say, "That was a wonderful shot you made at the fellow sittin' on the beef-head yesterday."

"You bet it was," George said with pride. "It's too bad you happened to be the unfortunate one there."

Hearing this, I almost broke concentration. Was the man who George shot telling George he'd made a great shot? Was everyone in here high on morphine?

"Oh, I'm not seriously wounded," Kruling said. "The ball went through both my calves and kept on goin'."

"I am sorry about that."

"Don't be. Besides, I had no business bein' up there. I think now I'll have brains enough to stay home and take care of my own business."

I finished my work on Ab quickly, and while George had Kruling talking, I told Frank I'd see him at the saloon and jumped out the window.

Landing sure and steady on my feet, I headed around the building only to stop dead in my tracks at what I saw. Moving along the building, I hid behind a big old tree, just close enough to watch as McSween, Doc, and Widenmann were marched onto the grounds as prisoners.

Not waiting to be added to the party, I rushed to Delaney's Saloon to tell Fred and Charlie what was going on.

"That's not all. We got news too," Charlie said, picking up his beer to finish it off.

Fred set his bottle down. "Seems that Lieutenant Colonel Dudley has already picked sides."

"And it ain't ours," Charlie added, belching loud and proud.

"I don't understand. McSween swore out affidavits—"

"From what we heard, so did Dolan's two top dogs, Billy Mathews and George Peppin."

"To who? What for?" I demanded to know.

"David Easton, who is a neutral justice, too," Fred said, shaking his head. "They swore out affidavits on McSween and the rest of them for riotin' and assault."

"That's ridiculous!" I blurted out.

"Like that's not bad enough, Dudley had his two lieutenants escort Copeland to San Patricio and made him arrest McSween and the rest, draggin' them all to Fort Stanton."

I sat down. "Son of a bitch!"

"That ain't all," Charlie said, waving at the barkeep, who nodded at him in return. "Seems Easton has now resigned his office. He didn't want to be seen takin' sides, so after he issued those warrants for McSween and company, he quit. That leaves only Trujillo in San Pat."

I breathed a sigh of relief. "Then McSween is as good as out."

"How so?" Charlie asked as the barkeep set a new beer by him.

"José will never hold McSween on that trumped-up charge. Those of you at the Ellis Store was just defendin' yourselves."

Charlie took a good swallow of his new beer. "But Coe shot first, so technically…"

"Technically, my ass, that's bullshit, and you know it," I said.

"I do," Charlie replied. "But that's the grounds Dudley is standin' on."

I grunted. "I hate that man, and I've never even met him."

Fred nodded. "Don't have to meet a man when his actions tell you all ya need to know."

"Hear, hear," Charlie said, and clinked beer bottles with Fred.

Feeling antsy, I stood up. "I best get movin' then."

"Sure you don't want to stay for a beer, wait on George and Frank?" Fred asked.

"Naw, I'm good. Seems to be gettin' a bit hot around here, and if Dudley is willin' to pull this kinda shit, God only knows what he'd do if he knew I was around. Besides, I need to see a woman about a horse." I set some money on the bar. "Frank and George will need a drink when they get here. Fill 'em in and use that to buy 'em what they want."

"Will do," Fred said.

I put my hat on. "You two should think of gettin' outta this area after that. If you're not careful, they'll lock you up, too."

"We'll bail," Charlie said.

"Good," I said. "Oh, and if y'all need me, send a message via Gaax. I hear he's still at the Ellis Store."

"Where should we tell him you are?" Charlie asked.

I grinned. "Eatin' apples. He'll understand."

"If you say so," Charlie said, and drank more beer.

Fred stood and slapped my shoulder. "You be careful."

"I'll try."

With that, I headed out to Colonel, and we began to work our way to Zahara. She was the woman I needed to see about my horse. I had an idea I wanted to run past her for him. Plus, it couldn't hurt to do more training. After all, the full moon was in two weeks, and something told me I needed to be ready for it.

5

BEING WATCHED

May 1878

A fter she gave a long goodbye, to Colonel, not me, Zahara let us leave and make our way back to Picacho. Gaax had brought me directions to Edward's home, and I arrived on the thirteenth around five o'clock in the evening. Though a good two hours until the sun set, I knew the moon was still in the sky even if I couldn't see it. This was supported further when I found two wolves staring each other down in Edward's front yard.

Recognizing Dick, I dismounted and said to Colonel, "Don't go far. We might not want to be around for all this."

Slowly, I approached as the two large wolves circled one another. Edward was a beautiful wolf, a silver-gray color tipped black and cinnamon in a pattern that appeared from this angle to not wrap around to his belly, leaving it a silvery white color. His tail was full and his ears furry. Though big, Edward was a bit smaller than Brewer. But really, who wasn't?

"Is everythin' all right over here?" I asked, hand on my gun.

Both wolves growled at me, barking something before they went back to staring one another down.

"All right then, I'll just let you two deal with this while I make us some food." I headed toward Edward's home, keeping an eye on the two wolves.

Edward's eyes flicked to me and back to Brewer. Then, as fast as flash powder, Edward was running toward me, jaws open wide. I didn't want to hurt him, but I didn't want him to kill me either. If his earlier friendship was a ruse, this was not the moment to try and figure it out.

Running, I headed for the house. Using a small tree near it, I catapulted myself up onto the flat roof of Edward's home. However, this still wasn't overly high, since his home was partially in the ground, and as I backed up, Dick ran full tilt toward Edward, bowling him over. Edward yipped in pain as Dick pinned him, grabbing Edward's throat with his enormous jaws. Eyes wide, I stared down in shock as it appeared Dick was about to rip Edward's throat out.

In the blink of an eye, Edward relinquished control by relaxing, and Dick let go, backing away from his elder, who smoothly shifted back into his human form. Edward's transformation was graceful and easy, almost beautiful to watch, even though he now lay there naked as the day he was born.

Dick followed suit, but his transition wasn't as clean or painless. His howl turned into a human shout as he completed the shift. Also naked, Dick leaned forward, hands on his knees while he worked through the pain.

Edward applauded and sat up. "Not bad. Seems you just needed some real encouragement. Transition was smoother, too. You're getting there."

Dick lifted a hand in thanks, still catching his breath. Finally, he stepped forward, offering that hand to Edward, who took it before allowing Dick to help him to his feet.

"Anyone want to tell me what the hell is goin' on?" I shouted down to the two.

"Hey there, Billy," Edward said, using my real name, which I appreciated. "Just been doing some training while you were in Lincoln." He stretched, popping his neck, and headed into the house, saying something about bugs and clothes.

Brewer's skin, usually white as rice, save for his farmer's tan, now showed signs of sunbathing in the nude. In fact, he was a bit pink-skinned from the waist down.

"Is your ass sunburned, Brewer?" I asked, trying not to laugh.

"Shut up," he said, and walked over to a bag beside the house.

I sat on the edge of the roof, legs dangling. "No, really, you look a bit red down there."

Dick pulled on a pair of knee length, summer undergarments. "Well, in case you didn't realize it, until the past few days, the moon has been up along with the afternoon sun, so while we worked on shiftin', I got a bit burned." He adjusted the V-ties in the back of the drawers for comfort and fit and turned to me. "Where've ya been?"

"Stopped to train with Zahara, helped heal Ab as best I could, and I stayed to bury MacNab. Not in that order."

Dick's face fell, and anger lit behind his eyes, silver glowing. "Who killed him?"

Edward opened the door. "Breathe, Richard. There is nothing you can do now. Let us eat, and Billy can fill us in on what's been going on."

"Sounds like a good idea," I said.

Edward looked up at me. "And get off my roof."

"Yep, sorry about that, but you were comin' to eat my face."

"I was not. I was trying to force your friend to attack me," he said and went back inside.

I looked at Dick. "Don't have it in ya to kill a wolf?"

Dick grabbed up his pants and put them on. "Not one like Edward."

I hopped down without the help of the tree, my ankles and knees accepting the weight of the drop without pain. "What about one that doesn't own his soul?"

Dick picked up his bag. "Not a problem."

He didn't sound as sure as his words, but I didn't want to argue with him. I just nodded and opened the door of Edward's dugout for him. "After you, red buns."

He stopped and grinned down at me. "Keep that up and next time, I'll let him pin you."

"Good to see you, too, big man."

Dick just shook his head with a laugh, then ducked under the doorway and went down the stairs into Edward's home. I set Zahara's gift just inside the door before shutting it and heading to sit down for a feast of venison stew, bread, and fresh fruit. As we ate, I told them of the fight at the Fritz Ranch, the Ellis Store skirmish, Coe's amazing shot, visiting the hospital, and the arrest of McSween and the rest.

"Well, now we know Dudley isn't on our side, that's for sure," Dick said.

"Understatement of the day," I retorted. "So now what?"

"Well," Edward said, "moon is still up, so Dick and I have more work to do."

Dick nodded in agreement as they both began to disrobe again.

"Are you two about to wander the world naked, or is this a wolf thing?"

"Hunting," Edward said.

"More trainin'," Dick replied.

"Am I required on this trip? If so, can I keep my clothes on?"

Edward grinned. "No, I would ask that you stay here and keep an eye on the property while we are out. We'll be back just before the moon sets."

I thought about what I'd read that morning. "Three in the mornin', right?"

"Close enough. Get some rest; we'll be back later."

With that, they stepped out under the light of the moon, shifted, and ran off into the night.

* * *

I awoke the next day before either of the wolfy boys, so I tended to the horses and other livestock Edward had. It'd save him time and earn me my keep for eating his food and all. Specifically, I checked in on Colonel and his new shoes.

"They feel okay?" I asked as I lay his saddle blanket across his back.

He pranced in place, making me chuckle.

"You know how lucky you are that a witch loves you, right?"

He whinnied, shaking his mane and swishing his tail.

I lifted his saddle up and set it in place. "She knows you love her, too. Don't worry. Hell, I'm pretty sure if you visited without me, she might not even notice I wasn't there."

Once he and Mattie were saddled up, I led them around to the front, not just as a warning system, but to be ready to head out. I wanted some time to talk to Brewer, and the best way to do that was to take a ride.

After breakfast, I got time to do exactly that.

"Moon rises quarter past five," Edward said. "Be back before then."

"Thanks, Mom!" I said in jest.

Eyes narrow, Edward added, "Be ready to go back out and work, Richard."

"I know," Dick said, and we headed off to hunt.

While riding, we got small talk out of the way. "How was the work last night?"

He grinned. "It was amazing! We've been workin' on recognizin' the difference between wolves, coyotes, and werewolves on sight and smell. I tracked down a two-man werewolf huntin' party, and we fought 'em. Richard had me deal with the smaller of the two, and we got the answer to your question."

"Which one?"

"If I had it in me to kill one."

"Good to hear! Of course, you're releasin' them from servitude more than killin' them. But still, good to hear you did well. You made sure no one followed y'all afterward, right?"

"Of course."

"Good."

Silence slid into place, and as I began to bring up what I wanted to talk about, he spotted a deer, and it had to wait. But once we were almost back to Edward's, I got back around to it.

"How long do you want to stay here?"

"As in here with Edward or here in New Mexico?"

"Yes. The longer we stay, the higher the chance someone who thinks you're dead sees you. We need to be gettin' on. I was thinkin' Colorado or Texas since I could still be wanted for murder in Arizona."

"*You* can't leave, not now," Dick said. "The Regulators will need ya now more than ever."

"You really want to stay here and take your chances?"

He shrugged. "For a while, but you're right. I need to leave soon."

"I'm comin' with ya, pal."

"William…"

"Oh, there's the full name thing again."

"You can't leave. Not yet. Join me later. I'll send where I'm at through Edward. When this is all over, you can join me."

I gave him side-eye. "You're not still freaked out, worryin' you'll accidently bite me, right?"

A beat passed, and he said, "No, I'm not. It's fine."

If Brewer ever told a lie, that was the one time. I was about to say so when my enhanced sight noticed the door to Edward's home ripped from its hinges, laying on the ground, five feet from the house.

"Uh, Dick. Edward's in trouble." I pointed to the door in the distance.

"Hey-ya!" he yelled out, snapping the reins and hitting Mattie's sides with his heels.

I did the same to Colonel, and we were flying across the land. Reaching the front of the house, we both dismounted quickly and ran for the front door. Sensing something was off, I shoved Brewer out of the way just as a bullet was fired from inside the house toward us. It missed my head by inches.

We both pulled our guns, and I raised mine to fire inside the house.

"Wait!" Dick said. "What if Edward is in there?"

"What if he's shootin' at us?" I countered.

"He's not. You know that."

"The big man is right," a throaty woman's voice said, and my blood went cold.

I stepped in front of Dick and backed him up along the front of the house, aiming my gun at the door as Scáthach walked out, a gun in her hand. Turning toward us, her brown eyes landed on my face. "Hello, Henry. It's good to see you again."

"I wish I could say the same. What are you doin' here? I thought you were happy pullin' the strings of the Santa Fe Ring and watchin' your puppets play?"

"I'm more of a hands-on kind of gal, but you know that, don't you?"

"Billy, who is this?" Dick asked.

She placed her gun into a shoulder holster and put her hand out, "Scáthach is my formal name," she said, being sure to pronounce it correctly as SKAW-huhck, so Dick would catch it. "But you can call me Mary, gorgeous."

I stepped back again, moving Dick farther away from her. "More like evil incarnate, but hey, the name Mary works too, for now."

Dick aimed his gun at Scáthach, and she laughed.

I pulled the hammer back on my revolver. "There's nothing here for you."

"Oh, I disagree," she purred, eyes on Brewer.

"Do not let her touch you," I told him.

"Don't plan on it," he said, sounding cocky.

"Oh, handsome, if you shoot me, he'll kill you. I can leave this body as it dies and find another, maybe even yours…"

"Doubt it," Dick said.

"If not, I could were-taint you, and then you'd be mine anyway."

I felt Dick inhale to say something I didn't want her to know, so I elbowed him. "She's right. You can't kill her and you don't want her to sic one of her mutts on you."

Scáthach wagged a finger at me. "Ooh, that was harsh, Henry. I thought we were friends."

"You left me locked up in an adobe prison surrounded by your monsters last time I saw you. The time before that? You broke my neck. So no, I don't think we're friends."

"You're not still holding that against me, are you? I mean, you were so rude. What else was I supposed to do?"

"I don't know, maybe *not* kill me, like you'd promised when I arrived at that bar."

Her smile lit up her face like it had when Mary's soul commanded the body, and my heart thumped in my chest. "I always did love your sarcastic humor. Now toss your guns aside and let's behave like adults, shall we?"

I sighed in irritation and did as she asked. "Why are you even here?"

"Why kill Edward?" Dick asked, tossing his guns into the brush by the house like I had.

"Kill him? Oh, I didn't kill him. He's one of my favorite children. He earned his freedom by killing a warrior. Not a simple task. I'd not take that from him. However, he killed two of mine last night with a partner my boys didn't recognize. Seeing this, my scouts came to get me. I want that wolf's name."

I crossed my arms over my chest. "Edward will never tell you. That's not how he works."

"I found that out. That blood you smell, it's his."

"You bitch!" Dick blurted out, looking toward the house to hide the silver glow of his eyes.

"Oh, he'll heal," she said. "But I did learn *some* things."

When she didn't continue, I rolled my eyes. "Why do you always have to be so vague? Just say what you mean. It's not so hard. I'd think someone of your age could figure out how."

She grinned, but this time it wasn't Mary's beautiful smile. Instead, Scáthach showed her real teeth, pointed like a shark's and razor sharp.

Her eyes bled into a red like embers of a fire while the skin she wore rippled like water as she moved. "It's time."

Trying to stay calm, I said, "That's not really your best look. Time for what?"

"The moon," Dick said, his voice low, showing strain as he fought the change that would give his secret away and likely bring about his death by her hand.

Howling could be heard coming from all directions, and wolves began to emerge from around corners, behind brush, and down the mountain. We were surrounded.

A man around Dick's height exited the house. His skin was the dark tan of the Mexicans who worked in the field, but his features were European, as were his blue eyes. "Alpha, he has not changed."

"Thank you, Kamil. Very interesting. Edward is able to fight the moon even while unconscious. Fascinating."

"Wait, is Edward inside?" Dick asked.

"Yes, but he'll be of little help to you," said Kamil.

Dick moved to stand by me. "We'll see about that." Slipping past the large man, Dick quickly went down the stairs and into the house.

Kamil began to follow after him, but I was faster and blocked his way.

"I might not be able to kill her, but I'll kill you if you so much as touch either of them."

With a laugh, Kamil took a step toward me.

"Stop!" Scáthach ordered.

Kamil obeyed and looked to her, confused. "Alpha, I can take this little man."

I laughed. "He doesn't know. That's beautiful."

Kamil growled and leaned in toward me. Channeling the power inside my soul-chamber, I hit him with both hands in the chest. Energy lifted him off his feet, and he flew backward about twenty feet and landed hard on a thorny bush. Jumping up, he shouted in pain, and I couldn't help but laugh.

"Henry," Scáthach scolded.

"What? It's funny. Now take your pet and go." An idea coming to mind, I repeated myself from earlier. "There's nothing here for you."

With a growl, she grabbed me by the throat and lifted me off the ground. "You don't tell me what to do."

Using a move Zahara taught me, I hit Scáthach's arm in such a way that her human body was forced to let go of me. Landing on my feet, I stepped backward, into Edward's home. Reaching in, I opened the jar that held the gift from Zahara I'd set by the door. I grabbed a handful of the blessed salt in the large blue jar. Laying it across the threshold between us, I said it for the third time. "There's nothing here for you."

A flash of light burst from the salt, shooting upward to the top of the door.

I bared my teeth at her. "Hurt them, and I'll end you, not just your monsters. I've not put any energy into figurin' out how to get you out of Mary's body yet, but I can and will if you so much as touch either of them. Do you understand me?"

After a beat, Scáthach laughed, throwing her head back, again exposing her razor-sharp teeth. My heart wanted to pound out of my chest, but I held my ground, trusting in Zahara's magic.

Stepping toward me, Scáthach hit the door of light. A wail like those described in banshee legends ripped from her as the smell of singed hair and flesh filled my nostrils. Backing away, her eyes lit red again. Pure rage seeped from every pore of her borrowed body until she appeared to vanish into thin air.

"Warrior of Scáthach or not, I can take you," Kamil said, stepping forth and reaching through the magic ward. Doing so, an emblem on his neck I'd not noticed before began to glow as if lit from a fire under his skin. Yanking his arm out of the ward, Kamil howled in pain, his hand rushing to grab the symbol burning him.

"Go. Do not come back here. Your kind took enough lives the other day at the Fritz Ranch."

"So you're saying we're even?" Kamil growled.

"Not even close, lap dog. But give me time. I'll make it equal. MacNab was a good man. His loss is worth a hundred of you soulless beasts."

THE TORMENT OF RICHARD BREWER

"I am not without a soul," Kamil argued.

"Wait, you serve her of your own free will?" I asked, honestly surprised.

"With pride."

"Then maybe yours should be the first soul I come for."

"I'd like to see you try," he said, baiting me.

I imitated Scáthach and wagged a finger at him. "I'm not stupid, Beta boy. I'm stayin' right here, behind my ward, all night. Now shoo, go on back to your bitch queen. I'll catch you later."

"Billy?"

I turned my back on Kamil to see Dick standing there. "Is Edward all right?"

"He's comin' to now. Rough but okay. I think he should—Billy! Watch out!"

But it was too late.

6

SECOND DEATH

May 1878

Opting for pain over loss of pride, Kamil reached through the ward and wrapped his arm around my neck. He dragged me backward through the open doorway and into the yard.

Kicking out, I tried to pry his arm off me as Dick ran out.

"Stay inside!" I shouted at him.

Biting down on Kamil's arm, my teeth sank in. I tasted blood and spit it out as he threw me into the side yard with a guttural wail of agony. I flopped like a rag doll being tossed by a giant, landing at the far end of the long house. Bones broke and healed, using souls from the well, as I tried to find the power to get up.

Standing, I watched as Kamil gave in to the magic of the ward and drop to his knees. Trying to catch his breath, the blue magics danced along his tan skin as the two dozen wolves surrounding the house closed in on us all. Whistling for Colonel, I made a run for it and this time, leapt to the top of the house without the help of the tree.

Running along the length of the roof, I saw my secret weapon approaching and jumped off the house to land in the saddle on

Colonel's back just as we'd practiced. Cringing from the land, I got my feet into the stirrups, found the reins, and used energy to tell him where to go.

Coming around the front of the house, a wolf leapt at us. Rearing up, Colonel struck out, hitting the wolf in the head twice just like Zahara had trained him this past week. First hit with his new silver shoes broke the wolf's skull, second crushed it in, killing him.

Unsure what would happen with the spirit of the wolf, I braced myself. Interestingly enough, it passed through Colonel and into me, lessening the effect of the dizziness I normally felt.

"Billy!" Brewer shouted as he stepped out of the protection ward and grabbed my guns from behind the brush.

Slowing down just enough, I was able to catch one as he tossed it to me but missed the second as a wolf leapt up and knocked it to the ground.

"Damn it!"

Colonel danced in a circle as I took aim and hit a wolf, killing it, shouting to Brewer, "Get back behind the ward!"

"The hell I will!" Richard grabbed his gun and fired on the wolves.

I did the same, taking the lives of three as Colonel killed another.

Out of ammunition, Dick became frustrated, his eyes going silver.

Don't you shift! I thought, as if thinking it hard enough would make him hear me.

Head dizzy from the souls I'd taken, I shouted, "Get back behind the ward, damn it!"

This time he listened to me, and I took a quick count. Colonel and I'd taken out five, Dick had killed four, and he wasn't the only one out of ammunition. I was, too. Feeling dizzy, I held onto Colonel's mane, but it wasn't enough when a wolf slammed into me, knocking me to the ground.

Rolling a few feet, we came to a stop with him on top of me, jaws snapping at my neck. Head still spinning, I had a hard time holding him back. Teeth inched closer, my arms beginning to ache and shake. Gasping for air, I heard the sound of a rifle shot rip through the air, and kill the wolf, causing him to fall on top of me.

Head whipping to my right, I saw Brewer now armed with a loaded Winchester in the doorway behind the ward. He began to fire at will, hitting wolf after wolf as Kamil finally regained his senses, standing up just out of Brewer's line of sight.

I saw my other gun lying on the ground at the corner of the house. Kamil followed my gaze, and as I ran for the gun, so did he.

Closer and longer legged than me, he was going to beat me to it if I didn't push harder than ever. Almost there, it became evident that wouldn't happen. Understanding this, I changed direction by climbing up into the tree just as two shots missed me. But now he was where Brewer could see him, and a bullet caught Kamil in the leg.

Screaming with rage so palpable I could see his body shake, Kamil looked up at me and grinned with such malice I was already shouting Richard's name before he'd done a thing. I had to stop him, even if it meant my life. Jumping from the tree, I heard the shot. I ran at full speed, but I was too late.

I watched as a silver bullet exploded from my gun in Kamil's hand, passed through the ward, and hit Brewer's neck. He fell back into Edward's arms, blood gushing from the wound.

Hate and fear filled me, and before I could stop myself, I ran for my fallen friend as Kamil put the fourth and fifth bullet into me. I kept running. He pulled the trigger again, but nothing happened.

Tossing the gun out into the yard, Kamil stood between me and my friend. We collided with intense force, him pulling me to the ground, slamming his fist into one of my wounds before it could heal. My blood spurted out at him, and he laughed before seamlessly shifting into a wolf almost twice the size of Brewer.

A rifle shot exploded again from the house, the silver bullet catching Kamil in the hip, throwing him off me as I felt the ground rumble.

"Oh, hell yes!" I stood and began to run, and soon Colonel was galloping beside me. Grabbing onto his mane and the saddle horn, I pulled myself up onto his back as another rifle shot fired. Riding in a large arc, I saw it was Edward on his knees inside the house, firing the rifle. But he kept missing, either due to Kamil's speed or the fact that he was still in pain.

My only chance was that last silver bullet in my gun that Kamil had thrown way out into the front yard. I hit Colonel's sides with my heels, and we headed straight for it as Edward ran out of ammunition.

Kamil's eyes glowed gold, and with rabid determination, he ran for the house.

Eyes on the gun, I urged Colonel faster as we rode away from the house. "It's just like a hanky," I muttered, and at full speed lowered myself along Colonel's right side, reached down, and as we passed, I grabbed the gun while still holding onto Colonel.

This was my gun that stuck at a certain round. Hitting it on the saddle horn like only I knew how, I took aim at Kamil as he rushed toward the house. With a prayer on my lips, I fired.

Kamil dropped, but he wasn't dead.

Leaping off Colonel, I began to run to finish the job when Scáthach appeared out of nowhere between us, and with one swift motion to my neck, took my life again.

* * *

April 1949

"D id they take anything, Mr. Kidwell?" Sheriff Apodaca asked. He'd seen my credentials, so the "mister" was a dig. "I don't know, Mr. Apodaca. As I told you, I touched nothin' while waitin' for you to arrive."

Sheriff Alfonso "Happy" Apodaca's dark eyes, set into a handsome face that seemed to be happy even when in rest, landed on mine with a snarky understanding of my passive aggressive remark. Little did he know that was an improvement. My aggressive behavior used to not be so passive. I could still be that person if I had to be, but I just chose not to.

"I've seen the room now, Agent," he said, correcting himself. "If you'd be so kind as to go through your things and verify they're all here, I'd appreciate it. Includin' openin' the safe."

If I thought it odd that the sheriff himself showed up to take my break-in report, this question triggered my sixth sense into full gear. "Didn't use it," I lied. Opening my luggage, I inhaled Apodaca's scent again. He wasn't a supernat that I could tell, but he smelled like a mix of a few. Meaning he either worked, lived, or was friends with one, or all the above.

"Calvin, the boy down at the front desk, said otherwise."

Rifling through my things, I couldn't help but chuckle at the lawman's twisting of my own words in order to find out if I'd had anything in there. "What I said to Calvin was that it's lucky about rooms havin' safes when stuff like this happens. I didn't have need of it, seein' as my weapon was on me."

In truth, I'd snuck all my items from the room's safe to my car before his arrival, disguising the trip as a coffee run while Calvin and I waited.

"Always carry your weapons on you?" Apodaca asked.

The corners of my mouth eased up slowly as I let a little bit of the devil who owned my soul shine through my eyes at him. "Oh yes, always."

After a beat, I went back to digging around in my luggage, wondering how much he knew about my world or what a Scáthach Warrior even was. If so, did he know he was talking to one right now? As far as I knew, Tom and I were the last two, but the world was vast, and Scáthach's evil reached far and wide.

Looking up at him, I could tell he was searching for where I wore my gun, but I wasn't about to show him Lilith. Instead, I smiled and said, "By the way, thanks for comin' personally to take my report. You saved me a trip."

Apodaca leaned his back against the wall, crossing one foot over the other as he pulled out a pack of smokes. Offering me one, he said, "How so?"

I took a cigarette and tucked it behind my ear for later. Pulling my wallet out as he lit his cig, I slid the picture of Agent Calhoun out and handed it to him. "I'm lookin' for this man. Fellow agent. Went missin' in this area." I didn't know that last part for sure, but I was beginning to suspect it more and more. Besides, Apodaca didn't know I was fibbing, and I wanted to watch his reaction.

He handed me back the picture. "Yeah, saw him once. He was eatin' at The DeLuxe Café when I was there. Heard someone call me sheriff and made a point of comin' over to introduce himself...courtesy and all. Lettin' me know he was in my town. Somethin' you didn't do."

"Well, I have now," I said, being cheeky. "Of course, if it matters, I arrived late last night and was headin' to you after I ate breakfast at the same fantastic spot. But hey, as fate would have it, you were brought to me instead. Besides, I'm leavin' as soon as we finish our business here. Drivin' to pick up a co-worker in Albuquerque and then headin' east to Santa Fe. Do you know where Agent Calhoun was stayin'?"

Apodaca shook his head. "Nope."

That smelled like a lie. Not figuratively, but yeah...big ol' lie.

"Well, I'm gonna go question each hotel in the area then, takin' me longer to get outta your city here." I paused so he could let that sink in. "Looks like nothin' was taken, suppose the SOB just wanted to see who I was and what I was up to." Without my usual smile or charm, I continued to face my luggage and slide my eyes to catch his gaze. Using a voice that hinted to a darker meaning, I said, "Hope he got all the info he wanted to satisfy his curiosity."

The sheriff's breath hitched just enough as he inhaled his cigarette, telling me he got my meaning. He held the smoke longer than usual, only exhaling once I looked back down. In the uncomfortable silence that hung in the air, I closed and fastened my luggage, picked it up, and turned toward the door.

"You might wanna check the Amador Hotel kitty-corner from my office," Apodaca said. "Now that I think on it, I do believe your friend mentioned stayin' there."

"Good to know. I'll check it out."

* * *

May 1878

L ooks like he's checkin' back in," I heard a man say as I began to
wake up. "Go get Scáthach."

Footsteps answered his request instead of words. Opening my eyes
fully, I inspected my surroundings. I was in a cave similar to Zahara's
but filled with elegance instead of nature. There was parlor furniture,
a wood-burning stove instead of a fire pit, and a delicate china tea set
on the coffee table.

I was, however, on a cot in the center of a cage of copper. Only
other thing in with me was a chamber pot. Groaning at how I felt and
my predicament, I sat up and cursed.

"Language, Henry. Language."

My eyes landed on Scáthach as she sauntered into the room, and I
had to do a double take. Gone were the typical long dresses with a full
skirt, popular for women her age, that she usually wore. In its place
was a fitted dress in red silk that ended just below her knees.

I flipped her off anyway.

"I taught you better."

"No, *Mary* taught me better. You're not her."

"Too true." She looked me over. "You're awake sooner than I
expected. You must have a lot more souls in the well than I
thought."

"Why? How many times did you kill me on the way here? Which
begs the question, where is here?"

Slowly walking around my cage, she let one hand travel from bar
to bar with a caressing touch. "Only once more."

That told me we weren't horribly far from Picacho, but I kept that
to myself.

"Do you know what these are around you?" she asked.

"I'm going to go out on a limb here and say bars?"

"You're not in a position to be flippant."

Exasperated, I said, "Yes, copper. They likely work like the bed did before since I feel human." Approaching her, I added, "If you wanted me dead, I'd be dead. So, what *do* you want?"

"The wolf. I want the name of the wolf that was with Edward. My minions told me he was special. I want to know how special. You're going to tell me about him."

Did it matter if I did, seeing as Brewer's second death was likely real this time? Probably not. Yet, if there was a chance in hell that he survived a silver bullet to an artery in his neck, I couldn't give his name to her. Not even if she *was* going to kill me without it.

"I don't know. He's a friend of Edward's. Never got his real name."

"Lies!" she screamed at me.

"What does it matter to you, anyway?" I yelled back at her.

Narrowing her eyes at me, she stayed silent. Again, she began to walk around the cage, eyes never leaving mine.

"If you don't tell me why you need to know, I won't try to remember his name," I said.

"Everyone leave us," she ordered.

A serious looking man stepped up. "But ma'am, with Kamil not back yet—"

"Now!"

No one questioned her again. Once they all left and the door shut, she stayed silent, walking back and forth, eyeing me. Without a response, I decided to do what I did best.

I went back to the cot and lay down, easing my hands under my head and crossing one ankle over the other. "I can do this all day."

"You really think you're in a position to be a wiseass?"

"But I do it so well," I said, grinning at her like a fool.

"Your charm won't win here."

I rolled onto my side, propping myself up on one elbow. "Kamil killed my friends, so I have no reason to hurry back to the stage you constructed. I have no desire to watch your puppets dance about the set of the play you've cast them in without their knowledge." I laid back down and stared at the ceiling, hands resting on my stomach, fingers woven together. "I refuse to be an actor in your show, Scáthach."

"Oh, but you already are," she pointed out, sitting down on the beautiful sky blue, low-backed chaise that was part of the elegant furniture just six feet outside the cage. "As a child, you were a natural on that stage." She laughed at a memory of Mary's. "In fact, you were excellent in the school play. But that shouldn't have surprised anyone. Not with the way you love to tell stories and act them out. You can imitate people to a tee, right down to their voice and walk."

I turned just my head to look at her. She was pleased with this memory, and it made me crazy mad to see she got to have it.

"From what I've heard, you sing like a songbird and are one of the best dancers in all of Lincoln."

I rolled my eyes. "So what? I like to sing and dance, so do most folks."

"What is it they would call you in the performing world? Oh yes, a triple threat...or is that a term that'll be used in the future? I can't remember now. Time is so fluid for me, you see."

This got my attention, but I didn't want her to know that. "If you are all knowin' of the past and the future, no wonder you're bored."

This made her laugh. "The past is set...the future is fluid. I can see many different futures for this world...that's what's so fun about being here. I get to push buttons and see what you humans bring to fruition."

"Sounds thrillin'," I said as blasé as possible. "Too bad you won't be around for it all."

She crossed one leg over the other. "Oh, but I will. I am eternal."

Watching her carefully, I said, "That body isn't."

"No...no it's not. Eventually I'll have to find a new one. I'm thinking a blonde next time around. What do you think?"

"I couldn't care less."

She stood and approached my cage. "Yes, you do. The name of the wolf, Henry, and I'll let you go and see if you can save your friends."

"They're dead."

"You don't know that. Tell me his name!"

Sitting up on the cot, I shouted, "Tell me why it matters!"

"Fine. From what I was told, he has a soul. I know all my children who've earned their soul back. None but Edward are in New Mexico. So, you see, he's a wild card, a loose end, and I don't like either. Can you tell me how Edward's friend earned back his soul?"

"If that's true, I have no idea," I said, laying back down.

Pain ripped through my flesh, and I fell off the bed.

Opening my eyes, I stared at four long slashes to my arm as they healed. A quick glance at Scáthach showed her hand pulling back in through the bars, her hand becoming human again, the claws she possessed in her real form retracting under Mary's skin.

"Impossible!" she whispered.

"That you can reach that far in here? I'd say so," I exclaimed.

Walking about the cage, she said, "The bars should remove your ability to heal completely! The only way you could still hold power is if…" An understanding of something flooded her face, and she threw herself against the bars, each eye looking at me from between them. "You made a Beta. Is it a man or a woman? Or is it an animal…like your amazingly talented horse?"

She cackled and clapped her hands together as she stepped away from the bars. "Having a Beta this early in the game? Why Henry, you have impressed even me."

"I don't know what you're talking about," I told her, and I meant it.

"Just remember, my little warrior, if he or she dies, you will be vulnerable in my copper cage. Until then…" She snapped her fingers, and the lock clicked.

Confused, I stepped to the door and pushed. It opened, and the souls the copper bars held slid back into me. Giddy, I began to slide to the floor.

Stopping my fall, Scáthach grabbed my arm and sat me down on her chaise. "There now, let them settle into place, and then you can go."

She walked away, and all I could do was laugh like a fool.

"You're just gonna let me go? That seems counterproductive."

She tossed my belt and guns to me, then opened a door and waved off my comment. "Not really. I learned things; you learned things.

Until we meet again, Henry, the exit is that way." She pointed at the door behind her and stepped out.

"Fair thee well," I said, my stupid grin still plastered to my face, for I was as high as a kite.

Leaning back into the room, she said, "Oh, one thing to think on— a Beta holds a lot of power. When he or she dies, no matter where they are in the world, you'll know…and though you'll surge with power, it'll render you emotionally useless."

"And?" I prodded.

She smiled with all her real teeth. "And I'll be waiting. Good luck keeping them safe from me, Henry. May the best woman win…"

With that, the door shut, and she was gone.

"She's crazy," I muttered. "She's downright crazy-town."

I worked to put my belt back on and checked my guns. "Empty. Of course they are."

Stumbling to the exit she'd pointed out, I shoved opened the steel door and found myself in a long underground hallway with light at the end of the tunnel. I moved as fast as I could down it, holding onto the cool stone walls to keep me steady as souls settled into place. Reaching the exit, I stepped out into the late day sun, with the moon in the sky, and ten werewolves sitting in wait, blocking my path.

"Guess she's not *that* crazy," I muttered.

The pack moved as one, surrounding me, leaving me no choice but to fight with my bare hands or run back down the hall to the door. I was debating my next move when my chest began to burn as if someone shoved a lit torch into it. All the air in my lungs rushed out of my body. Unable to inhale, I fell to my knees.

Heart beating faster, my head began to spin and crush inward. Shouting a curse word loud enough for those in Texas to hear, I covered my head with both arms. Power as heavy as a boulder hit me all at once. Unable to hold it all, my arms flung out to the sides, my chest jutted outward, pulled by an invisible force. I screamed, my voice echoing off the canyon walls.

One by one, the wolves before me fell. Blood seeped out of their ears and eyes until they moved no more. In death, they shifted back to their human form as their souls found home in my well. My eyes filled with tears as the only explanation of what had happened beat against my chest in agony.

With a hand on the wall of the canyon to hold me up, I let the tears fall for the first time since my mother died. Working my way around the dead, I realized my voice wasn't the only one shouting. For as her ten wolves died, Scáthach could be heard screaming in defeat. If I didn't leave now, I'd never get another chance.

So I ran.

I wanted to be there to bury Brewer myself. It was the least I could do for my Beta.

7

THE FERAL

May 1878

I stole the first horse I found and rode as fast as I could to Edward's. My heart was so tight in my chest from worry that I found it difficult to breathe. Why had I felt that enormous surge of energy and power if not from the death of what Scáthach called my Beta? How else had my voice killed ten werewolves? There was only one explanation.

My gut turned. I fought the fear and the need to vomit along with it.

Upon reaching Richard's home, I leapt off my borrowed horse before she'd come to a full stop, my feet running as they hit the ground. With consuming terror, I knocked hard and loud on Edward's newly repaired door. When Edward opened it, his face said it all. But I asked anyway.

"Is he okay?"

Edward laid a hand on my shoulder. "Come inside."

"No, tell me now. I felt a large life force go through me as I was leaving one of Scáthach's lairs. It saved my life. But it felt different...

She told me that if my Beta died…if Brewer is, was my Beta…I don't know, I just…"

"He fought hard, Billy. He left this all behind, but he didn't want to."

"No," I choked, stumbling back a few steps.

"I'm so sorry for your loss."

"No!" I shouted, stepping back from him again. My mother, John, MacNab, now Dick. It was more than I could take. Violently, I caved in on myself, hands on my knees, and emptied my stomach contents into Edward's yard. My chest hurt. I rubbed at it with the heel of my right hand, still propped up with my left.

I heard a crashing in the distance and hooves pounding the ground like the horse's tail was on fire. Wiping my mouth, I looked up to see Colonel come racing around the side of the home.

"Damn, he must've broken that gate again," Edward mumbled.

My stallion raced to me, stopping on a dime, nose low to bump my face. He blew hot air from his nostrils and made a sound of relief and comfort.

"Were you going to tell me you had my horse?"

Edward sighed. "Yes. He seems to be very concerned about you." He paused. "You two have a special bond, I see."

I stood to look Colonel in the face. "We do. How are your eyes, boy?"

Colonel replied with a slight shake of his head.

"The right one? Okay, hold still."

Colonel stopped all movement, and I carefully laid a palm on his eye, seeping healing energy into his cornea.

"Dick said you and Colonel could understand one another. He wasn't lying."

"When have you known big, honest, Dick Brewer to lie?" I asked, emotion almost choking my words off.

"All men lie from time to time," Edward said. "Especially if it is the honorable thing to do. Come, you should have some tea."

"I need to go."

"No, warrior child, you need to mourn. Sit, have some tea. I'll show you where I buried him."

"You buried him here? He would've wanted to be laid to rest at his old property," I explained, trying to focus on Colonel's eye.

"I promise to make a nice marker for him. I'll take you back there. But you are weary and brokenhearted. If you won't rest here, rest soon, Billy."

The use of my name startled me enough to look at Edward just as Colonel's eye was good as new. I took my hand back and stared into the gray eyes of the wolf who'd fought until he'd passed out that day.

"How are *you* feeling?" I asked. "From what I could see, they beat you badly."

Reaching behind him to something near the door, he said, "I shifted, hunted, and healed. I'll be fine." Turning back around, he handed me both of my guns. "All of your ammo is in the saddle bags."

"Thank you," I said, and numbly put the guns in their holsters.

He handed me Dick's favorite rifle and said, "Come, I'll take you to him."

I wasn't sure I could stand over Dick's second grave knowing he was really dead inside of it. But I nodded, took the Winchester, and followed Edward to the back, right side of his property. As we approached the mound of dirt in the distance, I froze. Feeling my hesitation, Colonel came to a halt as well.

Edward noticed we weren't behind him. "You need to have closure, Billy."

I tried to step forward, but my feet felt as if they were walking through molasses. I wasn't ready. "I can't. I just...can't." I attached the rifle to the side of my saddle, then hoisted myself onto Colonel's back. "I'm sorry."

Unsure if my apology was for Edward or Dick, I raced off into the night, my dark clothes and horse making me invisible to the naked eye as we rode far away from that place, and the truth it held.

* * *

April 1949

S tuck with Alfonso "Happy" Apodaca, the Sheriff of Lies, who insisted on walking me out, I couldn't speak to Calvin the way I'd have liked. However, as we walked through the lobby, I narrowed my eyes a bit and stared a hole through the young Korean boy's head, metaphorically speaking. He swallowed hard and found busywork to do. He knew something, and I planned to find out what it was. But first, I had to shake the sheriff off my ass.

"You parked nearby?" Apodaca asked.

"Nope," I lied. "I'm that way." I pointed the opposite direction from the sheriff's office and the other hotel. "I'm gonna put my luggage in my car and then go to the other hotel." I put my hand out to him. "It was great meetin' you, Sheriff. I'll be back in town in early May. If ya learn anythin' else about Agent Calhoun, you let me know then, all right?"

He shook my hand and met my strong grip with his own. "Of course."

I grinned at the undertone that said there was no way in hell he was going to do that, then mimicked his facial expression and tone, saying, "I'll be sure to let you know when I'm in town."

He nodded at me, very likely knowing it, too, was a lie. "Appreciate it. Travel safe."

"Thanks again."

We parted ways, and I headed in the wrong direction for two blocks, then turned about and headed to my car. Stashing my suitcase in the trunk, I locked her up and headed right back to my hotel.

Calvin's eyes widened when he saw me. "Agent Kidwell, I thought you'd left town."

A woman I didn't recognize stepped out of the office. "Cal, I was wonderin'—" She stopped when she saw me.

"Ma'am, you seem a capable young woman," I said. "Can you man the counter for a moment? I need Cal's help with FBI business."

"Of course," she beamed.

"I really shouldn't—" Cal began to say, but the woman insisted.

I smiled at her, keeping my tone easy and polite. "I'm sure this woman can do all you can do and more, Calvin. Come on, it won't take long."

He nodded. "I'll be right back, Marilyn."

She seemed not to care a lick if he did or not and took his position as he came around to my side. I placed a hand on his shoulder, quietly saying in his ear, "Run and I'll catch you faster than your momma could grab a switch to tan your hide as a child. Got me?"

He nodded, and we headed outside and around to the back of the building near the large, square trash bins.

I stopped and let go of him. "Talk to me about Apodaca."

"He's the sheriff 'round here."

"That's not what I meant. There's more goin' on here. What do you owe him?"

The young, cocky kid shrugged it off unconvincingly. "No idea what you mean."

Bingo. I was on the right track. Now to make him at ease. I remembered seeing him smoke out back earlier, so I took the cig from behind my ear and offered it to him. He stared at it like I'd offered him poison, and I casually tucked it behind my ear again. "Who'd you have watching me today and why?"

He looked around for help, but it was a slow day downtown.

I pulled out my hand-rolled cigs, selected one as I counted to ten like I'd been taught. "Look, I have to work hard to be a patient man. It won't take long for me to say to hell with my trainin' and beat the shit outta ya. That means, you can either talk to me, or you spend tonight in a hospital. It's your call." Putting the pack away, I lit the smoke with my Zippo. I inhaled on a five-count, then exhaled on a five-count. "No help is comin' for you, kid, so I suggest you tell me what the deal is."

"Kid? Hell, you're not much older than me."

"You'd be surprised," I said, leaning against a dumpster. Though I didn't think he'd believe I was ninety. "Quit stallin'."

"You don't scare me. In fact, I can take you," he said, taking a fighting stance indicative of martial arts. "I don't have to tell you—"

I moved with the speed of years of training while pulling on soul-energy for a little extra. In two seconds, I had his arm behind his back and his face slammed into the dumpster wall as he wheezed out the word, "nothin'."

"What was that?" I said around the cig still between my lips, bending his arm upward.

"He'll kill me, I can't."

"Then nod for yes and shake your head for no. Did you call Sheriff Apodaca after I checked in last night?" He nodded. "Would Sam have called him again when I left my room?" He nodded. "Why? 'Cause I'm FBI?" Calvin nodded again, and I let go of him. Pulling my cig out of my mouth, I asked, "He holdin' somethin' over y'all?"

He nodded and shook his head. "Some help because they like the perks."

"Perks?"

"A blind eye turned on gamblin' or a speedin' ticket. That stuff."

"You don't strike me as a gambler, Cal."

"No sir. But my dad..."

"I see. They made debts go away, and you feel you owe 'em. Oldest trick in the book."

The boy's brown eyes grew big and darted to something behind me. "Hit me."

"What?" I turned to see a mangy looking homeless man walking our way, someone you'd never look at twice. That's when I realized it —the mangy man was a perfect lookout. "Damn it." I turned back to Cal, desperate fear oozing out of every cell of his body.

Barely moving his lips, Calvin whispered, "He'll kill me if he thinks I said anythin'." The words were said so quietly that if I'd not been a supernat, I'd never had heard him.

The early spring wind blew, bringing the mangy looking man's scent to me, and there, under the filth, was wild dog.

"Great. A feral."

"What?" Calvin asked.

Ferals were something that'd only started popping up after the war—werewolves whose psyche couldn't handle the change.

Normally Scáthach's furry children were more man than beast. Ferals were more beast than man. Stronger for sure, but not as smart.

"Nothin', kid," I said. "Just, don't run. If you do, he'll chase you like prey. Got it?"

Calvin nodded, but I could see his adrenaline was too high to stay put.

"Sorry about this." I swung a calculated punch, connecting with his face in just the right way that he dropped to the ground, out cold.

I couldn't risk shooting the feral in broad daylight. Besides, the paperwork on that alone made me want to just walk away. But I'd put the boy's life in danger, so I needed to deal with it. Facing the feral head on, I said, "I'm FBI." I showed my badge, but he kept coming straight for me, or us, as I thought he would. "Yeah, didn't think you'd care, but protocol and all, ya know."

With a guttural yell, the man ran at me. Flipping my credentials into my pocket, I shoved a healthy dose of soul energy into my muscles. Picking up Calvin, I tossed him into the large garbage container to my left as I kicked out with my right, hitting the feral in the abdomen. He flew across the space, hitting the windowless section of the hotel wall.

Rising up before I could make a decision on fight or flight, the feral dropped to all fours, allowing himself to shift, but only partially, which I'd never seen before.

"Well hell's bells," I said.

Leaping high up into the air, I flipped backward and landed steadily on my feet atop the garbage bin. Dropping into a crouched position, I pulled both guns from behind me and took aim as he ran toward me. Using a bit of soul-energy to slow down how I saw his movement, I made a decision. If he went for me, I'd injure him with lead and leave. If he went for Cal...that'd be a different situation.

Standing, I controlled my breathing as the feral came closer. He would make the decisive move in three, two...there! Using my silver loaded gun, I aimed below me and shot him once into the top of his head. He went down mid-reach into the bin, his soul hitting me seconds later. Sitting down, I allowed the energy in, soaking it up without a fight.

Still a bit wobbly, I eased down off the container instead of jumping. Leaning in, I saw Cal was hidden well but still unconscious. Glancing about the streets, I saw no one had put their garbage out for collection. Cal would be fine here until he woke up.

Reaching in again, I touched his temple with a fingertip and inserted lies into his head as to what had transpired. I couldn't remove what he'd seen, but I could make him question it by stimulating the natural electrical current of his brain with alternate memories.

Grabbing the feral by the arms, I dragged his smelly ass where he couldn't be seen and hustled to the nearest pay phone. Dialing one of three numbers I had memorized, this one belonging to home office, I waited while the operator put me through to my contact, Margaret Olivia McNally, aka M.O.M.

"Hey there, Mom. I just wanted to check in, let ya know my stay at the hotel was great, but they don't clean up after me like you do."

Margaret laughed. "No one does, sweetheart. You sound like you're outside."

"Behind the hotel. Smells like trash back here."

"How bad on a scale one to ten?"

"Two...but one'll get worse as the day goes by. The other is fine."

"I see. Are you on your way home?"

"Not yet. Gotta swing by Albuquerque first, then I'll be home. I'm bringin' company with me though. My Oregon pal is visitin', and before you complain, I need his help."

"I'll let your dad know, and we'll prepare a room for him," she said, sounding less than thrilled. "Drive safe."

I laughed. "Will do, see you soon!"

Hanging up, I breathed easier knowing my boss would now be aware that my partner was coming to town and that a cleanup crew would be sent to snag my feral. Getting that all in one call was truly a gift. With how operators heard your calls, the drawn-out way of asking for anything or telling them your plans was tedious but necessary.

Hoofing it on over to the Amador Hotel, I hoped for better luck than I'd been having in this city so far, save for Miss Ovida. I needed answers about Fletcher, even though I was afraid to learn what I feared to be true—that he was dead, killed by the law of this town for figuring out something he shouldn't have. I didn't deal well with loss. Never had. Not my mother's death, not Tunstall's, and definitely not Brewer's.

* * *

May 1878

Not knowing what else to do, I rode to Brewer's ranch. There I ran into Robert Widenmann.

"I thought you were in custody at Fort Stanton," I said.

"Released. Held over to next term of court...if I live that long. Murphy left Lincoln for good, you know."

"He did?" I asked, grabbing some hay from the barn and giving it to Colonel.

"Sick as a dog, that man. Cancer has just eaten him alive. From what I understand, Dolan and Longwell went with him to his home on the tenth. I'm guessin' he went there to die. Don't think we'll be seeing him again."

"What are you doin' here?" I asked.

"Gonna gather up Dick's cattle and auction 'em off to get some money for his family. Least we can do."

I couldn't respond, so I just nodded and bit into the apple I'd plucked from one of the trees on the property.

"Word down the pipeline is someone from D.C. is comin' to investigate Tunstall's murder. Rumor has it, he'll be here sometime by the end of next week."

I nodded again. "He'll want to talk to all of us about it, I suppose. Wonder what side he's gonna take. Dudley obviously is already in Dolan's pocket."

"That son of a bitch can roast in Hell," Rob said.

"Why, Rob, you're startin' to sound like me."

He laughed it off and mounted his horse. "This is gonna take a bit to get them gathered up, so I best get to work. I can tell you that Doc and the rest are in town. Safer lately for us all with Copeland being sheriff and Doc his deputy. Even with Dudley bein' a snake in the grass, things are quiet again. You could probably come into town for some rest and good food. See no reason why you can't stay at McSween's if ya need to."

"Thanks, Rob. I appreciate the offer. Might even take you up on it. But I need a diversion right now…somethin' to keep my head busy."

"Well, Doc's puttin' together a party to hunt down the man who killed MacNab. That enough excitement for ya?"

This brightened my spirits greatly. "Yes, it is! Thanks for the info. I'll get washed up and head on into town."

"You'll beat me there for sure, so just let 'em know I'm on my way back if they ask."

"Will do."

With that, we parted ways. I cleaned up and headed into Lincoln to find Doc and get some closure for the death of MacNab, even if I couldn't fathom trying to find the same with concern to Dick.

* * *

April 1949

Hoping to get some closure about who had killed or taken Calhoun, I stepped into the Amador Hotel and found myself at one end of a long lobby. At the far side from me lay a set of stairs with a landing halfway up before splitting to take you up in either direction to the second level.

Taken by the older charm of the building, I couldn't help but feel optimistic as I moseyed my way to the check-in counter at the center right of the room.

"Hello," I said to the older gentleman behind the counter. "When was this beautiful hotel built, if you don't mind me askin'?"

The man, whose name tag read Manny, proudly smiled at me. "Original structure was built in the mid-1870s with the second level added in 1879."

"Ah, no wonder this place feels like home. I particularly love how open it all is." I brought my gaze back down to his. "Tell me, I'm lookin' for any information you might have on this man." I laid the picture of Calhoun on the counter. "Las Cruces was the last place Detective Calhoun was seen."

At this information, all the warmth and joy in Manny's face drained away. His eyes went flat, and his body became ridged as he crossed his arms, a classic closed-off stance.

"Never seen him before," Manny said, his accent becoming thicker, as if he spoke little English.

"You haven't even looked at him."

"*No puedo ayudarte,*" he said.

We were going to play this game. Fine.

With a sigh, I said, "*Hablo español fluido si eso es eaiser.*"

His face tightened. "I'm perfectly able to speak English."

"You were tryin' to evade me, hintin' to a language barrier. I assure you, good señor, I speak six languages fluently and more partially. Now, let's try this again, shall we?"

* * *

May 1878

I rode into Lincoln on the sixteenth and none of Dolan's crew were around. Not surprising though, seeing as it would be a full moon that night. My guess was that all of Dolan's muscle was in bed sleeping and getting ready to raise hell after the moon rose. I sincerely hoped we were out of here by then.

As I stepped into the McSween house, Frank and George Coe ran up to greet me. They brought me up to date on things before we all took a seat in the parlor to listen to Doc and Copeland's second deputy, José Chavez y Chavez, fill us in on the trip.

"Lucky for us, we have a first-hand account of what happened at the Fritz Ranch on April twenty-ninth from Frank Coe. We know exactly who killed Frances MacNab, and we're gonna go serve him an arrest warrant," Doc said.

I knew who it was, too, because Gaax had shown me, but I wasn't about to offer up that information to the group. Instead, I just listened as Frank told the story I already knew and gave the name of MacNab's killer.

"The person I saw kill MacNab was a man of many names," Frank said. "Some refer to him as The Indian, while others call him Juan Armijo, while some know him as Manuel Segovia."

His name didn't matter to me because there was now a warrant for his arrest in the hands of MacNab's friends. More importantly, if Segovia was one of Scáthach's cursed children, there was also a silver bullet with his name on it in the chamber of my gun.

8

THE MAN OF MANY NAMES

April 1949

M anny continued to fearfully say he knew nothing, and it smelled of Happy Apodaca's interference. If I were to guess, I'd taken too long at the Campbell and he'd had time to threaten the employees here. If that was true, he was more involved than he should be. Or I was being paranoid, which was always possible. If that was the case, then who were the employees at these hotels afraid of?

Soon, it got busy, and I left Manny alone, trying instead to talk to the bellboy in the lobby who also had no idea how to help me. I was about to call it a day when I heard a clatter above, and a towel landed at my feet.

Picking it up, I stared up at the second story, which looked down onto the lobby with only a railing to separate them. A red-headed maid peered over the edge down at me. Her cart was a bit too close to the balcony ledge, and it appeared she'd accidently knocked a towel off. That is until I realized she wasn't looking at me with apology or embarrassment. She placed a finger on her lips and gestured me to come up.

I didn't need to be asked twice, but I also didn't want to get her in trouble, so I gave her a barely recognizable nod of understanding so I wouldn't draw attention. Seeing this, she disappeared from sight, and I waited for a distraction so I could head on up the stairs without Manny noticing.

Thankfully, a large family came into the lobby a few moments later, with a dog and four kids, and pandemonium ensued. Taking that as a sign, I pulled on my speed and whisked up the stairs.

* * *

May 1878

"All right," Doc said. "We need to get outta town and to our first stoppin' point before that full moon rises around seven-thirty tonight. Last we heard, Segovia was at the Murphy and Dolan cow camp down in Seven Rivers. So that's where we're headed. Ride out!"

Sixteen men on horseback began to head out of town. Doc and José had each chosen eight men, Charlie and I being two of Doc's picks, along with John Scroggins, Henry Brown, George Coe, and two men I didn't know. I noted that one of the men chosen by José was a man named Francisco "Kiko" Trujillo. He was the brother to our friend and Justice of the Peace in San Patricio. Seeing him reminded me that I still owed the two of them a debt from back when we first met the previous October.

I hate owing anyone anything. I said so to Charlie, and he brushed me off.

"We got bigger problems on this ride than your sense of rightin' wrongs you done," he said. "Full moon all the way to the cow camp. Doc is a damn fool."

"Then why you here?" I said.

"Cause I'm spittin' mad at this son of a bitch, and we're gonna make him pay."

I couldn't fault him for that. Wasn't that why I was here, to take out my anger? Only problem was, by the time we arrived at the cow camp on the fourteenth, Segovia wasn't there. We did, however, find Frank Coe's horse and Ab Saunders's, too. Even some of Tunstall's herd was there.

"Doc! Billy!" someone yelled out.

I glanced over my shoulder as I finished securing Colonel's saddle and saw José walking toward us with his hand on a man's ear, bringing him along with.

"Who ya got there?" I asked.

"Meet the man who might know where Segovia is."

This captured my attention. Slowly, I turned from Colonel to look at the bleeding man. He was Mexican, so I spoke to him in his language to see if he spoke English. "*¿Habla Inglés?*"

"*No, señor,*" he replied.

I nodded. "*He oído que sabe dónde vive Segovia.*"

"*Si, señor.*"

"He knows where he lives," I told Doc as I pulled my tin from a saddlebag.

"I heard. But will he tell us where?"

José shook the man. "*Si quieres la vida, nos dice dónde está.*"

The man's eyes grew wide at the threat on his life, but he shook his head, determined to go to the grave with his knowledge.

I stepped closer to the man, my face not far from his, and I quietly said, "*¿De que estás asustado?*" He was afraid of something, but it wasn't us or the loss of his life.

Quietly he replied, "*Si no me matas, que, una vez que salga la luna.*"

"What did he say?" Scroggins asked.

I grinned, opened my tin, and put a toothpick in between my teeth. "He said exactly what I needed to hear," I said, touching my silver-loaded gun on my hip to explain.

Doc nodded at me, and I leaned into the man's ear, telling him in Spanish that the wolf would not hunt tonight, that he and his family would be safe, giving him my word.

The man looked from me to José and Doc. When we all nodded, he gave us the information needed, and we left. However, as we drew close to Segovia's home, Doc pulled the party to a halt and drew me, Charlie, and José aside.

"Problem, Doc?" Charlie asked.

"Dust. We got sixteen riders, twenty-five extra horses, and two mules. We're kickin' up a lot of dust. He'll see us comin' a mile away."

"You're right," José said. "We can't all go on in like this."

Doc squinted up at the sky. "Moon's not up until after the sun sets tonight, right?"

"That's right," I said. "They can't turn furry on us until then, but they're still fast, with acute senses. We need to go in with only a few of us, or he'll be gone before we arrive."

"I think we should—" Doc cut himself off when he saw my attention switch to someone approaching from behind him.

"Hey there, Kiko," I said to Francisco Trujillo as he rode on over. "What ya got for us?"

"Well, if you don't mind my interruption, I just thought that maybe I could be of help. I happen to know the man you call Segovia. I know he'd come quietly if I went to the door."

I shared a look with Doc and saw he felt the same way I did on this. "He's a dangerous man, Kiko. You know he could come out shootin', not carin' who's at the door."

Kiko adjusted his hat to block the sun. "I do. But, as a friend, I owe him this."

I nodded in understanding. "All right, but I'm goin' with you."

"As am I," Scroggins said.

"Atanasio Martinez also knows him," Kiko told us. "He should come as well."

José dismounted and said, "I know Atanasio. He's one of my men. I'll go get him."

Once he returned, we developed a plan, and the four of us headed in one direction while the other twelve took the horses and mules and went to station themselves at Good Bend Crossing.

Colonel was the fastest, so I stayed in the saddle while the other three approached the door on foot, Kiko yelling for Segovia to come on out.

The large man answered the door, a smile on his face when he saw who it was. "How are you, Kiko?"

"I'm all right, but I'm afraid I'm not here for a visit."

Segovia's eyes found mine, and they narrowed only for a moment as he sniffed the air once. Not smelling what he was looking for, he turned to his friend. "What's goin' on?"

Kiko sighed. "Ya need to come with us now. Ya killed MacNab."

It was my turn to appear confused at Kiko's pronunciation of the name, sounding more like Macky-Nane. But Segovia seemed to understand.

With a nod, Segovia said, "I was ordered to kill him by Robert Baker. He threatened me, told me I'd be prosecuted by *The House* if I failed."

"Robert Baker? I've never heard of him," John Scroggins said. "Could it have been Robert Beckwith? He was there that day."

"Maybe so," Segovia replied, then looked at Kiko. "I'll come talk to the law, since you have a warrant and all. Let me get my horse, and we'll go. But don't let them kill me, Kiko."

Kiko patted the tall man's arm in reassurance but didn't promise anything. Either he knew better, or he thought the worry to be unwarranted.

Segovia's saddle caught my eye, for it was a beauty, and as I watched him secure it to his horse, I understood his plan. He'd placate us until the moon rose, and then, when we camped for the night, he'd shift and disappear, or kill us all. I didn't plan on letting him get that far.

Scroggins moseyed over to me while Segovia fitted his horse for a long ride and quietly said, "Should he be comin' this quietly?"

I knew whatever I said, he'd hear, so instead I just muttered, "Count it as a blessin'."

Kiko and Scroggins flanked Segovia as we headed toward Roswell, with Atanasio Martinez out front and me in the back. About two miles south of our destination, at Good Bend Crossing, we came to a stop when Doc's large party came into view, obviously waiting for us.

At this point, I saw tension take up residence in Segovia's shoulders. This wasn't the small party he could overthrow at night; this was a hunting party, and he was the deer.

With my sight, I recognized the three from the large party who broke off and began to ride toward us. "It's José, Doc, and Charlie."

Segovia turned to his friend and said, "Kiko, don't let them kill me."

"We'll explain to them you are comin' peacefully, so don't you worry," Kiko said, urging his horse to hurry on ahead and motioning Atanasio Martinez to go with him, which he did.

Colonel needed no coaxing. The minute Kiko's horse moved, Colonel took his spot, placing Segovia between John Scroggins and me.

Once Kiko was out of earshot, I said. "Do you know who we are?"

"You're Regulators," Segovia said, then added, "I'll kill every last one of you and drink your blood from a chalice."

John and I turned to stare at Segovia, and then at each other. John laughed and shook his head.

"Now that is some imagery," I said. "It's cute that you think without the moon being up you can escape sixteen men."

"I only have to escape or kill you two, and the three comin' at us," he said. "Five is nothin'."

I gave him a narrowed stare from the corner of my eye, my lips turning up in challenge. "Oh, I'd like to see you try."

"You sure about that?" he asked, eyeing Scroggins, instinct telling him John was the weak link between the two of us.

"John, head on back to the group, would ya? Help Brown do a head and horse count for me."

"Billy, you don't have to—"

"Please? I don't trust Brown's countin' skills."

Scroggins had no misunderstanding to my real motive, and though reluctant, he headed off toward the posse.

"And then there were four," Segovia said, eyeing Doc, José, and Charlie as Scroggins rode past them and picked up the pace, Kiko riding along next to the three heading our way.

"I see you can't count. It's still five, unless you're gonna let Kiko live after seeing what you are and what you can do."

Segovia said nothing as the group got closer and we both could hear his friend pleading with Doc, saying, "Is it not better to take him in and let the law have its course?"

Charlie and Doc both looked at me, and I leaned my head to the left, then right, cracking my neck, my sign of saying, "No." Seeing this, Doc leaned toward José and said something quietly while Charlie replied to Kiko. "That all depends. Doc? José?"

"I'll go talk to him. Billy will keep me safe," José said.

Doc nodded to him and then me before turning around and heading back to the posse.

"Come on, Kiko, let us be runnin' along," Charlie said.

Kiko didn't want to. He looked toward his friend, but Segovia urged him on.

Once he left and couldn't hear us, I said, "That was a nice thing to do."

"Then there were two," Segovia said as José approached. "Besides, Kiko doesn't need an up-close view of watchin' you two die."

José came to a stop on the other side of Segovia. "Ride with us."

"With pleasure."

The three of us turned and headed away from the posse.

"You look rather pleased with yourself," I said to Segovia, then adding in, "José, do ya see how pleased with himself our captive here is?"

"I'm guessin' he doesn't have all the information," José said, humor in his tone.

"Nope," I said. "He has no idea."

"Shall you tell him or shall I, *espíritu guerrero de Scáthach*?"

The look on Segovia's face changed. His smugness transformed into fear, and all I could do was grin, saying, "I think he understands Spanish, José."

"I think you're right," José said with a laugh.

"You? You're her spirit warrior?" Segovia asked me, obviously stunned.

"Yes, and I carry silver, as does José, so why don't we all cut the bullshit and talk a deal?" I looked back and saw we were about fifty yards away from Charlie, Doc, and Kiko. "As much as I want to kill you, you're not the problem. It's more important I deal with Scáthach herself. If you'd be willing to help us—"

Without so much as a warning, Segovia took off, his horse moving faster than most I'd seen. José and I lit out after him, firing our six-shooters filled with silver, hitting him maybe once, but not anywhere vital. Soon, he was out of range, so I shoved some extra energy into Colonel and pulled Dick's silver-loaded Winchester. Seeing this, José pulled his too and fired on him, but soon his horse began to fall behind.

"Hold her fast and steady, Colonel," I said, and took aim.

Firing off at the same time José did, we both shot four or five times, one of our shots finally hitting home, causing Segovia to slump forward on his horse. I secured Dick's rifle quickly, in case it was me who made the shot.

Segovia fell to the ground, his horse still charging forward for a moment before slowing down and curving back toward her rider.

With a last breath that, somehow, I felt in my bones, Segovia died, and his soul energy slammed into me. I too fell forward, grasping onto Colonel's neck to keep from falling off as well. I whispered to Colonel, "Don't lose me."

Colonel eased up his speed to a trot as Doc, Charlie, Kiko, and a few others rode hard on past me to where Segovia fell. Taking my time in hopes of sobering up, I reached the scene once everyone had dismounted, and unfortunately, I was not fully myself yet.

Segovia's horse approached, and I remembered what a beauty Segovia's saddle was just as my eyes landed on Francisco Trujillo. "Kiko?" I said, but he didn't hear me. He was too busy staring at death.

"Francisco," I said this time, sliding off Colonel, attempting to get my feet steady under me and failing. Butt on the ground, I said, "I owe you a saddle and trappings. I've not forgotten, Kiko. I know you probably think I did, but I didn't. So, you should take Segovia's. He'd have wanted you to have 'em."

Charlie groaned. "Well, now I know who made the lucky shot." He came over and helped me up. "Ya know, Billy, he may not want 'em."

"Sure he does! That is a fine saddle! I'd take it, but Colonel already has one he likes. Besides, I owe him and his brother a debt. Right, Kiko?"

Kiko numbly nodded, asking Esequio Sanchez to do him the favor of removing the saddle from Segovia's horse for him, as he couldn't get himself to touch it.

Seeing Kiko's disgust at the blood, Doc stepped forward. "Take mine, for now, as a place holder. I'll have this cleaned for you." But Kiko only nodded and walked away.

I'd fulfilled my debt, but I felt horrible in how it had gone down. I was still too high on the soul to think of what to say, so I said nothing, sliding back down to the ground.

"We gave him the option," José started telling Doc.

"I take it he turned you down," he replied.

José nodded. "Even though he knew he'd be killed, he just ran."

"Did he ever! Woo-wee!" I hollered. "And how is his horse that fast? I'm telling ya, Doc, it's like, fast-fast."

"This is for your own good, Billy," Charlie said, and smacked me across the face.

The hit helped tremendously, and I shook most of the high out of my head. "No, but really, detain that horse. I need to have it looked at by someone." I rubbed my face. "That was a good one, Charlie."

"Thanks, I think. I'll have Brown secure Segovia's horse." Charlie headed off.

I looked at Doc, and the world spun. I leaned against Colonel's front leg and groaned. "He ran for it, Doc. How am I to save Mary from Scáthach if her own monsters are that afraid of her? I'm never gonna be able to save her…and until I do, we can't win this war."

Doc squatted next to me, a hand on my leg. "You tried. Try again, and again. You'll figure it out. I know you will."

I sighed, the weight of not only Segovia's death, but of others, weighed on my heart. I nodded for Doc's benefit, but all I wanted to do was trade places with Segovia. All I seemed to do was get people killed. I needed my head on straight, and in order to do that, I needed time to think.

Once steady on my feet, I excused myself from the group and headed to the Chisum Ranch, Segovia's weird horse in tow, to do as Edward had suggested: rest and regroup. Maybe if I could hide from what I was for a while, I'd see things from another angle.

Little did I realize that my prayers and my cry for help had not fallen on deaf ears.

9

TEXANS

May 1878

By the time I reached the Chisum Ranch, it was about ten o'clock at night. I had about forty minutes to get Colonel and Segovia's weird horse settled for the night before the moon came out. Sure, I had a lot of souls in me at the moment and could probably take on a small pack of 'em, but I didn't want to. I wanted to forget I was cursed and just be normal for a few days.

Dismounting from Colonel, I said hello to Chisum's foreman and began heading to the stable. I was about to cross the threshold when a voice in the dark startled me.

"Pushing it mighty close, aren't ya?"

I pulled my gun. "Who's there?"

A young man around my age stepped out of the shadows and lit the lantern he was holding. He was maybe an inch taller than me with a long face, a slight clef to his chin, and sharp, prominent features. The only thing that seemed to age him was his clear blue eyes; they held the seriousness of men in their later years, even when he smiled at me.

"Sorry to startle you, but I don't tend to stand around with a light on for any werewolf in the area to see me. Especially not right after the full moon or this close to the waning gibbous rising."

"Excuse me?" I asked.

"You like to live a bit dangerously I take it. That's all right. I did, too, back in my day. Here, I'll help you with one of them there horses and we can get inside before she rises for the night."

He stepped toward me, and I cocked the hammer back.

"Whoa now, I'm friend, not foe."

"Then you'll stop ramblin' and tell me who the hell ya are."

"Oh, I'm sorry. I thought the foreman told you I was here."

I stared him down. "What are you talking about?"

"My name is Tom Folliard. I'm Scáthach's other warrior. I got your letter."

* * *

April 1949

W alking down the open hallway of the Amador Hotel, I noted the maid's cart sat outside a room, so I figured she was inside. With a light tap on the cracked-open door, I entered. "Hello, I'm looking for some additional towels..."

She stepped out of the bathroom folding one and gave me such a look of indignation that I could do nothing but grin like a fool.

"Took ya long enough! Well, don't just stand there, cowboy, get in here and shut the door," she whispered haughtily, her Irish lilt charming me even if her words were demanding.

"My apologies," I replied as I shut the door. "But it wasn't like I could rush over here without givin' you away, could I now?"

Narrowed eyes gave me a once-over, and she went back into the bathroom. "I suppose."

I stepped farther into the room. "What's your name?"

Ignoring my question completely, she sprayed some god-awful cleaner on the mirror and began to wipe it down. "The man you were askin' 'bout, that detective? Did somethin' happen to him?"

"He's gone missin'."

She stopped what she was doing and stared at me through the mirror. "What?"

"And if we're bein' honest, he's really an FBI Agent."

Her hands dropped to rest on the bathroom counter. "Oh lordy..."

"Your help would be much appreciated if you know anythin'. Like your name, for starters."

She only paused for a moment before setting the cleaning cloth down and turning toward me. Offering me her hand, she said, "Sorry, my name's Catherine Bell, but my friends call me Kit."

I shook her hand. "Nice to meet you, Kit. I'm Agent William Kidwell, but you can call me Billy if you'd like. Now, I could use your help." I reached into my pocket and pulled Calhoun's picture from my wallet. Showing it to her, I said, "Is this the man you're talkin' about? I could really use your help if it is."

* * *

May 1878

I eased the hammer back into place carefully and slid my gun back into its holster as I stared at Tom Folliard, surprised not just that he was here, but that he was real, not something Garrett made up to make me feel better.

"Did you think I wouldn't come?" Tom asked.

"To be honest, I wasn't so sure you existed." I couldn't help but laugh at hearing myself say this. "I know that sounds ridiculous since I wrote you and all."

Tom placed a hand on my shoulder. "Naw, it makes sense. Scáthach Warriors are rare. You're still gettin' used to the idea of being one yourself, let alone thinkin' there are others out there. I've never met another one either, so this is interesting to me, too." When I didn't reply, he took his hand back and added, "Look, let me help you with these horses, and I'll explain as we work."

"That'd be mighty kind of ya," I said. "When did you get to New Mexico?"

"Not long ago. But got here specifically last night," he said as he stepped toward Segovia's weird horse.

"Careful with her. She's not normal," I told him.

Tom stopped in his tracks, his attitude changing from playful and friendly to serious business in a second. "How so?"

I filled him in as we worked as a team, Colonel included, to move her into the stable. Shutting the doors, I lowered the arm to lock us in and hoped Tom had some answers.

"It's possible he fed her some of his blood in her water," Tom offered as he began to rub her down, which was the first time I'd seen her be calm.

"She seems to like you doing that," I pointed out.

"Well, of course she does. You've had a long day, haven't ya, pretty girl? Your owner ridin' you like a hell-hound while gettin' shot at, then dyin' while riding ya, and then a trek across the countryside with this schlep."

"Gee, thanks," I said with a laugh as I took Colonel's saddle off him and put it away, but I wasn't upset. In fact, for once I wasn't feeling the weight of the world, and it was nice.

"She's a beauty though, even if she is hopped up on somethin' supernatural."

The mare blew air out her nose at Tom and bumped the side of his head with her nose.

"Well, I'll be. I think she understands us," I said.

Tom stepped around and looked the mare in the eyes, and she tilted her head at him. Before I knew the reason, Tom began laughing so hard he had to rest his hand on his knees. Head down, he shook it and said, "Well, I'll be damned, Billy. You gone and got yourself a—"

The horse hit him again with her head, and he shut up for a moment. Putting his hands up by his shoulders in surrender, he said, "Okay, okay, I'll let that be on you."

"What are you talkin' about?" I asked as I began to rub Colonel down, who kept his eyes on both Tom and the mare as I worked.

"Nothin' of note. Let's finish up and get inside. If we don't hurry, my buddy is gonna come out here lookin' for us, and I'd rather he stayed inside."

"You brought someone with you?"

"Yeah, pal of mine from down in Texas wanted to come with me. Figured the safest way to travel was with a warrior of Scáthach, so he tagged along."

"You didn't warn him that we attract trouble?"

"I did, but he was dead set on gettin' away from his family, so I let him come."

We chatted while we worked. Tom told me about where he'd been when he got my letter and their trip up from Texas. We'd locked the horses up for the night and were on our way to the house when I asked him how he'd been paying for his trip.

"Well, I had some money saved up, but I didn't want to blow through it all, so we did some cattle rustling for some guy named Dolan and his crew until yesterday. Got word some trouble was comin', so we got outta there and made our way here, like you told me to in the letter."

I stopped and looked at him.

"Don't just stand there. We need to keep movin'," Tom said, looking back at me.

"You do realize who you were workin' for, right?"

"Assholes. That much I know. Why? What are *you* gettin' at?"

I shook my head and whistled low as I walked up to him. Placing my hand on his shoulder I said, "You were in the devil's playground and you didn't even know it. Come on, I'll explain inside once Sallie is asleep. She's John's niece."

"Yeah, we met her earlier today. In fact, she was asleep when I headed out here," he said as we made our way to the ranch house.

I grinned and opened the fence gate. "Ya hear that piano being played? That's her. She sometimes plays when she can't sleep. Come on. She'll make us somethin' hot to drink, and we can pretend to be normal folks for a bit."

Stepping into the foyer of the house, I took off my boots as the piano stopped.

"Tom, is that you?"

"And friend!" I replied.

In seconds, Sallie came rounding the corner in a night dress and robe, her blond hair in a loose side braid, and a startled look on her face.

"Evenin', Miss Chisum," I said.

"Why, Billy Bonney, what in tarnation are ya doing arriving out here this late at night without lettin' us know?"

"Sorry, ma'am. It was a last-minute decision after a shoot-out at Good Bend Crossin'. I just wanted to get away from all the fightin' for a bit. If that's not all right with you, I can go sleep in the barn. I'd totally understand."

Her face softened. "I'm not makin' ya sleep in the barn, Mr. Bonney. Don't be silly. Just do me a favor and get cleaned up before you go sleepin' in the guest room. I'll have a bath drawn for you. To be honest, you look like you could use one."

I set my bag down. "Thank you, Ms. Chisum. I appreciate it."

"Now take off that hat and let me go fetch Miss Mary Ann."

Sallie headed off, and Tom just stared at me.

"What?" I asked.

"I heard you were a hard-ass cowboy. But damn the man, a woman steps into the picture and you are nothin' but a gentleman."

"My momma raised me right, Tom, God rest her soul. To be honest, I think if I wasn't right gentlemanly, my momma would find a way to come down from Heaven and whoop my ass."

Tom laughed and led me on back to the room he was staying in. There we found a young man reading by candlelight.

"Good, you're up. James, this is Billy Bonney. Billy, this is James Woodland."

The slender young man put a marker in his book and set it aside. Standing up, he was taller than either Tom or me by a good four inches. He offered me his hand. "It's nice to meetcha, Billy. Heard all about ya."

I shook his hand. "Sorry to hear that," I said in jest.

James appeared confused.

"I'm just kiddin'," I said. "I can't imagine hearin' about me was too interestin'."

"Depends on who's doin' the talkin'," James said. "Now, the guys who work for Dolan…well, they hate you."

"The feelin' is mutual," I said as I placed my bag near the straw mattress on a low platform against the wall by the door, like an afterthought to the room that already had two single beds on regular wooden frames.

A knock came at the door, and Sallie peeked her head in. "Your bath is bein' drawn now, Billy. If you need anythin' else, Mary Ann will be happy to help you. In fact, she's makin' some tea for y'all right now. I'm headin' back to bed seein' as I have a house full of guests who will be needing breakfast in the mornin'."

"Sallie, you know you don't need to be going to all that fuss," I said.

"Speak for yourself," Tom said with a wink at Sallie. "This mornin' Sallie and Mary Ann made the best breakfast I've had since hittin' New Mexico. It was like bein' home."

"Well, I *am* a Texas girl," she said with a yawn. "And I best get some rest. Goodnight, gentlemen. Billy, go get cleaned up."

I bowed my head to her. "Yes, ma'am. Goodnight, Miss Chisum."

The other two said goodnight, and I sipped on hot tea wile I took a warm bath, soaking until the water cooled. Once dried off, I put on clean clothes for the first time in ages and headed to bed. Entering with my candle, I found James had fallen asleep while reading, and Tom was out cold, snoring real quiet-like.

I sat on my mattress, happy to have it, and considered heading out to the enclosed patio area for a smoke. I reached into my sack for a book of matches and instead found something metallic that I'd forgotten was in this bag.

Pulling it out, I stared down at my mother's locket and got lost in thoughts of her until I fell asleep.

* * *

April 1949

K it sat on the edge of the sheetless bed. With one hand, she fingered a pendant around her neck; with the other she gently took the picture of Calhoun from me. Finally, she said, "Yeah, he stayed here. In fact, this was his room." Staring at the picture more intently, her face softened. "He's such a nice man. A real gentleman. Spoke to me and everyone else who worked here like an equal when it was evident he was a wealthy man from Scotland. In fact, it was my accent that got us to talkin'."

"He was born and raised there. And yes, he's a good man."

After one last look, Kit handed me the picture. She tucked a loose red curl, which had escaped the bun on top of her head, behind her ear and said, "He stayed here his last week in town. Had to leave the Campbell Hotel over yonder due to a weddin' party needin' the space. He was a tidy man, very meticulous. I would know, I cleaned his room. Ya learn a lot about someone when ya pick up after 'em, ya know? God, I knew somethin' was wrong. I should've done somethin'."

"You are now. Tell me, why'd you suspect somethin' was off in the first place?"

She reached into her front apron pocket and pulled out a necklace I recognized instantly. Calhoun always wore it. It was the Patron Saint of the Police: the Archangel Michael. "We got to talkin' one day when I came to clean his room. I told him I would come back later, but he insisted he was about to leave and invited me in. I like doin' my rooms in order, ya see? Anyway, he saw my necklace and asked about it." She pointed to a small silver pendant on a matching chain.

I assumed it was a Catholic saint of some kind, as I couldn't get near enough to read it without us getting intimately close. Nor could I stare at it, as it rested just above her cleavage. "Is yours also a saint?"

She smiled for the first time and said, "Yes. It's the Archangel Raphael."

Even I knew this one. "Patron Saint of Healers."

"Yes, sir. I'm in school to be a nurse, ya see? I've got a knack for healin'."

"Being a nurse is the toughest job there is. My hat is off to ya for it," I said.

"My momma, who lives in Texas now, she's a nurse, too. But she works with the little ones. I'm not all about that. But give me a good ol' bloody ER, and I'm as happy as a pig in... Well, you get my meanin'."

I couldn't help but laugh. "That I do. So are you from Ireland?"

"Actually, I was born in Texas, but my momma moved us back to Ireland to be near her sister shortly after I was born. We didn't come back to the States until I was in my teens. Only recently did I work my way up here."

I nodded. "You see yourself as a Texan then?"

She nodded. "Sorta. I was born there, so I got free college trainin'. But I love New Mexico. There's somethin' about it, ya know?"

"I do," I said. When she was quiet again, I sat next to her and asked, "You were sayin' somethin' about Fletcher's necklace?"

"Oh! Yes! Sorry, I'm such a fat head sometimes. So ya see, when he told me it had been handed down in the family for generations, I warned him of where in this room I tend to find forgotten jewelry and to be sure to check before he left. He then told me he never takes it off."

"He doesn't."

"And that right there is why I got to worryin' about him. See how the clasp is done up? I found it that way."

"Where at?"

"That's the thing, I found it right in the same spot I warned him about." She pointed to the crevice between the bed and the bedside table. "Just makes no sense to me at all. And stuff that don't make sense gets me to worryin'."

My sixth sense began to itch, and I had a feeling she was right to worry. Standing up, I began to pace. Fletcher wasn't one to do anything without a reason. I was beginning to sincerely believe he was dead. Problem was, how did I prove that? And if I did, who would've wanted him dead and why?

This whole trip was beginning to be a whole lot more complicated than I'd even thought when I called my partner. Now I was even more happy he'd be joining me. Without him, I was pretty sure this was going to be dead in the water.

* * *

May 1878

I woke up earlier than required when James headed out of the room. Ignoring him, I went back to sleep until there was a shake of my shoulder.

"Billy, if you be wantin' food, you best get up. Miss Sallie and Mary Ann have everthin' just about ready."

Blinking my eyes a few times, I grunted at him.

"Is that a yes?" Tom asked.

"Did you say food?" I muttered.

"Yeah…"

"Then it was a yes."

Tom laughed. "Then get up and into some respectable clothes. I'm gonna go find James."

"He left the room with the sunrise," I muttered as I sat up.

"Yeah, he's not a late sleeper."

I stood and pulled some clean pants on over the long undergarments I'd slept in. "Depends on when I hit the hay how long I can stay out. My buddy Richard, man, he'd be up before the sun and to bed after she set…never knew how he used to do that."

"Used to?"

I paused with my shirt in my hand. "He was killed recently by one of Scáthach's men." I put the shirt on and began to button it. "He was one of the best men I've ever known. Heart of gold, hard worker, honorable to the point of annoyin'…" I laughed, but it was stressed, and I knew Tom could tell.

Putting a hand on my shoulder, Tom said, "I'm sorry for your loss."

I nodded but said nothing, the words catching in my throat.

Once I was dressed, we headed out to the breakfast table to find Sallie, James, a few of the farmhands, and Uncle John Chisum himself.

"Why, Billy, it's good to see you."

"Good morning, sir. Sally and Mary Ann, this looks positively wonderful. Thank you so much for takin' such good care of us."

"Always the sweet talker," Uncle John said with a glint in his eye as he drank his coffee.

I pulled Sallie's chair out for her as she came to sit. "My momma was very particular in our upbringin'. We was to respect other cultures and those of different races, and above all else, never underestimate a woman or treat her with disrespect." With Sallie settled, I took my seat.

"Here I heard Billy Bonney was some crude outlaw killin' people left and right," James said.

Sally swallowed a sip of water. "Consider your source. Dolan's cow camp isn't filled with the best sorts of specimens."

"Why, Sallie Chisum," I said, "I think that's the first unsavory thing you've ever said about Jimmy Dolan and the Seven Rivers gang."

"Oh, it's not. And like every other time, I plan to ask for forgiveness for it later on today during my devotions," she said with a sly grin. "Shall we say grace?"

"We shall indeed," Uncle John said.

We all took hands, and Sallie thanked God for us visiting them and for the food, asking that it bless our bodies for the day's work ahead of us. Once finished, we dug in to some of the biscuits they'd likely made that morning, eggs they'd probably fetched from the chickens, and thick slices of bacon from a pig that Uncle John bragged about plumping up just right as we ate it.

My plate finally empty, I stood to fetch more coffee. Sallie attempted to beat me to it, but I insisted she finish her breakfast, grabbed the carafe, and went to the kitchen. After filling it with fresh coffee, I glanced out the window and noticed a stunning woman with dark skin and chestnut brown hair going by, riding bareback on Colonel.

"What the hell?"

I rushed back into the dining room and set the carafe on the table. "If you'll excuse me for just a moment."

"What's wrong?" Tom asked, setting his fork down.

"Well, that's what I'm fixin' to find out." I grabbed an apple from the basket on the table, hurried through the main room, and headed out the front of the house without taking time to put my boots on.

Stepping into the side yard, I saw them at a distance, so I whistled for him. Without so much as a pause, he turned on a dime, and against her urging, came right to me.

"Good boy," I said, rubbing his nose as I palmed the apple to him. "I know it's not as good as Z's, but it'll have to do."

I looked up at the rider to find myself face to face with a beautiful woman of mixed race wearing what appeared to be a bag or sack, likely stolen from the barn. "Now, who are you, and where do you think you were going with my horse?"

10

TOO MUCH BLOOD

May 1878

Tom came rushing out to stand beside me. "Well I'll be..."

"Woman was tryin' to steal my horse," I told him.

"I highly doubt she has need of a horse. Clothes maybe, but not a horse," Tom replied.

"Who are you and how did you get Colonel to let you ride him?" I asked, ignoring Tom. "He's not prone to lettin' strangers do that. Especially bareback."

Silently, we three stared at each other.

"You tell him or I will," Tom said.

I looked to my new friend. "Come again?"

Tom nodded to the woman. "We've met her before."

"I'd remember a woman that beautiful," I said. "No matter what she thinks is clothin'."

"If you'd not given my clothin' away to someone named Kiko, I'd not be wearin' this sack," she said with a hint of a southeastern accent and enough indignation that I couldn't help but grin.

I liked feisty women.

"If what you say is true, your clothes were in the saddle bags of

Segovia's horse. Why would they be there? Who keeps their clothes in…" I suddenly understood. "Well, I'll be damned."

Colonel fidgeted and whinnied, likely due to feeling a fight or flight response of his rider.

"We're not gonna hurt you," I said.

She musta known I meant it, for Colonel calmed down.

"Then you've met a shifter before I take it," Tom said to me.

"Yeah…long story. Fill ya in later. I did not, however, know there were horses in the mix."

"I'm one of a kind," she bragged.

"Sadly, you're not," Tom told her. "However, you *are* rare. What's your name?"

"Ianna," she said, pronouncing it "I-ah-nah."

"Well, Ianna, how about you come on inside and get some food, proper clothin', and tell us your story," I said. "Then, after that, you can tell Tom and me your real story. Not the others. They are not in the know, if you catch my meanin'."

"I do," she said, seeming to consider her options for a moment before dismounting with grace just as Miss Sallie came out into the fenced-in area of the front yard.

"Billy? Tom? What is going on?" Seeing Ianna, she stopped. "Oh, hello. Friend of yours, gentlemen?"

"New acquaintance," I replied. "But she *is* in need of clothes and food. Seems some idiot gave away her saddle that held her things."

"Well, that's downright low," Sallie said.

Making sure to hold Ianna's eye, I said, "I'm sure he's sorry. He wouldn't have done so if he'd have known." Turning to Sallie, I gave her my most charming smile I could muster. "Think you could spare some clothin' for her?"

"Well, I sure am not goin' to let her travel about in one of our grain sacks, Billy," Sallie said, opening the gate in the fence. "Come on in, Ianna. Let's get you somethin' to wear, shall we?"

Ianna looked to Tom and me. We nodded that she'd be safe, and without another word, she walked through the gate and followed Sallie toward the house.

"I'll take Colonel back," I said, using a bit of my power to jump up and land on his back. Clicking at him with a nudge toward the stable, we headed off to the barn as my head spun with the knowledge that Gaax wasn't the only kind of shifter.

"This world I've been pulled into is gettin' downright crowded with crazy, Colonel."

He whinnied in reply, and his feelings about Ianna came through from his body through the skin of my hand.

"You like her, do you?"

He whinnied, but it wasn't as joyous as when I asked about Zahara.

"You like her, but you're wary of her. Don't you worry. I don't trust her yet either."

By the time I got back to the ranch house, Sallie had taken Ianna to get bathed and dressed, and Uncle John had likely headed off to prep for his trip. That left me with Tom.

"Where's James?"

Tom sat on his bed. "Went for a tour of the property with Mr. Chisum. I stayed behind so you and I could talk."

I sat on James's bed. "You knew what she was last night, didn't you? That's what you were laughin' at in the barn."

"Yes. I had a feelin' that's what she was."

"Why didn't you tell me? We left her in a cold barn all night!"

"Don't get upset with me. She could've shifted then and there. That was on her. Question is, why did she shift and what does she want from us?"

"Why would she want somethin'?" I asked.

Tom raised an eyebrow. "She does. Trust me. She'd not have shifted and ridden Colonel if she just wanted to leave. She woulda broken out and galloped outta here herself."

"Meanin', we have to ask ourselves, is she friend or foe? What do you think?"

Tom looked out the window and then toward the doorway. Dropping his voice to a quiet tone, he said, "I think you killed her master, stole his saddle, took her things, and she let you bring her here when she easily could've given you the slip. That's what I think."

I nodded. "Okay. So yeah, she wants somethin'. What could that be?"

Tom shrugged. "Could be anything from food and clothes to money to takin' your life."

"One of those things is not like the other," I pointed out.

"Exactly. That means until we know what Miss Georgia has on her mind, I suggest we be careful."

"Miss Georgia?"

"Her southern drawl has that upper-class Georgia sound to it, where she could tell you to go to hell, but it'd sound as pretty as a rose."

"Woman of that colorin' from Georgia would likely mean—"

"Yeah, she probably was a slave," Tom said without hiding the anger he felt in his heart at the notion. He stayed silent for a few seconds, then added, "We also gotta remember that she knows what we both are. That's a problem."

Remembering our conversations around her before we knew, I groaned. "Son of a bitch."

Tom chuckled. "Is that your favorite sayin'? You say it an awful lot."

"Do I now? Got me all figured out in less than twenty-four hours, do ya?" I snapped as I headed toward the door, mad as hell, more at myself than Tom.

"Billy, there was no way you coulda known. Don't be too hard on yourself."

I looked back at him. "I shoulda known there was something odd. In fact, I did, I just didn't know what it was. I thought she was hyped up on werewolf blood."

"Well, until we know if she's friend or foe, don't let it bother ya too much."

I nodded. "I'm goin' to go check on her. You find James. Catch him up to speed."

Tom stood. "I'll do that now."

I headed toward the room I'd bathed in the night before, only to come face to face with someone else. "Miss Chisum, how is our guest?"

"Fine. Filthy, but fine. There's a beautiful woman under all that grime. I'm sure she'll be ready to join us by lunch. Until then, you leave her be."

I stared at the closed door behind Sallie, wishing I could see through it, and not for the reasons most would assume. Turning my attention back to Sallie, I considered telling her we couldn't trust that woman, but I didn't say a word. Instead I just said, "Yes, ma'am."

Turning on a heel, I headed to locate Tom and James. We needed to come up with a plan to find out her intentions without coming across ungentlemanly in case we were wrong. This was not going to be easy.

* * *

April 1949

I stopped pacing about the hotel room long enough to make a decision. Motioning to the spot where the necklace was found, I said, "Mind if I take a look?"

"No, go ahead." Kit stood and moved out of the way.

I knelt beside the bed, pulled out my flashlight, and turned it on. Using the normal setting, I examined the narrow area. The side table was basically a rectangular box, taller than it was wide, with a big bottom drawer, an open space below the top, and feet only an inch high. Thus, making this the perfect place to lose or hide things.

"There's something else," Kit said. "Fletch told me how long he'd be in town. Even had paid for the time in advance. If that's the case, then why would he leave early? That never set right with me."

"Sometimes agents have to leave suddenly. That's not rare."

"And not get his money back?"

"Fletcher's loaded. He wouldn't care," I said.

"And clean the room with bleach?"

I looked back at her over my shoulder. "You're sure the room was scrubbed with bleach?"

Hand on hip, she tilted her head. "I wasn't born yesterday, mister. That's not a smell you can cover up. The nose knows."

"You're not wrong." I twisted back to where she'd found the necklace and did the one thing I sincerely didn't want to do. I pushed extra soul-energy into my olfactory senses and breathed in slow and deep, my mouth open like a cat's would be when scenting an area.

It was not pleasant. First was the layer of daily cleaners, then the other humans who'd stepped into this room, including Kit's unique scent of herbs and plants. But under that, I found it. Bleach, and not a tiny amount. Then I smelled Fletcher. More specifically, I smelled blood, and a lot of it.

I sneezed. Multiple times. To the point of ridiculousness.

"Oh dear!" Kit said, bustling into the bathroom, returning with a tissue. "Here!"

I happily accepted. "Thank you." I blew my nose to expound all the scents I'd taken in and was surprised to find she held out the small trash can from the bathroom at me. I tossed the tissue and thanked her again.

"T'aint nothin', darlin'."

As she walked away with the basket, I twisted the tip of my flashlight, switching to ultraviolet light, and pulled out my small spray bottle of luminol. "Could you close the curtains and turn off the lights please?"

Anger and indignation lit up Kit's face. "Sir, I did not bring you in here for some hanky panky nonsense. You can just get your FBI ass out of this room!"

* * *

May 1878

B illy Bonney, if you can't behave yourself, you can leave this table," Sallie said.

"I apologize, Ianna. I didn't mean that the way it sounded."

123

Lunch was going as I'd expected. Not as Sallie had, obviously, but to Tom, James, and me, it was going as we foresaw.

"It's all right, Sallie," Ianna said. "Some men are just bulls in a china shop when it comes to tactful conversation."

"That's the thing," Sallie said, eyes narrowed in on me. "This one usually isn't." After a short pause, she added, "Billy, could you help me bring in the dessert I have in the kitchen?"

"Of course, ma'am." I stood and followed her out of the dining room, giving Tom a quick look as I did, his face the epitome of apology for the tongue lashing I was about to receive.

"What is wrong with you?" Sallie demanded to know once she had me alone.

"I have no idea what you're talkin' about, Miss Chisum. Now where is this dessert we're—"

"Don't you evade my question. You know darn well what I'm talkin' about."

I sighed. Tom was not going to be happy with me, but I wasn't getting out of here without telling the smartest lady I knew some kind of answer. Keeping my voice down, I leaned close to her and said, "Look, that woman was part of Segovia's team."

"How—"

"And don't you go askin' me how I know, I just do. All right?"

"Fine, but just because she worked with Segovia and the Seven Rivers boys doesn't mean she's a killer like him," Sallie whispered.

"Wouldn't you like to make sure before we get to nightfall and she's sleepin' under your roof?"

"James seems to like her," Sallie pointed out.

I was not going to explain we'd planned that out. James was to be the good guy so Ianna might open up to him. But I wasn't admitting to scheming in front of Sallie. I had my limits.

"Well, that's James. Tom and I are not as sure."

Sallie picked up a tray of scones and handed it to me. "Well, tone it down a bit while we're at the table if you would be so kind."

"Yes, ma'am."

She selected a container with clotted cream and another with jam and motioned me to go back into the dining room. We entered just as Mary Ann was pouring more coffee, and I thanked God for small favors.

For the rest of the meal, Tom and I did as Sallie asked, then politely stood as Ianna rose and left with James, who'd asked her if she'd like to go for a turn about the property. As James offered her his arm and they walked out, I shared a quick glance with Tom, and he nodded. Everything was going according to plan. Or so we hoped.

* * *

Upon return, James reported to us that she seemed to be just fine. In fact, he stated that she was happy to be out from under Segovia's thumb and could have her life back again.

"Oh, and you were right. She's from Georgia," James said, sitting down on my mattress. "Wow, this thing is way more comfortable than that bed."

I laughed. "We can swap out if you want."

"I wouldn't say no to that."

Tom just shook his head. "The harder the surface, the better that boy sleeps."

"Then living on the land will suit him just fine," I replied.

James's green eyes shone with the excitement of being a cowboy. "I just want to see the world. As much of it as I can, for as long as I can. I envy you both. You'll be around long enough to watch this country change and grow. Think of all the places you'll see!"

"I like just bein' where I feel I'm at home," I said. "That's why I love Lincoln so much. The people, the land, everything. I can't imagine living anywhere else. Not sure I ever plan to."

Tom raised an eyebrow. "You do realize that's an awfully long time. Right?"

"Maybe, maybe not. We'll see how it pans out."

Tom poked my chest. "You obviously have not come to terms with your gifts."

"Curse. It's a curse, Tom. To see it otherwise is ridiculous." I grabbed my bag and shoved it under the bed James had been using. "I'm gonna go for a ride."

Hot under the collar for a reason that escaped me, I headed out to Colonel. I rode him until late and had him settled for the night by the time the sun began to set.

Not ready to talk to Tom yet, I climbed up to sit on the roof and smoke a cigarette as the horizon turned the colors only a New Mexico sky could. A deep yellow blended up into orange, then pink, and then the deep purple-blue of the clouds. The colors were so vibrant, it felt more like a painting than real life.

"Ya know, you're not invisible up here," Tom said from behind me.

"If only. Hey, is that a power we can get? I could really use that. Especially right now."

Tom sat beside me. "I get it. Look, I'm sorry if I upset you this afternoon."

I inhaled on my cigarette and blew the smoke out. "Not really sure why I got upset and all."

"I do. I was insensitive. It's okay you've not accepted your…situation yet. I didn't either at first. It takes a bit."

"Why didn't you?" I asked.

"Well, I had a girl. I loved her more than anythin', and though I didn't leave her, I knew it was only a matter of time."

"What happened?"

Tom put his hand out for my cig. I handed it to him and lit a new one for myself. Inhaling, he held it for a second before slowly letting it out, puffing it to look like the dark clouds rolling in. "I stayed with her. Even married her, though there's no record of that. I made sure to destroy all evidence of it after I left."

"How long did you stay?"

"Until it was becomin' evident that I wasn't aging. Add that to bein' gone for days at a time and comin' home bloody or with blood-soaked clothes but no wounds, and well, she gave me an ultimatum. So, I left her almost all the money I had, put the deed to the house and land in her name, took all the pictures and documents that would tie her to me, and left."

"What did you do with it all?"

"Burned all of it except for one picture of her that I cut me out of." He inhaled again on his cigarette and then out, shaking his head. "That got destroyed not that long ago by an unplanned fight in a river. But I can still see her in my mind. That's the one good thing about our...predicament, Billy. We also get the ability to remember a lot more than most. Time bein' what it is to us and all, I suppose."

"She still alive?" I asked.

He nodded. "I check in on her without her knowin' it from time to time. She's married with kids, one of which has made her a grandmother. She's very happy. Married a good man."

"Oh, this was that long ago!"

"Yeah...yeah, it was. Sorry if it sounded like it was closer and all. But for us, time's like that. Whereas some will say three years ago feels like yesterday, our kind say that about thirty years."

"I don't want to live long enough to watch all my friends die, Tom. I've lost my mom and so much more than that. People I loved and admired...it's like a hole inside."

"And what, you think the more you lose, the more you'll be empty?"

I inhaled on the cigarette. "Yeah. That's what I see happenin'."

Tom nodded in thought. "Well, I suppose you can let that happen."

"Let it? You say that like I have a choice in the matter."

"You do. But that's a road you have to forge, Billy. I can't take you down a different path or instruct you how. And until you can see it differently, this is gonna feel like a curse."

Silence slid comfortably between us like it used to between Brewer and me. We sat there watching the glow of the sun shoot up from below the horizon like magic while we finished our smokes.

Hand on my shoulder, Tom said, "Come on, dinner should be ready, and I know how much you love food."

This made me laugh. "And how could you possibly know that?"

Standing, he put his hand out to me. "Same way I know how you're feelin' about losin' loved ones and livin' this life we were given.

Because I *was* you, because I kinda still am you, and we're hungry a lot of the time. Has to do with our *situation*."

I looked up at him and took his hand, not just so he could help me up, but in a way, to let him know I was willing to accept his help in general. Once up, I placed my other hand on his shoulder. "Situation. I like the term."

"Even if you do still feel it's a curse?" he asked with a lopsided grin.

"Yeah, even if."

We leapt down to the ground and headed in for dinner where we not only behaved but came up with a fun plan for the next day. As it would have us up early, we headed to bed shortly after the moon rose. But when we woke up, plans changed.

"Tom? Tom, wake up!"

"What? Why? Is breakfast ready?"

"James is missin'."

This made him sit up quick. Blinking his eyes to clear them, he looked at the floor mattress and found it empty. "Billy, he's an early riser, remember?"

"His bag is gone."

Tom rubbed his eyes and swung his legs out of bed. "But not his favorite picture of his family or his book. Maybe he just took his things to go wash up."

"I checked. He's not there. Neither is Ianna."

Worry like war-paint on his face, Tom dressed in a hurry, and we both headed out. Pointing to the sky, he said, "See it?"

"See what?" I asked at first, then I saw. The moon was still high in the sky even though the sun was up. With a second warrior around, I'd stopped being so meticulous about remembering when it rose and set. "Damn."

A scream filled the air, coming from the barns.

"That's Sallie," I said, before breaking into a run.

By the time Tom and I reached her, Sallie was crying in the arms of the ranch's foreman. Looking for what upset her, I quickly noted a large pool of blood on the barn floor and James's bag soaked in it.

That's when I noticed Colonel and his saddle were gone, too.

"I'm gonna kill her," I growled.

Tom spit on the floor. "Not if I get to her first."

"What are you boys talkin' about?" the foreman asked.

"She killed James and stole Colonel," Tom said.

"She'd never do that!" Sallie said, defending Ianna. "Besides, he might not be dead. If he is, where's his body?"

Tom, his face red with anger, said, "I don't know, but I intend to find out."

"I'm with you," I said.

"Take Samson and Delilah," the foreman said, pointing at two of his horses. "They're the fastest I got and already saddled since we prepped them for your trip today."

Without hesitation, Tom and I were in the saddle. Heading out, Sallie stopped us.

"I hope he's all right," she said.

Tom said nothing, putting spurs into the sides of Sampson, who took off. I followed right behind him without a word as well. Even though Sallie didn't realize it, Tom and I did. There was no way anyone who lost that much blood was still alive.

* * *

April 1949

K it's fury at the misunderstanding of my intentions had her face turning the color of her hair. Because of this, I shouldn't have laughed, but I'm not always bright, and I chuckled at the situation like a fool. If she was mad before, now she was steaming. Eyes wide with outrage, she turned on a heel and headed for the door.

"Wait!" I said. She stopped, hand on the doorknob. "I need it dark so I can look for blood spatter. It glows in the dark with the right treatment. Even after chlorine bleach is used."

"Oh," was all she said, and turned out the light before heading to the windows and drawing the drapes closed.

I stood. "Thank you. Do you want to see how it works?"

"Sure," she said, the word clean and crisp.

Once she was at the foot of the double bed, I sprayed the wood floor all around the bedside table and down along the side. Stopping once I reached her, I turned the UV light onto the space.

"Oh my God!" Kit said, her hands flying to cover her mouth in horror.

"I don't think God had anythin' to do with it," I said, looking down at a sincerely large smearing of blue that went from the bed to the bathroom and traveled halfway from the table to the end of the bed.

It was enough blood that even if Kit didn't realize it, I did. If this was Fletcher's blood, there was no way he was still alive.

11

GOLD DUST

May 1878

The beauty of Colonel and I being connected was that I could sense him, and he me. Because of this, we were able to follow Ianna's trail easily. That is, until we found him trotting back toward the Chisum's Ranch, alone and without a saddle. Calling out to him, he picked up the pace and came to a halt before us. I leapt down from Delilah and handed her reins to Tom.

"What's that on his neck?" he asked me.

Noticing the twine tied about Colonel's neck, my mind went back to that day I'd gotten a message from Scáthach attached to a wolf. Searching for a box that would hold a note, I found a rolled-up piece of parchment instead, likely purchased down the way at the post office and general store. "It's a note."

"What's it say?"

"I'm gettin' to it," I said, sliding the tiny scroll-like item out of the twine and unrolling it. "Shit." I handed it to Tom.

Reading aloud, he said, "Now we're even." Throwing the parchment at me, he yelled, "That fuckin' bitch!" A flash of his soul-energy escaped in his rage, causing Sampson to rear up, scaring Delilah and making Colonel anxious. Quickly realizing what he'd done, Tom tried to calm his horse down.

Placing a hand on Delilah, and then Colonel, I sent minute bits of energy into them as well, calming their nerves. However, when I did that to my stallion, he showed me something I didn't want to tell Tom. But if I didn't, he'd have us keep going.

"Shh… It's all right, Sampson. Sorry my energy flared up on ya like that," Tom said.

"Umm…Colonel showed me somethin' you should know."

Dread filled the warrior's face, but with a steady voice, he said, "Tell me."

"James was with her. Draped across Colonel as she rode him. He wasn't movin'."

"He could still be alive," Tom said.

"With that much blood lost?"

Tom's face fell. "I know. Damn it, I know."

"And if he is, he won't be for much longer. Maybe we should split up. You keep followin' this way, and I'll take Colonel back. Then I'll head to the store where she got this parchment."

"Okay, that sounds like a good idea. Especially since we were followin' Colonel and that lead is gone."

Getting back up onto Delilah, I said, "My sticking point here is why take a dead body with her? That makes no sense!"

"Unfortunately, it does," he said. "It'll be her offerin'. He's likely not dead yet, teeterin' on the edge. He'll be her offerin' to the pack so they let her back in. Showin' she got retribution for Segovia's death."

"I'm so sorry, Tom."

"I'll be back. You take Colonel and go learn things."

"Will do. Be careful!"

"Or heroically die tryin'!" he shouted, and was gone.

I looked at Colonel. "I thought by comin' out here I could keep the people 'round me from dyin'. I guess I was wrong."

And that hurt in the depths of my being in a way that twisted me up inside.

* * *

Returning to the ranch the following afternoon, Tom was filthy from the road and weary in his heart. Sallie, also beside herself, took his hands in hers the minute he was inside.

"I'm so sorry, Tom," she said, tears streaming down her face. "You two tried to tell me...to warn me...but I—"

"It's okay, Sallie," Tom said, his voice soothing even if the look of him wasn't. Letting go of her hand, he said, "I'm covered in grime, Miss Chisum. I'd rather you were not as well. May I please use your bathin' tub?"

"Of course. I'll have Mary Ann fill it for you."

"Thank you," he said, and walked past me to the room we'd been sharing.

I followed him in and shut the door behind me. "Did you find him?"

With his back to me, Tom removed his weapon belt and tossed it onto the bed. "No. Made my way all the way to Dolan's cow camp, but nothin'. I saw a new grave, but that coulda been for anyone. No one there knew anythin'."

"Bullshit. They had to know."

Tom spun to look at me. "You think I don't know that? I've been branded the enemy now, too. Not that James and I weren't already that way, but still...this was different. They acted like they'd never seen me before." He pulled his boots off and set them between our beds, and that's when he saw it. "You're all packed up. You goin' somewhere?"

"Yeah, away from anyone I care about. I thought out here I could stop gettin' people killed. But I'm not far enough out of the warzone. I'm gonna head north."

"Well, wait for me to get cleaned up, and I'll go with you."

This caught me off guard. "What? Why?"

"Uh, because we should stick together and rid this area of these vermin. I have some revenge to deal out to them bastards, and you do, too. Besides, neither of us should stay here. We are puttin' Miss Sallie and the rest in danger."

I sat on the bed I'd slept in. "Why would you want to come with me? I got your friend killed. Tom, I'm so sorry...I shouldn't have had you come out here, I shouldn't have—"

"Hold it right there! This is not on you. James said she was safe, not upset at all. We had our suspicions, and he's the one that read her wrong. Poor dumb kid." He ran a hand through his dark auburn hair. "I don't blame you. Did you think I was gonna?"

Standing up straight to face him, I said, "You'd have every right to."

"You have a good heart, Billy Bonney. But don't take on guilt that's not yours to bear or you'll go mad. She could've been free of that life, but she made her choice."

"Why not just kill me? Why James?"

"Easier mark. She had no idea how many souls are in your well. She coulda killed you and you'd come back over and over, and if you killed her, which you'd have done, she wouldn't come back. James was the weak link. I knew that bringin' him out here, but I still did it. So, you see, I could be placin' blame on my own head as well. But it's not on me. It's on her. And we'll find her, and we'll make her pay."

"That we will, brother. That we will."

A knock came at the door.

"Come in," I said.

The door opened. It was Mary Ann. "Mr. Folliard, your bath is ready for you."

"Thank you."

She nodded and walked away.

Following her out the door, he turned back to me and asked, "You gonna be here when I get done or am I gonna have to go hunt you down too?"

I sat on the bed. "Naw, I'll be here. We can both head out tomorrow."

"Good. 'Cause we got work to do."

"And you want whatever that amazin' smellin' dinner is," I said, teasing him.

He pointed at me. "That's no lie."

We both laughed, and he headed down the hall.

Going outside, I went to where I did my best thinking. I needed to figure out the next step now that there'd be two of us. After a bit, I decided on two things: we needed money and to know where we stood in the war. More importantly, I needed to figure out how to explain who Tom was and why he was with me. Now that was going to take some serious storytelling skills.

* * *

We were approaching the half moon, so that meant it would be in the sky until almost noon on the day we were leaving. So we stayed for lunch and then said thank you and goodbye to just Miss Sallie, since it turned out Uncle John had left town just before Ianna had shown up.

"Now remember, if anyone comes askin' about James…?" Tom said, prompting Miss Sallie as he made sure his wagon with things and equipment were properly hooked up to his ewe-necked gelding.

"I've never seen him," Sallie said. "All I know is that he was a pal of Tom's that split up after upsettin' Dolan and his boys."

"Good," Tom said.

I put my hat on. "That should keep you safe from Ianna and others like her."

"I don't like lyin', Billy," Sallie said, fist on hips.

"I know, and I'm sorry for that. But it's for your safety. For all y'all's safety."

Tom pulled himself up to sit at the front of the wagon. "Tell your uncle thank you when he gets back from wherever he went."

"I will. Not sure when he'll be back, but I'll tell him."

"Where'd he go again?" I asked as I mounted Colonel.

"Bosque Redondo to work with the Hunter and Evans Company again. Somethin' about all the cattle he sold them and clearin' them out from the Pecos Valley."

"Then I'll be sure either Tom, myself, or some of the other boys swing by occasionally to check on ya, all right?"

"I'll be just fine, Billy Bonney, and you know it."

"Even so...you be careful, and we'll be by to check in with you soon."

She shook her head at me. "You're not gonna take no for an answer, are ya?"

"No ma'am," I said with a silly grin. Tipping my hat to her, I said, "Till then," and turned Colonel, urging him onto the dirt road.

Tom took up the reins and reiterated what I'd said before urging his gelding up to the road. Once his wagon was alongside me, he said, "So tell me, with this war goin' on, where do you all usually stay at night?"

"We normally tend to camp in the hills between here and Lincoln, using the Chisum Ranch as our commissary."

"Then I'm surprised we didn't see any of the other Regulators while we was there."

"I got to wonderin' about that the other day, then I remembered that the new sheriff, Copeland is his name, is a Tunstall/McSween supporter. The boys are likely not as worried about bein' hidden and travelin' about Lincoln easier than before. Hell, they are likely gettin' some time at their own ranches."

"So then how do you plan to find 'em if they're all spread out?" Tom asked.

I smiled wide. "'Cause if they are tendin' their farms, I know one man who will be at home who could use some of your help around now."

"Oh? Where's that?"

"To one of the first folks I found work with: George and Frank Coe. They're cousins. Both have farms not too far from one another. One of 'em is bound to need help. More likely George due to his injury and the fact that Ab left for California to see his family."

"And you're sure he'll have work for me to do?"

"It's May. We're nearin' the end of plantin' season. But with all the fightin' we've been doin', they'll be runnin' behind, so they'll need help. And they'll pay ya for it, that's key. We're both low on *dinero*... that's why I'm headin' up to Fort Sumner. Got a guy I play cards with up there who owes me money. I'll fetch that, maybe earn a bit more, and head back down and meet up with you."

"Sounds good. We'll stick to the plan we discussed last night when you do?"

"Yeah. We only tell Doc Scurlock the truth. If you meet him before I get back, you can pull him aside. He's the deputy sheriff at the moment, and ya can't miss him. Sandy hair, big ears, missing his two front teeth, and a mind as sharp as an arrowhead."

"Sounds easy enough," Tom said.

The rest of the journey was idle chatter or discussions about the abilities we had. Good conversation makes for a short ride, and before we knew it, we'd reached the spot where we went separate ways.

"Ya got the directions I drew up for ya?" I asked.

Tom tapped his pocket. "Right here."

"Good. I'll be back down by the first of June, give or take a day. If you're not at Coe's, I'll head to Lincoln and San Patricio to find ya. You be careful."

"You too," he said.

We separated ways, him heading toward Lincoln and me to Fort Sumner. It didn't matter how powerful either of us were, without money to buy food and ammunition, we'd be dead sooner than either of us wanted to be.

* * *

I rode into Fort Sumner shortly after nine in the morning on the twenty-fifth of May and got to catching up with a few buddies of mine I saw on the way to my pal's house. They were all talking about some horse race going on later that day, but before I could get the details and place a bet, I saw the time and had to get moving. I wanted to find Pete because I'd bet all the money on me he was involved in that race for sure, and that wasn't the best idea.

Heading on over to the Maxwell mansion, I told Colonel, "Now

TAMSIN L. SILVER

you be on your best behavior. These folks ain't like you and me. They got money and high standards."

Pete's grandparents on his mom's side had received a land grant of a million acres in northeast New Mexico back in 1843. When their daughter, Pete's mom, got married, she and her husband were gifted fifteen-thousand acres. Only reason they were in Fort Sumner though was that when's Pete's grandpa died, his momma got the rest of the land. Gold was found on it, and that was that. They made a killing on it and bought land here. Never knew why they chose here, but I was glad they did.

"Here in the west, land equates to money," I told Colonel. "That's why men fight over it."

Colonel whinnied, and I laughed, catching his thoughts.

"I had no idea who Pete was when we became pals, and I've never asked for a dime. I never will. That wouldn't make me a very good friend. Nothin' kills a friendship faster than money." I paused and corrected myself. "Correction, money *or* a woman."

By the time I rode up, dismounted, and one of the servants took Colonel from me to the stable, it was approaching ten in the morning. I knocked on the door, and another servant opened it.

"Why, Mr. Bonney, it's good to see you," she said.

"Same to you, Sarah. Is Pete around?"

"I'm not sure if the young master is here, but come in. Luz is. Follow me." She shut the door and led me to the kitchen where Luz, Pete's mother, was making something that smelled delicious.

Looking up as she shut the door to the stove, Luz brushed the wood dirt from her hands. Eyes brightening, she gave me a big smile. "William, I didn't know you were comin' by today!"

Hat in hand, I nodded to her in respectful greeting. "No, ma'am, it wasn't a planned visit. I just wanted to run by and see how y'all were doin', what with all that's been going on 'round Lincoln County lately. Wanted to bring Pete up to speed."

"I'm afraid he's not here. Ran out this mornin'. Somethin' to do with that darn horse race. I suspect he'll be back soon. I know there's someone else who'd like to see you though. The child does not stop talkin' about you or your horse. You still riding Centauro?"

"I do, but he's not who I'm ridin' today. I was gifted a beautiful black stallion by Tunstall. I've got him with me."

"Aww, Paulita will be heartbroken to hear it. Always askin' if her horse Sugar could have a baby with your stallion." Luz laughed, then raised her voice and yelled out for her fourteen-year-old daughter.

"What is it, Momma?" Paulita asked before she entered the room.

"You have a visitor."

Stepping through the doorway, Paulita's eyes landed on me. "Billy!" She ran over and gave me a hug.

In doing so, I realized the young girl wasn't so young anymore. Taller and more filled out, she was looking like a young woman, and a pretty one at that. But I knew better than to bring *all* of that up, especially in front of her momma. So instead, I kept the hug short, took her hands, and stepped back from her. "Why, Miss Paulita, you've grown at least two inches!"

She beamed at me. "An inch and a half, but you can call it two if you wish."

"Got a growth spurt over the winter, she did," her mom said. "Billy, would you like some coffee? I got some cinnamon rolls about to come out of the oven here."

"Mrs. Maxwell, that sounds lovely."

The three of us sat down to rolls and coffee while Luz asked me about what was going on in Lincoln, and I told her about our latest victory.

"When the Regulators rode into Lincoln with the rescued horses, people cheered," I said, as that's what I'd heard from a passerby on my way up to Fort Sumner. I didn't tell her about killing Segovia. Not that she couldn't handle that, but I was sure she'd not want me saying such things in front of Paulita.

"Justice, at last!" Luz said.

"Are you the leader of the Regulators?" Paulita asked.

I laughed. "No. Doc Scurlock is."

"Oh," she said, looking a bit sad, and the conversation found its natural lull, making me wonder if I was possibly overstaying my welcome. "I won't wait on him much longer, imposing on your time and all. If the boy would just get back home and—"

Just then we heard the door open and shut with a heavy hand, and Pete Maxwell hurried into the room. He began complaining to his mother before he even realized I was there. "Damn crisis. Gold Dust has a problem, and I might have to pull him. This race was to fix that Fly fiasco, too." Noticing me, he smiled wide. "Well, I'll be damned, Billy. It's good to see you!"

I stood, shook his hand, and he pulled me into a brief hug.

"You Maxwell men never seem to learn," Luz said, looking from her son to me. "His father sure didn't."

"What is a fly fiasco?" I asked, sitting back down.

Luz stood up and fetched more coffee. Filling our mugs, she said, "Fly was a horse Lucien said was unbeatable. Because of that, in 1866 he set her up to race a bay stallion named Bald Hornet."

"In father's defense, Fly hadn't ever lost," Pete said.

"That's true, but your father failed to remember that all she'd ever run were half-mile races. Bald Hornet had won all of his races, too, but those were a mile long."

"And let me guess," I said, "this race with Fly was to be a mile."

She nodded and sat back down. Taking her coffee mug in her hands, she let the warmth soothe the aggravation she'd started to express. With a deep, cleansing breath, she said, "You are correct. Five thousand people showed up for this, and Bald Hornet won. Lucien lost a small fortune…which he didn't admit to me until later."

I winked at Luz and said, "That was probably a wise move."

She couldn't help but smile. "You are correct."

"You left out that Fly led for the first half," Pete said, standing up for his father's decision. "If she'd just been trained for a mile…"

"Yes, that big 'if' is always the question, isn't it?" Luz said, making her point.

"So, why is there crisis with the race today?" I asked.

Pete sat next to me. "My rider for Gold Dust won't ride in the race today."

"Won't or can't?" Luz asked.

Pete ignored his mamma's question and turned to me. "Billy, I've got a proposition for ya. Ride Gold Dust in the race today for me. I'll pay well."

"Do it!" Paulita said. "You'll win for sure. I'll even come watch!"

I looked between Paulita's smiling face to Pete's anxious one, my eyes stopping on Luz.

"Oh, don't look to me, that's on you, darlin'," Pete's momma said.

Being as that I could use the money, I half-agreed, stating a stipulation. "I'll have to take a look at your horse first."

Pete slapped my shoulder. "Great! I'm sure you'll like him! Come on!"

With quick goodbyes to Luz and Paulita, I followed Pete on foot over to the barn where Gold Dust was being kept. His handler, a man by the name of Jesús Silva, held the restless beast out back. The stallion was a flashy red-gold buckskin with a black mane and tail, a definite beauty whose name suited him well. As I began to examine him, Pete got called inside the barn to help with something, thankfully leaving me alone with Silva and Gold Dust for a few moments.

"Tell me, what happened to his rider?" I asked as soon as Pete was out of earshot.

"Betts?" Silva asked. When I nodded, he whispered, "The horse went crazy and threw him this morning. He's hurt pretty bad."

Pete returned and waited impatiently as I examined Gold Dust. Laying a hand on his neck, I released some energy into him, asking him what was wrong. The answer I got wasn't as clear as when Colonel replied, but I, at least, knew where to look and ran my hand along to his hip. Noticing the issue, I touched it, and Gold Dust kicked out in pain.

I calmed him down before turning to Pete. "He's got a really bad muscle spasm in his hip. It's hurtin' him pretty bad from what I can tell."

"Damn it," Pete said.

"I'll try some hot compresses and see what I can do. No promises."

Pete nodded, his hope dwindling. "Okay…I appreciate it, Billy."

141

Sending Silva to fetch the compresses, we took Gold Dust back into the barn where Pete and I caught up on each other's lives.

Once Silva returned and began to apply the heat, I told him I'd take care of it. This way I not only got to talk to Pete alone about things I felt he needed to know to stay safe, I had an activity that would mask what I was really doing, which was sending healing energy into the horse's hip.

By the time we needed to say yay or nay to the race, Gold Dust was doing fine. Not only that, but he and I had come to know each other better, so I agreed to race him for Pete.

"You're not gonna hold this against me if he doesn't win, are ya?" I joked.

"Naw," Pete said, but I could hear his wavering tone on that. "Or at least not for always."

I laughed. "Fair enough."

The things I get myself into.

* * *

April 1949

A re you all right?" I asked Kit, whose face had gone pale at the sight of how much blood had once been on the hotel room floor.

With hands still covering the bottom half of her face and eyes bugging out, she nodded.

"I'm going to see if it travels under the furniture, okay? You can step out if you want."

She shook her head, saying nothing.

"Okay," I said quietly, and stepped over to spray under the bed.

Shining the light, I could see the blood ran under a short way. Placing the small flashlight between my teeth, I moved the bedside lamp to the bed and turned the table out of the way. Spraying the mist, I immediately saw that the blood hadn't traveled farther, explaining why the necklace hadn't been found.

"What's that?" Kit asked, her voice quiet yet steady.

I took the flashlight out of my mouth. "What's what?"

She carefully stepped over, around the markings, and squatted beside me. Tapping a nail on the side of the table, she said, "These marks here."

"I must've gotten some of this stuff on here when I first sprayed it," I told her, coating the whole flat side of the mahogany with more of the luminol.

"Begosh, does that mean anything to ya?" Kit exclaimed.

I stared at the three words all in caps drawn on the side of the table, and my blood went cold. It said, "SCÁTHACH IS HERE" followed by a "BLO" and a trail off.

I pointed at the last three letters. "I don't know what this is, but the rest, yeah...yeah I do. And it's not good."

"Figures. I shoulda known somethin' was wrong."

"Why's that?"

"Cause as my momma is always sayin', 'The things you get yourself into, Kit...it's like trouble just likes to follow you.'"

This time, Kit's momma wasn't wrong.

* * *

May 1878

The racetrack was a straight shot from start to finish, and I led Gold Dust toward it, Pete and Paulita already in the crowd to watch.

"Contenders, please head to the startin' line," someone shouted as I got close.

With a nod toward the announcer, I got into the saddle and did as I was told, all the while thinking about the decision I'd made on my way over here: I wasn't going to help Gold Dust be faster with my gift. I wanted Pete to see the real speed of the stallion and not have false results that he based the future of this horse on.

Lining up with the others, I kept my eyes on the horizon in the distance, thankful that the sun was behind us. I'd given Paulita my hat to hold, and she gave me a handkerchief of hers for good luck. I'd put it into my pants pocket so her brother wouldn't see it and get the wrong idea. Yet, I found my hand on the outside of my pocket, feeling it there now. It made my heart flutter a bit, or maybe that was the impending race.

The man in charge stepped up, and I took my hand off my pocket, getting a good hold on the reins. Taking a deep, settling breath, I waited.

The shot exploded from the gun, and all of us took off like lightning had struck behind us. Gold Dust was fast all on his own, and we easily took the lead. But soon, other horses caught up. Two passed, and we were neck and neck with two more.

Still refusing to give Gold Dust any extra energy, I snapped his reins to urge him faster. "We got this, damn it! Just go for it!"

Next thing I knew, everything became a blur of people shouting, horses, and dust all around. We pulled ahead of those beside us and approached the two leaders. We rushed by one, then another, and kept going. We passed the finish line, but Gold Dust wanted to keep running, so I let him go a bit before turning him about and taking him back to the finish line.

Pete was screaming with joy, jumping around like a loon. Seeing me approach, he shouted my name as a ton of people surrounded us. Dismounting, Pete ran over to me.

"Woooo!" Pete shouted, and threw his arms around me. "You did it!" I could smell the alcohol on him, and one look into his eyes told me he was a bit drunk. "I'll never forget this... I owe you in a big way, Bonney! Anything you ask. Anything!"

I laughed. "Be careful, or I'll take you up on that someday."

Pete didn't seem to care. He'd just won so much money that his family didn't honestly need. But I understood. It was a matter of pride. Of setting his old man's wrongs.

The sun starting to set, it hit my eyes, and in the crowd, I looked for Paulita because she had my hat. Or, that's what I told myself.

Hearing her before I saw her, I turned in the sound of her squeal of joy. Before I knew it, she leapt at me, and for the first time, I truly hugged her. She returned it with unabashed fervor.

"I told you that you'd win," she said in my ear.

"How could I lose with your cheerin' me on," I told her, my dusty face buried in the dark curls of her hair. It smelled just like her handkerchief, which reminded me of it. Letting go, I reached into my pocket for it.

She stopped me with a hand on my arm. "You keep it." She put my hat on my head and winked at me before running off to her brother, who was calling for her.

This left me standing there, surrounded by people, yet seemingly alone. As my hand casually slid into my pocket to touch the handkerchief, I realized I had some unfamiliar feelings for Paulita and her new womanly body and attitude. All of which I'd not expected. She was too young for me to be feeling that way about, and I knew it. But she wouldn't be too young forever. I just needed to wait and examine if what I was feeling was real or just the buzz from winning the race. Only time would tell.

12

ANGEL

June 1878

I stayed up in Fort Sumner for a few more days and then rode down to the Coe farm as promised, getting there a day late due to weather. Hopping off Colonel, I noticed the beautiful roan-colored coat of Tom's gelding was now covered in mud and dirt as he grazed out front. Not far from him was Tom's worn-out equipment that'd been in his wagon. It was also muddy and looking a bit worse for wear.

Peering in the window of George's home, I saw both George and Frank sitting with Tom at the table eating lunch. I knocked on the front door.

George opened the door. "Billy! What a great surprise! Come in, come in! We're sittin' down to some grub, you hungry?"

"He's always hungry," Frank said.

I pointed at him. "You're not wrong."

"Have a seat, I'll get it for ya," George said.

"Ya sure?" I asked, looking at his injured right hand, still bandaged.

"It's healing better than you'd think," he said. "Thanks to you."

I nodded at him and said, "Is it still hurting ya?"

"A bit."

"Let me see?" I said.

George held out his hand. "Well, it's freshly bandaged right now so…"

I carefully took it and pushed a minute bit of healing energy into it, feeling a small bone move, making a tiny popping noise. George's eyes watered with the pain, but I soothed it as best I could. "I'm guessing whatever that was musta been what was causin' the pain. Take it easy today, and I'll get my own grub."

Blinking away the water in his eyes and holding the hand close to his body, he thanked me and headed back to the table. Once I had a plate full of beans with salted pork, I sat with the three men, Tom directly across from me.

"This here is Tom O'Folliard," George said.

"It's Folliard," Tom corrected. "Tom O. Folliard."

George raised an eyebrow. "That's what I said." Looking to me he explained who the clean-shaven, young man with the broad-featured face was. "Tom drifted from Texas lookin' for work and couldn't have shown up at a more perfect time."

"'Cause of him, we got our plantin' done by the end of May and then, like a gift from above, the rain came down the following day," Frank told me.

"Yeah, that's why I'm here today, was plannin' on yesterday but got caught in the storm," I told them, mostly just explaining to Tom why I was late. "Did you tell him we're in a war here?" I asked before digging into my food.

"We did," George replied.

"Still seems to be crazy enough to wanna stay," Frank added.

I swallowed my big mouthful of food. "Well, it just got worse. I rode through Lincoln on my way here. Everyone is upset about Axtell's latest proclamation."

Frank stood, picking up his dishes. "For the love of all that's holy, what's that bastard done now?"

"Seems a few days ago, a big printed notice with a big ol' eagle on it said that Copeland was no longer sheriff and appointed Peppin in his place."

George shot up out of his seat. "The hell he is! What was the reason listed?"

"Somethin' to do with not collectin' taxes in his first thirty days."

"How the hell was he supposed to do that?" Frank blustered, setting his dishes back down on the table harder than he likely meant to. "The conditions right now in this county make it impossible for anyone to even compile the tax lists needed to figure out the amounts owed, let along actually collect the taxes."

"Good news is that Peppin seems to not be in town at the moment *and* President Hayes's investigator will be in Lincoln this week. He's currently at Fort Stanton. I stopped by there and signed up to give information on Tunstall's murder."

George sat back down. "Like you're not already a big enough target for them bastards."

"The target on me can't get bigger than it already is, George."

Calmer now, Frank said, "I heard the attorney's last name and couldn't believe it. Right when we're needing a miracle, the powers that be send an investigator named Angel."

"Yeah, I thought that interesting, too," I said, shoveling more food into my face. I'd not eaten since breakfast the day previous, so I could've eaten my plate and theirs as well.

"Anyone else sign up?" George asked.

"Mac did. I visited him for a short spell on my way through town. He was makin' notes for his statement. He's real confident that President Hayes will help."

George huffed. "I never trusted no government lackey, but we can hope."

I laughed. "Did you just call the President of the United States a lackey?"

"Maybe," George said, not apologizing for it.

I sipped my coffee, my eyes on Tom. "Interested in fightin'?"

"Wouldn't mind," Tom replied, his voice gentler and more timid than I was used to hearing.

"What work did you do before you got here?" I asked.

"Farming at my uncle's in Uvalde. Parents died of smallpox, so he and my aunt raised me, but they didn't want me no more…said I needed to head out on my own. What's your name again?"

"Oh, I forgot. Sorry about that," George said. "Tom, this here is Billy Bonney."

"Good to meet ya, Billy," Tom said, extending his hand over the table.

I shook it and then took my last bite of food. "Let's see how you shoot, Tom. Wanna go fire a few rounds out back?"

"Wouldn't mind," he replied.

Standing up, I grabbed my empty plate and mug. "I'll take care of these. George, is the regular ammunition in the same spot?"

"Sure is."

"Good, you two wanna join us?"

"Afraid I can't, gotta get back home," Frank said. "You all have a good time though. I'll swing by a bit later on." He nodded at us and then took his dishes to the kitchen before heading out.

"Rest your hand a bit," I told George. "I'll take him."

George nodded. "That'd be best."

"Come on, Tom. Let's see what ya got."

Once we were a good distance from the house, we caught each other up on the past few days.

"Let me get this straight, I got dirty and exhausted plantin' crops here to make money," Tom said as he loaded his revolver with lead bullets, "while you got to win a horse race and play monte for money. Not sure that all sounds fair in the grand scheme of things."

I laughed heartily and shot a target off the fence. "We can't all be William H. Bonney," I joked. "But seriously, anyone coulda won on that horse. Once his muscle spasm was done, he was seriously fast."

"How long we gotta stay out here shootin' at stuff?" Tom asked.

"Well, if we're gonna stick to the story we planned out, we should stay for a few hours, you having limited firearm ability and all."

Tom chuckled and shot a target off the fence with no more than a second to aim at it. "Yeah, I'm horrible. You best teach me how to shoot properly."

I grinned. "Hey, it was your idea. We don't have to go with it."

"Naw, we stick to the plan of me acting all in awe of you and stuff. It makes the most sense on why I'd stick so close to you and gives the impression of me not being a warrior of Scáthach."

"Did you run into Doc at all?"

"Naw…guess you'll get to do that introduction."

I nodded. "Well then, since we gotta sell the story that there's teachin' goin' on out here, let's shoot more things and you can teach me some shit."

"That I can do, and same goes for you."

"Not sure what I can teach a warrior who's been around longer than me," I said.

"I've heard you're able to ride sideways on your horse like the Indians do."

I nodded my head toward the house. "Sure thing, but you'll not be able to do that on that ewe-necked gelding of yours. You need a better riding horse."

"He's a good worker though."

"That's all right, the horse I rode before I got Colonel is here. I'll introduce ya to Centauro."

* * *

We stayed with the Coes to help out a bit longer, then headed into town since my appointment with Attorney Angel was at eight-thirty in the morning on the eighth of June. We arrived at Colonel's secret stall in the stable just as the sun set on the seventh and was pleased to find Gaax hanging around outside.

I introduced him to Tom, telling my shapeshifting friend the truth, and vice versa. Even considered asking Gaax to shift to human form so Tom could meet him proper, when Ben came back to see what the noise was and found us sitting there smoking.

"And here I thought the neighborhood boys was out here causin' trouble again," Ben said.

"We are boys, and we've been known to cause trouble," I replied with a laugh.

"Tell me somethin' I don't know," Ben chided.

I introduced him to Tom and then explained, "You can't tell anyone we're here. Especially not now that Peppin is gonna be sheriff."

"And with him still not showin' up to cause trouble, we're all on edge," Ben said. "In fact," he began to add, when we all heard my stomach growl. "Billy, when did you eat last?"

A guilty grin filled my face. "This mornin'?"

"Well, seein' as it's *you* back here creatin' the ruckus, and you can keep an eye out for the boys that've been causin' trouble, I think I could bring ya some leftovers from supper."

"That would be heavenly," I said. "Just don't—"

"Tell anyone you're here. I got it," he said, waving off my worry and jogged back toward his house and store.

"I don't like that the sheriff is missing," I said.

"Same," Tom replied.

"Gaax, I need you to do me a favor. I need you to take a message to Doc Scurlock and then go see if you can find George Pepping. Can you do that?"

Gaax gave a loud *QUARK* and bobbled his head, so I set to writing a quick note to Doc. Once done, I quickly tied it to Gaax, and he took off.

We slept in the hidden room of the stable, and though Tom had assumed he'd be coming with me the next day to meet with Attorney Angel, I asked him to stay and watch the horses when I headed into town. I wasn't gonna ride Centauro or Colonel. Instead, I chose to ride one of Ben's fastest horses into town to meet with the inquisitor from D.C.

Seeing this, Colonel stomped his feet about.

"It's nothin' personal, boy," I told him. "I just don't want folks seein' you or Centauro and knowin' I'm in there. No offense, my black beauty, but you'd be a dead giveaway of that."

Colonel huffed air out his nostrils at me, and I pulled an apple from my pocket for him. "I know, big fella. Here...after this I'll see if we can find some time to take you to your favorite apple orchard, all right?"

Colonel nodded in his horsey way and took the apple, happy to munch away, his irritation at me clearly over.

Running a bit late, I hoisted myself up onto Ben's horse and headed down to the building Lincoln used for a courthouse, a meeting house, a dance hall, and anything else you could imagine. A long, rectangular, two-room adobe, it had a front door to each room, one more prominent than the other.

Leaving the horse tied out front, I headed through that primary entrance, entered the large main room, and let the person there know I was here to see Attorney Angel.

"He's in there," the man said, pointing to the doorway to my left.

I thanked him and headed over, my boots hitting the wood floor, announcing my arrival more than I'd have liked. Stepping into the smaller room about four minutes late for my appointment, I eyed the large, open window across from me as a possible escape route. Seeing as both the front and rear doors of the room were closed, that was my best bet. Finally, I let my eyes land on the only man in the room.

He was leaned back in a chair, one leg lazily crossed over the other, his light blue eyes looking right past me to the doorway. "I'm sorry, I'm waiting on a Mr. Bonney," the man said.

"That'd be me, sir," I told him.

He appeared taken aback.

"Problem?" I asked.

"I was expecting an older man."

Thinking his accent reminded me of New Yorkers I'd met, I thumbed over my shoulder toward the doorway. "I can go find you one if you'd like, but it's me you're needin' to talk to."

The man laughed. "Please, have a seat. I'm Attorney Frank Angel."

"Nice to meet you," I said, sizing him up as I made my way across the room.

Angel was a good-looking man with short, dark hair swept back from a face of square features and a protruding brow that made him appear more serious than he likely was. His beard was trimmed, and I'd have put him no older than his early thirties. He wore a wedding band and a nice suit, with shoes that appeared tailored for him, which said money and prestige.

"Tell me what you understand of our proceeding today," he said as I sat in a chair against the wall so I could see all entrances and exits to the room.

"To hear from me what happened to Mr. Tunstall," I replied.

"Yes." He dipped his pen into some ink and said, "For the record, how old are you?"

Being a bit cheeky, I replied, "A hundred and sixty-eight days short of nineteen, sir."

Amused, he wrote as he spoke. "I take it that you were born on November twenty-third of fifty-nine." His eyes then met mine, and I nodded. "That said, do you understand that the testimony you'll be giving today will be under sworn oath?"

"I didn't, but that's all right by me."

Once I was sworn in, we talked about that horrible day in February, and I told him everything I remembered. Afterward, he had me go wait in the main room.

I walked on over to the window to check on Ben's horse and found Tom standing outside. Opening the window, I said, "You're supposed to be at Ellis's watchin' the horses!"

"You might trust that attorney, but I don't. I'm here to protect you if *she* shows up."

I wanted to tell him he was crazy, but I could see his point, so I left him there and closed the window. That's when I noticed the long bar of the big room was covered in stacks of papers. Being as both the transcriptionist and Angel were in the other room, I began leafing through them and realized they were the other completed depositions.

I quickly read through Murphy's and then McSween's. I was just skimming over all the legal jargon for the Fritz estate when I heard footsteps approaching the room. Stepping away from the bar, I sat in the closest chair and pretended to be picking at my nails.

The transcriptionist walked in and handed me some papers. "I'll leave this with you for checking over. But don't sign it until Attorney Angel can witness that."

He left and I read through what they'd written down based on what I'd told him. Glad to see he'd gotten everything I'd said down right, I set the papers aside. With more time to kill, I skimmed through Gottfried Gauss's deposition and read things I'd never heard about. Mostly things Morton had said back at the ranch before they'd come out and killed John.

Slamming it closed with a rage at this new information, I walked away from it to collect myself when the door opened, and both Angel and the transcriptionist came in.

"Everything all right?" Angel asked.

"Yes. Everything looks to be in order, sir."

The transcriptionist handed me a pen with ink, and I signed the deposition in front of Angel.

"Thank you. Now, before you go, I wanted to verify...were you in the posse to capture John Tunstall's murderers until Justice of the Peace Wilson was removed by the governor?"

Thinking about Axtell's move to make us outlaws, I felt my mad creeping up, as George liked to say. "Sir, since Tunstall's murder, I've been an officer of the law. I was a deputy to Constable Martinez this February, then Brewer, and again with Deputy Scurlock's posse on May fourteenth. Hell, I'd still be, except Governor Axtell fired Sheriff Copeland a week and a half ago. But mark me, that doesn't mean my work's done."

Stopping, I stared at him good and hard to make my point. He nodded, thanked me for coming in, and I walked away hot and mad.

To see what Murphy's group was trying to pull off as the truth had my blood boiling.

Exiting the courthouse, I found Tom sitting, tossing small rocks toward a ring of sticks he'd set up some ways from him. "Told ya she'd not show up here."

Tom set the rocks down, brushing the dirt from his hands. "We can't be takin' any chances right now. Not with Peppin as sheriff and you indicted for Brady's murder."

I cringed. "You know there is no way of knowin' which Regulator made the fatal shot."

Tom stood. "And *you* know they don't care, right?"

"Yeah, I do. Don't mean it doesn't make me mad as a march hare though."

Tom laughed. "I hear that. Come on, let's get a move on. We have business to take care of."

"That we do. If Gaax got to Doc's fast enough last night, Scurlock will be arrivin' at the Ellis's anytime now, and he'd have sent a request for the rest of the men to be there an hour later. Time to tell Doc who you are, introduce you to the rest, and make you an official Regulator."

By the seventeenth, though Gaax had delivered our message and we'd seen Doc and the rest, we'd not seen Gaax or Peppin. To make matters worse, Attorney Angel had finished up his work and was heading back to Santa Fe that afternoon. Without knowing what else to do, Tom and I joined Reverend Ealy and his family to have dinner at the Ellis Store. Also in attendance were the carpenter that helped build the Tunstall Store; Lucas Gallegos and his wife; ex-Justice of the Peace Wilson; and fellow Regulator, Fred Waite.

On the walk back, after the Gallegos and Mr. Wilson split off, Reverend Ealy said, "Can you believe Wilson tried to sell me that house for two-thousand dollars?"

"Well, it's on eight acres of land," I pointed out, imitating Wilson to a tee.

Ealy swapped his eldest daughter from one hip to the other. "Still, I'm not buyin' anyone's home for that much. I don't have that kind of cash."

"Mac would probably lend it to ya, if he can," Fred said.

"Or see if the bank will give you a loan," Tom offered.

"That's not a bad idea," Charlie said.

"I mean, you are the new preacher in town, so you need a proper place to live. The Tunstall rooms here aren't big enough for you all," Fred pointed out.

"More space than the Gallegos have," I said. "By the way, did anyone else get the feelin' Lucas's wife was mad as hell at him?"

"Oh yeah, he's in the doghouse for sure," Tom said with a grin. "I could tell."

"Wonder what she's—" I started to say when pain ripped into my skull like a tomahawk had split it open. I dropped to the ground, forgetting what I was going to say. A vision of Peppin shoved its way into my mind's eye from Gaax, who he was with, and where. Then, just like that, it was gone.

"Billy! Are you okay?" Fred asked, carefully trying to help me up on one side as Tom did the same on the other.

With my own sight returned to me, I blinked and looked at the Ealy family. "Headache came out of nowhere. I'm okay."

"You sure?" Mrs. Ealy said. "The doctor could give you some—"

"No, no, I'm fine. Just need to go lie down."

Catching on that the Ealys didn't know about my abilities, Tom said, "Let's get you back to the McSween house so you can do that."

"Well, all right," Reverend Ealy said. "But I'll send somethin' down to you anyway. Get some water in him, too. Maybe he just had too much wine with dinner."

Tom and Fred nodded adamantly and whisked me down the road from them.

Once we were out of earshot, Tom said, "What did you see?"

"Was it from Gaax?" Fred added.

"Yeah, and we've got a huge problem."

13

TIME TO RUN

June/July 1878

Peppin is on his way back here with a military detachment," I told the Regulators, who were all gathered in the McSween patio area to discuss the issue. "He's campin' for the night, but he and his escorts will be here by tomorrow."

"That coward, of course he requires a military detachment," Charlie said.

"Well, coward or not, he'll swear in deputies and get to workin' on the Ring's business," Fred said.

"Bet I can guess what his first bit o' business will be," George Coe said. "We need to hightail it outta here."

"For once, I agree. We can't take on the military, or Dudley will get involved, and that's not a fight we can win. Not at this point," I said, looking up at Doc. "Where we gonna go?"

"Let's head back out to the hills," Scurlock said.

"No," Mac protested. "I can't do that again. We stay here."

"What's goin' on?" Susan asked, stepping out into the patio area as she wrapped a shawl around her shoulders.

"It's nothin', dear," Mac said just as I blurted the truth.

Susan knew bullshit when she smelled it, and she turned an accusing eye on her husband. "You are not stayin' here. You know damn well that idiot Peppin can't think for himself. He needs Jimmy Dolan to do it for him. He'll head straight here to arrest you." She looked to Doc. "What about San Patricio? It's close enough that if I need to get in touch, I can."

Doc opened his mouth to say it wasn't far enough when Mac piped in, saying, "It's San Patricio or here, Doc. You choose. I'm not goin' any farther."

Doc sighed. "Fine, San Pat it is. We leave before first light. Everyone pack up. We'll leave two men here as protection for Susan and the Shield family though. With Rob in Mesilla, we don't want the women and children left unprotected."

I nodded. "We'll leave men who don't have any warrants out for them. That'll give Peppin no excuse to pull 'em."

"Smart thinkin', Billy," George said. "I'll help spread the word to the others that ain't here to pack and meet up at Ellis's before sunup."

Everyone headed out to prep for our trip to San Patricio. Sure, we went there a lot, but this time we didn't know when we'd be back.

Gaax returned at some point in the night. By three in the morning on the eighteenth, he was perched on my shoulder as Tom and I flanked Mac heading east to the Ellis Store. There we found everyone loading the supplies we'd asked Isaac to put aside for us back on the tenth. We collected food and such, and thirty minutes later left for San Pat, leaving Gaax behind to find and deliver my note to Roy and bring me his reply. Which I received the night of the twenty-sixth of June.

Everyone gathered around a fire behind the home of a friend's house in San Pat as I delivered the news. "Roy, our Regulator Network contact, says that Peppin appointed Jack Long, Buck Powell, Marion Turner, and José Chavez y Baca to be his deputies."

"Well looky there," Fred said as he fed Gaax some eggs he made for him. "All men in the pocket of *The House*. I'm so surprised."

I fought not to grin at his sarcasm. "Oh, and it gets worse."

"Of course it does," Tom said.

"That rumor we heard a few days ago that Kinney and his gang arrived in Lincoln to join up with Peppin and his men is true."

"Well, isn't that just swell," George said. "There's not an eviler man than Kinney in all of New Mexico, that I know of at least."

"I can think of a few," I muttered, but no one paid me no mind.

"Kinney's probably there at Dolan's request to keep Peppin in line," Fred pointed out.

"So now what?" Charlie asked. "Do we wake Mac up and see what he thinks?"

Doc scratched at the stubble upon his face and sat. "No, let him sleep. Thing is, with the Santa Fe Ring officially takin' control of Lincoln County again with the likes of Kinney, it's gonna be bad. They'll split into huntin' parties and come lookin' for us all. We covered our tracks leavin' town, but they'll check here for sure, and soon."

"Doc's got a point," George said.

"What about Susan? We can't just leave her there to deal with it all," I stated.

Tom stepped up. "Let's go get her." Everyone turned to him, and he continued. "We send Mac out of here first thing in the mornin' with some men and the wagon Isaac Ellis gave us, then a few go get her and meet up with the rest of ya at a designated location."

That sat on our heads for a moment before I piped up. "Sallie said Uncle John would be back in time for the Fourth of July and that we were all to come out. I say we head there a bit early."

"They'll go there lookin' for us, too," Fred said.

"Not if we spread word we're somewhere else," I said. "You know they'll question everyone here. We let it be known we're headin' someplace different...and trust someone to break."

"Or order someone to if no one else will," Tom suggested.

"Exactly," I said, pointing at him.

Doc nodded. "I'm good with the idea. So we send Mac off tomorrow and then we fetch Susan that night and meet him at the South Spring Ranch."

159

"I think that's our best bet," I said. "Tom and I will get Susan, bring her back here, and then we'll leave town."

"That sounds like the best option," Doc replied.

Everyone nodded, and silence set in as one question was on everyone's mind: who was going to tell Mac?

"I'm not tellin' him," I said quickly.

"Not it!" George and Frank said at the same time.

"I've got to work out the trip to Lincoln with Billy," Tom said, grabbing my elbow and starting to pull me off as I heard each person give an excuse followed by Doc regretfully saying he'd do it.

"That should go well," Tom said in jest.

"Oh, I'm sure."

It did not, but Mac finally agreed it was best and with mighty reluctance left the next morning. Tom and I left after just after five o'clock in the evening as the moon set and began our trip toward Lincoln.

"Why are we in this get-up?" I complained.

"It's not a costume or anythin'," Tom scolded.

"It feels like one. What am I wearin'?"

"You're wearin' Regulator attire. The Network men and women own this type of stuff, too."

"Wait, women? Women are Network Assassins, too?"

"Yeah, you didn't know that?"

I grinned, something now making sense. Instead of mentioning it, I said, "But all black?"

"Well, once that sun sets, we'll be invisible to the naked eye. That's why we ride dark-colored horses," he said, motioning to the dark gray mare he'd swapped Centauro for, just for this trip.

"Um, I chose Colonel because we have a connection and John left him for me, not because of his color."

"Well, a lot of our kind tend to live in the shadows, Billy. A dark horse helps."

I rolled my eyes. "I think a fast gun helps more."

He laughed. "Sure it does, but shootin' your way out of somethin' isn't always the answer."

"I know. That wasn't my point."

"Oh, then what was, Mr. I Practice Shooting Every Chance I Get?"

"Shut up will ya? I don't—" I stopped, noticing Colonel's ears raise up. "What is it, boy?" I asked, placing my hand on his face. He replied, and I looked at Tom. "We have to head back."

"But why would—"

"Now, Tom!" I whispered loudly as I spun Colonel around. "We got company comin' our way."

"It might not be the Murphes," he said as we began a steady pace back while on hard ground.

"We can't take that chance," I replied. "We'd be outnumbered. Come on."

With a nod, he followed me a different way than we'd come, onto softer ground. This meant less sound, so we picked up speed, riding hard and fast into the center of town.

George Coe saw us first from his spot on a rooftop. "What ya doing back here, Billy?"

Doc stepped out the door of Juan's home. "Is there a problem?"

"Gaax!" I shouted, and he came swooping down to perch on Colonel's head. "Find out who's comin' this way."

With a QUARK, he beat his wings and took off the way we came.

To Doc, I said, "Colonel felt the vibration of a bunch of horses, plus the smell of men and gun powder headin' this way."

"That means we got trouble comin'," George Coe said, before shouting down to his cousin to throw him up some cartridges for his carbine.

"Heads up!" Frank yelled, throwing a bag up from the back of the adobe house.

Pain eased into my skull, Gaax merging his sight with mine, showing me the leader of the group heading our way.

"Aww, hell...Doc, it's José Chavez y Baca and his scoutin' party."

"Then let's go be hospitable and greet them with some holiday fireworks," he replied with a grin, holding his gun up to clarify.

"Guess you're gonna get to show us if ya have what it takes sooner than we thought, Tom," Frank said.

"More than happy to kill me some demons on any day that ends in Y."

I laughed. "Ya good up there, George?"

"Just make sure my lady is tethered at the other end of this place where she'll be as safe as she can be, and I'll be ready."

"On it!" Fred said, urging his horse to the far side of the house to check on George's mare.

Dropping to his belly, George Coe took aim toward the dust cloud heading our way as regular townsfolk disappeared into their houses and the rest of us pulled our guns, looking to Doc to give the orders.

"On my lead," Doc Scurlock yelled out.

"We can't let them get into town," I said.

"Don't plan on it. Let's go."

With a shout, we rode toward the small group of men, out-numbering them by twice their size, if not more. My enhanced eyesight made it possible for me to see faces of the small posse, and none of them were friends to us. I told Doc as much, and we picked up the pace, shooting at them as soon as they were in range.

José Chavez y Baca's men pulled up short at the sound, their horses' front legs lifted, kicking out in front of them as their riders pulled them to a halt faster than they were ready for. A bullet of mine hit a man I didn't know in the shoulder. As no wave of energy hit me, I switched to my gun with lead.

"Human scoutin' party!" I yelled out.

Men who carried both types of loaded weapons switched to lead as well and continued to fire on them until George took a shot from the roof and hit one of them in the head. That stopped their advance, and Baca quickly tucked tail and ran, heading back toward Lincoln for sure.

"They'll go get reinforcements," I said.

"And we won't be here when they come back," Doc said, turning his mare around.

"We gonna leave early? What about Susan?" I asked.

"Nothin' we can do about that now," Doc said.

"She's gonna think Mac's dead, Doc. We can't just—"

"We don't have a choice, Billy. We need to go."

"Then you can tell Mac it was your decision," I said.

Doc looked torn, but said, "Guess I will. Let's go!"

And just like that, we collected George, and the whole lot of us eased our horses down to the Rio Ruidoso and followed it to hide our tracks. Once that got to be more trouble than it was worth, Doc eased us, one here and one there, up onto the main path. Once on dry land, each of us began our journey to South Spring Ranch to see Uncle John Chisum.

It wasn't the first time, nor would it be the last, where I had to head in one direction but wished I could stay where I was.

* * *

April 1949

Leaving the Amador Hotel, I glanced across the street and to the right. There sat the courthouse and the sheriff's department. To justify my staying put, I pulled out a cigarette and lit it. Inhaling, I focused on the men standing about outside. Exhaling, I pulled on soul-energy to enhance my vision more than it already was, making my eyes work like binoculars.

Apodaca stood with three men. Two of them were your typical officer in uniform; the other seemed to be just a regular local guy. None were looking my way, except Apodaca, and he didn't appear to see me. I turned right and headed to the next intersection. Taking a right onto Water Street, I walked the length of the hotel to get an idea of her full circumference. Seeing all I needed, I made my way back to Main Street, where I'd parked my car.

Looking about, I saw no one, so I got in and headed out of town. It was only a three-hour drive from Las Cruces to Albuquerque, and I considered stopping in to see Cricket again. As I drove up Main and parked near the diner, I was pleased to see the raven-haired beauty step out. I rolled my window down and yelled out, "Miss Ovida!"

Her dark eyes found me, and the worry on her face slid away.

Running out into the street without looking either way, a car nearly hitting her, she came over to my car window and leaned down. "Hey there, cowboy. I thought you were leavin' town."

"I'm headin' that way now. Did you get what I left you?"

She looked around and then back to me. "I sure did! You are too kind."

Something was off, but I didn't say anything. "Naw, you earned it. Meetin' you has been the best part of my trip to New Mexico."

This finally softened her features to how I'd seen her earlier that day. "You really mean that, don't ya?"

"Miss Ovida, is everything okay?"

She lay her left cheek on her arm that rested on my door and laughed, making my heart sing. Then, without warning, she leaned into the car and kissed me on the lips. When she stopped, I placed my hand gently on the side of her face, urging her to stay, and she kissed me again. This time her mouth opened, as did mine, and the kiss deepened. Tongues found one another, the passion behind the deepened kiss radiating heat while the kiss itself hung on the edge of control.

Slowing it down, she pulled back and looked into my eyes. "I just wanted to do that in case I…" Her voice faded.

"In case you what?" I quietly asked, my fingers playing with the dark curls along her neck.

She gently brushed the hair across my forehead. "In case I don't see you again."

"Do you doubt that I'll be back? I keep my promises, Miss Ovida," I said softly, still in a daze from her lips on mine. "My momma taught me right."

"That's good to know, lawman."

"How'd you know that—"

She glanced over at my passenger seat. "Your badge is a giveaway."

I looked over where I'd placed it in case I got pulled over again. "That it is. Sorry I didn't—"

"Don't matter to me none, as long as you ain't a cop from 'round here," she said.

"I'm not. I can promise ya that."

"Good."

"Cricket!" I heard someone yell from across the street.

She sighed. "Gotta go." She planted a quick kiss on my lips, pulled her head out of the car, and began to back up into traffic.

"Be careful, Miss Ovida," I said. "You're gonna get yourself killed. Not all drivers pay attention."

"If I die, will you avenge me?" she said playfully.

"To the end of my days," I replied.

"Good to know!" she yelled out to me, her eyes darting to her right and back to me.

Horns honked at her, and she smiled at my answer as she backed up more, getting out of the way, but the hint of sadness behind her eyes was there.

"Are you sure everythin' is okay?" I yelled out to her.

"Cricket!" the voice shouted again.

"Gotta go!" she yelled out to me, her eyes darting to her right and back to me. "Here's to hopin' I see you in May!" She blew me a kiss and ran back to the diner, leaving me wanting more of her, but it would have to wait until May. I cranked the car, pulled back into Main Street traffic, and headed for Albuquerque. But my heart was still in Las Cruces.

* * *

July 1878

Arriving at South Spring Ranch that evening, the Regulators placed our horses in the stable or corral out back of the house. With just the essentials for the night, everyone headed up to the main house. Sallie was happy to see us, and as we all knew the rules of entering the house, everyone took off their shoes and cleaned the dirt from their britches.

Sallie happily directed everyone into the main part of the house, her eyes lingering on mine and Tom's longer than the others. We

TAMSIN L. SILVER

quickly understood she had something to tell us, so we held back at
the door, pretending to dawdle with our boots, as the rest of the
Regulators headed into the main part of the house.

"What is it? Everythin' all right?" I asked her.

She looked about and whispered, "You said to tell you anythin' out
of the ordinary that I saw after you were gone, right?"

"Yes, ma'am," Tom replied.

"Well, the Saturday after you left, I woke up earlier than usual. I
got up, made a fire, and read until the sun started to rise. I put on a
coat and grabbed a bucket to fetch water from the stream. But the
minute I stepped outside, at least fifteen wolves came walkin' past.
Huge wolves. Larger than ones I've ever seen."

"Did they see you?" Tom asked.

"Not that I know of. Thankfully, I was in the shadows and they
were upwind of me. But they moved funny."

"How so?" I asked.

"Like a flock of birds. You know, when you see them fly in forma-
tion and turn all at the same time, as if it's choreographed?"

"Yeah," Tom and I said.

"Like that."

Tom and I shared a look but said nothing.

"Is that of any importance? Could one of those have killed James?"

"We're still not sure he's dead," Tom told her.

She nodded. "I know. I just had never seen anythin' like it."

"Whatever you do, please don't go near those things if you see
them again," Tom said.

"I don't look that stupid, do I, Tom?"

He laughed. "No, ma'am. I just wanted to reinforce that."

"Good to know," she said, smoothing her dress skirt nervously.

Someone in the other room called to her. She excused herself,
leaving Tom and me in the foyer.

"They were checkin' to see if we were still here," I said. "The whole
pack!"

"Which means every minute we are here, we put that woman in
danger."

166

I nodded. "I'll do my best to convince Doc that we stay as short a time as possible."

"That'd be best."

"But for now," I said, "we got food to eat, music to dance to, and a good night's sleep to get so we can celebrate the holiday tomorrow!"

* * *

That night we all bunked in the cow camps, and the next morning Uncle John, who had returned just the other day from his trip, came to see us all.

"Now, boys, it's time we have a big celebration. We'll throw the camp cooks with the ranch cooks and have a real feed, so get ready for the frolic! Clean up, and let's get this movin'!"

Everyone cheered and needed no other persuasion to get up and get ready for the day.

"Billy, you got any tobacco left?" Frank Coe asked.

"Not much. Why?"

"George and I are out, too, thought maybe we'd ride on over to the little grocery Ash Upson runs and get some, and some other stuff for the day."

"Like beer!" I heard someone chime in.

"Sounds like a solid plan." I turned to Tom. "You stay here, keep a gun with silver loaded on hand, even if you have to hide it from Sallie. If I'm leavin', I want to know this place is protected."

"Consider it done. Oh, and Billy, last night Miss Sallie mentioned wantin' some—"

"Candy, I remember. I'll get it for her. Least I can do."

He handed me a dollar. "Least *we* can do."

George, Frank, me, and two other boys mounted up with money from others and headed to the store. By about ten in the morning we'd finished our shopping and were loading up our saddle bags with our purchases as George noticed something in the distance.

"Hey, Billy? Take a look over there," George said, pointing west as a dust cloud was rising up.

"I don't like the look of that," I told him.

"Me neither," he said, then turned to the rest of the group. "Boys, we might have some trouble comin'. Let's finish packin' up quick and get on our way."

By the time we were in the saddle, I could easily make out what was causing the dust. "It looks to be about fifteen to twenty men on horseback."

"That's too many to be an ordinary band of cowboys," Frank said.

"Agreed. And no matter who they are, there's only five of us," George pointed out.

"We can't hold our own with them. Let's get movin' out. They're almost in firing range if they got rifles," Frank said.

I'd left Colonel to rest at the stable, opting to ride Delilah again. Turning her about, I said, "Don't rush though, just move leisurely, or we'll draw attention to ourselves."

Heading toward the ranch at a steady pace, we kept an eye on them from time to time, making sure not to let them gain on us.

"The minute they reach the store, Ash is gonna tell 'em who we were," I pointed out.

George scoffed. "Not if they don't ask."

"They'll ask," Frank said, dryly.

"I shouldn't have come. I've put you all in danger," I said.

"Stop that. Everyone knows we Coes are Regulators, too," George said.

"But neither of you are wanted for the murder of Brady," I pointed out. "That gives 'em an excuse."

"Well, here's the moment of truth. They're at the store," Frank said.

We kept riding, but it didn't take long. Soon the men who went in came out, hurried into their saddles, and bee-lined for us.

"Time to haul ass, gentlemen," Frank said.

In full agreement, we picked up the pace. After only a short distance, they opened fire on us.

"Damn it!" I shouted, and pulled my gun, firing back at our pursuers. The others did the same, and we hurried as fast as the four legs under us could go.

Riding into the ranch area, I noticed one of the female servants was in the front yard doing laundry. I shouted for her to get inside and kept going.

Leaving the horses with the stable boy, we gathered our things and ran for the rear entrance of the ranch. Once inside with the door shut, Tom and Uncle John came around the corner.

"Heard gunfire, what's goin' on?" Tom asked.

I explained.

"We've got the whole party set up in the patio area. Nowhere safer. Let's send everyone in there," John said.

"Good. I'm headin' to that part of the roof you built for just this reason," I told Uncle John.

"There's ammunition up there if ya need it," he told me, which was his way of giving me permission not only to go on up, but to shoot at the sons of bitches chasing us.

Tom, George, and Frank followed me on up to a part of the roof that looked over the front yard. It had a four-foot high adobe wall with portholes at the top. Looking down, I noticed the woman washing clothes in the front yard was still there. But it wasn't one of the servants.

"Miss Chisum," I shouted down to her, "please come into the house at once. Those dirty curs can't tell whether you are a man or woman from that distance, and they likely don't care much neither. They may take a shot at you any moment."

Sallie looked up at me and smiled. "Thank you, Billy, but I don't think for a minute that they would shoot me."

"Well hell, now what?" George asked.

I glanced down to see Sallie hang her last piece of clothing on the line before picking up her basket and heading for the house, leaving her large copper washing kettle in the yard. Once she entered the house, I let go of the breath I'd been holding just as a shot was fired at the house, hitting the copper kettle.

With my elevated hearing, I heard them laugh as water poured out the hole in the side of it. Mad they took a shot toward her at all, I took aim with my rifle and fired. Tom did, too. That was the last they shot at us for a bit. Not that they didn't get courage later on.

We all took turns that day at returning fire whilst still making time to eat and enjoy the day's festivities. Approaching evening, Tom and I went up to the roof to have a look.

"Damn curs have been just out of range all day," Tom said.

I pulled on some extra abilities and watched as they appeared to be moving. "Tom, what are they doing?"

Tom watched with me for a minute. "Well, I'll be damned. They're trying to creep down a low spot on the South Spring River. Use the cover of the reeds to come in closer to us I'd bet."

"Sons of bitches," I said.

"There's that favorite curse again," Tom joked.

I flipped him off and grabbed my rifle. "Care to play with them for a bit?"

"Whatchu thinkin'?"

"Shoot at them, but don't hit 'em. Ruin bags and anythin' else you see."

Tom slid the tip of his rifle into the porthole. "This'll be fun. A point per item."

"Done."

We took turns shooting, announcing the number of points we had each time we hit something.

"Woo-wee! Did you see, his hat just flew off his head!" Tom shouted.

"Nicely done, they're changin' course. Gee, sorry to ruin your plans there, fellas."

"You don't sound very sorry," Tom said.

"Why, whatever do you mean?" I replied, sounding as innocent as I could.

We laughed and headed back down to the party as others came up to watch in our place. Wasn't until nightfall that the Murphes tried to get to the barns and corrals. We did the same thing to them then as we had that afternoon, and they gave up.

Temporarily secure, Tom and I entered into the fun going on in the patio, forgetting about the band of cowboys stuck sitting out in the heat for the holiday, and had a great Fourth of July.

* * *

The next morning, we arose to find all points of attack were evacuated. Tom and I rode out to track where they'd gone. Once we had an idea, we returned to the ranch.

"Well, what did ya find?" Uncle John asked.

"Looks like they took the back trail to the Upson Store," I told him.

"Best we get out of your hair," Tom said.

I nodded, happy to have a legitimate reason to drag trouble, supernatural or otherwise, away from Sallie and John. "We'll follow their tracks and see where they went from the store."

"Sounds smart," Uncle John said. "We've packed up some food for y'all to take along. Just be careful out there."

"Thank you," I said.

"Will do," Tom said at the same time.

Everyone mounted up, and Doc led us along the path out back to the store where we picked up their trail and followed them west.

"Looks like they're headin' for Lincoln," I said, "by way of Black Water Canyon."

"I agree with Billy," Doc said. "George?"

"As do I."

"Then what do we wanna do?" I asked them.

"Head home?" Frank offered.

"Not safe to do that yet," Doc said. Turning to McSween, he added, "It's best if we head up into the mountains for a few days, Governor. I know you'd rather not, but I'd prefer we all stayed alive. We need to do some investigatin' on Peppin before we head into a trap."

McSween wiped the sweat from his brow. "As much as I hate it, and you know I do, I agree."

"George and Frank, will your farms be okay? Charlie?" I asked.

Charlie nodded. "Yeah, I got some help for while I'm gone."

"Us too," George said. "We got a new threshing machine. Hired a man to work it. Got a crew to bring the crop in."

"All right," Doc said. "Billy? Tom? I want y'all to find out what Peppin's up to. Make sure Susan is all right and report back. If we're not here when you return, come find me at my place."

I hated leaving the whole group without me or Tom, but we were the best to go get the information and still return alive with it. Or so I hoped.

14

TIME TO FIGHT

July 1878

T om and I went to Lincoln and back, only to return and find a note at Scurlock's on where they were. By July ninth, we arrived at an adobe ranch in the mountains, tired and hungry. Entering the home, we found both George and Frank Coe beside themselves in grief as they spoke with McSween.

"What's goin' on?" I asked.

George looked to me. "Thank God you're back. We gotta do somethin' about them sons of bitches."

Tom placed a hand on George's shoulder. "What happened?"

"We stopped by the farm to see how the threshin' was goin'," George started to say.

"But the farm is gone," Frank added.

"What? How does a farm just disappear?" I asked.

"Not gone like that, Billy," Frank said. "Word is John Selman and his pals invaded our place, robbed it, and then burned it to the ground."

"I'm tellin' you," George said, "they got tipped off we was gone by Dolan and The Boys. Selman is from Texas, just like Evans."

"Texas is a big state, George," his cousin said to him.

"Yeah, but bad men tend to find other bad men. I tell you, if I see either of them sons of bitches, I'll put a bullet in 'em so fast they'll be talkin' to the devil himself before they even knew death was comin' for 'em."

"Thankfully Grey, the man we hired to do the threshin', convinced Selman it was his machine and it was all he had to make money for his family, so that was saved," Frank said.

"My good violin, pictures I treasured...damn it! Our homes are gone, Frank!"

"You can stay with me and Fred if you want," I said, knowing there really was no room and that they'd never take me up on it. But they'd taken me in when I'd had nowhere, so I was good with sleeping outside if I had to so they had a roof over their heads.

"Thanks, Billy. We appreciate that, but we have some family who can take us in."

I nodded. "Well, if you need my bed, it's yours."

George looked touched and, with a heavy sigh, said, "We've got to do somethin' to make this stop. I can't see any hope of a peaceful settlement in all this. We need to organize our forces and go into Lincoln and fight it out till it's finished. It's time for action!"

"George, I'm not so sure that's a good idea," Frank said.

"You don't? I do!" Henry Brown said, walking up to us. "Sorry to interrupt. I couldn't help but hear what y'all were sayin'. I agree."

"As do I," Big Jim French said. "We go take Lincoln, and we end this."

Doc walked over. "I'm not against the idea myself. But we need a leader for all that. That is not my forte."

Fred spoke up. "We need someone who hasn't been as involved, who won't have a personal agenda, if we're goin' to do this right."

"He's got a good point. It should obviously be one of the McSween sympathizers and someone who's not been directly involved with us so far," I suggested.

"It should also be someone in law enforcement," Charlie Bowdre said, joining the conversation, along with John Middleton.

Frank Coe was nodding through all this, and with his opinion outnumbered, he'd stopped protesting. Then, out of thin air, he said, "Martin Chavés. What about him? He's a prominent native, lives in Picacho. He's a deputy sheriff, a conservative, and I know he's not satisfied with how the conditions of things stand in the county right now. I think he'd be open to leadin' us."

Just hearing the word "Picacho," where Brewer was truly buried, my heart squeezed in my chest, making it hard to breathe.

Charlie spoke up first. "Then let's go ask him. Can't hurt."

"All of us?" I asked. "I don't recommend a huge posse of us go ridin' up to his home with how tense things are."

"I have a friend who owns a ranch not far from Chavés' place," Henry said. "He's got a big extra buildin' for family when they visit, but they don't come this time of year. We can likely stay with him and send a few to talk to Martin."

"Sounds good to me," George said. "But it's a few hours to Picacho from here, so we should get movin' if that's the plan."

Everyone agreed, so we packed up our things and were on the road in the next hour. I'd not been back to Picacho since Dick died, and I didn't want to go back, but I had no choice.

Thankfully Henry's pal, an older gent with ten kids and a multitude of grandkids, was happy to see us.

"Been downright quiet around here," he told us. "Me and Rose hate it when it's like that for too long. Please, feel free to stay for a few days. You'll have to chop your own wood though, can't say that I have a lot right now."

"We can handle that just fine," Henry said. "Don't you worry about it."

Fred walked over and handed his wife, Rose, some money we'd collected amongst us before we'd arrived. "Ma'am, this is for using up your food stores while we are here. Hopefully we'll not eat more than that can provide. If it is not enough, please be sure to let us know."

Rose blushed and patted Fred's cheek. "Well, aren't you a well-spoken gent. Thank you but we don't—"

"Take it," Henry said. "We're not here to put y'all out more than we already are. We just need room to make plans."

"Speakin' of, who wants to come with me and Frank to talk to Martin?" George asked.

Doc stepped up. "I suppose as current leader of the Regulators, I best go with y'all."

John Middleton stepped up. "I'll go as look-out so you three can talk without worryin' about unexpected company."

"He's right, we don't know where Peppin and his men are right now exactly," Tom said, giving me a look that asked the question, "Where is Gaax when we need him?"

"I'll see if I can get us some help on that front," I said before excusing myself from the group while they figured out the rest of the logistics for the trip. With things in motion, I asked Tom to stay put and excused myself to go get Gaax. But once I was on Colonel, I found myself taking a short ride to see a friend for a one-way conversation.

* * *

Riding up to Edward's place, I dismounted and left Colonel on lookout while I walked to the one place I didn't want to go. Seeing the cross stuck in the ground, I took a seat beside it. For a moment, I just pulled at the grass that was growing in patches on the fresh dirt, while trying to figure out what I wanted to say.

"Hey, Dick, how are ya, pal?" I paused. "Well, we're all about to do somethin' stupid, as you would say." I laughed. "You called it, you know. You told me that this whole thing could only end in war, a big battle between the two sides, and that's what it's come to as sure as I'm sittin' here talkin' to a dead man."

My throat threatened to close up, and I swallowed. "Damn it, Dick! Why'd you have to give up? Why? God knows we could use you right now. I think the boys would even have accepted you as a werewolf. They'd see it as an advantage in the battle we're about to walk into."

With a loud sigh, I fell backward and lay there, staring up at the summer sky as clouds began to form. "Seems as if monsoon season is

176

gonna start. Look at them clouds gatherin' up. We'll get that late afternoon shower for sure!"

Laying there, I just watched the clouds and thought about the battle to come. "You know, I used to do this with my mom, too. I'd go to her grave in Silver City and talk to her. Last time I was there musta been the night I escaped jail for the first time, out that chimney." I laughed. "Man was I filthy, but I was free, damn it. Free to go wherever I wanted. A young man on the run just like those dime novels I liked to read. An outlaw at the age of fifteen, I thought I was...what's that phrase John would say? Oh yes, I thought I was the bee's knees."

I burst into heavy laughter. "What about bee's knees is so great to create that sayin' anyway? Do bees even have knees?" I rolled onto my side to look at the grave marker. Edward had used a nice cross of wood with the initials, RMB, on it. "And what the hell is the M for?!" I threw grass at the cross. "Shit, you never did tell me. Now I get to spend eternity wonderin'."

I stayed another half hour talking about the upcoming battle idea and asking questions he couldn't answer. Standing, I placed a hand on the top of his cross. "I miss you. But hey, maybe you're in Heaven tellin' my mom all about our silly adventures. She'd like that. Tell her I love and miss her, too, would ya?"

I wiped a tear away and pulled myself together. "And who knows, maybe I'll see you both again someday. Stranger things have happened than Billy Bonney gettin' into Heaven, right? Anyway, I gotta go. Love ya, pal."

I turned and began to walk back to where I'd tethered Colonel, only to run right into Edward. "Hey, I didn't know you were home. Sorry to trespass on your property."

"It's okay, William. Sometimes I need to talk to my friends who have crossed over as well. What brings you to talk to Richard?"

I told him of the developments. "I sort of figured I should come say some things in case I can't after this is all said and done."

"How many souls you got in the chamber?"

"Enough."

Edward rubbed the few chin hairs he had. "Be careful not to kill those who have their own will and choose the way of peace, William."

"I promise. They'll have to try and kill me before I'll take their spirit. You have my word."

Edward pressed his thin lips together, causing them to seem to disappear completely as he gave me one large, slow nod.

Since he said nothing else, I mounted Colonel. But before I could go, Edward lay his hand on my horse's neck. "Don't take Colonel into battle."

"What? He's my horse. He and I have a connection. I'd only be safe on him."

"This battle you speak of. It could kill him or put him in the hands of Dolan and his men. He's too special for that. Find a way to hide him, William."

"I need him if I'm gonna survive this, Edward. I'm takin' my damn horse." With that, I took the reins hard and tapped Colonel's sides, yelling out an encouragement for him to go before Edward could say anything else to me.

Yet, as we rode away like a werewolf was on our tail, Edward's words sounded in my head like the bell of a church tower, and it rang true, which made me mad. By the time I got back to the ranch, I was happy to learn some good news: Martin had agreed to help us and would be here the next day.

With Edward's words still dancing about in my brain, I headed to bed, evading Tom's questions as to what was wrong. I had no interest in talking about it. But that didn't stop him.

"Billy?"

I took off my ammunition and sat on the bed to remove my boots. "I just want to get some sleep. Tomorrow is gonna be a long day."

Tom sat on the bed across from mine. "What is goin' on?"

I fell back on the bed. "It's just been a difficult day. I'll be fine once I sleep."

"All right," Tom said, and got ready for bed. However, once the lights were out, he said, "We need to find Gaax."

"I know," I said. "Tomorrow after we talk with Martin, we'll know more and then we can find him." I paused, then added, "I hate to say it, but we need him for this fight."

* * *

April 1949

I brought the car to a stop at the red light just as bird shit landed on the right side of my windshield. A second later, a black bird swooped down to land on the left side. It looked at me through the glass, pecking at it like an idiot.

"I just cleaned this," I complained and reached for the windshield wipers when the bird backed his butt up and shook it right in my line of sight. He then turned to stare at me, his look indignant. That's when I realized. "Gaax? You son of a bitch!"

"QUARK-QUARK! QUARK-QUARK!"

He flapped his wings and flew up into the air, half of my vision suddenly not my own as pain ripped through my skull.

"Dear God Almighty, I've not missed this pain!" I complained as I watched him fly low over the car behind me, and the car behind that to a truck. Gaax landed on the man's side mirror and stared right at him.

"QUARK- QUAAAARK!"

"Damn crow, get out of here!" the man said, and that's when I recognized him. It was one of the men I'd seen Happy Apodaca talking to when I exited the Amador Hotel. The guy that didn't look like a cop.

"Well I'll be damned," I said. "That ass had me followed, and I was too wrapped up in my own thoughts and feelings about Ovida that I wasn't payin' close enough attention."

Gaax flew back and landed on my side mirror.

"Thanks, Gaax. I appreciate the—"

He flew off as a horn sounded behind me. The light was green, and I drove north toward Albuquerque with an eye on my tail while keeping track of Gaax because I knew I was going to have to deal with both soon. Funny thing was, I'd rather fight my tail than apologize to the raven…but I was going to have to do both.

"Damn it."

* * *

July 1878

With a groan, I pried myself out of bed as the sun slapped me in the face. I washed up, dressed, and was heading toward the main house when a Hispanic man rode up on a beautiful gray stallion. I thought it best if I greeted him and asked how I could help.

"*Mañana, buen señor. ¿Puedo ayudarte?*"

"*¡Hola! Busco alto Scurlock y George Coe.*"

That was fine by me, but I wasn't about to take the man to see them until I knew who he was. "*Por supuesto por supuesto. ¿A quién debo decir que está llamando?*"

"*Martin Chavés, me están esperando. Ah, y por cierto, es tarde.*"

"What?"

"They're expecting me."

"Oh, no no, I understood you, but is it really the afternoon?"

He laughed. "Yes, it's almost one o'clock."

"Wow, I really overslept. Come on, they're expectin' you."

He dismounted and walked with me. "Late night I take it?"

"I had trouble sleepin'." I yawned. "Hope they have some food left over from breakfast."

He laughed, and I saw the youth in him that his unsmiling face hid in a way that surprised me. I guessed him to be in his early twenties. It appeared he wore his dark hair short and hidden under a black cowboy hat, making his dark eyes prominent. "I hope they do, too. I'm starving."

We gave his horse to the stable boy, and I escorted him into the house, where I quickly introduced him to the Regulators who didn't know him.

"Let's have some lunch," George said. "We can discuss the best strategy to take Lincoln back."

Martin explained his idea while we all filled our bellies, and after he finished, he said, "The only way I'm agreeing to do this is if you all promise to follow my lead."

"More than happy to," Doc said.

"There's only one problem," I pointed out. "For all that to work, we'll need to be able to get into town unseen, and it's a full moon that night. There's no way we'll not be seen unless it's cloudy. I mean, it is the top of the rainy season, so we might get lucky."

"The only way we have the element of surprise is if we can take positions without bein' detected," Martin said. "That's the key to keepin' the casualties down."

He had a point. If we came barreling into town, Peppin's men would start shooting, and it would get bad, and fast, likely killing innocent people who had nothing to do with this war and just happened to be on the road.

"We wait until a cloudy night rolls around, and then we go in," Frank offered.

McSween sighed. "This is our one openin' since the majority of the sheriff's men are out of town lookin' for us in the mountains. It's now or never."

I finished my bread by scooping up the last bit of chili and washed it down with the rest of my iced tea. Standing, I carried my plates over to the washing bin in the kitchen as they began to discuss a route into town that would disguise them the best.

I had an idea of how to help, but it wasn't something I could just share with the whole group, for not everyone was aware of the supernatural side of this war. Grabbing my hat, I headed to the door.

"Billy, where you goin'?" George asked.

"It's better y'all don't know," I said, putting my hat on. "Plan on there being no moon and organize us gettin' into town accordingly."

"It needs to be tomorrow night, the fourteenth," Martin said. "My sources say that Kinney and his men should be back to Lincoln by the day after."

"Then I guess I'll be back before we set off tomorrow. If I'm not, go without me, and I'll meet you just outside of town. George knows the spot, but I'll need you to bring me a horse, and not Mattie, leave her here." Saying nothing else, I went out the door into the warm summer night air and mounted Colonel.

Tom followed me out. "Where are you goin'?"

"To get us that help we talked about last night. Keep them safe while I'm gone."

Tom nodded, and I raced off for the long ride, pushing energy into Colonel more than usual due to time. As we got close to the orchard, I heard a *QUARK-QUARK* above me.

"Tell her I'm comin' to see her," I yelled out, and Gaax flew off.

Colonel whinnied, understanding where we were headed, happy to know he was going to see Zahara.

"And she'll be happy to see you, too. Now, take more of my energy. It's yours, use it, and let's be like the wind."

* * *

By the time we reached Zahara's orchard, it was way past midnight, and I was almost asleep in the saddle. In fact, as we wove our way through the grove, I relaxed against Colonel's neck and let him take us the rest of the way. In a haze of exhaustion, I heard Gaax and knew we'd made it.

"Poor boy, so tired," came a soft voice. "Come with me, you big beauty."

I opened my eyes to see Zahara's smiling face. "You got my message."

"I was speaking to Colonel," she said, a wicked grin on her lips.

I rolled my eyes. "Of course you were."

"But yes, I got your message. Come with me and rest."

"There's no time—"

"Shhh...sleep. We'll talk soon." She waved her hand in my face, and everything went dark.

I awoke inside the Forest of Truth, staring up at the stars that were or were not real, I was never sure. Sitting up, I noticed I was in the armor again. "How did they move in this stuff?"

"They were used to it, just like you're used to wearing your two belts of ammunition, two guns, and all the rest of your cowboy attire," Zahara said. "Come, I have food and drink to revive you."

I stood and peeled out of the chainmail before making my way to the cushion by the fire. I sat, and she handed me a bowl filled with stew and a wooden spoon. I took a bite and swallowed, the warmth of it replenishing my tired bones. "I have no idea what this is, but it is fantastic."

"I thought you might think so," she said, and sat down to eat some as well.

I glanced at her fingers but remembered that in here they would be fine. "How are they doing?" I asked, motioning to her hands with my spoon before scooping up more of the stew.

"They've been hurting again," she said. "Though, the minute you rode into the orchard, they felt better. It would seem that your healing powers on others are not permanent but that you being near them helps sustain the repairs done."

I thought of the healing I'd done for Ab Saunders, who was now in California, and worried that this was true. Swallowing my stew and my fear for my friend with it, I nodded. "So you're sayin' I should not go gettin' myself killed and maybe try to visit more often."

She ate some stew but kept her eyes on me while she chewed, giving me the willies. Swallowing it, she paused and said, "That would be a big thing to ask of you. But you are here to ask for something you need. Is it big enough to trade on?"

I thought on this as I ate another bite, for two could play at this game. "It's big, but it's not that big, Zahara."

"Hmmm…" was all she said and ate more. "I feel you have a heavy heart."

I could've lied, but she'd know in seconds. "Dick's been killed."

Her face fell. "I'm so sorry, Henry."

I nodded and ate, still unwilling to talk about it.

"When you are ready, we can do a ceremony for him, in his honor, to the earth that now holds him in her arms."

Again, I nodded, and we ate in silence. By the time we finished, she looked to me and said, "So tell me, what is this big, but not that big, favor you need? Maybe we can work out a deal."

I explained our problem.

She set her empty bowl down. "May the bargaining commence!"

* * *

By the time I left Zahara's orchard, it was too late to head back to Picacho, so I turned Colonel toward the meeting spot just outside of Lincoln and hurried onward. By the time I arrived, most had gathered.

"Billy, you made it," George Coe said. "But this all might be pointless if we don't get some cloud cover soon. We might as well enter with guns firin' if we go into town with that full moon shining down on us."

I smiled. "We'll be fine. Did you bring what I asked you for?"

George paused, then said, "No, but Frank did. Why would you want a horse, Billy? You have a great one right here."

"Not for much longer," I told him and hopped down off Colonel. Removing my needed ammunition and guns from him, I set them on the ground with my old war bag, my new one still on Colonel with the charm in it. I walked round to his head and lay my hand on the side of his face.

Pushing energy from me to him, I cleared his eyes again and said, "It's time. Go be safe like we talked about. I'll come for you if I live through this. When the charm takes hold, you go."

Colonel whinnied, and I felt his understanding pass under my hand along with his affection and desire to stay.

"I can't take a chance you die here or they get you. Tunstall wouldn't have wanted that."

"Billy?" George prompted. "Here comes McSween."

I looked at the group of us, easily forty, maybe more, and Martin Chavés at the helm. "Does that mean we're all here?"

"I think so, but I'm not sure." He paused and then called out to Martin. "Are we waitin' for anyone else, Captain?"

Martin came over. "Oh, good, Billy, you made it back. Yes, George, this is all of us. Now we just wait for some clouds to roll in. If the hour gets too late and none come, we'll ride into town as quietly as we can."

"We'll have cloud cover," I said. "Just let me know when."

Martin raised an eyebrow at me and then looked to George, as if he could make sense of what I was saying. Finally, he turned back to me. "Oh hell, Billy, I don't know, now would be good."

"All right then," I said and went back to my newer war bag. Opening it up, I pulled out the milky white stone Zahara'd given me and hid in the shadows. "Here goes nothin'," I muttered, and cut myself with the blade she'd given me. Wiping my blood on the stone, I said, "Blood and stone, white to black, air thick and moon dark, clouds of night, find their mark." I placed it back into the pouch and hid it in my old bag.

I then pulled a separate charm from my pocket and wiped the remaining blood on it before the wound healed. Stuffing it into Colonel's saddle bag, I said, "This will hide you from the wolves. Now go. I'll miss you." With that, I gave Colonel a swat on the rump. "Now!"

Turning about, Colonel bumped me with his nose and left, disappearing into the night. My heart broke to watch him leave, but I knew this was part of my promise and trade. I'd healed Zahara's hands again and promised to send Colonel to her for safe keeping.

I heard a gasp from someone behind me followed by more. Turning, I watched as dark clouds began to fill the sky, covering the moon so well, it was if there were no moon out at all. With a nod and a grin, I muttered, "You ain't half bad, Zahara, you ain't half bad at all."

I heard loud *QUARK-QUARK* and laughed. "She ended up sendin' you to help me, did she? Doesn't trust I'll stay alive otherwise, huh? Well, all right, come on."

I couldn't see him, but I heard his wings beat twice before he took to the air.

"Is that enough cloud cover for ya, Captain Chavés?" I asked, picking up all my things.

"I don't want to know who you sold your soul to, Bonney, but thank you for doin' it."

"Not sure how to take that, but you're welcome, I think. Let's ride! We've got at least two hours. George, my horse?"

"Right here," Frank said, riding over, bringing an extra horse with him. "Sent Colonel off to keep him safe, I take it?"

"Yeah," I said, throwing my bags up and attaching things to the saddle. "Keeps him out of Dolan's hands as well." I mounted the horse and calmed her with a touch.

"I get it," Frank said.

Martin mounted his ride and yelled out, "Everyone knows their job. Let's head on into town!"

"And take it back!" I heard Jim French yell out.

There was a cheer, and we all headed to Lincoln...where many of us were prepared to die, me included. It was time to fight.

15

THE TRUTH ABOUT SUSAN MCSWEEN

July 1878

T he night of the fourteenth, as darkness enveloped the one-
street town, we quietly rode in, stopping first at the Ellis
Store. Here we left most of our horses and placed key
people like Middleton, Bowdre, Scurlock, Stevens, Frank Coe, and
eight to ten folks made up of new recruits and Hispanics native to the
area. Placing good men here not only fortified this entrance into town
but protected the Ellis family.

From here, many moved on foot, including myself, into other positions in town. The main two being the Montaño Store, since the
owner was in Santa Fe for supplies, and the McSween residence. The
store was a prime location because it was connected to Ike Stockton's
saloon, and Ike was a known McSween sympathizer, and it sat close
to the center of town. Because of this, the Montaño Store is where we
dropped our leader, Martin Chavés, along with George Coe,
Fernando Herrera, and nearly twenty Hispanic men from the area.

I was supposed to stay at the Montaño Store as well, but as
everyone began to head in, I peeled off.

George Coe followed, stopping me with a hand on my arm. Keeping his voice low, he said, "Billy, where you goin'?"

I glanced at McSween standing there, nervously looking around, then back to George. "Tell Martin I'm goin' to go with Tom to escort McSween home to make sure the house is safe." What I didn't say was how I needed a word with his wife before one shot was fired.

"Good call. I'll let Martin know you'll be back before sun-up."

I nodded, then turned to Alex. "Come on, Mac. Let's get you home."

Silently, the two of us and fourteen more Regulators walked into the heart of town. Five of whom took their place at the Torreón. Not only was it a prime location, being built for battle, it sat on McSween's land. After that, Henry Brown and Sam Smith headed into the Tunstall Store. Their job was to locate Dr. Ealy, tell him what was going on, and to find a good advantage point to take aim at anyone coming at the McSween home. By the time we snuck through the back yard and into the patio area of the McSween/Shield home, it was just Tom, Mac, me, and six Regulators.

Entering through the door to the west kitchen, we found Susan standing there, anxiously waiting. Mac had barely gotten his hat off his head when she pulled him into her arms and held him tight.

He did so in return, saying, "Now, now. I told you I'd come back to you safe and sound, didn't I?"

"That you did," she said, but her eyes were on me as she mouthed the words, "Thank you."

I nodded to her as my reply before saying, "We need everyone who is livin' in this buildin' to meet in the parlor."

"I can make that happen," Susan said. "Give me a few moments to fetch my sister."

"Is David here?" Mac asked.

"No, he's in Santa Fe to attend court."

"Damn, we could've used him," was all Mac said before pulling Susan in and talkin' to her in hushed tones.

I moved on through the U-shaped house with Tom, leavin' the two McSweens to talk. I knew she'd ask why we were all here and he'd tell her, for they had that kind of relationship, a partnership of two equals. I thought highly of them for that. Men who thought women were just to be pretty, quiet arm decoration they took to bed on lonely nights made no sense to me. Some of the strongest people I knew were women, Susan being one of 'em.

Everyone gathered in the parlor. Not counting us Regulators or the McSweens, the only others in the house were Susan's sister, her three kids, and a man I'd not met before by the name of Harvey Morris. It appeared that he'd moved to Lincoln to work with Mac and David at their law offices, so I didn't question his existence too much.

As efficiently as I could, I explained the gist of what was about to happen in town. At the end, I added, "Tom and I are stationed at the Montaño Store, but we are goin' to be leavin' these six men with you for protection. This here is Francisco Zamora, Vincente Romero, Tom Cullens, Joe Smith, George Bowers, and Yginio Salazar."

"He's just a boy," I heard someone say. It was Elizabeth, for her eldest son was older than Yginio by two years, if I remembered correctly.

Before I could stand up for him though, Yginio stepped forward and said, "I'm fifteen. I'm not a boy, thank you. And please, call me Eugene."

"Eugene it is," I said, tryin' to stop any argument from transpiring further. "Look, we're hopin' y'all don't need 'em, but if so, these men are here for your protection."

"You really think this is enough men for what is about to happen here, Billy?" Susan asked. "The inhabitants outnumber them."

I heard a tone in her voice that screamed experience and dread, with a dab of fear thrown in for good measure. "And what *is* about to happen here, Susan?"

"War. By comin' back here like this, Peppin and his men will converge here, and this place will become a battlefield."

"That's not the plan," I said. "Mac got tired of bein' on the run, so we are here to make sure he doesn't have to be anymore. Plus—"

"And if they fire at him, at this house, with my children here?"

189

Elizabeth Shield asked, her big brown eyes even larger than normal as she stared me down.

I placed my hand on my six-shooter. "Then we'll fire back at them sons of bitches."

The men all agreed in kind. After explaining that there were more in town and where, I realized no one had any idea what to do first. So that Mac could go relax in his own bed, I began to dole out positions for the men. "Tom?"

"Yes?" both Tom Folliard and Tom Cullens said.

I sighed. "You, I'm gonna have to call you just Cullens, all right?"

"Fine by me."

"Great. Tom, you work to fortify all the windows and other openings to the house."

Tom nodded and left.

"Cullens, get a head count and names of all in the house so we can keep track of who is where and when. This isn't goin' to be a one-day affair. It's important we remember that. People will come and go as is possible, and I need you to keep track of that."

"Yes, captain!" Cullens said and ran off.

"Captain, like I'm some leader or somethin'," I muttered to myself.

"Well, aren't you?" Susan said behind me.

"Ha, no." Emotional pain slammed into my gut. "Dick, he was a leader. MacNab, he was a leader, too. I'm just here to keep as many alive as I can while we take those that killed them and John down."

"That's a leader's job, Billy," she said. "However, this idea you have is not goin' to work. You know that, right?"

I stepped in toward her and quietly said what I'd come here to say. "As an ex member of the Regulator Network, I'm countin' on your help here, you know."

Her eyes grew wide at first. Then they narrowed in on me, her hand snatching my shirt front faster than I'd foreseen. Dragging me from the one room into another, she shut the door between us and all the others. "Talk."

"Uh, about what, ma'am?"

"When did you figure it out? Did you tell anyone? Does Mac know?"

"Whoa, whoa, whoa... No, Mac doesn't know. I'm the only one who's figured it out."

"Damn," she muttered.

I grinned. "And then there's the subject of your colorful language and outspokenness for a woman," I said with a wink. "We all know the Network men and women tend to be rather ruthless, even with their language."

"Shut up, Bonney. How did you figure it out?"

"When I saw Roy's bag on April first. It had the same initials embroidered into it that the trunk hidden in your closet has. Are you still active?"

"No, haven't been since shortly after I met Alex. That's why I was in Kansas. I was workin' for a Regulator who'd been sent there. But I met Alex, and then my Regulator died, so I decided to have a normal life. I quit."

"They just *let* you quit?"

Susan looked guilty. "I might've had some dirt on the director."

I shook my finger at her. "See, you're a resourceful lady, and I know you don't like me much, but I believe in you and your talents. Question is, why do you still have the trunk?"

She opened her mouth and then shut it. Stepping away, she crossed her arms over her chest as she watched the activity going on in the patio area through the window. "Just because I stopped dealin' with the supernatural doesn't mean I quit believin' they exist, Mr. Bonney."

She was quiet for a moment, as if making decisions about things. Turning to look at me, she added, "And just because I never again wanted to fight doesn't mean I won't protect what's mine, and that includes Alex."

"Good, because we're goin' to need you. If nothin' else, we may ask that you get messages to people. All right? I promise I'll never reveal the truth of your background if you'll help us."

"Deal."

"Oh, and one more thing, Susan," I said.

"What?" she snapped.

"Why or when did you start? I'm just curious."

She sighed, dropping her arms to her sides. "Battle of Gettysburg. I was a teenager livin' there when the battle happened, and I saw things...had to deal with seein' creatures I never would have believed were real." Her eyes met mine. "You understand that. You know what that's like, to see and deny and then believe the horror of the truth. To realize you can't just do nothin'."

Her voice was sincere in a way I'd never heard before, so all I could do was nod.

"After the battle, I ran to family in Michigan, but the horrors followed me, so I did somethin' to make those nightmares die—I got into the game."

"Then you got out," I said.

"Didn't do me a damn bit of good, now did it? Here I am again..." She sighed and then set her shoulders, almost seemin' to grow two inches taller. "If we live through this, I'll be out again. Got that? I don't go in your report to Garrett, you understand? That's the only way I'll help."

"Fair enough."

Susan opened the door and stepped out to run face to face with her sister. "Lizzy, there you are. I was comin' to see if you want to take the children somewhere else."

"Where would they go?" she asked. "They are awake and huddled together in the east bedroom as it's the safest spot for them, for us all, as there are no windows that face anywhere but the patio."

"Smart thinkin'," I said. "Let's make sure that we set up both you ladies and the children in there for the duration of this...this...whatever this is."

"I think the word you're looking for is battle, Mr. Bonney," Susan said.

"If it is that, it'll be the final one, I hope."

"Final? You really think this will end all the bloodshed that this city feeds on?" Elizabeth said. "If you do, you've not been payin' attention." Turning on a heel, she headed back to where her children were.

"I'll talk to her," Susan said. "Thankfully, Roy was here two days ago, and we got the word you sent. Elizabeth, Suzy, and I went to the store and bought food for a group. We don't have a lot, but we'll work to keep y'all fed as best as we can."

"Nice cover. It keeps you in their eye, but the men will group you in with the womenfolk and not pay you much mind."

"Well, that and you do need to eat. Right?"

I laughed for she wasn't wrong. "Right. And we all know I like to eat."

"When's the last time you all ate somethin'?"

"Not since this mornin'."

"We'll get to feedin' everyone who's hungry. It'll keep my hands busy and give me an excuse to pull the trunk out. Top of it has a few pots and pans to dissuade nosy folk."

I couldn't help but grin. "I can see why women make great Network folk. No one suspects y'all, and they are either dead or fooled before they even know it."

"Someday women will stand up for their rights, and when that day comes, Mr. Bonney, men will see that a woman can run somethin' just as good as a man can," Susan said.

"Ma'am, some of us already believe that. But I hope you see it in your lifetime."

"I plan to *do* it in my lifetime," she said with flare and walked from the room.

With nothing else left to do, I helped Susan move her trunk into another room, stayed to eat, and headed back over to the Montaño Store with Tom.

"Everythin' okay?" Tom asked.

I told him what Elizabeth Shield had said.

"She's right. It's almost like this street feeds on the blood that's shed on it. Like it's a hellmouth or somethin' of old that *The People* talk about."

I shuddered. "God, I hope not."

193

"We'll soon see," he said, and with that, we entered the store and got ready for war.

* * *

The morning of July fifteenth, the first full day in town, was quiet. We in the Montaño Store were itching to let Peppin know we were in town and get the ball rolling. Not many had slept, but those who had were awake with the sun and had taken places at their stations.

Not long after, George came to sit with me. "Did you have them drill portholes last night?"

"Tom helped 'em do some last night. They'll do more once they know which way the enemy is goin' to come at 'em. No need to turn the house into Swiss cheese just yet, George."

"True," he said, and glanced out the window. "It won't be long now until some of the folks try to come to Ike's for their mornin' appetizer, if you get my meanin'."

"On a Monday mornin'?"

"Day don't matter, kid. Trust me. Hell, Dolan would probably already be down here if he wasn't lumberin' around with that broken leg."

"Still on crutches?"

"Not from what I hear. That stubborn little Irishman is walkin' around on that cast."

"I'd say I'm surprised, but somehow, I'm not."

George laughed and then was quiet, which meant something important was coming, so I sat still and waited. Finally, he took a deep breath and said, "Be honest with me. What are our chances? What moon cycles are we lookin' at? Is the full moon up right now? Don't say you don't know 'cause I know you do."

I did know. Zahara and I had looked at that the night before. "Good news is that until the twenty-fifth, the moon is primarily at night, with only a few hours up in the sky during the day."

"Like how many hours?"

"It changes by an hour each day. The moon set this mornin' around six, it'll set tomorrow around seven, and so on and so forth."

"You're sayin', there'll be a lot of moon every night, but by late mornin' each day, they can't change."

"Yes…but they'll have advantage on us every night."

"Except between the hours of sunset and moonrise, right?"

I smiled. "You are learnin' this, aren't ya?"

"When your life depends on it, you tend to get to learnin' pretty quick-like."

"Too true," I said, thinking about how fast Dick and I had set the moon schedule to memory. "Also, since the sun'll set around seven every night this week, while the moonrise changes, we'll gain thirty minutes of no moon from the previous night," I told him. "For example, tonight it rises at twenty after eight. Tomorrow it'll rise around ten to nine."

"Meanin' we need to make our moves durin' the day. Got it." He paused again, and I waited. "Ya know, Billy, no matter what happens here, you've been a good friend."

He took me off guard, and I stammered for a second. "Where's that comin' from, George?"

"I don't know, it's just that the odds here are—"

"Now don't you start that shit, George. None of us is gonna die today, all right?"

"All right." He paused, but I could feel he wasn't really done. Before I could head him off at the pass, he added, "But still, I just wanted you to know that. Hell, if you'd not stepped in, I might not have the use of my hand at all."

I remembered Zahara's realization and said, "Yeah, about that… I've learned—"

Something caught George's eye, and he said, "Get your gun ready," and then ran off to get Martin. I looked up and saw a couple fellows approaching the saloon.

"This is as good a time as any to start the fight," Coe said to Martin as they walked toward me, and he pointed out the approaching men.

"Now it is," Martin replied.

The three of us grabbed our guns and headed for the door that led from the Montaño Store into the saloon. Others saw our actions and took that as a cue to grab their weapons as well. Walking through the door, a few of the women in the saloon saw our guns and stepped in our way, keeping us from moving through the room.

"*Por favor, no disparen! Te lo ruego, por favor!*" one of the women said over and over as the others parroted her.

"They're beggin' us not to shoot," I told George.

"Well, they're gonna get their way. Those men got their drinks and are headin' on out."

"What now?" I asked, as gunfire outside erupted.

Running to the door, we saw our boys in the Torreón had also spied the men and had the same idea. They'd opened fire, and then the men on the roof of the McSween home did as well.

Surprised, the two men turned and ran right back into the saloon, and right into us.

"Hi-ya doin', boys," I said, and cocked both my guns at them.

Dropping their beers, the two turned around and ran out, taking their chances with gunfire from the Torreón versus up close and personal with me and the others.

I laughed. "Is it something I said?"

* * *

By mid-afternoon, high winds kicked up clouds of dust outside, making it hard to see for those without abilities. Tom and I though, we saw the minute Sheriff Peppin and a few other posses clattered into town from the west. They stopped by the Wortley Hotel, halted by someone we couldn't see, and were likely being told we were in town.

Moments later, they reined in their mounts, pulled their rifles, and began to fire at the McSween house, splintering slats on the drawn shutters.

"What in the blazes?!" I muttered, grabbing my rifle.

"They're shootin' at the McSween house!" George yelled out.

"What for? No one fired at them," I said, heading for the door.

"Where are you goin'...damn it, Billy."

I ran out the door and down the street to protect them like I'd promised, and a dozen or so men from the Montaño Store filed out behind me into the street. Running past the Torreón, I saw Jack Long had taken up position there.

"Halt!" Jack yelled out.

We turned as a group and opened fire on him and whoever else was with him. We kept firing as we continued toward the McSween home, where our men inside fired off a fusillade that spattered the Wortley, its corral, and sent the posse scurrying for cover.

Taking advantage of this, Tom, me, José Chavez y Chavez, Ignacio Gonzales, José Sanchez, and Big Jim French ran for the McSween home, entering through the door to the east kitchen. Immediately, we headed into the main sitting room of the Shield family, where we found one young man.

"Eugene, what happened?" I asked.

"Gun fire erupted to the west side only, but they told me to keep an eye out over here in case that was a distraction for somethin' else."

"Smart move," José Sanchez said.

"Yeah, I agree," I said. "Tom and Jim, come with me. The rest of you, stay with Eugene."

I didn't wait for anyone to reply. I headed off for the other side of the U, where most probably were. I found Cullens first.

"What the hell?" I asked.

"Billy! How'd you..." He then saw the others. "Oh..."

"Why'd they start firing?" I demanded to know.

"We don't know. I told Eugene to—"

"We know," I said, then saw Susan. "Is everyone alright?"

She nodded. "I think we need more men here with us, Billy."

"I'll stay," Tom said.

"As will I," Jim said. "It's best to keep the governor and his wife safe. We need more eyes on what's goin' on closer to Wortley, too."

"I'll stay, too," I said. "In fact, all of us who came in will stay. Tom, go get an update from Cullens on who is where, and I'll go talk to the men who ran in with us."

We parted ways, and I ran back into the parlor of the Shield side of the house. "José?"

Both José Chavez y Chavez and José Sanchez stood up and said, "Yeah?"

I looked to ceiling as if patience was located somewhere up there. With a sigh, I said, "Okay, same deal with the multiple Toms. Chavez y Chavez, you'll go by José. Sanchez, you'll go by that, all right?"

"Sure thing," Sanchez said.

"Jeez… Two Toms, two Josés… If we get another Billy in here, I'm gonna…" I let that trail off. "Never mind. Where was I? Oh, we're all goin' to be stayin' here. If you have things at the Montaño Store you need, tell José. He and I will get it for you and bring it back tonight."

"And how are you gettin' back to the Montaño Store?" Tom asked from behind me.

I turned to him. "More importantly, where are our men that were at the Torreón not that long ago? I saw Jack Long is there with a few men."

"I counted seven at the Torreón," José said. "I recognized Billy Matthews and Jim Reese."

Sanchez joined in. "The two I knew were Sam Perry and Jim McDaniels."

Ignacio walked over to me. "I saw George 'Roxy' Rose and Dummy."

"Dummy?" Tom and I asked at the same time.

"He can't hear or talk none," Ignacio explained.

Tom's eyes met mine. "And yet he's good to have in a fight? He must read lips like a champ and have great aim, or somethin' isn't sittin' right."

"All of it over there isn't sittin' right with me," I said. "We need to find out what happened to the men we positioned there."

Tom pulled me aside. "Are we sure the firin' from the Torreón earlier at the men from the bar were our men?"

"What are you gettin' at?" I asked.

"Sun rose just a couple minutes before five this mornin'. What time did the moon go down?"

"Shit."

"That's not an actual time, but yeah, it set an hour and three minutes later."

"So you're sayin' our boys are—"

"Dead or they've been bit bad enough to be out of commission and stuffed into the Torreón for safe keepin'."

"How would they have known we had men there? No one saw us come into town."

"That we know of. All it takes is one person wakin' up to take a piss in the middle of the night."

"No one is close enough to have seen shit at the Torreón except those that live on either side. That'd be the carpenter, Daniel Huff, or..."

"Saturnino Baca," both Tom and I said at the same time.

"I'd bet all my money on Baca," Eugene said.

"What? Why?" Tom asked the young man.

"His wife just had another child, on the eleventh. I'm sure they're up and down all night."

"We need to check on Daniel, then. Make sure he's okay," I said.

"Why? Is he a McSween sympathizer?" Tom asked.

"He's who built the Tunstall Store," I replied. "Chances are the men Martin sent to the Torreón alerted the Huffs to their presence in order to ask for help gettin' food and water while holed up in there."

"None of us can go near that house or we're signin' death warrants," Ignacio reminded us. "If he's not dead, or dying, you go near his home, and he will be."

"Agreed. Well, while I figure that out, we need to tell Mac 'bout losing the Torreón."

Steppin' into the parlor, I found Susan sitting with him in the corner, and Mac holding his Bible. "Sir? It appears that Jack Long and his men have taken the Torreón at some point this mornin'. That cuts us off from the rest of our men except the few at the Tunstall Store."

Mac sat up. "If they've taken hold at the Torreón, where they getting' their food and water? Daniel Huff wouldn't supply it to them."

I thought about that. "But Saturnino Baca would. He owes *The House* in a big way."

Mac's face went red with anger as he stood. "That's my house he's living in! Come, we'll send a letter." Mac headed to the room on the west wing that housed his small office, but before I followed him, I looked at Susan.

"What?" she asked.

I leaned down and whispered, "I need you to deliver that letter, and while you're at it, oh ex-Regulator Network employee, I need you to see if you can get another letter to Roy. He can't come up to the spot at the store, but there's the old box that John installed before the store was built, and it's at the house you were stayin' at when you first arrived in Lincoln."

"Lucas Gallegos's place?"

"Yes, right next door to Baca's east side."

"Billy?" Mac yelled from the other room.

"I'll tell you where the spot is when I get back."

I sat with Mac as he wrote the short letter to Saturnino Baca. When he was done, I read it to myself quickly.

Sir,

   I want you to vacate the property now occupied by you at once. Unless you leave the house within three days, proceedings will be instituted against you without further notice. You have consented to improper use of the property by murderers for the purpose of taking my life, and I can no longer consent to your occupancy thereof.

"Three days?" I said. "We need those men at the Torreón gone tomorrow."

Mac folded the letter and said, "By law, I technically need to give them three days. If the captain is a smart man, and he is, he'll find a way to stop helping Dolan's men or vacate the premises. Besides, by sending this notice, we will legally justify any assault on my land there, including the Torreón, which is also technically on my proper-ty." He handed me the letter. "Who is delivering this?"

"Oh, I have someone, don't worry. It'll get there safe and sound, I'm sure."

"A member of the Network?" Mac whispered.

"Exactly."

"Good. Good. I'm going to head on in and lay down for a bit. My head hurts."

"Of course, sir. I'll take care of this."

He went in to the parlor, spoke with Susan, and then went into their bedroom.

"Do you need anythin' before you take this?" I asked quietly.

"No. Write the letter for Roy, then help me suit up while you tell me where the box is."

Susan walked from the room with anger-filled poise and a sense of urgency that only gave me a glimpse to the kind Network Operative she must've been.

"Now, Mr. Bonney."

"Yes, ma'am."

16

THE DRAMA OF DANIEL HUFF

July 1878

Not wanting to keep Susan waiting, I ran back to the room I'd been in with Mac and shut the door.

"Lock it."

"Um, okay."

She slid a trunk out from under the bed in the corner and opened it. Inside were blades, Network message boxes, guns, ammunition, and something I'd not expected to see.

"You have a sword?" I said, staring at the long blade in the trunk.

"It's an 1862 Calvary Saber, thank you very much, Mr. Bonney."

"Can I—"

"And no, you cannot touch it."

I narrowed my gaze at her. "Fine. But does it have silver in it, or is it just for killing humans?"

"It's just steel, but I have a silver resin that I used to wipe it with and a silver tip. Of course, if you remove their head with steel, they're still dead, silver or no."

"Good to know."

"Turn around."

"Like I've not seen a woman in her petticoats before."

She motioned for me to spin around. "Whores don't count, Mr. Bonney."

I did as she asked. "I've never gone to a whore, thank you kindly. Not my style."

"You have a style?" she retorted.

"Ya know, sometimes you're complimentary to me, and sometimes you're as cold as a fish. If I didn't know better, I'd say you don't like me very much."

"No, I do not. Not particularly."

I thought for sure she'd expand on that, but she didn't, prompting me to say, "What, no reason behind that?"

She was silent at first, then said, "I don't approve of your lifestyle, mainly."

"Says the woman who used to live my lifestyle."

"That's not the point. I never killed so recklessly and without any regard for human life like you do. You kill without a second thought. I guess that's why Scáthach cursed you, isn't it?"

I spun about. "How dare you claim that I'm some heartless killer that deserves what was handed to him! She cursed me at the age of fifteen after my mother died in front of me. She played on the connection I had with a teacher, and she took advantage of that."

"I'm sorry to hear about your mother and how Scáthach took advantage of your situation. But she'd not have cursed you if she'd not seen somethin' of value in you."

"Yeah, a hero, which I don't agree with, but that's the tale I was told."

She laughed. "Then maybe you should really look at the qualities you possess that would have attracted someone who creates monsters, Mr. Bonney. Now, if you would please tighten my laces in the back, I would appreciate it."

"Of course," I said and stepped toward her.

"Not too tight. I need to be able to reach my knives if need be."

After lacing her into the dark blue dress, I watched in silence as she went through testing if she could reach all her hidden weapons, including the silver sticks she'd slid into her hair.

"Perfect. Now write the letter."

I quickly wrote a note to Roy listing our needs. "Here. And if you can, swing by the Huff residence and see what is going on with them. If our men are no longer at the Torreón, we fear that somethin' happened to Daniel and his wife."

She took the paper and slid it into a pocket I'd not even noticed in the material folds of her dress. "Now, where exactly is this Network box?"

* * *

Because she was a woman, the minute Susan stepped out of the house, the shooting came to a halt. Stepping quickly, Susan headed east past the Tunstall Store and disappeared around the curve. No shots were fired as we stood by the window waiting for her to return, but thirty minutes later, a horse rode by. The rider didn't stop at Wortley, just kept on moving, and still, not a shot was fired.

With no idea who'd ridden past, we all began to worry about them and Susan. In fact, I was just about to send someone to go find her when a knock came at the front door.

"Who is it?" I yelled out.

"Lieutenant Appel. I need to speak to Alexander McSween concerning his eviction notice to Captain Baca."

"Military don't get involved in landlord/tenant disputes," Tom yelled to Appel.

"We do when asked by a retired captain of the military. Please open the door."

"No. Come 'round to the west kitchen, Lieutenant," I said. "We'll have Mac meet you there."

"Very well."

I heard his heavy but sure footsteps walk away while Tom and I flipped a coin to see who got to wake Mac up. I lost.

Mac was upset and appeared to get more so with each step he took as he moved with purpose to the back end of his wing of the house. By the time he spoke to Appel, he was more brash than I thought necessary.

"He is on my ground, harboring my enemies, Lieutenant. You tell him that if he does not leave, I will burn him out." Mac walked off, but as he reached the doorway, he turned back and added, "I've been out in the hills long enough. I'm in my home now, and they will not drive me away again, not while I'm alive."

With that, he left the room, leavin' me standing there. I nodded to Appel, who said he'd be back. By the time he returned, Mac was pacing about his living room asking for his wife.

"I told you, she is tendin' to matters with the chickens and the garden so we can eat later."

"Then you tell her that I—"

A knock came at the front door again. "It's me. I'll meet you where we met before."

Mac hurried to the west kitchen. Once Appel was inside, he said, "Well?"

"He has asked for a military escort to take him and his family to the Wortley, but there is no room for them there at this time. So, what can be done while we find them a place to go?"

"You can get Peppin's men off my land at the Torreón, that's what you can do."

"I know the minute I do that, your men will take that location, and then Baca's life is truly in danger. I can't let that happen. What if I removed them and put a few military men there? They won't fire upon anyone, but they'll remove those who wish to kill you off your property."

I shook my head at Mac, but instead of listening to me, he agreed, and Appel left.

It was almost six o'clock in the evening, Susan wasn't back, and I still needed to get back to the Montaño Store. The dust storm going on outside would give me some protection, but I was going to need more than that. I told Tom as much, and he, of course, disagreed.

"You cannot go running back there right now," Tom said.

"I have stuff to get and to let Martin know what's goin' on. Besides, we need someone to go check on Susan, and she is likely at Daniel Huff's. If she walked into a bad situation there…"

"I'm mightily sure if anyone could get out of that, she can," Tom said. "I've known Network folk a lot longer than you have, Billy, and they are resourceful bastards."

I cringed. "I didn't tell her you knew."

Tom rolled his eyes.

"Look, either way, I have to get the war bags of all the men now here. Better I run now and return after the sun sets versus tryin' to fit the trip in that twenty-minute window between pure darkness and the moon rise."

Tom sighed. "Yeah, you're right. How you wanna do this?"

"I got an idea," I said. "I'll need some cover fire."

"Easily done. But where are you goin' to head?"

"There's only one person I can think of who can go check on Susan, so hear me out."

By six o'clock, I was ready to run and had my hand on the door when bullets started flying at the house again, splintering shutters and scaring the women inside. Since everyone was already in place to give me cover fire, they let loose on those shooting at us.

"Who is it this time?" I yelled out.

"The Powel-Kinney posse has arrived at the Wortley!" Jim French yelled.

Without a second thought, I waited for us to let out another round of gunfire, and I made a run for it. I bolted from the front door straight for the Sisneros's home across the street and a bit to the east. Between the speed I could run and posse retreating from gunfire, I was almost there by the time the men at the Wortley caught a glimpse of a random person in a tan cowboy hat running for cover. But by then, I was completely hidden.

Catching my breath along the back side of the Sisneros's house, I banged on a window.

Lola Sisneros, a fifteen-year-old girl, opened the window a crack. "*¿Quién es?*"

"La esposa de Daniel Huff está pidiendo ayuda con su esposo. Es urgente. ¿Puede alguien aquí ayudarla?" I asked, telling her how Daniel's wife was asking for help with her husband.

"¿Cómo? Cualquiera que salga está loco. ¡Les dispararán!"

"Yeah, crazy to go out, I get that," I said to myself quietly. However, women and children would be safe to go. So, I mentioned that. *"No si una mujer fuera a ir. Todos los disparos cesarían."*

She finally agreed to see if someone could go help and left the window.

It was the best I'd get, so I focused on my mission. The next closest building was Wilson's home, but it was a long run, and I was going to have to burn a soul to move fast enough. Pulling on the same amount of energy that I would've to heal one of Zahara's hands, I flooded it into my muscles and ran. The world moved in a blur, but I was safely behind his place without a shot taken.

I didn't want to burn another one to get to the Montaño Store since it was so close; however, Jack Long and his posse, who were still at the Torreón, would have a clean shot at me if I didn't.

Wilson opened his back door. "Billy, what in tarnation are ya doin'?"

"I was never here. You never saw me. I ran to Lola's to ask her to check on Daniel Huff 'cause we think something has happened to him. I have to..." I suddenly realized how silent everything was, and I snuck a look around the corner to see Lola herself walking down the street toward Daniel's home. "I didn't mean her specifically, damn it all!" I said, then added to Wilson, "I gotta go."

As Lola walked by the Torreón, telling me that fifteen-year-old girl was made of some stern stuff, I bolted for the Montaño Store. Again, I was either not seen or mistaken for someone else due to the hat. Once inside the store, I filled Martin and the rest of them in on what had happened, including the idiotic agreement McSween made.

Feeling restless and inhibited by all the folks piled into the Montaño Store, George said, "Captain, when Billy goes back tonight, I'd like to change my position as well. Time is passin' and we're not getting anywhere."

"Where to?" Martin asked.

"I'll head to the store. There's an old warehouse Tunstall used for grain. It has air vents on the side that faces McSween's and gives a good view of things going on behind the house."

"That's actually a really good idea," I said. "They don't seem overly worried about anyone here—they just want Mac. It's important we get more protection for that property."

"I'm good with it," Martin said.

I showed the captain the list José gave me. "George and I will need this stuff to take the men now at McSween's, since they left without it."

"Can you run with all of that?" Marin asked.

"We'll be good," I said. "I'm stronger than I look."

George coughed to cover a snicker, and I "accidently" hit him while stretching my arm.

"You boys best get ready to make a run for it. Sun is close to settin.'"

We walked off to gather the bags for my third run across the street in one day. We needed to start thinking smarter, or this was all going to fall apart.

* * *

The sun set around quarter after seven, and we stood by the door watching the sky grow dark. By eight o'clock the lingering summer light was gone, and no moon shone in the sky.

"Let's go," I said.

George and I headed back the way I'd come earlier, and once we hit the McSween house, George headed on over to the store with just his war bag, rifle, and six-shooter.

"That was close," Tom said to me as I walked in to the front corner room of the east wing. "Moon's comin' up."

"I know, but we'll have bigger windows the next couple of nights if they're needed."

"True. By the way, have you seen Gaax since last night?"

I rolled my eyes. "You know, that damn bird is around when I don't want him to be, but when I do…he's nowhere to be found."

"We need to get word to him and to the men at the Ellis Store. They're so far down there I bet they have no idea what to do. I wish we could see it from here."

"No way with the 'S' shape of the street," I said.

"With our enhanced vision, I can at least see the front west corner of the courthouse."

"Same here," I told him. "I need to see farther though. Once Gaax shows up, that's what I'm gonna do."

A lull in conversation caused us to look out the window in time to see Wilson crossing the street.

"Damn it, what is that old man doin'?" Tom blurted out, pressing his face to the glass.

"Shit. He's headed to Daniel's house. Lola's not come out, so I bet he's worried."

"Did you tell him we thought Daniel was in trouble?"

"Yeah, but I didn't think he'd go over there once the moon was up."

Nervously, we watched as he walked up to the door and was let in. Breathing again, we both sat down.

"Damn fool!" I said.

"You say that like he knows there are werewolves out to kill us," Tom said.

I laughed. "You're right. He don't know nothin' about it." I sighed. "By the way, did you fortify the house more while I was gone?"

"Not yet. We were able to get a few more adobe bricks just before moonrise though. They're stacked in the west kitchen."

"Good, let's get some of the boys to start piling them in front of the windows, but they can't cover the whole thing. We need to be able to see out of part of them from time to time or we're shootin' blind. Remind 'em of that."

"On it now," he said, and left.

Not long after he did, I heard Elizabeth announcing food in the east kitchen. I was about to go get some when I noticed movement outside. I pulled my gun, then realized it was Wilson, heading to the Tunstall building.

"Now what's he up to?" I muttered to myself.

Afraid to walk away and miss what was goin' on, I stayed to watch. About five minutes later, Wilson appeared from the opposite side of the Tunstall Store with a man. Looked to be Dr. Ealy, and he was carrying his medical bag and a lantern.

Gunfire erupted from the Torreón, and I pulled my gun. Was about to run out the front door to help until a voice was heard.

"Don't shoot, I'm takin' the doctor to see a dyin' man!" Wilson shouted.

"Damn it all to hell," I said.

"That does not bode well for Daniel," Tom said.

I turned around to find him with two bowls of food. "Hungry, are you?"

"No, smart ass, one is for you. I knew you wouldn't leave the room. Here, eat."

I took it. "I don't need to be babied."

"You're welcome," he said with a laugh and sat.

It was cornbread and a fish stew with fresh vegetables, likely from the garden Susan kept. I was so hungry it could've been half raw cow and I'd probably have eaten it. Thankfully, it tasted just as good as it smelled.

Between bites, Tom said, "If Daniel is dyin'—"

"Might not be him. Could be one of our men who'd been at the Torreón for all we know. We just gotta wait and see."

"I hate waitin'."

"Yeah, so do I. Here, I'll take these back." I stood up and took his bowl, along with mine, to the kitchen.

There I found Elizabeth and her daughter tidying up the kitchen. Setting the dishes by the wash bin, I turned to them just as gunfire erupted outside. Pulling both my guns, I opened the kitchen door and rushed out into the night where there was shouting and more shots, but I saw no one. Worrying about Susan, I went back inside to go fetch Tom when Elizabeth grabbed my arm.

"Don't you ever do that again! Do you hear me?"

"Ma'am?"

"Pull your guns near me or my daughter and take shots with us in the line of fire."

"I didn't take any shots, ma'am."

"Either way, you put my child in harm's way again, and I'll kill you myself." With that, she walked off, pulling her daughter behind her.

I looked up to find Tom staring at me with a stupid grin on his face.

"You got told," he said.

"Shut up. I was worried for Susan. She shoulda been back by now."

"If anyone can handle themselves, it'd be her, so let's go over to the other side of the house and see what everyone is wantin' to do about the night shifts."

I nodded and followed him around the U-shaped home to the other side, and we worked with the other Regulators to figure out who'd be where and when. About an hour later, we heard gunfire again, this time from the Torreón for sure, and I looked to Tom. He nodded, and I ran out of the parlor, into the east bedroom, and turned left to follow the west side. Guns drawn, I ran out one of the doors that led to the patio area to see Susan running our way, holding her skirts high as she ran.

"Shoot him!" she yelled.

I saw nothing behind her and wasn't about to shoot at her, so I shot around her, hoping to scare off whatever was on her heels. She continued to run until she screamed out and fell forward, an enormous wolf now standing on her back. Without hesitation, I fired, and it hit him square in the head; however, the spirit of it didn't hit me.

Confused, I ran toward her as her arms, which appeared to be behind her back like she was cuffed, spread out to either side. As she straightened her arms, a six-inch silver hair stick slid out from his chest on both sides, one in each hand.

"You could be a gentleman and help get the thing off me," she said.

"Uh, yeah," was all I could say. Holstering my gun, I rolled him off before offering her my hand and helping her up.

Pulling out a hanky from her bosom, she cleaned the blood from the weapons that'd killed the beast. "Thanks for shooting toward us. I needed him to believe I'd fallen. That shot was well done."

I raised my eyebrows. "That fall was intentional?"

"In case you've not noticed yet, Mr. Bonney, all werewolves are male. They carry over their perceived human notions about women into their wolf form. It's a weakness I exploit on a regular basis. It's why I'm still alive." With that, she turned on a heel and walked toward her home. "Oh, and Daniel Huff is dead. Poisoned, it seems."

"And our missing men from the Torreón?"

"No one knows. They seem to be missing. My guess is they've been killed or bitten."

"Damn it," I muttered. "And the gunfire?"

"Dolan's goons shootin' at our servants, Washington and Bates, while they attempted to bury Daniel near John. Sadly, they just dropped him in the hole and ran for it when the bullets started to fly."

Without another word or look back at me, Susan McSween, who'd just killed one of the biggest werewolves I'd seen yet, besides Brewer, with what could've been mistaken as knitting needles, walked into her home with poise, leaving me with the dead body of what was now a large, naked man in the yard.

"How do I always end up with disposal duty? Tom!"

* * *

The morning on July sixteenth, Deputy Long tried to serve warrants at the McSween house, so we shot at him and he ran back to the Torreón. At some point, it seemed that Peppin sent a few men into the hills south of the Montaño Store to fire down on the boys there.

With a yawn, Tom looked at me. "It's been a quiet day."

"Shhh!" Jim French said. "Don't be temptin' the fates like that."

"And here I thought only Brewer was superstitious," I said.

Big Jim stared me down until I felt like a bug.

"But you probably have good reason to believe what you believe, so...I'll just be over here, and Tom will keep his mouth shut."

Big Jim grunted in reply, and Tom yawned again, closing his eyes as he leaned back in his seat on the couch.

"I'm headin' to the roof," I told them. "Sun will start settin' in an hour. Be ready. Bein' that Peppin and his boys—" I felt Big Jim give me a look, so I altered my words to say, "haven't been as busy as usual today, I'd bet money that they got a plan cookin'."

Once up top, I focused my rifle on the Wortley and waited. Not an hour later, a rider approached from the west. With the setting sun in my eyes, I wasn't sure who it was, but it appeared to be a Buffalo Soldier from Fort Stanton, so I did nothing but tell those on the roof with me to save their ammunition.

Shots fired anyway though, and from our direction, spooking the soldier's horse and throwing the man of color to the ground. Looking for the culprit, I saw one of Dolan's pecker-heads on the roof of the Mills's home, and he wasn't facing us. I took aim and shot the man, first in the leg, causing his next shot to go flying past the officer. My next shot hit him somewhere vital, and he rolled to his side, holding his guts.

Without warning, a few more shots followed toward the man in the blue uniform, and those were definitely coming from below me. I stomped on the roof and the shooting came to a halt. Jumping down into the patio area, I ran in through the closest door and headed straight for where the men would be firing from.

Bursting into the front room of the west wing, I yelled, "Who the hell fired on that officer? What dumb son of a bitch did that? I want to know now!"

A man whose last name was Bowers stepped forward. "You all began to fire from the roof, so we followed suit."

"I was firin' at the man on the roof of the Mills's house who was shootin' at the soldier. I did not fire at the soldier. Do you want to bring the wrath of all of Fort Stanton on us? If so, keep firin' at his men. Damn it all to hell!"

"Obviously that nigger is on Dolan's—"

I punched the man in the face, knocking him back into Cullens, who caught him. "Say that word again, and I'll put a bullet in ya." The room went silent. "No firing at the soldiers, do you hear me? I don't care what color they are, no shootin' at them, period."

The men in the house muttered an agreement, and I cursed a few more times before walking off, but not before I saw a look from Susan that I couldn't read as good or bad. Tom followed me out into the patio area where I pulled out a cigarette and lit it.

"Are you out of your fuckin' mind?" Tom yelled at me.

"What?" I demanded. "He shot at a military officer."

"So?"

"Look, I don't like Dudley any more than the next Regulator, but if the military gets involved in this, Dudley won't be neutral, he'll take Dolan's side, and we'll be screwed."

"I don't mean that. You punched one of our own men, Billy."

"How observant of you, Tom. And ya know what? Now he'll think twice before shootin' at someone because of their color." I turned to leave, but my head began to swim, causing me to sit down on the ground.

"Billy! You okay?" Tom asked, crouching down to look at my face.

I tried to shake it off, but it was hard, it always was. I laughed and said, "Guess that son of a bitch on the Mills's rooftop was a supernatural."

"How many do you have in the chamber now?"

"I have no idea," I said, giggling like a young girl.

Tom smacked my face. "Pull yourself together. That euphoric feelin' shouldn't make you totally stupid."

I swatted his hand away with the least amount of grace and then stood, stumbled, and caught myself easier than usual. I slapped my own face, and it dissipated even faster. Getting solid feet under me, I said, "I honestly don't know how many, Tom. I wasn't tryin' to be a pecker."

He stepped into the sun, making the red in his hair shine like a new penny. "It's very important you keep track. If not, you could run out at a very inconvenient time. That spirit energy doesn't know the difference between a papercut and a hole through your chest. It's going to use whatever portion of it that's needed to heal you. We got a long battle ahead, best you not lose track."

"I hear ya, I do. I'll start countin'." Not wanting to continue this conversation, I climbed back up onto the roof to watch the Wortley.

As the sun went down and the man from Fort Stanton got on his horse and headed back the way he came, my mind began wondering who the man on the Mills's roof was, and why he was there in the first place. The only idea that came to mind made me realize we needed to start playing smarter, or it wasn't going to matter that there were twice as many of us as the Murphes, we were gonna die here in this house.

17

LEAVE NO MAN BEHIND

July 1878

T
ired from a long night of volleying shots between us and the Wortley, the Torreón, and the Montaño Store, everyone slept in the morning of July seventeenth. Well, all besides me. I was awake, sitting on the rooftop with coffee I'd made in the west kitchen so I'd not wake people, as most slept on the east side for safety.

I sat facing south so I could not just watch the sunrise in the east but keep an eye out for movement from the west. As the sun came up and washed the mountains on either side of the valley that was Lincoln, I couldn't help but feel the power and awe of her beauty. A bird sang as the wind blew the trees and long grass. I could hear the rustle of them both it was so quiet. Hell, I could've probably sneezed and the men at the Ellis Store would've heard me.

Enjoying the silence, my coffee, and the sunrise, I felt better than I had in a long time. Since I'd been on that mountaintop with Brewer. Oh, how we could've used him right now. Drinking more coffee, I caught the sight of movement over the ridge of my mug. Slowly lowering it, I watched as two of the men Peppin had sent into the hills south of the Montaño Store casually walked down the hill like nothing was going on.

I was too far away to make a shot, but I set my coffee down and grabbed my rifle in case they came my way. I was just taking aim when a shot rang out, sending birds flying from trees and local dogs to barking. One of the two men went down while the other ran for his life.

It didn't take more than a moment for Tom to appear beside me, in his long johns no less, saying, "What the hell was that?"

"Nice outfit."

"Piss off. Did you shoot someone?"

"All the way over there? I'm good, but that's about a half a mile from the Montaño Store, let alone from where we're at. But gee, Tom, thanks for thinkin' I'm that talented."

Tom picked up my coffee and drank some. "Ooh, this is still warm." He drank more.

"Hey, that's mine," I said as I watched him finish it. "*Was* mine. No really, help yourself."

"Oh, don't pout. I'll get you more."

"I don't pout."

"I beg to differ."

"Shut up," I said, turning my attention to the man lying on the hill. "Can you tell who it is from here?"

"No more than you can."

I grunted in reply. "It seems not a soul is comin' to his aid. Maybe he's already dead... Nope, he just moved."

"You really think anyone is goin' to go after him when someone made a shot like that? No way." Tom walked to the edge of the roof. "I'll be back with more coffee." He jumped off.

"And clothes, clothes would be wise."

"I heard that," came his voice from below.

I grinned and sat back to see what would happen, but nothing did. Not a soul moved in town until around noon when eight men on horseback approached from the west. Each of them wore a blue uniform, and not a soul fired on them.

"Who's that?" Tom asked.

"Looks like Lieutenant Appel," I said. "He's the assistant surgeon over at Fort Stanton. He's a good man underneath that outfit."

They stopped at the Wortley before taking a ride through town. As they passed, I recognized Lieutenants Purington and Blair as well, along with five troopers. The posse went all the way to the opposite end of town before returning to the Wortley. Dolan limped out with Peppin at his side, and they spoke to the men, pointing toward the McSween house as they did so.

"That doesn't bode well," I muttered.

"Why?" Jim French asked.

"Well, Dolan is the king of lies and misdirection. He's likely tellin' them about yesterday. Hell, that's probably why Appel is here. He's one of Dudley's favorites."

"I still don't understand," Jim said.

I decided to throw my theory out into the world. "I think that Dolan was expectin' that Buffalo Soldier yesterday and planted that man on the Mills's rooftop to fire on him."

"Why would he do that?" Eugene asked.

"To implicate us, and in turn, show Dudley he needs to get involved."

"That's ridiculous," José said. "He can't. There's a law that forbids him to get in the middle of this type of thing."

"That won't matter," Eugene countered. "If they can convince Appel that we fired on the soldier, Dudley will find a way to show up in town."

"We did fire on the soldier, though," Jim said.

I ground my teeth in irritation at the missed point. With a sigh I said, "But you all only did that when I shot the man on the Mills's roof."

Tom patted my shoulder. "If you'd not taken that man out, he might've killed the trooper, which would've been even worse than being accused of shootin' at him."

"I know. But you can bet your britches they're gonna come over here and ask about it."

"We'll tell them that we didn't fire on the soldier. Simple as that."

"It won't be as simple as that."

Sure as the sun rises in the east, Appel and his two fellow officers came to question McSween and he told them it wasn't us, but Appel didn't believe him, so I stepped in.

"Lieutenant, on my honor, the person shootin' at your soldier was a man on the Mills's roof."

"Do you have a name or any proof?" Appel asked.

"No," I said reluctantly. "But I shot and killed him to stop him. That should account for somethin'."

"I'll go over there, take a look, and talk to Peppin. See if any of his men were over there."

"Like he'd admit to that!" I said.

Appel just raised an eyebrow at me and left.

"He didn't believe us at all," Tom said.

"Nope." I left the room and headed back up to the roof where I watched Appel and the two other officers ride to the opposite end of what must've looked like a ghost town.

Everything was closed, and no one was on the street. Even in the heat of mid-July, no one had their doors or windows open, not even the businesses. This made spotting the man shot that morning on the hill easy. Then, because Appel was a good man deep down, he and Blair headed up the hill to help him while Purington headed farther east.

"They better not fire on them," I muttered. "If they do—"

"They won't," Tom said. "Martin knows better."

Gun blasts went off, causing me to stand up and shout for them to stop.

Tom pulled me down. "They can't hear you, and you're just making yourself a big target. Stay down."

"Damn it all to hell! Why are they firin'?"

"They must have a reason," Jim said.

Watching in horror as the bullets flew, Purington returned with a wagon he likely borrowed from Isaac Ellis. Appel and Blair pulled the injured man safely to the wagon, and the three of them loaded him onto it before heading our way.

"Thank God they didn't hit any of them," Eugene said.

"Which is interestin' to note," Tom pointed out. "If someone inside the Montaño Store can hit a man at that distance, they could've hit Appel and Blair, but they chose not to. That tells me they weren't firin' to hit them."

"Then why?" I asked.

"No idea. No idea at all."

* * *

F rustration running high, I was at a loss of what to do. So that night, in the break between actual darkness and moon rise, Tom and I headed to the store. We needed to talk to Martin and ask them not to fire on soldiers.

The sun set at quarter after seven as expected, but the summer light lingered until about eight o'clock. That was when we made a run for it. Shots fired at us from somewhere near the wall, and I took two hits and picked up speed. By the time we arrived at the Montaño Store, they'd healed, and I was even more angry.

Bursting through the door, Tom and I threw our hands into the air as twenty guns aimed at our heads.

"Damn it, Billy, what are you doin'?" Martin said.

"Me? What are *you* doin', firin' on two officers? Do you think they won't go back to Dudley and tell him? Trust me, he's lookin' for a reason to come get involved."

George pulled us aside as the rest lowered their guns. Keepin' his voice low, he said, "It was Crawford. We were tryin' to scare the officers away from him until he died. We didn't want him bitin' them. It was all we could think to do to save them from being turned."

"Shit," I said, shoving my hair back from my face. "Damn it all to hell!" I walked away and began to pace.

"It worked in a way," George said. "The bullets flyin' by kept Crawford from attackin' them."

"Yeah, but they aren't going to think you were trying to save their lives," Tom said.

"We know. And we weighed the consequences and made a call."

"It was a bad call," I said.

"Not necessarily," Tom corrected me.

"Only time will tell."

Tom nodded, then walked back to the group of men. "Who shot Crawford?"

"That'd be me," said a man we knew well. He was Charlie Bowdre's father in law, Fernando Herrera. He held up a buffalo gun. "Charlie loaded it for me. Said this ammunition was better."

"It is," I told him. "Keep usin' it."

"That was one hell of a shot, Mr. Herrera," Tom added.

They'd done everything for the right reasons, but we knew it wouldn't be seen that way. We left there around eight forty-five, and since we had another forty-five minutes until the moon rose, we chose to head to the Ellis Store.

Stepping inside, the Regulators gave us a warm welcome while berating us with questions to what was going on at the other end of town. We filled them in and encouraged a few to come down closer to the middle of town. If not tonight, on the night of the eighteenth, when there would be no moon until after nine-thirty.

"We'll do that," Scurlock said.

"If you can't get down our way, for whatever reason, ride around. It'll take time, but you should be able to take the long way and come at us from the other side of the river. With the Torreón still held by Long and his men, you'll need to be very careful. If you can find a way to keep hidden, you should be able to take positions on the other side and lend aid," Tom said.

"We'll figure something out," Doc said. "Good to see you both and hear no one has died over there yet. We feel a bit separate from the fight all the way over here. No one has come this way."

"They will," I said. "It's just a matter of time. Remember, stay in after the moon is up and no shooting at the military."

Ike came over and handed us each a bag. "Here are some food

stores for you. With all of you there, it must be hard for the McSweens to feed y'all."

"Thank you," Tom said, taking his sack.

I took mine as well. "Much appreciated. We were runnin' low on water, but once we realized no one fired on the women, we were able to send the ladies to fetch it from the river."

Ben stepped over, hand on my shoulder. "I'll walk ya out. Gotta feed the animals anyway. Come on." Once we were outside, he said, "Well, did ya ask her?"

I nodded.

"Were ya right? Is she a member of the Network?"

"She *was*," I said, and told him the rest as quick as I could, keepin' my voice low.

"Well damn," Ben said. "She must be as hot as a pig on a spicket. Thinkin' she left that life behind to have it come and bite her in the...backside."

With a quiet laugh at Ben changing his language due to Susan being a woman and all, I set my bag down and began to help him feed the animals until a shot hit me in the shoulder.

"Damn it!" Tom yelled, taking a bullet to the arm.

"Run!" Ben yelled, just as a bullet hit his neck.

"Ben!" I yelled, and ran for him.

"Leave him be," Tom shouted. "We need to go!"

"The hell I will. Ike!" I screamed, laying my hand on the blood gushing out of Ben's neck. I pushed energy into the wound and felt the artery heal as gunfire erupted from the Regulators, shooting out into the dark in the direction the bullets came from.

Tom yanked me away before I could finish. "We need to go now!"

"We'll cover you!" Middleton said, taking aim and shooting into the black.

"But Ben needs—"

"We'll get Ealy to come down," Charlie said. "Go!"

He shoved the bag of food at me as Tom grabbed his with one hand and me with his other. Yanking me with him, we ran at full speed all the way back to the McSween patio, where I stopped to catch my breath.

"You can do that inside," Tom said.

"Fuck you," I muttered.

"Excuse me?" Tom said, stepping in too close for my anger level.

Swinging fast, I hit him with an uppercut to the jaw, sending him flying. "How dare you choose to leave Ben injured when we could've stayed and saved him for sure. Now they need to try and get Ealy down there, past the Torreón! That'll never happen, not in the moonlight." I pointed as the white orb began to show in the sky.

Rubbing his jaw, Tom said, "Ben is not important to this fight, you are. I had to get you back here in case—"

"Everyone is important to this fight," I corrected him. "Numbers is all we got, in case you hadn't noticed. And there's no reason you couldn't have come back here and let me stay to fix him, or vice versa."

"I'm on strict orders from Garrett. I'm not to let you out of my sight."

This was news to me. "Well damn him and damn you!" I said, and yanked open a door to a room when I heard the one thing I didn't want to: a wolf. Tossing my bag of food inside, I shouted, "Pull your gun, now!"

Tom didn't falter. He dropped his bag of food and pulled his six-shooter. I spun back around, shut the door, and pulled the gun from my holster as three wolves entered the space, one from each opening and another from the rooftop.

"See, this is what happens when you don't listen to me," Tom said.

"Oh, piss off. Let's just kill 'em and go on in…we need to replenish anyway. Here puppy puppy puppy," I said. One wolf turned toward me, and I slid the gun back into the holster. "Look Ma, no hands," I said, and put them behind me. "I can kill you without 'em."

The wolf didn't hesitate; he had me pinned against the house and knew an opportunity when he saw it. He jumped at me, and I pulled on the power of their magic inside me to watch things in slow motion.

The second he was too far into the leap to change direction, I pulled the gun from my back, stepped to the side, and shot him in the head.

He landed where I'd been standing, dying real quick-like. His soul slammed into me, causing my head to spin enough to lean against the house to hold me up. Slapping my face to break the euphoria, I laughed and shook it off. Still feeling wonky, I pulled my second gun.

Walking over to Tom, I said, "Two on two, little bit better odds."

A loud shot rang through the space, hurting my ears, and a wolf dropped.

"Two on three," came a voice behind us.

"Why, Sue, how nice of you to join us," Tom said.

Two more wolves came around the corner.

"You were sayin', Sue?" I said.

"Damn," she muttered and went into the house.

"Did she just really leave us *two* to go up against four wolves?" Tom asked.

We both began to move toward a door of the east wing, and I said, "She went to get help, I'm sure."

"You don't sound sure," Tom pointed out.

"Only one way to find out." I began to shoot at the wolves, hitting one but missing the other. Jumping with a good push, I leapt to the roof and twisted my ankle on impact. I hobbled myself about to look down on the scene and fired again at the injured wolf, killing him. The wave of giddiness hit me, and I toppled backward. Ankle popping into place, I watched as the next wolf leapt up and flew over me. Rolling so I could see over the edge of the roof, I heard a blast go off and watched the wolf's head come nearly clean off.

I looked to my right and saw our youngest fighter hiding in the small, shadowed corner made by the chimney. "Nice shot, Eugene. Very nice."

"You okay?" he asked, helping me up and steadying me.

"I'll be good in a sec."

Below, I watched as Tom killed one with a shot, but it was his last. I was about to toss him a gun when Sue came back out.

"Tom! Catch!" She threw a rifle to him perfectly, and he caught it without trouble. "There's one in the chamber. Send it to Hell."

Tom pulled the trigger, and the blast tore open the wolf's chest, dropping him where he stood and causing Tom to need a moment to settle.

Eugene suddenly screamed out, "Sue! Above you!"

A fifth wolf we'd not seen jumped from directly above her, and there was no time to get to her, for me or Tom. I pulled a gun and took aim but was afraid I'd hit her in my current state. Yet, as I contemplated jumping down as a distraction, her right arm swung out, and in one swift motion, she took the wolf's head with the saber I'd seen earlier.

Sue stepped back inside. "Now get in here before more decide they want to decorate my yard," she said and shut the door.

"Did that just happen?" Eugene said.

"Nope. You didn't see anythin'. Got that?"

"Ummm...uh, okay."

I helped Eugene down, and we headed into the house. One look at Eugene, and Sue's eyes grew wide. Before she could freak out, I said, "Eugene, go make sure everyone is all right. I'll be there in a moment."

"Of course," he said, and quickly left the room.

Eyes still on him, Sue whispered, "What did he see?"

"Nothin' at all. He was behind the chimney when that all went down. You're fine," I said, and turned to Tom. "You got that food from Ike?"

"Really, that's your concern? Not, are you all right, Tom?"

I sighed. "Are you all right, Tom?"

"I am, thanks for askin'."

"You're welcome. Now, did you save your bag of food or not?"

Tom sighed and held up the sack. "For you, Sue, from Isaac."

"To go with the one I tossed in here before it started," I added.

She took it but looked from me toward where Eugene had disappeared.

"You have nothin' to worry about, Sue," Tom said. "He doesn't know."

225

I wanted to hit him. Again.

"Excuse me?" she said, slowly turning to him. "And what do you know of my worry?"

I sighed and heard Tom curse. "Well done, idiot."

Eyes closed, a thumb on one eye and a forefinger on the other, Tom dropped his chin. "I *am* an idiot."

"Mr. Bonney, we had a deal... My help will end here."

"Wait!" Tom said, hand down, eyes now on her. "Don't punish the cause because I'm tired and runnin' high on adrenaline and... Look, a secret for a secret."

"Tom..." I said, my voice leery. "You said that—"

"It's only fair," he said, and before I could stop him, he cut his arm with a knife and made sure to hold it in the light so she could watch it heal. "I, too, am a Warrior of Scáthach. Been around a bit longer than Billy here, but that doesn't always equate to bein' smarter, obviously. We've told no one other than Doc, and now you. Your secret is safe with me, Mrs. McSween."

The silence was painful as we waited to see if she would accept the trade and continue to help us in this war.

"*Two* of you? I have to deal with *two* of you pains in my ass?" She looked upward. "What did I ever do to You? No, don't answer that. It's obviously somethin' bad." Eyes back on us, she just said, "Fair enough, we're even," and walked off.

Releasing the breath I'd been holding, I smacked him in the back of the head.

"I deserved that," he said. "Look, I fixed it, and she'll not tell anyone. Besides, it's probably best we have an ally here at the house that knows. Doc is all the way at Ellis's...so this way we both can work with her."

"I'm not going to agree or disagree with you...as one would validate your idiocrasy and the other would invalidate your point, which I think is not far off. Come on, let's help with dinner and get some rest. I got a bad feelin' about tomorrow."

18

BACKUP

July 1878

The eighteenth dawned bright and clear, and after I'd cleaned up the best I could with a wash basin in one of the rooms, I got a flash of the view of Lincoln from the roof in my one eye. This told me that Gaax wanted me to know he was up on the roof. I put on some clean clothes and made my way up top to find Tom lying there on his back and perched on the edge of the house like a watchdog.

"Got your message. What's goin' on?"

"They seem to be mobilizing over there behind the Wortley," Tom said. "No idea what they're up to, but I thought you'd want to know."

"I do. Got any idea of what we should do next?"

"Yep," Tom replied. "Gaax could go hang out on the Wortley property and feed us information."

I nodded. "Probably a smart idea now that they're not all holed up inside. But let's add more to it. Hey, Gaax, you up for a mission of sorts?"

QUARK-QUARK!

He hopped over and shook his tail feathers in what I could only assume was excitement.

"Head on over to check on those at the Wortley…if nothin' really is goin' on there, head to Fort Stanton."

"Why Fort Stanton?" Tom asked.

"I just got a bad feelin', ya know? Especially with the soldiers thinkin' we was shootin' at them and all." I looked to Gaax. "Only person there you can trust is Roy. I think Juan Patrón is there too, but don't go to him unless ya have to. Let me know if you hear or see anythin' peculiar, all right?"

QUARK-QUARK!

He bobbed his head, flapped his wings, and took off toward the west.

I prayed he saw nothing of interest. "Come on, coffee should be ready. Let's go see what we can do to help Susan and Elizabeth with this mornin'."

"You thinkin' she's still mad at us?" Tom asked as we both leapt down.

"Not sure…but it never hurts to hedge your bets."

We entered the east wing and headed to the kitchen for coffee. No sooner did we have a cup in our hands, but someone was calling our names from the front east corner of the house. We hurried to see what the ruckus was about, and as soon as we stepped into the room, Big Jim pointed out the window to people in the street.

"What in the hell are they doin'?!" Tom said.

Standing on the street in front of the Tunstall Store was Dr. Ealy and his wife with their two girls. Their youngest, Ruth, was nestled in her mother's arms, while their eldest, Pearl, stood there holding her dad's hand. As we watched, they all began to walk east down the street. At first, I didn't understand, then I noted what the Reverend held in is free hand: his medical bag.

"Now that is one gutsy Reverend," Jim said.

"You have to respect that," José added.

"They shoot at that family, we kill 'em all, here and now," Jim said.

"Agreed."

We watched in silence as not a shot was fired and they disappeared around the bend.

"Well, if nothin' else, they'll get a good breakfast from Isaac," Cullens said.

I smacked his arm. "Really?"

"Ow! What?"

"They don't know, Billy," Tom reminded me.

"Oh. Sorry. Ben was shot in the neck last night as we was leavin'. The doc is likely headin' down there to tend to him, hopefully to save his life."

"Oh," Cullens said as he wandered off looking like a sad puppy, making me feel like crap.

"Billy..." Tom said, prompting me.

"Yeah, yeah, I know." I followed after him. "Cullens, wait up."

He stopped and turned. "Yeah?"

"Hey, don't feel bad about all that. You didn't know."

"Really?"

"Yeah," I said, hand on his arm.

"It's just, I feel like I've done some stupid stuff and I'd hate to be the reason—"

Gunfire erupted outside, slamming into the house. Cullens knocked me down, landing on top of me, as others took cover. A few of our guys returned fire out the portholes until it all calmed down. Even so, Cullens wouldn't let me up.

"Cullens, you weigh more than you look. Let me up, man. It's over, we're good."

But he didn't move, and I quickly rolled him over to see his blank eyes staring up at the ceiling. "Tom!"

He came running into the room. "Holy shit, what happened? You didn't kill him, did you?"

I glared at him. "Tom, you idiot, no, I didn't fuckin' kill him. He was standing right here and..." I walked over and saw there was just enough space by the window where the shutters had been damaged on the fifteenth that a bullet must've made it through.

Tom sighed. "Nothin' to be done. Looks like it hit his heart and passed on through."

"Damn it!" I said. "If I'd not had him stop there…"

"Don't start that," Tom said quietly.

"Yeah, Billy, you can't take the blame for everythin' that happens. It's not always on you," Jim said. "Come on, we'll bury him out back."

"Not safe," Mac said. "The cellar, you can bury him in our cellar."

Jim nodded as José stepped up to help as well.

We weren't up from burying Cullens for more than a minute when Gaax's view of things took over half of my sight. Quickly heading to the west wing kitchen, I sat down to watch and listen as best I could.

John Kinney and George "Roxy" Rose, two of Dolan's crew, were standing there talking.

"I'm gettin' tired of this fight," Roxy said. "We came for the purpose of makin' a raise, but at this rate, we ain't gonna see that. There's no use in in waitin' any longer if we don't get help from the military."

John Kinney leaned against the building that Gaax sat on and said, "Wait a day or two longer. We were assured help if they can give it."

"Until then, why not start with the friends of the McSweens here?" Roxy said. "We kill them here first, and then go to town for the rest?"

"No," Kinney said. "We deal with them in town first. The rest can be attended to afterward."

"But—"

"Here comes Jimmy now."

Gaax looked up long enough to show Dolan, Sam Perry, and an older gentleman in uniform joining them. The latter sported a big mustache, a frustrated scowl, and walked with an air of arrogance as thick as a winter coat. He looked to Dolan and said, "Get on your horse and leave. Stand them off. I'll be there by twelve hundred hours."

"Yes, sir," Dolan said.

"And take all your men away from here. If I find any of them by sundown, I'll put them in the guardhouse. You hear me?"

"Loud and clear, Colonel Dudley." Dolan gimped over to his horse and, using his good leg, hoisted himself up into the saddle.

Kinney, Rose, and Perry followed suit, and all of 'em rode off.

Dudley turned about just as Juan Patrón had the misfortune to step out a building. Seeing him, Dudley cut him off. "You, I want you off my post today."

"Excuse me?" Juan asked.

Stepping into his face, Dudley said, "I do not want anyone spyin' on my movements and actions for the McSweens."

Juan, totally taken aback by this, refuted the accusation. "I have no idea what you're talkin' about. I'm no spy! I don't—"

"If you don't leave right now, I'm going to send you to the McSweens' house in a wagon."

Juan must've seen truth in the threat, for all he said was, "Yes, sir," and headed off.

Gaax took flight, and as Juan left, and I caught sight of an actual spy listening in on the conversation and fought not to grin. Photographer, James Tomlinson, had obviously stopped and listened in on it all and now was trying to decide which way to go so that Dudley didn't see him.

Knowing Juan and Dudley would go in opposite directions, James followed Juan and disappeared from view. Gaax returned my sight to me, and I filled Tom in.

"He could've just been sayin' that to get Dolan to leave. He has no reason to come to town, and there's a law that states he cannot get involved."

"Somethin' tells me he doesn't give two shits about that law. We need to warn Mac."

"And how are you goin' to say you know this information?" Tom prodded.

"Well, shit."

* * *

With no good idea, we gathered everyone and explained we'd seen Dolan and his men ride off toward Fort Stanton. We then proposed that we should possibly leave, as the military might get involved. McSween refused to listen to that and instead wanted to discuss the possibility that more Regulators were coming to help.

"Yes, if the information Dr. Ealy got to us is right, Doc and a few of the others are goin' to try and get here between sundown at quarter after seven and when the moon rises just past nine-thirty tonight," I told the men. "We need to be ready to help them."

"Summer light takes a while to be gone," José said. "They'll only have an hour at best."

"I know. From what the Reverend said, they're goin' to head up into the southern mountains and come down behind Wilson's place."

"Why not just follow the river in the dark?" Eugene asked. "They should be safe from those still near the Torreón."

"That was their original plan, but when Ealy couldn't get past there with his medical bag to treat Ben last night, they scratched the idea."

"So that's why he had to protect himself with the womenfolk this mornin' out on the street."

"Seems so," Tom replied.

"Best thing we can do is get men on the roof and positions at all portholes to help fire at the Murphes when they start comin' out of the hills. My guess is it'll be around nine o'clock."

Everyone agreed, and at a quarter till, we took our places. We waited and waited, but no one came. That is, until a knock came at the back door at nine-thirty. I quickly opened it to find a Hispanic woman out of breath and agitated. She began to rattle off things in Spanish so quickly that even I wasn't catching everything.

"*Por favor, venga por un minuto,*" I said, quickly ushering her in as I looked to see if anyone else was around. The yard was empty.

Once she was seated, I handed her water to drink, and she explained slower, starting with, "*Necesitas irte. Vendrán mañana.*"

I translated for those in the room. "She says we need to leave, that they are comin' tomorrow."

"Who's they?" Tom asked.

"*Militar,*" she said.

I didn't need to translate that.

"The military can't get involved in this. It's against the law!" McSween said.

Ignoring McSween, Tom knelt beside the woman. "Where did you learn this?"

"*Los oficiales estaban jugando al billar...no sabían que podía oírlos hablar.*"

"Make sense," I said. "Officers were playing billiards and talkin'... didn't know anyone could hear them." I looked at her and asked what exactly she'd heard. "*¿Que dijeron?*"

"*Todo el commando se movera temprano en la manana a Lincoln.*"

"All of them are coming to Lincoln tomorrow?" I asked.

She shrugged, obviously not knowing what, "all the command" meant in numbers, but added, "*Los oí decir gatling arma...cañón howitzer...*"

Tom stood. "Gatling gun and a Howitzer cannon? Sir, we need to move you out now."

Then, speaking in English with difficulty, she said, "They are coming to kill you."

The room erupted in conversation, many men waving arms and shouting back and forth. Seeing this scared her, I ushered her out of the room and asked her if she was sure no one knew she'd heard them.

"*Había uno. Tal vez.*"

"Why do you say maybe one?" I said.

She tried to reply in English. "One man. Tall...rubio, er...umm..."

"Blond?" I asked, helping her with the English word.

When she nodded, I grinned. I knew exactly who'd made sure she heard...the questions now were, would Mac listen? Would we move out, or would we stay? And where were our reinforcements? The moon had risen, and they were nowhere to be seen.

"Billy?" Tom said with trepidation in his voice. "Listen."

I was about to say, "to what?" when I reached out with my hearing and heard it. "They're not comin' from the north, and they've got company." I ran into the west kitchen and shouted above the arguing men, "Everyone, guns to the river!"

Running out of the kitchen door, a gun in each hand, I pulled on my gifts for speed, sound, and sight. Rushing across the yard and through the center gate of the back adobe wall that ran along the river, I froze in my tracks.

"Shit," Tom said from directly behind me.

"I had a more colorful word in mind, but that'll do," I said as all the Regulators joined us, taking positions to fire out of the holes drilled into the adobe wall.

Spread out before us was a standoff. Wolves lined the opposite side of the river's embankment blocking the other Regulators from coming to us.

"Don't waste your bullets," I shouted to the men. "They're out of range on purpose."

"What the hell is goin' on, Billy?" Eugene asked as he and Bowers approached the doorway.

"Stay back," I whispered.

"Why aren't they attacking?" Bowers asked.

"Hell if I know," I replied.

"Billy!" Susan shouted from the door of the kitchen. "We're surrounded."

"I'll go look," Tom said.

I nodded, and he left, motioning a few Regulators to follow him.

"We should start shootin' at 'em," Bowers said. "A well-placed rifle shot might make it."

"No," I said. "We do that, and they'll attack Doc and the rest...and we'll be powerless to help. Hell, for all we know, they have more behind them. I don't know what's going on...but—"

"Oh, Henry..." a voice trilled from the opposite side of the river.

"Fuck. Scratch that, I totally know what is going on."

"You do?" Eugene asked.

I shrugged. "Well, sorta."

Scáthach stepped out of the shadows in a dress the color of blood and a bhava lamp in her hand. The light from it bounced off her dress and pale skin, causing her whole body to appear to glow in the dark. "It's good to see you are alive and well..."

"Why, do I smell sarcasm?" I retorted.

Eyes narrowed on me. "Because you killed my Beta, Kamil. I am very displeased with you, warrior child."

Had I? I'd shot him, but there was no way I'd taken the killing shot. I'd have felt it, and I didn't. So who killed him? Edward? Richard? It could've been either.

Tom ran up behind me. Seeing Scáthach, he said, "Fuuuuck."

"Now you're pickin' more colorful words. And yes, we are. We are fucked."

"Why is she here?" he whispered.

"She thinks I killed her Beta, and she's mad as a march hare."

"Damn it, Billy," Tom said.

"Key word of that sentence was *thinks*. I didn't kill him." I turned to Scáthach and shouted across the river, "Did you hear that? You're confused. I didn't kill him. You took me from the fight that day before I had the honor. Edward must've killed him, not me."

"Why would he do that?" she replied.

"Because Kamil killed our friend that day."

Scáthach stood in quiet reflection, and no one moved. All I could hear was the unsettled hooves of the Regulators' horses across the river, the panting of the wolves, and the crickets who sung to us their evening song.

A wolf padded up to her side and bumped her hand with his nose. She absentmindedly scratched his head as she thought about what she wanted to do. Finally, she asked, "So you didn't feel a rush of power that embodied you to kill all of my wolves outside the cave?"

That'd been the death of Brewer that empowered me to do that, but I wasn't going to admit that, especially not with all the Regulators listening in. "No. I fought them, using the rest of my strength. I'm lucky to be alive, and you're holding a grudge about something I had no part of."

She stared me down, and I returned the glare with fervor.

"Just go and take your demon squad with you," I said. "This isn't your fight...unless you're now pulling Dolan's strings, too."

She grinned. "I told you, I only put things in motion. Men will do what they do."

"I don't think men orchestrated this surrounding of the McSween home!" Tom shouted out.

"Ah, yes...Tom. I almost forgot you were here. How are you? It must be nice to have another man like you to fight with. Are you playing big or little brother?"

"Ignore her," I said.

Tom flipped her his middle finger, and she cackled with laughter that turned my stomach.

"Isn't that what got you into trouble in the first place, Tom?"

Before I could ask him what she meant, he shouted, "Billy didn't kill your Beta, so take your revenge-needy entourage with you and go. We have a war to fight here...one you started."

"Yes, and if I'm lucky, you all will kill each other. Come, my pets, let's go."

Six wolves immediately followed her, one of which lagged behind, eyes on me.

"Samuel, now!" Scáthach shouted at him.

The wolf hesitated but began to slowly follow the other five.

"Looks like only six of your men listen to orders," I said.

A creepy grin spread across her face. "These six are my chosen, the rest are not. Normally, I have eight. All of these others are vying for those two positions."

"Oh? And how will they do that?" I asked.

"By killing a Regulator."

"You had to ask," Tom muttered.

"Your friends here on my side of the river have two choices, leave or die by their jaws. Whoever kills a Regulator is up for promotion." She looked at Doc Scurlock, John Middleton, and the rest of our team on her side of the river and snapped her fingers. An hourglass appeared, and she set it on a stump of a dead tree. "You boys have an hour to get far enough away that my boys can't find you. If you move more than five feet closer to the river, that hour is over immediately. You choose."

With that, she motioned to her six, and the first five began to follow her, the sixth lagging behind again.

"Samuel…he didn't kill Kamil, come with me now."

The wolf lowered his head to me, growling with teeth bared.

"Sam! Come!"

When he didn't respond, I said, "Didn't you hear your master, Sammy? Be a good boy and go…or have you not learned the trick of comin' when called?"

"Billy…don't provoke him," Tom said.

"Fine. Whatever." I raised my voice to Doc and the rest on the other side. "We got Dudley and his men comin' tomorrow. Leave now and come back later when the moon isn't in the sky."

"We can take them, Billy!" Middleton yelled.

"No, you really can't," I said. "Go!"

Doc spoke with the men, then said, "Until tomorrow, then!"

I nodded, and he turned his horse around. The Regulators reluctantly rode off, and Scáthach started her walk along the riverbank toward the east end of town, a smile on her face. She'd won this round, and she knew I'd never forget it.

"You're just lettin' them go?" Eugene blurted out.

I turned around, shoving one gun into its holster. "Yes. They'd be slaughtered. We can't—"

"Watch out!" Bowers shouted.

Instinct kicked in, and I grabbed Eugene around the waist with one arm, twistin' him away from the danger behind me as I lifted my gun and turned to face the danger Bowers saw. Samuel had changed his mind, jumped over the river, and leapt at me, teeth bared.

Taking aim, I was about to pull the trigger when Bowers catapulted Eugene and I backward. My back slammed into the ground as a scream pierced the air, followed by a single gunshot.

Sitting up, I saw that it was Tom that killed the wolf, but Bowers's arm was bleeding, teeth-marks evident in his flesh.

"Fuck," Tom and I said at the same time.

Then, as if words upon words passed silently between us, we nodded and helped Bowers back into the house. We had no backup coming, Dudley and his men would be here by noon, and now one of our men was tainted with werewolf venom. We were looking down the barrel of a loaded gun, and everyone knew it. Everyone but McSween, who refused to leave.

"Now what?" Eugene asked.

"We sleep," I said. "We rest and we see what comes. Tomorrow is a new day. We pray it's not as bad as today."

"It'll be worse," Tom whispered as the young boy walked away.

I nodded. "Yes…yes it will."

* * *

April 1949

I pulled into Albuquerque, checked into my room, and headed to the Alvarado Transportation Center where I waited for ages. Finally out of patience, I found the information table and inquired about the train coming from Portland, Oregon.

"I'm sorry, sir. Did you not hear the announcement?"

"No, must've been before I arrived."

"Due to a broken rail, they are stuck in Colorado for the night. They should arrive tomorrow at some point."

"At some point?"

The station employee looked a bit petrified, but I stared him down anyway until he said, "We are not a hundred percent sure of the arrival time. They are sayin' around ten in the mornin' at this point, but that's not a promise."

I sighed in frustration. "Fine. Here…" I pulled out a pen and jotted my name on a slip of paper, along with the phone number at the hotel, and my room number. Handing it to the man with a five-dollar bill, I said, "Call me if that time changes in either direction, would you? There'll be another five in it for ya."

The man looked a bit less nervous as he took the items from me. "Yes mister…Agent Kidwell. I'll be sure to do so as soon as I hear."

"Thank you."

With that, I headed back to the splendor of the Alvarado Hotel and got a bite to eat. Sittin' there, I considered heading back to Las Cruces to spend that evening with Cricket. She'd likely be somewhere downtown at this point and not hard to find. I got as far as the hotel doors when I considered the hours driving, the cost, and the already paid-for room. I sighed at the horrid notion of being a responsible adult, and I headed back up to my room to get a good night's sleep.

19

MILITARY COME TO LINCOLN

July 1878

T he morning of the nineteenth was full of sunshine as I lay on the rooftop thinking about the night before. Bowers was still out of commission downstairs with a bite wound that would eventually turn him. I couldn't tell him that. I figured, let him survive this battle, and then I'd tell him. Either way, it brought back memories of the night and days of Dick's first few changes and how hard it had been on him. Could Bowers survive that? Dick was in prime condition and it about killed him, so I wasn't sure Bowers would make it. Would I be smart to kill him and save him all that pain? God only knew.

The loud *QUARK* of a raven interrupted my thoughts, and at first, I thought nothing of it, then I realized I knew that particular call. As I sat up, Gaax landed in front of me, fluffing his feathers.

"I am glad to see you! Where the hell have you been? Do you have any idea..." I let that drift off. "You know what, that's not important, you're here now. I need to see what is going on over at the Wortley. Can you do that?"

Instead of replying, Gaax swiftly shifted into his young human form. Noticing my coffee, he took up the mug. Feeling its warmth, he hummed in pleasure, then drank.

"I swear, I really should always just have two cups up here," I muttered. "Where have you been? Are you okay?"

He swallowed and sat. "It's good to see you too, Henry," he said.

I raised an eyebrow. "You do know by now that's just my middle name, right?"

"It's what the mistress calls you, so it's what I call you. I apologize for my absence; I was captured as a child's plaything at Fort Stanton last night and shifted to escape. Had to wait until morning to shift back. I was put in a cage." Gaax shuddered. "However, it is our fortune that I was still there. For there was a lot of commotion on the grounds all night."

"I bet," I commented. "I heard and saw what you did."

Gaax glared at me. "Then why are you still here?"

"Long story," I muttered. "What did you see this mornin'? Anythin' that could help us out?"

Cracking his neck, Gaax began to stretch his shoulders and arms out. "Yeah, I did, and you're not going to like it. At seven-thirty, 'Boots and Saddles' played, and thirty minutes later, the cavalry was on their way. Henry, you need to leave Lincoln, now."

I looked at my watch. "It's eight-thirty in the morning, so we can't go anywhere. You might not see it, but the moon is up and will be until about ten."

"Then leave at ten. You might get out of town before the military arrive."

"How many are comin' with Captain Dudley Blowhard?"

"I counted thirty-five in total. Four officers, one company of cavalry, and another of infantry."

"Son of a bitch..."

Gaax drank more of my coffee. "You caught that they're bringing a Gatling gun and a Howitzer, right?"

I nodded. "Yes."

"Well, they also have a huge container of ammunition," Gaax told me. "This fight is over. You all need to leave. In fact, I'm surprised you're still here."

I rubbed my face. "We tried to go, but we were surrounded all night by wolves. They wanted to make sure we were here for this."

"Your deduction is sound," Gaax said before downing the rest of my coffee.

Drumming on my leg with my thumbs as I thought, I said, "My question is, how is he justifyin' gettin' involved in civilian matters? The new Posse Comitatus Act forbids it."

Gaax shrugged. "I don't know, but he's on his way. Best you go start moving McSween out of town."

I chuckled. "Like they're gonna believe me. It's not like I can say, 'my shape-shifting bird pal here says'..."

Gaax nodded and pulled the paper scroll off his ankle. Handing it to me, he said, "No, you cannot, but you can get a letter from Roy."

"You are one smart bird...man...birdman? Whatever. Thank you." I took the note and scooted to the edge of the rooftop. "Oh, and either put some clothes on or shift back into your raven."

I jumped to the ground below and headed into the house. I found Tom and pulled him into the small west kitchen since it was empty and still had hot coffee on the stove. Pouring a mug for both of us, I sat at the table with him.

"Moon sets at ten a.m. We need to get everyone out of town at that time."

"Why?"

I informed him of what I'd learned from Gaax.

"So they left the fort at eight o'clock?"

"Yeah, here's the note from Roy."

Tom took it. "If only we'd had this earlier."

I nodded. "We don't have a shot against all of that artillery."

Tom rolled the note back up. "I agree. We leave and live to fight another day. I'll start wakin' 'em up, and we can all form an exit plan."

"Wait," I said. "Only bring in Eugene, José, Big Jim, and the McSweens. Too many cooks and all."

"You got it. I'll have them all come back here. Elizabeth will have started breakfast in the other kitchen anyway."

"All right."

He left, and I sat there wondering what to do. Why the hell was I in charge anyway? Why wasn't Mac doing anything? It was like the fire in his belly to fight had vanished almost completely. Even though I was some cursed being, I wasn't anything but a nineteen-year-old.

My head dropped back, and I stared at the ceiling, my mind reeling on what to do, how to get us past the Torreón without dying. We could leave from the east, ambush them, and from there, run like hell. No guns at the Wortley could hit us at that distance unless they had a guy like Herrera, and they didn't. Sure, Kinney and the rest were lacking in morals, but not in courage or a desire to kill things. Shoot first, tell lies later. That was their motto; I remembered it well.

By the time Tom brought them all into the kitchen, I'd almost formulated a plan. The look on their faces told me that Tom had at least told them I had bad news. Sue was the first to sit and tell me to spit it out. So, I did.

"What's the difference between a Gatling gun and a Howitzer?" Mac asked.

I opened my mouth to answer, but Sue beat me to it. "Both are long barrels on two large wheels that the military drag about with them to battles. The Howitzer has a shorter barrel, looks like a small cannon. It's optimized for firing small explosive shells that can blow through a wall easily while a Gatling gun is a rapid-fire weapon. Its operation centers on a circular, multi-barrel design, and can fire up to three-hundred and fifty rounds per minute."

"And how do you know all this?" José asked.

"I was at the Battle of Gettysburg. I've lived with military around me most of my life."

I knew the second part of that was a lie, but it was a great cover, and she explained it better than I could've.

Mac patted Sue's hand. "My wife, sometimes I think she is smarter than me, Billy, I sincerely do."

I raised an eyebrow at Sue, and the corner of her mouth went up, as did mine, in our own private, internal laugh.

"I think, instead, maybe she's just a perfect match and equal for you, Mac," I said.

That softened Sue's face, and I knew she appreciated the sentiment. But it washed away, replaced by her training. "All right, the moon sets at ten this morning, so we'll carry a white flag and go."

"I am not going to jail, my dear," Mac said. "They'll kill me there. We both know that."

"Then we go on the run," she said.

"No. Not again. I say we stand our ground. Sure, Dudley's forces add to the mess, but he cannot get involved, and even if he does, his forces do not give Peppin more men to fight than we have. We can still stay here, tucked in, and he will eventually leave. He cannot babysit us forever."

"The guns he brings are the issue, Alex," Sue said.

Mac stood, his hand pounding the tabletop. "I will not be run from my home again. I have done nothing to warrant any of this. I've killed no one or stolen anything! I'll be damned before I surrender myself! I'm in charge here, and that is my decision."

He turned and left, leaving us all to stare at one another with perplexed expressions. Sue stood to follow him, but before leaving, she looked back at me and said, "I'll try to talk to him on this. You formulate a plan in case I can get through to him."

She left, closing the door behind her, and I knew she'd not waver his resolve. I said as much to José, Jim, Tom, and Eugene.

"So, do we run?" I asked them.

"Hell no," Jim said, and José echoed the sentiments.

"You all could die here." I looked to the fifteen-year-old at the table. "Eugene, go home to your family. You're too young to give it all up over Dolan and his need for power and money."

"We all are too young for that," he said. "We leave now and Cullens died for no reason. We leave now and we are all labeled quitters and outlaws. I say let Dudley come and we see where it goes before we make decisions."

"Besides," José said, "we walk away from this post now, they'll raid this house and take the governor by force, likely killing him and maybe Sue as well. Then we'll be arrested or shot by the men at the Torreón."

"He's right, Billy," Jim said. "We have to wait this one out."

Tom and I were outnumbered and had to relinquish to Mac's wishes for now. They all left to get breakfast except Tom.

Lookin' him in the eye, I said, "What are *you* going to do?"

"I go where you go."

"Don't you dare put that on my head! What would you do if you weren't Garrett's babysitter for me?"

He paused long enough to confirm my statement.

"It's okay. If I was in his position, I would've sent you, too. I don't care. But you don't have to die here with me, too."

Tom cleared his throat. "At first, yes. But other than my letter to say I was here, I've not sent him a thing. It's none of his business. He's not a Warrior of Scáthach. He doesn't know the weight that carries. So he can kiss my ass."

I laughed. "Tell me how you really feel, Tom."

He smiled, and it was one of kindship and loyalty. Finishing his coffee, he took his mug and mine to the stove for more. "Jim and José are right. Hell, Eugene is right. You know that, right?"

"Yeah, I do. If Mac won't leave, we can't leave either, or he's as good as dead for sure."

"Exactly. So, we wait, and in the meantime, we devise a plan of escape for when and if it's needed. I'm guessing you already had an idea in mind."

When I nodded, Tom returned to the table and sat, placing a full cup of coffee in front of me and himself. "Good. Tell it to me."

* * *

Around noon, the unmistakable sound of a marching, military regiment could be heard. They pounded into Lincoln like unwanted visitors on your one day off, and I cursed as I took a seat in a quiet room of the house. With me were the few who knew of my connection to Gaax, and they sat quietly by waiting for me to impart what I saw. Gaax was already in place on a low tree limb in front of the Wortley Hotel. Thus, as he witnessed Colonel Dudley and Captain Purington lead the column of blue into town, so did I.

"I want you to understand that I have not come to Lincoln to assist you in any way," Dudley told Peppin. "I have come solely to protect the women and children; the men can take care of themselves. I propose to go into camp within a half-mile of the town. If my camp is attacked, or anyone in my party is killed or wounded by a shot fired by either party, from any house, I shall demand the parties be turned over to me.

"In the case where that fails, I shall request the women and children leave the buildin', and then I shall open fire on it with my Howitzer and arrest the parties inside. I do not know what houses your party or McSween's party occupy; I shall treat both parties exactly the same."

Without another word, the troops made their way through town without stopping in front of the McSween house to deliver the same warning, telling me all I needed to know. Gaax took flight, and we both watched as they marched past the Tunstall Store, the Torreón, the Baca residence, Lucas Gallegos's house, and stopped at the vacant lot that followed.

This land belonged to McSween, but he was currently leasing it to one of his servants, George Washington. The land ran from the Gallegos's home all the way to the jail. On it stood the beginnings of an adobe building that was supposed to become the Presbyterian church that McSween had promised Dr. Ealy.

I couldn't hear the words, but I was able to read body language as Dudley spoke to George. "Don't do it, George!" I said.

"What's goin' on?" Tom asked.

"Damn it all to hell!" I said as Dudley appeared to get permission for his men to camp just east of the unfinished church, which sat directly opposite the Montaño Store.

I relayed the information to those in the room with me.

"Well, on the plus side, with how the ground slopes between here and there, all Dudley will be able to see is the roof of this house, not the actual building itself," Eugene pointed out.

Suddenly my view changed from camp being set up to something much more dire. Gaax was swooping here and there to show me things, making me a bit nauseous. Feeling that from me, he slowed down, and I saw what he was trying to show me.

"Damn it," I whispered. "We have a problem."

"You mean other than thirty-five men with guns taking up residence across from where our captain is along with the majority of our fighters?" José said.

"Yeah...seems that the marching of the troops past the house was done as a diversion. It looks like separate, small groups of Peppin's men have taken positions around us. If I'm seein' this right, Peppin made his way to the Torreón, but Bob Olinger and some other men took the house across the street from us."

"That's Steve Stanley's house," Eugene said.

"Johnny Hurley has taken over Wilson's abandoned jacal, and we've got Andy Boyle and some others in Mac's stables here. Dolan gimped on over to the Mills's place and the home behind that, the one that lines up with the stables here. I see Billy Mathews, Pantaleon Gallegos, and Sam Perry."

Susan nodded. "That's the Schon residence. We're surrounded."

A knock came at the door, and Susan opened it a few inches.

"A red flag has just been hung outside the Stanley house. I thought you'd want to know, ma'am."

"Yes, thank you, Ignacio," she said.

Tom cringed. "Shit."

"Shall I alert the governor?" Ignacio asked.

"No, I'll go talk to him. Thank you." Susan shut the door and leaned her back against it, the look of utter defeat on her face.

"Y'all know what that means, right?" José said.

"Yes," Tom replied. "Just like at the Alamo, Peppin's men are tellin' us we'll be given no quarter."

Eugene looked perplexed.

"It means there is no surrender," I explained to the young boy. "Fight to the death."

He swallowed. "Mac should've listened to you when you said we should leave," Eugene said, fear thick in his voice.

"This isn't about who is right or what should've been done," I said. "We just need to figure out what to do now. Does anyone—" I stopped short, seeing what Gaax was showing me now.

"Billy? What is it?" Tom asked.

The door burst open, and a panic-stricken Ignacio ran in. "Look out the window!"

Everyone did but me. I already knew.

"What are they doin'?" Eugene asked.

"Surrenderin'," Tom said quietly.

He wasn't wrong. All our men positioned at the Patrón's house were abandoning their post and heading down to the Ellis Store.

"But the army hasn't even finished pitchin' their tents!" Eugene blurted out. "Why would they just abandon us like that?"

"Because of that," Tom said.

I could only assume they were noticing Dudley as he ordered the Howitzer be trained on the door of the Montaño house.

I fought not to curse as the gun crew shouted the cadences of their loading drill as Dudley dispatched Captain Blair to the Montaño house. I couldn't hear over the drill going on, but from the look on Martin's face, it was likely a repeat of what Dudley had told Peppin at the Wortley Hotel. I did catch the end of it.

"We would advise the women inside to leave immediately."

"What is he telling Chavés?" Ignacio said.

"I can't tell," Joe Smith replied.

I kept my mouth shut since not everyone in the room was privy to why I'd know.

Martin shut the door, and it didn't take long for it to reopen.

"What are they doin'? What's on their heads?" Joe asked.

"Looks like blankets," Sue said.

One by one, our men at the Montaño house and Store exited. Susan was correct: they all wore blankets or bags of some sort over their heads as they exited and followed Martin down the street to the Ellis Store.

"Why are they wearin' those?" Eugene asked.

"Probably to conceal their identity from everyone watchin'," I told him.

"They left us!" Smith said, utterly flabbergasted. "They up and left us high and dry, ma'am. I best go tell the governor."

"No," Susan said. "I'll go talk to him."

She left the room, and it was silent.

"The women didn't exit," I mentioned to anyone listening.

"What?" Tom asked.

"The women stayed in the Montaño house. Only our men left," I said, pausing to watch Dr. Appel and another man mount horses. Appel headed to the Ellis Store while a man in a basic uniform rode to the Torreón.

Follow Appel, I thought, and Gaax understood.

While everyone else was talking amongst themselves, I kept my eye on the doctor. He went into the store but came back out to fetch medical items from his saddlebags before going back inside. I whispered this information to Tom.

"He's likely tending to Ben."

"Good point."

Gaax then took it upon himself to fly back toward Dudley, but as he did, we both noted a man in uniform slinking along the back of the property toward the Ellis Store. Gaax needed no instruction. He immediately swooped down toward the private, with a loud *QUARK-QUARK!*

I laughed as the man waved at the bird. "Roy is here," I told Tom.

"Thank God. Where is he?"

"On his way to the Ellis Store for whatever reason."

There was a commotion in the parlor, so I rose and carefully maneuvered to the door between it and us with Tom making sure I didn't run into anything. There we found Mac handing a note to Elizabeth Shield's eldest daughter.

"She is not going out there for you," Elizabeth was yelling.

Sue tried to calm her down. "She's the only one who can run this without drawin' fire."

"I'll go," Elizabeth said. "Or you go, for goodness sakes, but not Minnie. She's only ten!"

"She'll be perfectly safe," I said. "What are you sendin', Mac?"

"Just a letter askin' Dudley why they are here in town, since he didn't bother to stop here."

Minnie took the piece of paper. "I'll be fine, Mama. It won't take long at all."

"Be sure you bring back a reply from him," Mac said.

"She sure as hell does not need to wait around that camp!" Elizabeth said. "Minnie, you come right back here. He can send his reply with someone else."

"What does it matter if I wait a few extra minutes for a response, Mother? Really now." She turned and left out the front door, while we all stayed back and out of the line of sight.

"You have to give that girl credit! She's the courage of her aunt," I muttered to Tom.

"Agreed."

As Sue, Elizabeth, and Mac argued, I watched as Roy approached the back of the Ellis place and ran into Charlie and Isaac. I was happy to see they both were alive, but Gaax wasn't close enough to hear what was said. Isaac told Charlie something before heading back into the house, and Charlie headed to the stables as Roy headed back the way he came.

I pulled Tom aside. "Gaax was too far away. I have no idea what he told Isaac and Charlie."

Gaax perched on top of the Ellis building, looking left, then right, showing me what all was going down on either side of the building. At the front, Isaac and Dr. Appel were leaving together while all of the Regulators made a mad exodus out the back to the stables.

"They're leaving!" I said in a voice that went up in pitch due to my surprise.

"What's done is done, Lizzy. She'll be fine. Sit down and relax," Susan said before coming over to me. "What did you see?"

Tom and I pulled her back into the room, and I said, "Our men at the Ellis Store are leavin' town. They are all getting on horses as I tell you this."

"There must be a good reason," Tom said.

"I don't see one...I don't...oh wait."

Gaax left the rooftop and flew down the street heading west, and that's when I saw it. "Peppin and five others are running up to the Ellis Store fully armed, and the Howitzer is now trained on the store."

Before my eye, or rather Gaax's eye to mine, I watched as Charlie and the rest rode out of the Ellis coral, shooting and hollering at Peppin and his men. A bullet hit one of Peppin's men while a few bullets hit ours as they rode off, but no one fell off a horse, and they all got away.

"We're all that's left now," I said.

Susan stood and walked out, the swish of her skirts the only sound she made on her way to impart the news to Mac. He was not going to be happy. Hell, I wasn't happy. We were now not only surrounded, but we were alone in this, and with the red flags flying, we had nowhere to go.

20

VIOLATION OF THE POSSE
COMITATUS ACT

July 1878

Time passed quietly as we all sat and waited for Minnie to return. When she did, the response wasn't from Dudley, but from someone named Lieutenant Goodwin.

"They wouldn't give it to Dudley," Minnie said. "They wouldn't let me see him at all. I was told he was too busy. I saw him talkin' with the sheriff though, right before they left to head toward the east end of town."

"What does it say?" I asked.

Sue read it aloud. "I am directed by the Commanding Officer to inform you that no soldiers have surrounded your house and that he desires to hold no correspondence with you; if you desire to blow up your house, the commanding officer does not object providin' it does not injure any U.S. soldiers."

I could tell that Sue was seeing red as her hands shook with anger.

"Can I see that?" I said.

She thrust it at me and turned on a heel to go somewhere else in the house. I looked it over, and that was exactly what it said.

"Mac, did you tell him you were goin' to blow up the house?"

"Of course I didn't! I simply asked them, before they blew up my property, if they could tell me the reason."

I raised an eyebrow and noted the Bible in his hands, which also seemed a bit unsteady. "Sir, why don't you sit down for a moment. Elizabeth, could you get him some tea? Maybe somethin' to eat? When's the last time you ate, Mac?"

"Who can eat at a time like this?" he asked, motioning toward the military down the street.

"You do. Please, Elizabeth, get him some tea, would you?"

I could see her anger and resentment in the pause that followed.

"I'll get it," Minnie said, and ran from the room.

"Someday, I want that girl on my team," I said.

"You stay away from my daughter!" Elizabeth yelled, and ran from the room after Minnie.

"All righty then," Tom said. "Now what?"

Placing my attention on what my other eye was seeing, I focused on Gaax as he flew low and landed on the top of a tent in the military camp. He appeared to be near Dudley, since I could hear him having an argument with someone I couldn't see at first. Finally, I saw Justice of the Peace Wilson ushered into his tent.

"I'm going to go sit and think," I said, my code words to tell Tom I was needing to listen in on what Gaax was watching.

He ushered me into the easterly corner room. I sat by the window and placed all my attention on what Gaax was listening to.

"You must issue a warrant for McSween's arrest," Dudley told Wilson. "I asked you for it this mornin', and I will not ask again."

"I cannot do that without a necessary affidavit," Wilson said. "I told *you* that this mornin'."

"Fine, I'll send my officers with you to your office, and they will make one."

"Sir, I do not have the authority to issue such a warrant anyway. That is the duty of the U.S. Commissioner."

The look on Dudley's face made me afraid for Wilson.

"You know what you are, Wilson?" Dudley said. "A coward. You've issued warrants like this over the past few days and months for others.

If you don't do this right now, I'm going to put you in double irons and report you to the Governor of New Mexico for neglect of duty."

"You can't do that!" Wilson yelled at him.

"Oh, but I can. And you know what I think. If it was one of the McSween party asking you, you'd have that warrant done by now. So, will it be irons and imprisonment, or shall my officers escort you back to your office to get me what I asked for?"

"May you burn in Hell," Wilson said. "I'll do it, but then I'm done doin' anythin' for you, *ever*. You will leave my family and me alone. You hear?"

"You have my word."

Wilson stormed out of the tent, and I watched as Purington, Appel, and Blair followed Wilson toward his office that now stood just outside of town.

"Warrants are being drawn up for Mac's arrest," I said.

"What?!" Susan exclaimed from the doorway between the parlor and us, wearing something more befitting a Regulator Network Liaison.

I told her and Tom what had transpired, then asked about her attire.

"I'm goin' to go talk to Peppin. This is gettin' outta control."

"Wait on Gaax to get back," I told her. "I want him to go with, so I'll see if you need help."

"I do not need a babysitter, Mr. Bonney," she said, looking out a broken window in time to see movement near the house. "What on earth are George, Joe, and Sebrian doing?" she muttered, and marched out of the room.

I asked Gaax to come back, and he returned my sight to me. Finally able to see out of both eyes for the first time in hours, I took advantage of the moment. I found some of Mac's stationary and ripped it into three pieces. Sitting down, I wrote a short note to Doc and one to Edward.

As I rolled them both up proper for Gaax's legs, in walked Sue with a beautiful raven on her shoulder.

"He suits you," I said.

Face and voice flat but stern, Susan said, "Get this bird off of me."

"Gaax, come down from there."

With a *QUARK* that sounded more like a laugh, he swooped down to walk around on the table.

Sue glared at him and then me. "Just so you're aware, Sebrian Bates and George Washington, our two servants, and Joe Dixon, were bein' forced at gunpoint by three of Peppin's men to stack wood up against the east side of the house."

I groaned. "I take it you put a stop to that?"

"Yes!"

"Good. Gaax, come here, I have need of your delivery services." He came over, and I tied them on. "Right leg Edward, left leg Doc. Got it?"

He bobbed his head up and down and added a loud, *QUARK!*

"Good. But before you go..." I let that hold and sat back down, picking up the last small piece of paper. "Sue, are you still plannin' to go talk to Peppin or Dudley? If so, I need you to get a note to Roy." I began to write as I continued, "If you *can't* find him, put it where you put the other message earlier this week, in the old Network box."

"Talk to *Dudley?* Ha!" she said. "If that bloated, pompous old man wouldn't talk to Minnie, he surely won't listen to a grown woman, let alone me! I told the officers I wanted to speak to *Peppin*."

"Problem is, Peppin isn't the bigwig in town right now, and he's quite likely followin' Dudley's orders instead of Dolan's at this point. You need to go to the biggest cock in the field, so to speak."

"Mr. Bonney!" Susan exclaimed.

Tom laughed. "He means roosters, biggest chest-puffed-out rooster in charge, Mrs. McSween."

"Oh...well..."

I fought back a grin as I folded the note for Roy. "Look, we need to ask Dudley why he's in town. If we don't, they could get suspicious. I mean, he's not stopped here, and common sense says we'd ask."

I handed her the note for Roy. "Please?"

She hesitated but took it, sliding it into a pocket on her dress that, again, I couldn't see. "Let me get a few more supplies and I'll go."

"Thank you! Gaax will follow along to make sure I can keep an eye on you."

"Mr. Bonney, I am perfectly capable to do my job."

"Your ex-job," Tom corrected.

With a huff, Susan turned and left the room.

I looked at Gaax. "Follow her until I let you know it all seems good to go, then take the notes to Edward and Doc before comin' back here. I have a feelin' that I'm gonna need you if we're goin' to get outta here alive."

Gaax nodded and hopped onto my shoulder. I walked to the east kitchen and opened the door a crack to let him out. Walking back is when I saw Susan out the window, crawling on her hands and knees from the house until she was safely on the street where she stood and began to head east. I found a quiet place to sit down with my eyes closed so I could track her and hear what happened.

Sue moved quickly for a woman in heeled boots and was almost past the Torreón when she saw Peppin and diverted her path. I groaned, but she was going to do what she was going to do.

"Peppin! Peppin!" she called out.

Tall and lanky with short, light brown hair and a full mustache, Peppin turned toward Sue, his exceedingly light blue eyes zeroed in on her, yet he said nothing. However, eye contact was all she needed to feel empowered to proceed.

"Why are you attemptin' to set my house on fire? Why are you allowin' your men to attempt to burn my home? And don't say you aren't. I caught 'em red-handed!"

"If you don't want your house burned down, I recommend you make the men inside leave. I hold warrants for half the men in there, and I'll take those men today, dead or alive."

"And how do you suggest I get them to leave? I alone cannot make that many men leave my home."

"No idea, but don't go lookin' for help from Dudley. He's not about to assist with anythin' as this is a town matter."

"Then what would you have us do, Sheriff?"

"That's up to you."

"You're a monster," Sue said.

"Your point, Mrs. McSween?" he said, drawing her last name out in a whining tone.

"You say my last name as if it were a terminal disease. I tell you, I am proud to be married to Alex. He's a good man. I'm honored to carry his last name...something I'm sure your wife knows nothin' about."

Peppin's face flushed with anger. Leaning toward her, he stuck his finger in her face. "Figure it out, for I'll have them dead or alive, *today.*"

Susan didn't flinch. "Even if it costs the lives of your men in the process?"

"Yes."

"Interesting how I don't see you gettin' anywhere near the fight. So, what, everyone can die but you? What a brave man you are, Sheriff..." she said, her biting sarcasm hitting its mark before she walked away.

I applauded her, for not many women would have the gall to say such things. I relayed what had transpired to Tom while Sue and Gaax moved farther east past the Baca home to the military camp. She stopped and surveyed all the men roaming around. Many glared or laughed at her.

Noticing this, she put her hands behind her back and messed with her belt briefly. Then she set her shoulders and headed right for the troopers who were laughing at her.

"Excuse me, where might I find Colonel Dudley?"

The man to her left ignored her and just lifted his mug of coffee and drank from it carefully, before setting it down on the wagon bed. The other two men did the same.

With a smile, she said, "Well, if you won't tell me..." She drifted off, and her eyes locked on something behind them. "Oh dear God, William Bonney, you idiot!"

This got my attention, and I started looking everywhere for what she was seeing, as did Gaax. So much so that I almost missed the best sleight of hand I'd ever seen.

While the three soldiers turned heads to see if I was really behind them, she dusted all three of their cups of coffee with a dark powder before they turned around.

"Made you look!" she said with a laugh. "Like I really need your help figuring out where the colonel's tent would be. You all set up the same every single time."

"Wait, you saw nothin'?" the pompous man on her right said.

"Maybe...maybe not. Guess you best stay awake and alert or you could end up surprised in the night." With a big grin she walked away, head high, shoulders back as they downed their coffee in case she was correct. Once far enough away, she said, so Gaax could hear and relay the info, "They'll live in the shitter for days."

I burst out laughing.

"What is it?" Tom asked me.

Leaving my eyes closed, I said, "She just dowsed some rude soldiers without their knowledge. Man, I wish she wasn't retired, we could use her."

"She's a pain in the ass, Billy."

"The best of us are."

"You speak from personal experience without a doubt," Tom said.

"Shh...she's walking up to Dudley's tent."

"Excuse me, Colonel Dudley? May I have a word?"

He was speaking to a man inside his tall tent and ignored her. When she repeated herself, he dismissed her with a shrug. She then said it a third time, and a fourth, until he realized she wasn't going to go away. Stepping outside of the tent, his uniform excellently pressed and his chest perfectly puffed up, he glared at her.

"Colonel Dudley, thank you for a moment of your time," she said. "As you stopped everywhere but at my home, I wanted to inquire to as to what your object in bringing your troops to Lincoln is."

"Mrs. McSween, I don't know if you are aware, but I am not obligated by law to report my actions and their meanings to you. However, as you will not leave until I tell you, I am here simply to offer protection to women, children, non-combatants, and to prevent the wanton destruction of property."

"Then why do you not protect myself, my sister, and her children? Or our home?"

"I cannot protect them while they are in that house with *those* men. Your sister or your husband or anyone else who comes to camp will be given protection."

"May I remind you, neither Mr. McSween nor any of those who live in my house have been found guilty of a crime. April court exonerated Alex and, in fact, indicted many of Peppin's men for Tunstall's murder. Yet here you have soldiers surrounding my house!"

"I know nothing about soldiers surrounding your house, Mrs. McSween."

"Well, they're Peppin's men really. Now, since we know he can't think for himself and takes orders from whoever is the biggest dog in the courtyard, which at the moment is you, they might as well be your men."

He began to interrupt her, but she continued.

"Now, Colonel Dudley, you must know that my husband and I hold you in high regard."

"I thank you, madam, for the compliment," he said, lifting his hat, a smirk on his face as nearby soldiers watched on with a laugh.

Holding it together, she said, "Will you not at least assist in having the gunfire stopped so that I can remove my things from my house, seeing as your stooge is determined to destroy it?"

"I am sorry, but I cannot interfere with the civil authorities."

"Like that has stopped you before," she muttered.

Either not hearing her or ignoring her, he said, "I understand that the sheriff has warrants for various parties of those inside your home, including your husband, and he must be the judge of the means to be used in serving them."

"Those arrest warrants are nothin' more than death warrants with a judge's signature, and you know it."

Dudley appeared unconcerned. "At least they are signed by a judge."

Beginning to lose her temper, she shouted, "So you think it is perfectly all right to burn down my home and kill two women and five children in order to serve those warrants? Colonel Dudley, what will your superiors think? I'll make sure they know of your stance on this." She paused, and even from where Gaax perched, I could see the tears in her eyes. "Why have you allowed Peppin's posse to try to burn our house? It's all I have in this world, it and what is inside of it."

I knew she meant Mac, not her organ or clothes, but her husband, and in that moment, for some reason, I understood her reason for leaving the Regulator Network.

"I am not aware, madam, that your house has been set on fire by Peppin's men," Dudley said, blustering at her comments.

"Not yet, but they are trying to. I've been told you are going to blow up my house."

"You've been misinformed, I am afraid, Mrs. McSween. To be frank with you, madam, a few hours ago, I received from your husband a note saying that he was going to do that himself. When I see smoke, how am I to know that he has not begun to carry out that intention and started that fire and not Peppin's men?"

Tears slid down Sue's cheeks, her face becoming pink with anger in seconds. "My husband would never write such a thing! I demand to see this so-called letter! For if you received one at all, I do not believe my husband wrote it."

"I will read it to you." He stepped into his tent, fetched the letter, and came back out, reading loudly for the troops who were being entertained by the show she was putting on. In fact, it was such a commotion that most of the men with any interest in what was going on in the town had converged on the area, including a blond-headed man I spotted around the time Gaax did. The raven changed location with a QUARK, knowing Susan's eyes would follow him. They did, and she spotted Roy not far from the huge Gatling gun, standing between it and the road.

With her eyes on him, Roy nodded once at her. She returned the gesture but made it appear as if she was merely motioning for Dudley to read on. Which he did.

"Per your husband, 'Would you have the kindness to let me know why soldiers surround my house? Before blowing up my property, I would like to know the reason. The constable is here and has warrants for the arrest of Sheriff Peppin and posse for murder and larceny.'"

"I do not believe that my husband wrote that. Let me see the hand-writing," exclaimed Sue, reaching for the paper.

Dudley slapped her hand away and lifted it high, just out of the tall woman's reach, like dangling a carrot in front of a rabbit. "I would never trust you to handle this. I believe you would tear it up if you had the chance."

"Oh, for God's sake, why would I do that?"

Some of the men nearby exuded short gasps hearing her speak this way.

She rolled her eyes and sighed. "Please, let me see this note from Alex."

Motioning to two men to come forward, Dudley said, "Shoot her if she so much as tries to destroy or leave with this letter."

Susan's eyes grew large, but instead of saying anything, she accepted the letter and read it. Then she burst out laughing.

"Is there something funny, Mrs. McSween?"

"You, you are who is funny. What he obviously means here is before you blow up his property, he'd like to know why. A solid question and for you to be so idiotic to think he means to blow up his own house is absolutely absurd."

Blustering again, Dudley took the letter from her and stuck it in his pocket. "You are mistaken, madam. I know exactly what this letter says. If you are unable to see your husband is a danger to you, then your fate is not my fault. However, if you come to your senses and can convince your husband to surrender, I give you my word of honor as an officer that he will not be hurt in any way. I will take him to the post and give him all the protection that I can."

"We both know that if he were to surrender, Peppin's men would kill him before you got the chance."

She looked toward Roy, and I realized he was in the opposite direction she needed to go in order to head home. I began to panic when she began to walk toward the large piece of artillery. "You claim protection, Colonel Dudley, so why then do you have a cannon pointed toward our house? If you do not intend to take sides in this fight, why bring this at all?"

I heard her almost cringe at calling the Gatling gun a cannon as she feigned female stupidity.

Colonel Dudley became amused at her, his pompousness vanishing in laughter as he said, "Madam, if you will take a careful look, you will find that gun is not pointed toward your house at all, but in the exact opposite direction. Please, step away from what you know nothing about."

"I believe you know more about guns than I do," Sue said with a laugh.

Roy stepped up to lead the "misguided woman" from the large military weapon, and while everyone laughed, looking at one another in bemusement, the note switched hands without being seen.

I grinned like a kid on Christmas morning. "She's brilliant."

"How so?" Tom asked.

I held a hand up to him to tell him I'd let him know in a moment. I needed to keep ears and eyes on Susan.

"So really, tell me, why bring it all if you aren't planning to fight?" Susan asked.

Still laughing, Dudley spoke to her as if she were a child. "I did intend to use it, if need be, on the men I found this mornin' in the Montaño house and store, for Mrs. Montaño had sent me a letter requesting my help removing them from her establishment. I expected trouble from them, but they took the hint and vamoosed. Now, if you would do the same, so I can get back to my job, madam, before anything else here befuddles you to the point of no return."

This made the troops laugh, and again, Sue's eyes narrowed. I saw temper rolling off her and wondered what she was going to do this time.

"Oh, I shall. But I must say one thing before I leave, Colonel. Your being in town with your troops looks a little too thin, in my opinion. Good day." She turned on a heel.

Dudley blinked, his smile gone, and his irascibility came bubbling to the surface. "What did you say? Will you repeat that?"

She turned toward him and walked over. In his face, she said slowly and quietly, "Your reason being in town with your troops today looks a little too thin."

Standing tall with indignation, Dudley said, "I do not understand such slang phrases, Mrs. McSween. The ladies with whom I am accustomed to associate do not use such language, and I do not understand what you mean by, 'too thin.'"

So quietly that I only knew what she said because I read her lips, she said, "Yes, you do. You know exactly what I mean." Turning to leave, she paused again to say one last thing. "You are a cruel and hard-hearted man, Colonel Dudley, to sit here in your camp and allow Peppin and his men to do what they please when you know it goes against the exact reason you are supposedly in town. Someday these deeds will recoil on your head, and if I live, I will do all in my power to bring that about. You have my word as a Regulator. Good day."

She then hustled off so fast that it left Dudley standing there befuddled. Gaax flew over Roy's head, and the Network man looked up and gave me and Gaax a nod before walking off, note in hand.

"I shouldn't have lost my temper like that," Susan complained to herself, and me, as she walked down the street. "He just makes me so angry with his holier than thou attitude and the whole, 'I'm a man so I know better' frame of mind." She groaned and kicked a stone. "Fuck."

"Oh my," I said.

"What?" Tom asked.

"Don't you dare repeat that!" she said.

"Nothin'," I said. "She's on her way back. We need to have a meetin'. Gaax, take the notes and return quickly."

My sight was fully restored, and I rushed to the door to open it for Susan. Once she was inside, Tom and I selected the usual few to discuss our next move and what we should do, shutting ourselves in the dining/drawing room of the east wing. There, Susan filled everyone in on the gist of her meeting with Dudley and how our men were now nowhere in the town but here in this house.

Just as she was finishing, gunfire erupted outside.

Tom and I ran to look out the east kitchen.

"Gaax flies fast," I muttered.

"Or they were already close by," Tom replied.

"It's the combined Scurlock-Chavés group," I shouted back to the others. "They're on the crest of the hills on the other side of the river. They're shootin' at the men that have taken positions around the house and at the Torreón."

I watched as Peppin's men fired back, but neither our men nor theirs hit anyone due to the distance between them. That wouldn't stop Frank Coe or Charlie, I knew. In fact, they were beginning to fire rifles when suddenly all the Regulators on the other side of the river began to back up and run northeast, away from town. Before I could ask, Gaax showed me.

I stood in anger. "That son of a bitch!"

"The firing has stopped. What happened?" Susan asked.

"Pecker Dudley had his soldiers wheeled that Howitzer around to point it at our men," I told her. "His gun crew is making a big show of swabbing out the barrel and such." I looked to Mac. "We are now vastly outnumbered, Governor. What do you want to do?"

Gunfire erupted again, and we all could tell we were being fired at as well as returning it in kind. As I was already standing, I made it to the door that led to the rest of the house first. Opening it, I ran into Ignacio.

"It's Marion Turner and a dozen or so men," he told me. "They were across the street and just made a run for it."

The shooting stopped.

"We have warrants here for all of you!" came Turner's voice from just outside the front wall of the parlor, heard clearly as the sound of it carried through the broken window.

Big Jim French came running into the parlor, yelling, "We've got warrants for you, too!"

"Oh yeah?" Turner said in disbelief. "Where are they?"

"In our guns, you cock-sucking bastards!"

A scream erupted from way back inside the east wing.

"Oh God, Minnie! She went to get water!" Elizabeth shouted from the couch where she was resting.

I pulled my gun and ran at full supernatural speed into the dining/drawing room, where I saw two men in the east kitchen dashing small firecrackers called torpedoes onto the floor of the dining area trying to catch the room on fire. Between them and me stood Minnie, yelling at them to get out of her house, throwing water at the little explosives.

I cocked my guns. "I suggest you listen to the girl," I said.

"Billy! Don't!" Elizabeth yelled from behind me.

I wouldn't have. I'd made that woman a promise to not shoot near her children, and I planned to keep it. But they didn't need to know that. Thankfully, they didn't know I was lying, and I knew they weren't about to fire toward a child and a pregnant woman, so I wasn't surprised when they high-tailed it out of there.

"Mom! They poured coal oil on the back windows!" Minnie shouted. "We're on fire!"

21

THE BIG KILLING

July 1878

Elizabeth grabbed a potted plant and was about to go outside when gunfire could be heard.

"Get out of this wing!" I yelled at both of them, ready to run outside.

"Set fire to my house? I don't think so!" Elizabeth said, and pushed past me and out the back door she went.

"Stay here!" I told Minnie, and ran after her mother. Once in the kitchen, I saw what the gunfire was all about. George Coe, Henry Brown, and Sam Smith were shooting at the two who'd tried to start the fire, and they'd taken refuge in the privy.

Elizabeth walked in, plant and dirt now gone. "Fire is out, but we still need water."

"I can go. They won't shoot with me out there," Minnie said.

"No, you are not goin'. I will go," Elizabeth said.

"Mom, you and my brother are not goin' out there."

She said it so matter-of-factly that I laughed. But when Minnie gave me a glare, I held up both of my hands, guns and all, and said, "You just remind me of myself at your age." It wasn't a lie. She had no

266

fear, that girl, and she said things as she saw them. Minnie smiled wide, and I knew I was forgiven, so I lowered my arms and put my guns away.

"That is not a compliment, Minnie. Now go get your aunt. She will come with me."

With a dramatic sigh, the ten-year-old set the pail down and trudged past me on her way to the parlor.

"You think she's goin' to have a boy then?" I said, tryin' to cheer her up.

"I don't think, I know, Billy Bonney. Look how Mom waddles. He's sitting back on her hips. Besides, other than me, she's only had boys. If you could do math, you'd see it is evident that she is carrying my little brother."

Without another word on it, she left the room, head held high. I watched her go with a grin on my face. One that vanished the minute I turned back to Elizabeth. She was inches from my face, and less than pleased.

"What did I ask you about firin' near my children?!"

"I wasn't going to! I damn well know my promise. But if they'd pulled a gun on her, wouldn't you have been happier if I was ready to kill them first?"

Eyes narrowed on me as she pressed her lips tightly together. Finally, she said, "If they tried once, they'll try to set us on fire again. We need to get water and sand."

Susan walked in. "What's going on here?"

"Mom is givin' Billy the business," Minnie said.

I took that as my cue to leave and high-tailed it into the parlor, calling Tom over. "Man, that was scary."

Tom seemed confused. "That Minnie was almost hurt? Of course it was!"

"No, man, I mean Elizabeth Shield. I recommend we just send her to Dudley. He'll leave town in minutes."

"It's the hormones," Tom said, nodding in understanding. "Never upset a pregnant woman if you want to live. That's what my dad used to say to me."

"What did your father say to you?" Elizabeth said from behind us.

"Nothin'," we both said, and headed for the west side of the house where we had a greater chance of being shot. In our eyes, that was a lot less scary than what we'd face if we answered that question.

We found Mac sitting in the drawing room, his head in his hands. We sat with him in silence at first, then launched into the discussion we'd been having before Turner and his men had tried to serve warrants.

"We need to convince the Shield family to take Dudley up on his offer of protection. Three children with one on the way and David Senior in Las Vegas is a recipe for disaster," Tom said.

"Susan should go, too," Mac said.

"Uhhh...maybe we should let her decide that?" I suggested, mainly because she was our only way to move information to Roy or anyone else on the outside, but I couldn't explain that to Mac. However, he heard what he wanted to.

"You're right. It'll have to be her decision, or I'll never hear the end of it."

* * *

Each time things got too quiet out there, gunfire would erupt from the Tunstall Store again as they fired on the privy. By now there were three in there, Buck Powell joinin' the other two when he attempted to get water from the river.

"Either them boys are dead or been drivin' down below ground to stay alive," Tom pointed out.

"So, they're either dead in the shitter or standin' in shit," I clarified.

Eugene laughed, and I couldn't help but chuckle at the notion, too.

"I do not see how any of you can be laughing at a time like this," a man whose name I forgot said to us.

"And you are again?" Tom asked.

"Harvey Morris," the man said.

"Oh, that's right. Your brother knows Elizabeth's husband, David."

"Yes, I came out here for my health and to work with him and McSween."

"Bad timin', that," Jim French said.

Harvey coughed into a white hanky before using it to dab the perspiration on his forehead. "I didn't have much choice."

I recognized that cough. I'd lived with it for many years, and my heart ached. "You have consumption."

Taken aback by my candidness, Harvey stammered a noncommittal reply of, "Why would you say that?"

I stood. At this angle, I noticed the bloodstain on his handkerchief. "My mother had it for most of my childhood. She died of it when I was young."

The room went silent, and I walked out before anyone felt the need to give their condolences to me for her passing. It was just after two in the afternoon, and I'd not slept in so long I'd lost count of the hours. Deciding on some coffee, I headed to the back of the west wing, to the wooden framed lean-to we called the summer kitchen. Opening the door, I discovered Peppin had finally gotten his way.

"FIRE!" I shouted, and everyone came running.

Minnie brought water, and her brothers brought sand, but as they got close, gunfire erupted outside, aimed at those in the kitchen. Quickly, we all pulled back.

"Tom and I can take it," I said.

"But you'll be shot," Minnie said, worry in her eyes.

I took the water bucket from her. "We heal quicker than most, so we'll be all right."

Elizabeth's sons, George and David Curtis, who were strapping young men, were having a bit of trouble carrying the sand, so Tom took it off their hands. Carrying it like it weighed no more than a housecat, he joined me by the door.

"Everyone get back!" I ordered them. "They're gonna fire on us, and I don't want any of y'all to get hit."

I needed to say no more. They all swiftly retreated into the house.

"Water first or sand?" Tom asked.

TAMSIN L. SILVER

"Sand," I replied. "If we can put it out with sand, we'll still have some drinkin' water."

"Good point. On three then?"

"On three!" I said.

Tom nodded. "One, two, three!"

We burst through the door and with superhuman speed, set the pails on the ground, scooped handfuls of sand, and began to throw it on the fire.

"It's not enough!" I shouted over the gunfire as another bullet ripped through my arm. Shouting in pain, I grabbed the water pail.

"Stop! Don't use that!" Tom ordered.

"Why?"

Without answering me, he pulled me out of the kitchen.

"What are you doin'?" I yelled.

"Can you not smell it?"

"Smell what?"

"Oil! They used coal oil to start the fire. If you throw water on that, the fire will spread everywhere!"

"Are you sure?" I said.

Tom nodded. "Oh yeah, I'm sure."

"Is it out?" Susan asked, the door open only a tiny bit to the next room.

"Do we have more sand?" Tom asked.

"That was the last of it," Minnie said. "Mom used the rest on the other fire."

Mac stepped up. "Is my house still on fire?"

I looked at Susan, and she knew the answer before I said it. "Yes."

Minnie ran for the pail of water. "You didn't use the water, Billy!"

Quick as lightning, I snatched it up away from her. "They used coal oil, so the fire will just spread if we throw water on it. Tom smelled it and I trust him."

Everyone was quiet. Seconds went by like minutes as the truth of the matter sank in: our shelter was going to be gone and soon.

"So now what?" Eugene said.

270

"Once it runs out of wood, gets to the adobe part of the house, we can try again with the water," Tom said.

"Dependin' on how it spreads," Susan said, "it won't matter anymore by then. But we'll wait and see."

Time passed, and when the time came, Susan was right. One look and we could tell the small amount of water we had left wouldn't make a dent in the slow burn of the house, so we began to grab possessions of importance and move them from room to room as the fire spread. Even Susan's new piano was moved, making quite a musical ruckus as we shoved it from room to room. Eventually we had to give up on the beauty, since it wouldn't fit through the doorway of the next room.

As the flames advanced from room to room, Peppin's men closed in, firing at the home without caring if they hit a woman or child. Smoke was so thick that it was getting hard to see and breathe for everyone, but mostly for Harvey. I sent him to the farthest point from the fire right away, along with the children and Elizabeth. Not long after, the rest of us joined them in the largest room of the east wing.

The men gathered around Tom and me, and we started to discuss a plan. I looked over and saw Susan sitting in the corner with Mac. He sat with his head down. I didn't know if he was in prayer or just too upset to talk anymore.

We needed to keep the morale up, so I stayed lively and positive with the boys as best I could. And once we had a good plan mapped out, I bounced on over to Mac and Susan.

"We have a plan. We're gonna make a break for it. If we all go out with the women, we have a larger chance of not bein' fired on."

"No," McSween said. "I'm not puttin' my wife in that kind of danger, or Liz or her children."

"But sir—"

"I will not discuss it further!" Mac said.

"Somethin' is goin' on next door!" Millie blurted out.

Elizabeth went as white as a sheet. "Get away from the window, child!"

I got a hand under each of the young girl's arms and spun her away from the window, depositing her with her mother and brothers before looking outside for myself. "Looks like three men and a wagon are pullin' up and around the Tunstall Store."

"Why would they—" José began to say.

"This is our chance!" I interrupted. "There's no way Dudley is goin' to fire that Howitzer or Gatling gun toward us with his own men in the way. Susan, Elizabeth, and the children, you should all leave now."

"I'm not goin' anywhere without Alex," Susan said.

"Oh for the love of—" I stopped and said, "Look, you need to make a decision. The window on this won't be long."

And it wasn't. As soon as the wagon was full with the Ealy's belongings, the three men drove it away to the camp, and they didn't return for the Ealys until about an hour later. When it did, there were more than three men this time, but even I couldn't see who it was through all the smoke. This worried me.

"Tom, I can't see who it is. My well is low."

"I can't either, so it might not be that."

Reaching out mentally, something I'd never initiated myself, I looked for Gaax. "I need you, pal! Where are you?" When he didn't reply, I covered my one eye and focused on the fire with just the eye we shared, shoving the image out toward him. I felt a quick connection but couldn't hold it.

"Damn it," I said. "I tried to—"

A birds-eye view of San Patricio came into view, and I knew he was almost here. As he sped toward town, I saw the glow of the fire from his perspective and knew our situation was more dire than I'd thought. He swooped into Dudley's camp where he and his men now hid behind the partial adobe building to stay out of the way of bullets flying at the house from all directions. Before Gaax left camp and headed here, I caught only one thing Dudley said, and it resonated with me in a big way.

"My God, why does that woman not come out?"

I knew he wasn't talking about the Ealys or Susan Bates, for as Gaax took flight again, I could see, Lieutenants Appel and Blair,

Corporal Pergold, and five enlisted men helping them and the rest of their things into the wagon that had returned a short bit ago.

I ran over to the McSweens and told them what was going on.

Susan stood. "Mac?"

"Go," he said. "It's best you go."

Torn between stayin' with the man she loved and savin' her own life, Susan paused, until Elizabeth shouted, "There's room for us on that wagon! Susan, I need your help."

Susan looked to me, her sister, and children, and back to Mac. With a kiss on his head, she said, "I love you. Do what you have to in order to get out of this alive, Alex. I have to save the children." Without waiting for a reply, she ran for the door to the eastern kitchen.

I took Mac by the shoulders and shook him. "Get up! We're goin' to make a break for it!"

When he didn't move, I looked toward the door, eyes locking with Susan's.

"Save him for me," she mouthed.

"I'll try my best," I said.

With a single nod, she left the room and ran out the door of the east kitchen.

Gunfire became sparse due to the soldiers, but it came to a complete halt the minute Susan was outside. I watched her from above as she ran to Captain Blair and begged him for his protection for herself, her sister, and the children.

Seeing him agree, I shouted to Elizabeth, "You have safe passage, go! Go now!"

Susan ran back as Elizabeth and her three kids exited the burning house. Without hesitation, the five of them ran to the wagon waiting for them and piled into it with Miss Gates and the four Ealys. I could see the eyes of the frightened children and felt unmeasurable guilt. This was because of me. My curse led to this. The loss of their home, everything they owned.

"It's time to put this plan in motion," Tom said. When I didn't reply, he said, "Billy?"

"Yeah, I'm here. I'm just...I feel..."

"Act now, feel guilty later if you live through this. The fire is startin' to take this room."

This snapped me out of my guilt, and I grabbed Mac, who was lethargic from the intense heat. "Come on, Governor, we have to move!"

With Tom's help, I got him and the rest into the east kitchen, the last room of the house, where he immediately sat in a corner, his Bible in hand.

"Everyone, gather round!" I shouted. Once they all appeared to be listening, I said, "Okay...let's go over the plan one more time."

* * *

As darkness fell, things inside and out had reached a desperate place. From Gaax's point of view, the blaze lit the hills on both sides of the structure, which appeared about to give way and disintegrate with us still inside. From my point of view, with Mac near a state of collapse himself, and the fire eating at the wall between us and what had been the dining room, it was up to me to decide for all of us. Swallowing down my fear of making the wrong decision, I stepped into the middle of the room.

"Time to run or die!" I shouted. "Tom? You and I are goin' to run out first and draw the fire, just like we discussed. Everyone else, follow after and go the other way."

"But we don't know where they all are," Ignacio pointed out.

He was right. Gaax couldn't get close enough to see where all Peppin's men were.

"That's why Billy and I are goin' as a diversion," Tom said.

"He and I will try to make it to the Tunstall Store," I told them all. "Everyone else, while we have their attention, you run for the gate in the rear adobe wall. You'll be shielded by the chicken house. All you need to do is get across the river and run into the hills. Okay?"

"Two isn't enough of a diversion," José Chavez y Chavez pointed out.

Jim French stepped forward. "He's right. I'm comin' with you two."

"So am I," José said. "What's important is we get McSween to safety."

"I am goin' with you, too," Harvey said.

"No, you're not," I told him. "Your lungs can't handle it. Smoke rises, so you need to get down to the river, away from it."

Harvey began to argue, but I spoke over him, sayin', "Okay, on the count of three. One, two...three!"

I stepped out the door, and before I could run for it, Harvey Morris pushed past me and ran, out of fear, not smarts, that was for sure. I quickly pulled my guns and began to fire to keep him safe, but he'd only gone three yards and a bullet took him down. He fell dead at the opening of the eastern fence, and as much as I didn't want to leave the poor man behind, I had a job to do. So I jumped over him and kept on going, as did Tom, José, and Jim.

Dodging bullets, I lost count of how many hit my body as the fire consumed the rest of the house behind me. Very quickly I realized I wasn't going to make it to the Tunstall Store. With George and Henry giving us some cover fire at the back, I switched trajectory to the river.

I fired wildly, killing at least one werewolf, his essence flowing into me as I reached the downward slope of land filled with tamarisk trees. The dizziness hit me at the wrong moment, and my foot caught on a root of one. I fell, tumbling down the embankment, landing near the river with a horrible sound.

The snap of my leg was first, and the life I'd taken healed it. However, when my left arm broke, nothing happened, telling me one thing: my well of souls was empty. It was dark out, my sight and hearing were back to that of a human's again, I was almost out of bullets, and now I had a broken arm.

Thing was, empty well of souls or no, if I stopped now, I was dead.

"Tom!" I shouted.

"Down this way!"

He sounded like he was upriver, but I wasn't a hundred percent sure. Looking behind me, my human eyesight saw nothing. "Shit." I carefully moved upstream, cradling my arm, and as I did, Gaax took half of my already bad eyesight, causing me to stop in my tracks and sit on the wet ground.

I watched for what felt like hours as McSween and two Mexicans who had made it to the back wall with him stood frozen due to the bullets flying by. They tried again, only to have more bullets shot at them. They couldn't get to the river, but I couldn't see why. Shortly after, I realized there were men, most of whom appeared to be in blue uniforms, behind the back wall.

Finally, McSween backed up toward the house, yelling out, "I will surrender!"

"I can accept your surrender," Robert Beckwith, a Deputy U.S. Marshall, replied from behind the back wall.

Stepping into the firelight, Beckwith approached the back door of the last burning room of the McSween home. As he did, movement behind and to Beckwith's left caught Gaax's attention, and for a moment, I saw the horror before it happened.

John Jones lifted his rifle, and I honestly wasn't sure who he was aiming at, Beckwith or McSween. Sure, Jones and Beckwith were both Murphy men, but the Beckwith family and the Jones's had been fighting over cattle for close to a year. Either man could've been Jones's target.

Thinking nothing of Jones, Gaax turned his eye back on McSween, where Beckwith also must've noted the raised rifle, for he raised his arm up as if to block a shot just as Jones fired. The bullet slammed through Beckwith's wrist and into his head, dropping him where he stood.

The Murphes, seeing Beckwith go down, opened fire on McSween. Those who'd been backing Beckwith up were so close to those huddled by the remnants of the burning home that bullets hit targets easily. McSween was the next to fall, landing on top of Beck-with as the rest of the men who'd been in the house tried to make a run for it.

Eugene and Ignacio fell between the door and the back of the burning east kitchen. Seeing this, my heart broke. I could barely watch as two more of our men ran into the chicken house, which immediately was shot at, riddling it with bullets, very likely killing all inside.

"No no no!" I shouted, before a wet hand slapped over my mouth.

"There you are! Shut up! Why are you on the ground?"

"Gaax…"

"What?" Tom asked.

"Gaax, I need my sight back."

He let me have it, and I looked at Tom. "They killed McSween, Eugene…all of 'em."

22

REUNION

July 1878

Tom stood there stunned for a moment, then said, "Can you move?"

"I broke my promise," I muttered.

"What promise?"

"I told her I'd keep him alive."

"No, you said you'd try to…and you did. Now can you walk?"

I couldn't think of anything except Susan. How I'd let her down, after all she'd done for me.

When I didn't answer, Tom squatted to face me. "Billy, you can't focus on all that right now. Fight that inner battle another day. We have to go. Can you walk?"

"The well is empty, and my arm's broken…but yes, I can walk."

"Shit. Okay, let's get across the river and find a demon or two for you to kill."

I nodded, but I worried it wasn't going to be that easy. Even so, I took Tom's arm for balance, keepin' my injured one bent and close to my body as we stepped into the river.

The water felt good after the heat of the day and the break of the lower leg bone. I desperately wanted to lay down in the river, play dead, and float downstream. But Tom said that wasn't a good idea, so we finished crossing the river and scrambled up the embankment, past some brush, only to collapse behind it to catch our breath.

Tom stood and carefully helped me up. "What did I tell you about lettin' the well get empty?"

"I took too many hits tryin' to put out the fire and on that run just now."

"That's what you get for tryin' to be the hero."

"Ha! Me? That'll be the day," I said. "Did you see where José or Jim went?"

"I didn't hear or see them die, so there's that."

"Good," I said, as we walked into the small clearing and stopped in our tracks.

"Well, that's unfortunate," Tom said as we stared down three large wolves blocking our way.

"Uh, Tom, how many in your well?" I whispered.

"If I counted correctly, I'm down to one," he quietly replied.

"Wait…" I said, raising my voice. "You lectured me before but you're—"

"Can we fight about this later, Mom?" Tom countered.

I let go of him and began to walk to my left so as to give the wolves more than one target to run at. "Mom? You compare me to that horrible hag?"

Catching on to my way of thinking, Tom moved to his right. "Horrible hag? How dare you—"

We sprang into action simultaneously, pulling guns at the same time. I dropped to my knees, took aim, and shot the wolf coming at me in the head. The dizziness only lingered a moment as his soul immediately had a purpose, healing my arm. However, that meant the well was empty again.

I turned toward Tom. The two other wolves had chosen him, which made sense, since I was the injured of the two upon arrival.

Taking careful aim with human eyesight, I shot, hitting the wolf that lunged at Tom in the ass just as he dodged Tom's bullet and sank his teeth into my pal's arm.

"Noooo!" I yelled.

A gunshot went off. Blood and tissue flew as the bullet exited the back of the wolf's head.

The third wolf circled toward my pal as Tom writhed on the ground, the severe pain of the bite being healed rendering him useless.

I checked my gun. I was out of bullets.

"Aw hell, here goes stupid!" I said, and jumped between Tom and the wolf. "I was thinkin' we could talk about this. I have a bullet or two left that could be yours *or* you can leave with your life. What do ya say?"

"What are you doin'?" Tom groaned out. "Shoot him!"

I couldn't admit aloud to having no ammo left, so I just smiled and blocked Tom as the wolf moved to my left.

We were screwed. This night wouldn't hold just the big killing of our leader, but of both of the Scáthach Warriors. I wondered if she'd be happy or sad, chuckling at the fact that I didn't know the answer.

The wolf was about to strike. I could feel it more than see. The best I could do was protect Tom and pray for a swift death. Backing up, I stood my ground and kept my eyes open as the reddish-brown wolf leapt high into the air with triumph. I pulled my gun, planning to hit him with it, when another wolf, more of a shimmering silver-gray, emerged like magic over the brush from behind Tom and me. He met the other one in mid-air, his speed and mass hitting with such momentum that they both flew back from us, landing hard and rolling farther away, the gray wolf on top of the other.

I watched in horrid fascination as the gray wolf's jaw opened wide and bit down on the neck of the smaller, reddish brown wolf that only seconds ago thought it was going to take the lives of two Scáthach Warriors. The smaller wolf squealed in fear and pain as the larger shook the smaller wolf like Punch used to do with a stuffed toy. But instead of cotton flying out, the neck of the smaller wolf snapped, and as the gray wolf let go, it lay dead and limp on the ground.

THE TORMENT OF RICHARD BREWER

Turning his focus on Tom and me, blood covering his teeth, the gray wolf cocked his head sideways as I stared at him in disbelief.

A shot rang out, and the wolf dodged the bullet easily. Growling, eyes sliding from me to Tom, the wolf hesitated.

Praying I was right, I reached out and shoved Tom's arm down. "Don't shoot."

"What are you doin', Billy?" Tom demanded to know. "Are ya crazy?"

"I hope not." I looked at the gorgeous creature and approached slowly, squinting to see better as I pulled out my lamp.

Holding it out before me as I moved toward him, the wolf held his ground. In two steps, I saw what I needed and collapsed to my knees. "You son of a bitch! Damn it, Dick. I thought you were dead! Man, are you a sight for sore eyes."

The wolf's mouth opened into a grin, his tongue lolling out to one side, and emotions hit my chest, pressing in. "Come here, you bastard!"

The wolf looked past me at Tom and tilted his head in question.

"He's like me." I kept the wolf in my sights but spoke to Tom. "Stand down, brother. This beast isn't an enemy to fight. He's a fellow Regulator. See the pattern like flames on his face? Those match my hands. He's my Beta. Tom O. Folliard, meet Richard M. Brewer, the first leader of the Regulators and my good friend. Dick, this is Tom. He's good people."

Dick growled lightly.

"Put your gun away, Tom. He won't hurt us."

"I don't understand."

"I know, but you trust me, right? Holster your weapon."

Tom hesitated but slowly slid the gun back into its spot and sat there petrified. Seeing a chance to prove himself, Dick padded over to me and lay down, resting his head on my knee.

I reached out and placed my hands across the wolf's wide face showing Tom how they matched up to the markings. Staring into the wolf's blue eyes, I quietly said to him, "You have a lot to answer for, jackass."

The wolf smiled again and rolled over, exposing his belly and wiggling on the ground to scratch his back.

With a laugh, I lay a hand on his barrel chest. "Oh, don't pull that shit. You know you have a lot to explain. For example, if you're not dead, what was the surge of energy that I thought was your death?"

Since I was touching him, I could hear Brewer's thoughts. "Your shot to Kamil, Scáthach's Beta. Edward knew it would hit you the same way, if not harder, than my death. I used that to leave, so you'd be free of me."

My chest tightened. "I don't need that."

"I'm tormented by the idea that if my tooth were to accidently pierce you, you'd be forced to kill me or die. I never want you to have to make that choice."

"Then I won't. We'll make sure of it. But damn it, Dick. I need you in this fight. We could've used you the past five days, that's for sure. Shit."

Dick rolled back so his belly lay on the ground and just before I took my hand away, I heard him think, "I'm sorry."

I patted his shoulder. "I suppose I can forgive you since ya saved our lives. Come on, before Dudley and Dolan send any more henchmen to see what's goin' on."

Dick stood up on all fours and shook off the grass and dirt.

I did the same, in my way, and turned to Tom. "I'll explain further when we get to a safe location. Can you walk?"

Tom stood slowly and looked from me to Dick. "I can, but know I'm not one hundred percent sure of this idea of yours."

"I know. But trust me."

"It's not you I don't trust."

I nodded and took one of Tom's guns. Checking it, I saw it had two silver bullets left. "Then let's make this pact. If Dick is dumb enough to go at you, I'll shoot him in the ass."

Dick huffed but seemed to understand.

Seeing Tom's healed arm twitch near his other gun, I pointed the one in my hand at him, cocked and ready to go. "And if you even look like you're gonna go for yours, I'll shoot you without hesitation, and I'll choose somewhere painful."

Tom didn't hide his surprise. "Billy, you can't trust these things..."

"He's not a *thing*, he's a *man*," I told him. "He owns his own soul and he's my brother. Now let's get our butts movin'. We need to meet up with the rest of the gang and let them know McSween is dead."

"Then what? He was the leader. With him gone, isn't the war over?" Tom asked.

I felt the rage in me build until the glimmer of revenge shone through my eyes. "We gotta plan our next move. 'Cause if I got anythin' to say about it, this ain't over...not by a long shot."

* * *

April 1949

Waking up the next morning in Albuquerque, I received a call from the man at the train station. My partner's train was going to be in around noon now instead. Because of this, I took my time getting ready, dallying over breakfast and a good conversation with the waiter who served me, and headed on out to the parking lot, only to find my tail from Las Cruces was still there.

"You have got to be kiddin' me! I'm over this."

I snuck over to find him sleeping. Using my speed and my favorite blade, I slashed his tires, got in my car, and left, arriving at the station just as the train from Oregon pulled in. People flooded off the train, obviously happy to finally be at their destination, but I didn't see my pal.

For a moment, I thought my partner had blown off the ticket I'd sent him, but as the last person cleared the doorway, I saw him. His long, strong legs moved in that rangy way cowboys walked when they were reluctant but willing. He wore his usual cowboy hat and boots, but he'd added some style to his wardrobe. He now sported mirrored sunglasses, well-worn jeans, a fitted white t-shirt, and a brown leather aviator jacket.

With a large duffle slung over one shoulder, he stepped through the doorway, and took off his hat, exposing his hair that appeared recently buzzed and cleaned up for his journey. He must've seen me because a half-smile slid into place on his handsome face, telling me he was happy to see me, but not to be in New Mexico. Who could blame him?

Without a word, he came over, dropped his bag, and pulled me in for a hug.

I wheezed. "Dick, you're squeezin' the air outta me again."

He let go and pulled his glasses off. Blue eyes looked down at me and he grinned. "Serves ya right, draggin' me into this hellhole again. What's so important that you needed me, anyway?"

I frowned. "She's here."

"Come again?"

"Scáthach. She's here, and I'm pretty sure Fletcher is dead. It's time I take care of her once and for all. You in? You ready for this?"

Dick's grin widened as he slid his sunglasses back into place. "Brother, I was re-born ready." He picked his bag up. "Lead the way, and let's get to work. Where do we start?"

"Santa Fe, believe it or not. Need to check in with home office."

"That sounds swell," he said, obviously meaning just the opposite.

"Have no fear. We won't be there long. The trail leads to Las Cruces, and I lined us up some hot dates there for Cinco de Mayo… it's not gonna be all work and bad memories, ya know."

"Dates?"

"Yeah, I almost went back to see the girl I met when your train was runnin' late…but I figured, best to leave as is…give us both somethin' to look forward to and all."

"I'll take your word for it."

I slapped my hand onto his shoulder. "I know I stole you away from your vacation and all…"

Dick raised both eyebrows at me. "Oh, is that what home office is callin' it now? Vacation?"

I rolled my eyes. "Ya shoot one upper muckity-muck and they get all pissy, I know, but Mr. Earl Gray deserved it. He shouldn't have been in that fight to begin with and he knows it."

"I believe his last name is Whimbley," Dick said.

I let go of him and walked onward. "Ugh...Mr. Earl fucking Whimbley," I said in a heavy British accent, "Can suck my—"

Dick smacked my chest with the back of his hand to shut me up.

I faced my partner. "I'm just sayin', he's an asshole and the investigation into his bullshit claim will be over any day now and you'll be cleared."

"And if I'm not?"

"Then you're still comin' with me to Las Cruces. I'm not facin' that bitch alone. I'm not. If they think I am, they'll have another fight on their hands they don't want. Now come on, get in the car and let's go."

"What's yours?"

I stepped over to my beautiful, special order, black 1950 Aston Martin DB2 and made a grand motion toward her. "Tada! Isn't she gorgeous?"

Dick stared at her and with hands in his pockets slowly turned to look at me. "And what in the name of all that is holy made you think that your six-foot four friend would fit comfortably in that car? Hmm?"

I'd not thought of that.

I gave him a sheepish grin. "The seat goes back a good way and it's not far to Santa Fe?"

Dick sighed, took off his hat, and rubbed his hand over his newly short-trimmed hair. "Shit. Fine. But we get me something of normal size if we go to Las Cruces."

I opened the trunk. "Deal, now let's head to home office and see where we're at."

Richard put his military style duffle into the trunk. "Have you told them the news yet about Scáthach?"

"Nope," I said, shutting the trunk. "I decided to save that for in person."

He let out a low whistle, followed by a laugh. "You aimin' to piss 'em off?"

I grinned and winked at him. "Maybe."

We both got in my DB2, and after Richard fit his legs in and shut the door, I started her up. We were on our way to home office, and if my vision served me right, and it always did, we traveled with a big black raven on our tail the whole way.

* * *

Driving through the big, black metal gates of the estate, we made our way up the long driveway to the old, New Mexican-style mansion. The severe lack of a welcoming party as we got out of the car told me that our arrival was not as celebrated as it once had been.

We gathered our bags and went up the stairs to the main entrance. Before I could ring the bell, the door opened to show Collin, the butler and all-around man of the manor, standing there with a grin on his face.

"Good afternoon, Collin," I said.

"Master Kidwell and Brewer. I was told you would be arriving today. Please, come in. I've had your rooms prepared for you."

"Thank you, Collin," Richard said as we stepped into the home, his tone of voice expressing his appreciation of Collin's friendly and polite greeting considering the situation.

A fire was going in the fireplace of both the living room and kitchen to fight back the chill the cool morning had laid upon the house. I remembered the first time I'd come here, and even now it had the same effect on me. It felt like home in a way no building had really ever done for me, with its wide arches between rooms and the warm environment of the décor.

"Oh, and Master Kidwell?"

"Yes?"

Collin looked one way and then another before stepping in closely. "Master Whimbley has already arrived for the hearing. I made sure to put him in a different wing than you and Master Brewer, but he is on the grounds. I thought you'd like to be aware."

"I would. Thank you, Collin. You're a good man."

Collin beamed with pride though he didn't smile. With a nod he said, "I'll leave you to get settled. Tea will be in an hour."

"Thank you," Richard said again.

With another nod, Collin disappeared to do butlery type things, and we headed up the stairs to our rooms.

"Whimbley's here?" Richard whispered. "Well this is going to be 'fun.'"

"Exactly what I was thinking."

He was right. Tea was the epitome of 'fun,' as was dinner. However, seeing as Whimbley was also on a probation of sorts, he was not with the board when I took my news to them about Las Cruces.

"Are you certain that Fletcher is dead then?" Madame Dixon said.

I nodded. "He lost too much blood to be alive from what I saw. But there's always that small chance he's alive, or turned."

"Here's to hoping the latter is not the case," she said, shaking her head, which caused her dark auburn hair to float about her well-aged face of forty-nine years.

"I agree," I said.

"And Magoon?"

"That'll need more footwork. He's not in Lincoln or Las Cruces anymore though, I can tell you that."

She flipped through the papers I'd submitted and took her glasses off to look at me. "William, the board fully authorizes you to go into Las Cruces for a full investigation either alone or with a new partner."

"No can do. If I'm fighting Scáthach, I need Brewer with me."

"I understand, but he isn't cleared yet. The final determination will not be until Saturday the sixteenth of April. That's fifteen days you'll have to wait."

"I don't mind, madam chair. I can rest up for a few weeks and do more research. I'd prefer to wait on headin' back, if that's all right with you."

With a heavy sigh, she said, "Yes, it is the opinion of the board that you should go right away, but having time for research is wise. You have until Easter Sunday and then, no matter the determination of the hearing, you will need to head to Las Cruces."

"Yes ma'am. Thank you."

"You're dismissed."

With a bow, I stepped out of the room and went to go fill Brewer in on the news.

* * *

Two weeks passed by faster than one might have thought. Richard and I had traveled to libraries and to secret SIS locations in the city to research for our trip to Las Cruces. Sometimes I had to go alone because Richard was giving testimony on his own behalf. In fact, today had been one of those days, since it was the sixteenth of April and the final arguments were being given.

I'd been told to make myself scarce and had plopped down onto the couch in the rear parlor to read. Getting nervous for Richard, I decided to turn the TV on low so as to catch anything worth knowing on the evening news and went back to my book.

Hearing something about a body having been found, I glanced up. There I saw a picture on the television that I recognized. Below it was a caption that shook me to my core.

Had I read that correctly? I couldn't have. To make sure, I walked toward the TV just as Richard rushed into the room.

"Billy, I've got good news. I've been cleared of all charges and reinstated."

With no more than a nod, I held up a finger toward him and turned up the volume on the TV.

"Sad and disturbing news in Las Cruces tonight," the news anchor said. "While out rabbit hunting with his friends near the village of Mesquite, nineteen-year-old Gerald Smith came across the body of Ovida Coogler. Missing since the night of March thirtieth, the manhunt for Coogler has been extensive since she was reported missing by her mother to Sheriff Apodaca in early April.

"Thought to have been last seen wandering the streets of downtown in the wee hours of the morning of March thirty-first, it has been weeks without so much as a clue, but now she has been found.

According to Smith, he was the first to see Miss Coogler, stating it was hard to tell she was even a human being after spending weeks decomposing out in the New Mexico sun. He said that it was her painted fingernails and toenails that keyed the boys in that it was a woman."

"Dear God," Richard said.

I backed up and sat on the couch, for my legs didn't want to hold me up anymore.

"A team to investigate Ovida Coogler's death is being gathered at this time. Anyone who knows any information about her where-abouts on the night of March thirtieth or the wee hours of the thirty-first is asked to come forward and talk to someone at the sheriff's office. Happy Apodaca is running point on the case at this time."

"Isn't that the girl who—" Richard began to say.

"Up next, the weather for your Easter Sunday tomorrow. Stay tuned and we'll be right back after these words from our sponsors."

The sound of buzzing in my head was so loud I couldn't hear a thing Richard said next. I could see his mouth moving, but he could've been speaking in gibberish and it would've meant the same. In a daze, I sat there with my head in my hands, elbows resting on my knees.

A moment or two later, the big man sat beside me. Leaning forward like me, he clasped his hands together and waited. After a few minutes, he simply said, "Billy...?"

I was afraid to say anything for fear I'd not be able to hold my anger in check. I shook my head as the anguish built. My chest became tight, and I bolted from the room. Out the door into the back yard I went, as if my ass were on fire.

I ran through the elegant gardens in their early spring bloom until I was as far from the house as I felt I needed to be for this. I came to a stop, and much like when Tunstall died, I shouted out my grief at the top of my lungs. This time, I also followed it up with as many curse words as I could string together until I ran out of breath.

I heard Richard enter the small clearing I stood in. I turned to face him. "I should've been there. She asked me to stay. I could tell some-thing was wrong and yet, I left. Why? Why did I leave?"

"I don't—"

"I almost went back! Your train was late and I almost drove to Las Cruces. God, I should've gone back!" Tears came to my eyes, and I wiped them away. "Damn it!"

Richard took a seat on one of the stone garden benches to wait. I paced around, then sat, then paced a bit more, and he waited.

Finally seeing a chance to speak, the man of great patience said to me, "Well then I suppose it's a good thing our mission got cleared about fifteen minutes ago."

I turned to look at him. "That's right, you were saying you had good news. Have you been cleared and reinstated?"

He nodded.

"I'm so sorry I didn't respond to that. Congrats, my friend, though I had no doubts you'd be cleared."

Richard stood and gently placed his hand on my shoulders. Looking me in the eye, he said, "Apology not required, my friend. I understand this pain. Tunstall's death felt like this. It still torments me to this day."

"Yes, and like then, this feels like my fault. God, Richard, my card was on her. What if they found that and that's why—"

"No! No doing that. We go and we get ourselves invited to be part of the investigating team. We'll find who killed her, Billy. I promise."

"She was a sweet, lovely girl, and I'm going to make them pay, Richard."

He nodded and put his arm around me. "Come on back to the house. Let's get packed and head on out."

I nodded, and we began to make our way back through the gardens.

As we walked up the stairs to the back porch, I said, "Who'd have thought, the first two New Mexico Regulators are about to be back in business where it all began."

"Las Cruces has no clue what she's in for, does she?" Richard said.

My stare went cold with determination. "No way in hell, but she's gonna know soon enough. I can promise you that." I walked away from him and into the house. However, I wasn't so far away that I couldn't hear what he said next.

"They have no idea of the Hellfire that's comin' for 'em. I'd say God help 'em, but even He can't save them from you."

He was right. I was going to get revenge for Miss Ovida. Obviously, we didn't know for sure that Scáthach was involved in her murder, but I'd bet every dime I had that she was. So yes, I was going to rain hell down on the evil of that town...and I was going to enjoy every last minute of it.

THE END

To Be Continued in *The Murder of Cricket Coogler*

ACKNOWLEDGMENTS

First and foremost, I'd like to thank my support system: my parents, my best friends, my writing group, my wonderful editor, and those who live in Lincoln, NM. If it wasn't for the people in Lincoln, taking me in and helping me learn about Billy, this book never would have happened.

I'd like to lift a glass to all the people of Lincoln for sharing their knowledge, hospitality, and affection for Billy the Kid with me. Specifically, we should toast to, Drew & Elise Gomber, Marilyn Burchett, Jens Klingshirn, Bev & Bill Strauser, Tiffanie Owen, Beau Lucas, Annmarie LaMay, Kenneth Walter, John Schultz, Victoria Kubica, Marilyn & Murray Arrowsmith, Marla & Brandon Caughron, Sumi Ayame, Mitchell Harper, Nina & Brett McInnes, Rick Garcia, Tim & Ashley Roberts, and last but never least...Katherine, Troy, Willa, & Prue Nelson—your family is my heart.

I'd also like to thank Frederick Nolan. Most of my preferred research came from his books. If he'd not done so much leg work years ago, I'd not have had such a rich group of books to pull history from. So, a huge thank you to him and the other writers on my list of books listed at the back of this novel.

ABOUT THE AUTHOR

Tamsin Silver is a Fantasy author currently based out of Albuquerque, NM. Her Urban Fantasy works include the **Windfire** saga, **Mark of the Necromancer**, novellas based on her **Skye of the Damned** web series (*which can be seen free online*), and the **Moon Over Manhattan** series (*Falstaff Books, fall/winter 2020*).

She is also a writer for Faith Hunter's **Rogue Mage Anthologies** with *Lore Seekers Press*, the **We Are Not This** anthology for *Falstaff Books,* and the **Storming Area 51** anthology with *Bayonet Books.*

Tamsin graduated from Winthrop University in SC with a BA in Theatre and Secondary Education, along with a minor in Creative Writing and Shakespeare. She's taught middle school and high school drama in the Carolinas and run two successful theatre companies (one in NYC), where she holds awards in directing for both.

You can learn more about Tamsin by visiting www.tamsinsilver.com and www.skyeofthedamned.com.

Books Used and/or Recommended for fans of Billy the Kid

Billy the Kid - A Short and Violent Life by Robert M. Utley

Billy the Kid: The Endless Ride by Michael Wallis

Frontier Fighter by Frank Coe

High Noon in Lincoln - Violence on the Western Frontier by Robert M. Utley

Historic Lincoln NM - The Buildings and People by Rich Eastwood

History of the Lincoln County War: A Classic Account of Billy the Kid by Robert N. Mullin

Images of America - Lincoln by Ray John de Aragón

Images of America - Towns of Lincoln County by John LeMay

In the Shadow of Billy the Kid by Kathleen P. Chamberlain

Joy of the Birds by Gale Cooper

Lincoln County and Its Wars by Nora True Henn

Lincoln County, New Mexico, Tells its Stories by the Lincoln County Historical Society Publications

My Own Story - The Autobiography of Billy the Kid by Ralph Estes

Nuestros Antepasados (Our Ancestors) by Ernest S. Sanchez & Paul R. Sanchez

Such Men as Billy the Kid by Joel Jacobsen

The Billy the Kid Reader by Frederick Nolan

The Illustrated Life and Times of Billy the Kid by Bob Boze Bell

The Life & Death of John Henry Tunstall by Frederick Nolan

The Lincoln County War: A Documentary History (Revised History) by Frederick Nolan

The Story of Richard M. Brewer by Harry Leighton (and Elise Gomber)

The West of Billy the Kid by Frederick Nolan

These Were the Regulators (Lincoln County War) by Philip J. Rasch

They "Knew" Billy the Kid (Interviews with Old-Time Mexicans by Robert F. Kadlec

To Hell on a Fast Horse, The Untold Story of Billy the Kid and Pat Garrett by Mark Lee Gardner

REFERENCES

Violence in Lincoln County by William A. Keleher
Cricket in the Web by Paula Moore

FRIENDS OF FALSTAFF

Thank You to All our Falstaff Books Patrons, who get extra digital content each month! To be featured here and see what other great rewards we offer, go to www.patreon.com/falstaffbooks.

PATRONS

Dino Hicks
John Hooks
John Kilgallon
Larissa Lichty
Travis & Casey Schilling
Staci-Leigh Santore
Sheryl R. Hayes
Scott Norris
Samuel Montgomery-Blinn
Junkle

Made in the USA
Monee, IL
20 September 2020

42801231R00184